PURELAND

PURELAND

PURELAND

Zarrar Said

GLOBAL COLLECTIVE PUBLISHERS

Philadelphia

Published by Global Collective Publishers
2628 West Chester Pike, #281
Broomall, Pennsylvania 19008, U.S.A.
www.globalcollectivepublishers.com

First Published in India by Harper Collins India in 2018

Copyright @ Zarrar Said 2020

Print ISBN: 978-1-7344019-0-5
eBook ISBN: 978-1-7344019-1-2

This is a work of fiction and all characters and incidents described in this book are the product of the author's imagination. Any resemblance to actual persons, living or dead, is entirely coincidental.

Zarrar Said asserts the moral right to be identified as the author of this work.

All rights reserved. No part of this publication may be reproduced, stored in a retrieval system, or transmitted, in any form or by any means, electronic, mechanical, photocopying, recording or otherwise, without the prior permission of Global Collective Publishers.

for Dr. Abdus Salam,
who loved a nation that never loved him back

Prologue

I think you were expecting someone else—a monster perhaps. Sorry to disappoint you, sir. I'm not who they say I am. Please, have a seat. I will tell you more.

In a few days, as you know, I'll be executed for the murder of Salim Agha. The charges levelled against me are of terror and barbarism. They say I am the Scimitar, the Sword of the Caliphate, sent forth by a brutal empire to unleash horror upon the West. Perhaps there's some truth to that claim, perhaps not. I'll let you be the judge. It's true that I murdered Salim Agha and I alone will take the fall.

But I believe we were all responsible for his death.

Because we, the people of his nation, stood silently when the storm arrived, watching our culture and our way of life vanish before our eyes. The black flag of the Caliphate approached us like a giant broom and, just like that, swept everything away. They seized town after town, levelled our buildings, and snatched children from their mothers' bosoms. That's when entire nations faded. Darkness fell.

Since then, every anecdote has been rewritten, our histories altered, and whatever lay there before is lost forever.

We know that out of all the forgotten homelands this storm devoured, there was one that was revered by all. Yet the world didn't even notice when, with an almost suddenness, Pureland disappeared.

Salim's legacy, and that of his beloved nation, Pureland, will perish with me when I die, and soon it will be as if he never existed at all. I have been unable to live with this reality. Had I gone to a hypnotist, instead of sitting here in your pleasant company, he might have extricated from my mind these taunting thoughts and absolved me of this remorse.

But you're not here to listen to a remorseful plea. You're here to learn about the Caliphate, the assassin they call the Scimitar, and what compelled me to carry out this archaic execution. After all, it's not every day that a person of your distinction enters these daunting walls.

I see you are a bit overdressed for this place. Please, take off your jacket, loosen that tie, it gets quite warm in here. I would put away that pen and notebook too; you won't need them. Just listen.

You see, sir, at this very moment, Salim Agha lies in an abandoned cemetery in a forgotten town of this dominion we now call the Caliphate. On any given day you will find his grave pitilessly surrounded by trash and shit. The epitaph is obscured. Ruthless chiseling has left the inscription unrecognizable. For the townsmen, it's just another heretic's grave; no one knows who lies below the headstone, only that its violation is a celebrated custom.

I can tell from your face that you find all this deeply unsettling. What was his crime, you ask? The answer: he fell in love.

Sometimes, in a world like this, that's all it takes.

Part I

*Thousands of desires, each worth dying for,
Many of them I have realized ... yet, I yearn for more*

—Mirza Ghalib

His Birth—Summer, 1950

All that matters in life is our desire for one another. That was how Salim Agha saw this world. Before havoc was wreaked upon us, before the evil of the Caliphate descended, this was how our world was—a world of lovers. Strangely, all that mattered to Salim was a nation that never loved him back. In order to understand this paradox, you need to abandon your view of reality. Forget what you know about time, space, what's true, what's fantasy. More importantly, forget all you know about love. Because more than anything else, this is a story about love. And to truly understand love, you must first set it free.

It is a strange tale I'm about to reveal—one rooted in mystery. Such mystery that you might start to question my state of mind. But I assure you, sir, my sanity is intact. Prior to your arrival, I had thought about where to begin this story; whether or not to reveal its obscure mysticism. I don't want to hide anything from you though. It's clear to me that to understand this tale in all of its cosmic relevance, we must begin with the prophecy, which was delivered through God of Abraham's most trusted emissary. Our journey begins here.

It was in the minutes before Salim's birth that it all started. In the summer of 1950, deep in the drapery of starlight, further than any man can see, celestial beasts gathered. One of them wore the look of hurried excitement as he prepared to welcome the final savior.

"I can't believe the time has come for us to welcome the trusted one! I can't believe the time has come!" the archangel Gabriel sang, dusting his wings while the others huddled around him tapping their foreheads in nervous panic.

"Hurry! You have no time. Look below, he's about to arrive!"

"Yes, I know. I'm not blind. Believe you me, I've done this many times." A portal swirled around his fingers. The dial was stuck. Gabriel fidgeted with intensity, wrinkling his forehead. "Seven ... one ... no, where is it, ah! Ground floor!"

"He's going, he's going! We can't believe the time has come for us to welcome the trusted one!" the others sang, dancing in a circle with their elbows interlocked.

Their feet began to tap to the marching tune they had rehearsed earlier, as white dust flew in plumes around their toes. One beast screamed into the shrinking portal, "Wait! Do you remember His instructions?"

"What bloody instructions?" Gabriel looked at his palm where his short-hand notes had been smeared by sweat. "Oh yes. Of course, I remember: to blow into his ear. Or was it his nose?" The portal shut as he chimed in with his comrades, "Oh when the saints ... oh when the saints go marching in."

It suddenly dawned upon the archangel that he would have to employ his powers of improvisation—a talent only a real actor could boast of, and in his mind, he was the finest thespian in the entire cosmos. Down below his feet he could see the world of Abraham, wrapped in its blue blanket, welcoming him as he closed his eyes and drew a breath. At the height of the Himalayas, he twisted into a ball, diving further south into the creamy hue of the night sky.

"Oh when the saints go marching in, ta ta ta ta tu ru tu tu..."

Piercing cloud after cloud, he sang as he entered the place where no man or archangel ever cared to venture. It was a place where moonlight was the only guide. Gabriel was terrified, but he clasped his hands together in a *namaste*, muttered a prayer, put his chin to his chest and plunged into the darkness. The kino trees broke his fall as he bounced into the air and smashed against a corrugated iron roof. He came to a stop as another prayer fell from his lips. Turning sideways, he slipped through rusty holes into Jaaji the Painter's home.

Jaaji was asleep on the floor. Gabriel saw where it was he had to go. A woman, Jaaji's wife, was crying out in pain. The archangel took his mark and ran towards her.

"Marching in," he shouted, blinking in urgency as he squeezed himself through wide open legs towards the womb. Cradling the unborn babe in his arms, the archangel blew into his nose, the final revelation, a prophecy revealed to him by God of Abraham himself, and moments before the birth took place, he wriggled back out, gathered his wings, and rocketed up into the night sky.

It was there, in the flickering light of a kerosene lamp, in a small earth-packed corner of a village named Khanpur, that Salim was born.

His mother wailed, "He is coming ... I'm going die! Do something, Jaaji! Wake up you drunk fool. Your child is coming!"

That clamor echoed throughout the village as Salim tumbled forth into this world. His mother yanked him by the shoulders, delivering him onto the packed dirt. The motherly smell of his nation's soil made the newborn smile. He tapped the floor with his palms, took his fingers to his lips and kissed them gently. At that precise moment, during his first kiss, Salim fell in love.

The Prophecy

You're leaning back in your chair with your hands on your head. I understand your apprehension, sir, I honestly do. I may be a murderer, but I'm not a madman. If you wanted to know about the evils I've been accused of, you could have easily read my file or watched those painstaking documentaries on the Scimitar, the Sword of the Caliphate, but instead you agreed to hear my testimony. And, therefore, you must allow me to reveal things the way they happened, because believe me when I say that Salim's life was stranger than you and I could possibly imagine. All this talk of angels and demons? That is just the beginning. May we continue?

Here he was, Salim, just two days old. His mother's face was varnished with concern. She held this expression for a while, as her child had refused to make a sound since his birth. Her husband was no help. For two whole days, Jaaji the Painter had been sprawled out on the floor, tanked up on sugarcane ale, tongue out. He didn't notice the new tenant in the house. Hell, he could barely see where he was going as he clawed his way outdoors like a zombie to relieve himself. Then he collapsed onto the floor again. That morning, as his mother lugged a bucket of water into the house, Salim shrieked so deafeningly that she slipped, falling headfirst into the bucket. It might have been the shock, or perhaps it was the water that poured into the void of her final gasp, but she died immediately.

The villagers gathered around the house, whispering amongst themselves. Salim's mother's death became an enigma. She was discovered bent over in a prayer position, head in a bucket. What could cause such a thing, they wondered. Like purposeful detectives, the villagers examined the crime scene delivering their own verdicts. By the time Jaaji was slapped awake, consensus had been reached: the boy had brought with him a bad omen.

Jaaji never named the child. Names in the village were not given at birth, they had to be earned. Like that of his eldest son, Tamboo the Camel, who had the unfortunate appearance of a desert beast, and whom the village had mocked from the moment he took his first steps. There were more pressing matters at hand, like the immediate need for a replacement wife. So, to simplify his burdens, in an act of great urgency, Jaaji married again.

As Salim's stepmother shuffled into her new home with her nose ring bumping against her cheek, she stopped to look at him. "This child ... this child is like a potato," she said, squinting at him as if he were a circus freak. "I've never seen one this fat." It was her first contribution to Salim's life. The name Potato stuck, and Salim had earned his label.

It wasn't long before death was forgotten, and the house became alive again. The house was the only treasure Jaaji the Painter really had. He had built it with his own hands. It had many oddities. The wooden door, which clung to the mud walls, had cracks so large you could push your fingers right through. The holes in the corrugated iron roof sliced sunlight into beams during the day and escorted mosquitoes in at night. And when it rained, tiny puddles formed on the earth-packed floor below, and if you let your tongue hang out like a catching mitt, you could taste the rust in the water. They added to the house's character. It was easy to be forgotten here and, as such, the first three years of Salim's life passed by as if he were raising himself.

Sometime around his third birthday, his stepmother stormed up to her husband yelling, "This one is still not talking! What use is this fat Potato if he is deaf and dumb?" Jaaji never paid much attention to his youngest son who always kept to himself in a corner. He looked away as his wife continued her rant. He was good at that. He typically ignored her cries as one would the wailing of mourning crows. But soon enough, rations dwindled, and appetites swelled. Hunger hit the painter's family hard in their bellies. That's when his wife revealed her crafty plan.

"Look, Jaaji. Why don't we auction the boy off in Kidney Town? You'll get a good payment for a healthy child. The brick kilns give two meals a day. He'll be better off ... and this way, so will we."

Kidney Town. You could sell anything there: organs, children, buffaloes. In this unique village, indentured servants could settle their debts permanently. Jaaji pictured the brick kilns of Kidney Town with their smoking red towers that were visible from miles away. He imagined the burning furnaces under which the space was so cramped that only workers with tiny bodies could fit. It wasn't ideal, but the pay was good, and the meals were regular.

The brick kilns, Jaaji muttered to himself as he looked up from his hookah at the fragile figure of his wife. Her eyes were sunken into her face, and her nose ring had been pawned and replaced with a toothpick.

"You look like an Indian film star, you know? From a Bombay talkie, I tell you," he said, grabbing her ankles and stroking her leg with his coarse fingers. This gave rise to a dull ache in his groin. That is to say, he was sober enough to get it up and there was little time to waste.

"Stop this nonsense! You've never seen a movie in your life," she hissed. "Can never get it up when it matters and now, when the children are awake, so are you? God forgive me." She put her fingers to her ear lobes, because even the thought of the painter's naked body felt like a sin.

That night, Jaaji convinced her to allow him to rub his delinquent erection between her legs, and he pondered her earlier suggestion between untimely thrusts.

Everyone, Jaaji thought to himself, should pitch in. Even Tamboo the Camel, had reached the formidable working age of eight and had begun to contribute to the household. And it was no secret that the painter's livelihood was in jeopardy. There were only so many signs he could paint in a town where four people could read. He couldn't possibly continue to sustain a household. In such dire circumstances, the youngest child almost always met a sickly demise. To trade Potato in Kidney Town was to buy his survival. It was the best solution. Sell a child, save a child: sheer genius, he thought.

His excitement didn't last long. He climaxed, plopping onto his wife's breasts, and went to sleep as she wriggled out from under his bony torso.

The next morning, when the blazing sun was at its peak, Jaaji walked his son down the dirt path leading out of the village. Potato held on to his father's hand. He was intrigued by a wing-shaped paint stain on Jaaji's wrist. He stroked it gently as they turned on to the main road and walked towards the canal which ran along the sugarcane field. Suddenly, the boy stopped to stare at his reflection in the brown water.

"What is it? Why have you stopped?"

The rushing canal reflected in his son's eyes and the look on his face made Jaaji's heart swell. He had seen this before. It was a look of curiosity, of promise. Many years ago, before he fell in love with the bottle, Jaaji himself had those eyes, that trenchant smile. It's what drove him to the zenith of his ambition: painting imitation Mughal miniatures. He made them with the most intricate of brushstrokes and sold them in the city to Englishmen. Such was his talent that often his fakes were better than the originals.

Doubt settled into the painter's heart as he sat on his haunches, lost in his son's giggles. His wife's Kidney Town plan didn't seem so brilliant to him anymore. How could he even fall for it? There was clearly something mysterious about his son he himself did not know.

Below them, the canal charged through at great speed, smashing against the small bridge. Above them, crows flew in circles.

"What do you see?"

"Aaah. Aaah!" he cried, holding up four little fingers.

Salim looked up at the birds and then down to his father's wrist— right at the converging black wings. Like a sudden storm, an emotion he had not felt before, came rushing from within. Jaaji began to cry, pulling his son to his chest, kissing his hair. "Yes, I see it too. Four wings," he said.

At that moment, he didn't know what the future held for his son, but he knew someone who would. Rising to his feet, he mopped his tears with his sleeve and took his son's hand. His feet twisted in the soft morning dirt as he marched away from the canal towards the shrine.

The Floating Pir lived in a white brick temple halfway to Kidney Town, where devotees brought offerings in handmade baskets and sought remedies for their ailments in exchange. Hope was sold there. Outside this establishment, the white paint was jagged and crumbled under the slightest touch. Leather slippers lined the steps as visitors were ushered in through its wooden doors.

Jaaji entered the shrine, pushing through the velvet curtain towards a dimly lit room decorated with maroon tapestries, rug-adorned walls, and a baroque arrangement of candles. In the middle of this peculiar den was the majestic Pir, whose silver hair cascaded like a waterfall down to the small of his back. His eyes were shut tight, creating a constipated expression. He counted beads on a string and muttered phrases in an unknown tongue. As anticipated, his ass was elevated two feet clean off the ground, and Jaaji passed his hand underneath to make sure he wasn't hallucinating.

The Pir's eyes opened, finally, and looked at Potato whose cheeks were lifted by a probing smile. After placing his hand on the child's head, his eyes shut again.

"What do you see, Pir Saab? The child doesn't speak. Is he deaf? Is he dumb?"

After a pause, the Pir cleared his throat and said, "No drunkard, your son is not a mute. You will see, he is destined for greatness!" He took a deep breath. "God has given you a gift, Painter! The only obstacle in his life is you. Yes you. Because you're the chieftain of imbeciles, the monarch of morons, the father of fools, the Shah of shitheads! Free him from this village and he will deliver his true promise. O foolish Painter, he will change our world forever. He might not speak now, but when he does, the whole world will listen."

With those words, uttered by a levitating saint, Salim Agha's destiny was foretold. The Pir gave Jaaji a glimpse of the future his son could have; a way out from a life of hereditary destitution, away from the gloomy town where a man's fate was decided in his mother's womb, and where his future was as dark as his skin.

For this was no ordinary land: it was a place where men owned men. Where, at birth, one was handed a prescription for life. It was where one knew nothing but to be servile. And without servitude, as the village imam would say at Friday sermons, man was nothing but a hollow carcass, an infidel with no soul and no purpose to live.

Potato

———• 🙢 •———

Sir, it's difficult to describe darkness. I want to tell you about it without sounding like I'm preaching. But there's something about the village and particularly about darkness that you should know. It's here that our story begins to take a bit of a bend. Similar to the Canal of Fables that ran through the village of Khanpur, making its way down from the river, towards the city of Lorr.

After sunset, there was a suddenness of night in the village, when the moonlight shyly kissed the fields, grassland, and ponds. In this darkness, the trees trembled as winds whispered deviously through the leaves. When the sun dipped, a black silk tapestry covered the sky, and, with the night, came a terrifying silence, a time of nothingness. Even the flickering flame of a lantern was not enough to ward off this uncertainty. Leaving the village was unheard of. The village was all anyone knew. Birth, life, and death all took place in this, the only universe.

In such a place, one can easily get carried away by magical notions. Notions of a prophetic light that could one day pierce through the darkness and eliminate all grief and misfortune. The floating Pir had injected Jaaji with such a dose of optimism that day as he returned gleefully to the village. With his son on his shoulders, the painter cried out to anyone who would hear him, "A promise of greatness! Did you hear me, you illiterate donkeys? Greatness!"

As he made his way down the winding road, Jaaji made engine sounds from his mouth, squeezed his son's feet with both hands, and bolted into the rice paddies pretending he was a motorbike. Salim, with his arms around his father's neck, chuckled as the painter kicked the muddy water like a child.

On his return home, as he charged through the front door, the painter suddenly became still. His wife's shock transferred to him through her eyes. Much to her dismay, Potato had returned home un-auctioned, with his kidneys intact. Jaaji, in a pleading appeal, cried, "I saw something in the boy's eyes. He's not a mute! The Floating Pir says he brings a prophecy of great promise."

"You're full of shit!" she shouted back, clouting his ears with her rolling pin. At night, however, when everyone was asleep, Salim's step-mother walked towards him with her arms crossed, pondering the words of the soothsayer. She knew that such prophecies were not to be taken lightly. She gave up the idea of auctioning the boy hoping greatness would show up at their door one day. Because she, like the other village folk, knew that when you have nothing, promises are your only treasure and this promise was worth the wait.

In a feudal town, hope dries up fast. The painter's family held on to it until they forgot what it was, they were holding on to. A year trickled by, then two, then five. Then, on the eve of Salim's eighth birthday, something remarkable happened. The mute child finally began to talk. And boy, did he talk. It was as if he had been swallowing words, waiting for the opportune moment to spit them out. Once he started yapping, it was difficult to shut him up. He talked and talked, sometimes even in his sleep. His parents, who were excited at first, became annoyed. Endless inquiries fell from his mouth repeatedly.

"Maa, why do you burn buffalo dung?"

"Baa, why is the earth brown? And the sky ... why is it blue?"

The words who, what, where, why echoed in the painter's house throughout the day. When his interrogations would become unbearable, his stepmother would shove him out the door to accompany his father at the dera. There, in the evenings, he sat with the townsmen hunched in a corner, quietly ingesting the gossip. He would absorb every blithering tale, every slurring gag, and would then regurgitate it without discretion in the morning.

"Wait, Billa Cycle! Why was your wife in the sugarcane field with Wannu the Weasel? Khassi Kasai says she's the village bicycle. Why is she a bicycle? Is that how you got your name?" Upon which, Billa ran to his wife and questioned her illicit behavior only to be reprimanded by a swift slap across the head.

Even the village butcher wasn't spared, as Potato approached him at the water pump one day where he was chatting up the ladies. "Khassi Kasai, why do you crush goats' nuts before slaughter? Pappu Uncle says it's because you don't have any balls yourself." To which Khassi Kasai smiled and quietly retreated from the giggling women.

Then there was Pappu Pipewalla whose coveted sex organ was thought to have made donkeys whimper with envy, "Pappu Uncle, Pappu Uncle, why do they call you Pipewalla? Billa Cycle says it's because you have a two-foot pipe between your legs. Does it protect you?"

Secrets, truths, and lies were all under siege. Potato the painter's son questioned everything and everyone. When he waddled into the dera with a smile lifting his beefy cheeks, people scurried in the opposite direction.

It was during those days that the painter had managed to land a new job in the city. He hadn't had work in a while, so he felt the need to celebrate with his friends. But when he made his way to the dera, brimming with excitement, he was cornered by the villagers. "Jaaji, do something about Potato for the love of God's prophet. He is going to get me killed," said Wannu the Weasel.

"Your son's going around telling people I have no balls. How am I ever going to get married in this fucking village?" wailed Khassi Kasai.

"Yes, Jaaji, he also told the blind man we brew ale at his mosque. Do something before we're all fucked," cried Pappu Pipewalla. The thought of Unna Huneira, the old blind mullah, snuffing out the only supply of alcohol in the village, sent Jaaji into a nervous panic. He realized something surely had to give. At the St. Andrew's Church in Lorr, Jaaji had just been hired to paint the new church dome. The only way he could keep Potato out of trouble was to take him along and leave him at the church while he worked. Surely the nuns would take care of him, he thought.

Unwittingly, that was Jaaji's greatest gift to his son. The church became fertile ground for the child's inquisitiveness and the nuns took a liking to him, spending hours cushioning his curiosity with their love and patience, a virtue they'd taken an oath to uphold.

That was where Potato found literature. The nuns taught him how to speak English and read. And once he started reading, he devoured books by the kilo. For Potato, every day orbited around the desire to swallow the universe, one bite at a time. With each bite, the cosmos revealed itself, so he went on eating. Over the year he spent at the church, Potato pawned Pappu Pipewalla, Khassi Kasai, and others for Kipling, Joyce, and Thackeray. But when that year ended, around the time the church prepared for the Christmas sermon, a budget cut from the governor terminated the dome's redecoration project. Without warning, as the government changed hands, the church was taken over by a new administration and Jaaji's paintbrushes dried up for good and that meant, Potato's encounters with the outside world also came to an end.

That year, Potato turned eight—an age when boys in Khanpur became men.

"Get this Potato a job, he eats more than all of us combined," his step-mother cried.

Jaaji admitted to himself, albeit reluctantly, that she was right. Since his gig at the church concluded, hunger had returned, and something had to be done. Also, it had been many years since the Floating Pir's prophecy. Even promises had an expiration date and for Potato, that date had long passed. At night, gathered around a fire at the dera, he asked Pappu Pipewalla for help.

"There is one thing," said Pappu. "The buffaloes need tending in the morning. This way, Potato stays out of trouble, and I can catch up on my sleep. What's the worst that can happen? It's not like he can annoy buffaloes with his words." They both laughed, touching their ale bottles.

When the sun rose in the morning, it stretched its limbs, rousing each living being it embraced. Sugarcane stood tall, while gaunt, sunken-eyed farmers returned to chiseling the earth with heavy plows hanging from their shoulders. Nearby, the children ran barefoot on the pebbled dirt road that snaked through the village.

Along the side of the road was a shallow ravine where blue water buffaloes stood with their swooping horns and savage eyes. Potato, the painter's son, barely reaching the buffalo's nose, stamped his authority by wielding a bamboo stick.

The ravine glistened as the buffaloes waddled out of the water and the sun bounced off their wet backs. They meandered towards the winding dirt road as Potato ran up behind one as fast as he could, grabbed his tail and tried to mount his back, slipping right off, thudding on to the ground.

"You have to help me out here, Baloo. I'm counting on you," he said, recovering from his fall. He took a deep breath and using a large rock as a launching pad, planted himself on top of the animal. Waving his bamboo stick in the air, he yelled, "Go forth, my trusted steed! Yield forward, Baloo!"

Gathering his cattle, he made his way towards the dera where the elders met on the first Sunday of every month to discuss business with their landlord. He peered through his bamboo-stick telescope, smacking his tongue against the roof of his mouth as it moved towards the target: General Zafar Khan, the feudal king, owner of all land, men, women, children, and buffaloes.

"Baloo, what say you? Should I do it? What's that you said?" He scrubbed off the mud from his shins with his fingernails. "That's right, Baloo. I think we'll have a chat with the General today." He dropped his stick and headed towards the gathering.

"What can we say, General Saab? The rain hasn't come timely this year and crops aren't yielding like they used to," said Kaana Munshi, General Khan's one-eyed accountant.

"Saab, just think of it this way, when the rains do come, we will bring you double than last year, Kaana Munshi has it all worked out," said Wannu the Weasel.

Potato approached the huddle of bowed heads, quiet as a whisper. Between the collected shoulders, a cool breeze of cologne floated from the General's cheeks, entering Potato's nostrils. The elders conducted business as usual, grumbling of arid spells, ailing cattle, and crops destroyed by wild boar, while Potato lined himself up to walk through an open passage to the throne.

"Good afternoon, General Khan. I hope you've had a wonderful morning," he said in perfect English, extending his hand towards Khan's face. Gasps followed, as everyone looked up.

General Khan turned to glance at the boy's mud-caked legs.

"Get out of here, you fat good for nothing! This is the elders' meeting. You know well not to come here!" shouted Khassi Kasai, the ball-crushing butcher.

The General's hand rose and Khassi's eyes fell to the floor.

"Who are you, boy?" he asked.

"General Saab. I am Potato, son of Jaaji the Painter. I take your buffaloes out to drink every day. Baloo is the fattest of them all. He's my friend. You know, like Baloo from *The Jungle Book*?"

This was the closest Potato had come to the General. Looking up, he saw his slant emerald eyes and his bushy moustache that lay like stacks of hay by the sides of his lips, and his white safari suit with tan leather shoes, the kind English people wore. He held a walking stick which had a golden pigeon's head on the handle.

"Who is this child? And where's his father?"

"Sorry, General Saab. He talks shit all the time, don't you mind him," said Wannu the Weasel.

"We'll take him back to his mother. I don't know what he said, but he will apologize!" yelled Pappu Pipewalla.

"He is the painter's son, Saab. This Potato is nothing but trouble. Please don't mind him," said Unna Huneira, the blind cleric.

"Be quiet you imbeciles. You! Come here!" With two wagging fingers, the General signaled to Potato, who walked up to him with a smile, holding out his hand like he had been taught in church. "Can someone bring me this painter?"

Within a matter of minutes, as the elder's meeting came to a premature close, a skinny cadaver, freshly awoken from under a kino tree, entered the dera.

"Does this boy belong to you, painter?"

"Yes, Khan Saab. He's my son," mumbled Jaaji, continuing with rehearsed precision, "I'm sorry if he's offended you. He didn't mean any harm ... Potato, apologize."

"Yes, apologize, son," said Cut-Two Naii, the barber who could perform two haircuts simultaneously.

"Yes, go on ... say you're sorry," said Billa Cycle, who had finally realized that he'd earned his name not because he owned a bicycle but because he had married one.

"That will not be necessary, painter! I want to know where this boy learned to speak English."

"I used to work at the church, Saab," began Jaaji. "The nuns taught him, gave him books and things. The boy loves to read, sir. He reads all night."

"And you don't find this the least bit astonishing?" asked General Khan. "What's his *real* name?" To which everyone responded with confusion and a cool silence fell. "Wait. So, you haven't even named your child?"

"General Saab," began Jaaji while, around him, the others shook their heads as if to show their disappointment, "I wanted to name him Salim, but my wife started calling him Potato. Then all of Khanpur started calling him Potato and the name has been with us ever since."

As the name fell on the ears of every Khanpur man like the first droplet of morning dew, Salim looked back at Jaaji with surprise.

"Your boy seems to have more brains than you or anyone in this entire village. Salim, come with me. Let's take a walk."

General Khan leaned over to grab his walking stick, covering the pigeon head with his large hands. As Salim saw the grand figure standing in his polished boots, the tale of Deema Engine raced to his mind. Legend had it that Deema was obsessed with making hand-powered machines and had once exhibited his creation to General Khan: a small car that would run for miles using nothing but a hand crank. Khan, awestruck, made a vow to pay for Deema's education at the engineering university. You see, the General's vow was imperishable; to be on the receiving end of one was truly a blessing.

Salim had never met Deema Engine. In actuality, no one really remembered what he looked like, but his heroic tale had remained, lingering in the village where stories and promises were sacred and stories of promise even more so.

"Come here boy, don't be shy. Let's walk down to the canal. As a boy, I was once told that if you swim in it you can hear stories," General Khan said, while shooing away his valet who tried to jolt open an umbrella above his head.

"The canal only speaks to those whom it deems fit, sir," replied Salim with an unshakeable smile.

"Is that so?" asked General Khan as he carefully avoided a puddle. "Tell me, how did you learn English?"

"I used to go to the city with my father," Salim began as he jumped over the puddle, pretending he too had precious boots to protect. "The nuns gave me books and taught me the alphabet. I love reading, sir. But there are not many books around here."

The General listened in amazement as he became more and more convinced of the role he had to play. For he was General Khan, protector of the weak, owner of men, father to Khanpur's children. And this boy was no ordinary child, he was a gem that needed a good old polish. Deema Engine had never looked back to even thank him for the life he had been gifted. He was, after all, an ungrateful servant, Khan thought to himself. But Salim's eyes spoke of sincerity, and sincerity was the only thing that Khan truly valued.

"Tell me, boy. Would you like to come to the city with me? To Lorr? You can live in my house, work for me. I promise to send you to the best school in all of Pureland. As long as you study hard and prove your worth, you can stay."

"Oh, of course, General Saab. I am your humble servant already. We live on your land. To come to your home will be my family's honor," he said. "Of course sir, of course."

"Jolly good. It's done then. I will speak with your father and you will come with me right away."

"General Saab, there's one thing though," he said, while peeking at Khan's enormous vehicle as the village children gathered around it, licking its door handles, giggling at their reflections.

"What is it, boy?"

"Sir, I like to eat, as you can tell. Will I be allowed to eat twice a day?"

The General burst into a laughter that made his belly dance. He tapped his round midsection and said, "Three times. You'll be given three square meals a day, don't you worry. Run along and get your things. We'll be leaving shortly."

Before Salim could gather his excitement, news spread and the villagers gathered near the sparkling Mercedes Benz to watch Khanpur's son being hosed down under a hand pump by his brother, Tamboo the Camel. Salim waved at his onlookers as soap was daubed on his face. Among the spectators was his father, who clutched on to his son's belongings: two books, a clean set of clothes, and a pair of slippers. There, in attendance, stood Wannu the Weasel, Cut-Two Naii the barber, Billa Cycle, Pappu Pipewalla, and Khassi Kasai, the butcher. As much as they despised Salim's interrogations, they all felt that a part of them was being anointed and each one secretly claimed responsibility for his upbringing.

And as he watched his son walk towards the car, the Floating Pir's prophecy became obvious to Jaaji. He pulled Salim close, holding him near his heart, kissing his cheeks. The car doors shut. Through the window, Jaaji stared at his son's eyes. He tried to hold his tears back, tears that would have revealed his own incompetence to himself. The words of the Floating Pir came from nowhere, lodging like a stone in his throat: *the only obstacle in his life is you, yes you.*

"You go now, Potato! Get out of here and eat all the books you can eat," he said as he hardened his heart, twisted on his heels, and walked away before the car left a trail of dust and running children far behind, speeding away from the village, towards the city of lights, the city that awaited its adopted son.

The Emperor's Kingdom

———•⚜•———

Excess was something Salim had never encountered before. It burned his eyes as he entered the Khan House later that morning. The twelve-foot gate with its interwoven iron snakes creaked open, revealing an elevated driveway of cobblestones; they made the car wobble as it climbed up. Rows of exotic flowers stood in welcome, and in the center sat a neatly manicured lawn whose fragrance punctured the car windows. Cradled in the corner of the estate, behind a large banyan tree, was the castle—a concrete pyramid wrapped in creeping leaves. It had already devoured Salim before he could fully take it in. Just when he was about to blink, his gaze was yanked upwards, apprehended by pigeons so white they looked as if they had been dipped in cream. He watched them as they swooped down onto the roof. On the ground below, Bally the cook scurried towards the veranda from the servants' quarters. He was followed by an army of servants running in frenzied excitement towards the car. This was no mere abode for humble beings, it was an empire constructed by a dynasty, an emblem of the Khan legacy. And Potato, the painter's son, longed to be a part of it.

It's difficult to adjust your eyes to such extravagance. Which was why Salim stood blinking at the Khan House, knowing that the only way to consume its enormity was with the first bite. Clutching the threadbare remains of his village in his hands, he stood beside the General as a growing group of onlookers amassed in reception.

"Salim will be with us from now on," Khan began, pointing the pigeon end of his cane towards an old man with a hunched back, "Bally here is a house servant, and the best cook in all of Lorr. Italian, Chinese, local, you name it, he makes it."

Khan spoke facing towards Salim, but his words were loud enough for the others to be reminded of certain things. One of these things was access. This was crucial. The outside servants, needless to say, remained outdoors, while their in-house counterparts had territorial demarcations. Bally's claim extended to the kitchen and dining hall only, but free to roam among the masters inside were the Christian maids, one for each of Khan's sons: Khalil and Gibran. Then there was the older handmaid for his daughter Laila. Her name was Bilki and, despite her unlikeable character, she had been rewarded her own private room for sustaining years of torture from the General's mother. The mother is important, but we shall get to her later.

Before he continued, Khan paused to deliver a word about cutlery. "In the Khan House, there are sets for everyone," he said. "One, of course, for the family, a set for the house servants, one for the outside servants, and one for the Christian maids." Why, you ask. I assume because a fork can taste quite foul once a Christian has touched it.

Outside the mansion, there was Maali the gardener, the guards, Khan's batman Abbas, Chaku the driver, and a group called the *velas* or idlers—rotating servants with no clear designation, who slept out on the lawn. Lastly, emerging from a kennel behind the garage to be alongside his master, a German Shepherd named Jabberwocky. He was different from any dog Salim had ever seen before. His muscular body and shiny coat revealed the complexity of his diet. What the village kids would do to be that dog, Salim thought.

Chaku, the driver, ground his teeth upon hearing that he had to vacate his room for a child and was further irked by Khan's final announcement at the foot of the lawn. "One more thing. No one is to give this boy any chores. Anyone who does will get the whip."

So Chaku did as he was told and relinquished his room but waited to welcome Salim as he arrived taking small cautionary steps. "So, they say you speak the Saab's language," he said, as Salim sat down on a bed for the first time. He looked up. Chaku was a young man barely past puberty and had thick brown hair and golden eyes.

"Yes, sir. I speak English. My name is Salim, pleased to meet you," he said, extending his hand only for it to meet a protruding oddity. He felt a fleshy knob extending from a black bush of hair. It frightened him. He pulled his hand away with great speed and drew his gaze away from the throbbing organ to its owner. Chaku grinned. His teeth were so brown it seemed he had bitten into a dung cake.

"Don't be scared, fat boy. Just wanted to give you a welcoming present," Chaku whistled through his russet fangs. The room began stinking of sweat and sandalwood. A sound outdoors startled him as he collapsed the clothing around his crotch and breezed out of the room.

Salim's face began to burn with a strange sensation. Was it anger? Or perhaps nausea? Either way, he fell towards the tap in his toilet and washed his hands raw.

For days to come, the villagers back in Khanpur huddled around the dera mouthing their versions of Potato's story to each other. Gossip in the village was bartered like cigarettes in a prison yard, it was currency, and before anyone knew it, the decaying legend of Deema Engine was forgotten altogether. Through Potato, the painter's son, they all imagined living in the Khan House—a fantasy which required a pinch on the arm.

"Did you know he gets three whole meals a day ... with meat? Oh Allah, truly a miracle," said Wannu the Weasel.

"I actually saw him sitting on General Zafar Khan's lap one day. Can you bloody imagine? Our very own Potato, who used to smell of buffalo piss, sitting on the General's lap! I heard he only has to wash his car once a week," muttered Cut-Two Naii.

"You're all wrong," said Khassi Kasai. "I deliver meat to the house. I've seen it myself. Khan Saab gave him no responsibilities. He only sits and reads all day. Truly, God is great!"

As the days elapsed, the tale of Potato, the painter's son, snowballed. In reality, no villager had ever been inside the mammoth gates of the Khan House, not even Khassi Kasai. The closest they would ever come to it would be through the stories they told themselves and, sometimes, that was as good as the real thing.

Those stories made Jaaji's heart swell with emotion. One day, he came to see for himself what had become of Salim. Peeking through the iron gates of the Khan House, the painter saw his son on the veranda, dressed in a school uniform. He pushed his arms through the gates as if to touch him, but immediately pulled back. The Floating Pir's words warned him once again. Jaaji closed his eyes and let the tears fall, as he got on his bicycle and pedaled back to the village. He never spoke about Salim again.

There at the Khan House, out of all the amenities, Salim became fond of one in particular. It was behind the back garden, this chamber, and it connected to Khan's study through a slim corridor. Inside, sunlight fell through the prisms of the glass ceiling in fractured rays making patterns on the floor. Glass bouquets hung from the walls and the ceiling, and, with the flick of a switch, could light up night time. Persian rugs over cool marble floors, exotic creatures stared back in stillness from their mounts, their eyes delivering their final chilling glances. Along the walls, oak shelves nestled miles of endless leather-bound volumes. It was heaven, and Salim held a VIP pass.

"This is our family library," said Khan, thumping his cane on the marble.

"I can't believe it, sir. I've never seen so many books in my life ... and I can take any of them?" Salim asked with widening eyes, as he stared at a stuffed bustard displayed mid-flight on the wall.

"Of course, you can. You can take any book, as long as you put it back when you're done."

"Oh sir, thank you, thank you so much," cried Salim, kissing his hand.

"For God's sake, boy, stop thanking me ... I might change my mind and send you back to Khanpur!" He sat down at his desk and leaned over to say, "I've been thinking about something. It's important that a man have a surname, not random monkey tags that you villagers go by. We need a name that is above all, creed and caste. Something royal. Something..." He paused, tapping his chin with his fingers, "I know ... Agha, the king, the warrior ... yes, that shall be your name."

In the coming days, and before Salim could manage to fully take in the Khan House, General Khan enrolled him in St. Walter Blisschesterson

College for Boys, a seminary of refinement and epicenter of prestige. This crimson brick palace stretched for acres in the heart of Lorr. After all, Blisschestersonians were no ordinary brethren. No sir, they were handcrafted casks of influence, prepared to become men of Scotch tumblers and imported cigars, of Italian shoes and silk ties, to captain cricket teams and govern empires, to marshal armies and wage wars. To sit in the red colosseum was to become a future owner of men, with the power to hold destinies in the hollow of your palm; and the more you could hold, the greater the itch to squeeze your fist closed. It was the only power in the world worth having. Dry-eyed, standing under the red towers, Salim Agha was in awe, acknowledging that, in his new identity and his boundless acumen, he himself had a power of his own, unlike the pitiful herds that stampeded through the city daily, pawning their integrity, consuming humiliation as if it were a vitamin supplement.

"From today onwards, if anyone asks, you are my orphaned nephew. Do not reveal where you come from or who you really are. No one will understand," General Khan said, as he escorted Salim to the boarding school. "Just keep your head down and focus on your work."

It was an awkward thing to ask for, to expunge his origin, but Salim accepted guiltlessly.

"Of course, General Saab," he replied without hesitation. "You will see, I will not let you down."

Shaking Khan's hand, he turned and headed down the curving campus road towards the boarding house, walking fearlessly, to be among sultans, and to complete the extermination of the drunken painter's son.

The Princess of Eden

I know what you're thinking. This is not the story you were expecting. You probably suppose that I, an assassin for the Islamic Caliphate, shouldn't be trusted. People who look like me are seldom trusted in this part of the world. Yes, it is true. I do come from an empire lost in confusion about origins; where followers of modernity are hung from trees and women are flogged for revealing smiles. But I'm nothing like those merciless fiends who forced their ethereal reckoning upon us. In fact, sir, I am a victim. In a way, we all are—victims of forced identities.

When the Caliphate arrived, it was like a vicious white light, so strong that it cast no shadows, there was no refuge for miles. And as it burned through our selfhood, we became ghosts, phantoms unsure of our identities.

I had become one of those phantoms, programmed to act upon hatred. So, it is understandable that you question why I, being aware of this identity crisis, exhibit such tenderness towards my victim in this story. That is because I only came to this realization after I had murdered Salim Agha.

You will have to trust me.

Sir, we find ourselves seven years on from where we left off.

Salim is a teenager now, a teenager who has extinguished the remains of his past with his heel and has allowed his knowledge to catapult him over rows of boarding school dimwits. This was truly a novelty in such a school as Blisschesterson since he did not captain a cricket team, like his mate Mitti Pao, nor was he bequeathed national treasures like Prince Azim Molkheiah of Brunei, and he surely wasn't gorgeous enough to peddle sexual favors in the quiet depths of the junior school locker rooms. No sir, his was a distinct, intellectual propensity, one which helped him build a new frontier of friendship using his academic persona as a counterweight to the politician-spawn, the sport ace, and the feudal princeling. It helped him create his own legion, allowing him to vacation on summer ranches, ride thoroughbreds, and sip colas at pool parties. And after all, he was only executing his general's orders.

"Peer into the heart of each soldier. What does he desire? What does he have to offer? Guide him yet use him in whatever manner you need in order to win the war," General Khan said to him one Sunday night, after the drinks trolley was rolled into the study. It was pertinent advice, as a boys' boarding school can be a war zone. And in this battleground, Salim's secret tutoring service became an unlikely safe haven where excellent exam results were bartered for favors, such as Mitti Pao adding his name to the cricket team roster, or Prince Azim gifting him a record player. Consequently, similar to the levitating saint who had once prophesized his life, Salim promulgated the sacramental wafers of wisdom from his dorm-room pulpit, chalking inscriptions on walls while the surrounding devotees bobbed their heads. He was the bootlegger of knowledge.

But how did it all come to this? How did a boy from the village acquire such charm? You see, Salim saw the world differently from everyone else. The Floating Pir was aware of this when he saw a remarkable world simmering behind his eyes. He could sense that the boy was special. That is because, since he was a child, Salim saw the world in numbers. Distances, words, and energy spoke to him mathematically. His teachers also picked up on this when he was a young child. When he first arrived at the boarding school as a timid eight-year-old boy, Mrs. Alam, the geography teacher, realized his unique gift. One day in her class, Salim had calculated the length of Africa from North to South on her world map by using just his forefinger and thumb. "Eight thousand kilometers. Yes, that's how tall Africa is, Ma'am," he claimed, eyeballing the map from the back-bench.

Mrs. Alam immediately pulled out her notebook and ruler and started scratching out calculations. Then, without uttering a word, she took the boy to the headmaster's office where a faculty meeting was called. There, Salim sat doe-eyed in the middle of the room, answering absurd questions.

"What about twelve times ninety-three?"

"How far is that tree, Salim? How about the ceiling?"

"Wait, wait. Ask him how far you're standing from him in millimeters. Go on, ask him."

This went on for a while until Salim felt overwhelmed and his eyes began to well. The teachers retracted immediately, patted him on the back, and escorted him to the hostel.

"Don't worry, son," they said. "There's nothing wrong with you. You're just very special."

Special. He didn't like that word. Special meant that he was different and different sticks out of the crowd. Different was precisely what General Khan had asked him not to be. He had to be careful. He didn't want his specialness to give him away. And he didn't want to come across as being cocky in front of the other students either because he saw what happened when the dorm lights were switched off at night. So, over the next seven years, he used his uniqueness to his advantage, to help others and to buy their friendship. It took a bit of time, but eventually the boarding school became his kingdom.

You might ask whether the boy ever missed his family in these seven years. He did, of course, and asked about his father from time to time. But Jaaji had made General Khan deliver him a cold message—that the village had no room for him anymore. Salim felt a lump in his throat when he heard that but vowed to himself to never talk about the village again, believing that he had to completely adapt to his new world and forget the old one.

And there was so much to love about this new world of his. For example, the game of chess was something he valued immensely. In Khan's study, he would pull out a battered wooden board from under the crystal cupboard and tenderly align the porcelain pieces in their rightful squares. Then he would give Khan a cheeky smile and say, "What say you, General Saab? Ready for battle?"

To which Khan would reluctantly oblige, "Oh alright, but just one game." One game would turn into two or, on a good day, four. Salim cherished those moments. Their games would often take on multifaceted narratives and, over the years, the pieces evolved into intricate characters. They even came up with their own poem:

The knight might be cunning,
The bishop may be sly,
But the rook's a real prick,
Watching as they all die

Chess was more than just a game to Salim. It was why, often in school, Mitti Pao would enrage him by insisting on playing morbid games like Snakes and Ladders.

"But why not?" Mitti would ask, pouting through his winding locks.

"Why not? Because Mitti, I fucking hate that game! Instead of using your mind, you would rather roll the dice?"

He wondered to himself why he despised this board game so much. The whole concept of it irritated him. Yes, it was true that Mitti Pao's intellect could only stretch as far as a throw of the dice, and it was also true that Snakes and Ladders was the only game in which other boarders could pose a challenge to him, but he hated the duality of the game—the bipolarity of it, if you must. That at every ladder there lurked an imminent threat waiting to offset your advance, a Ying to every Yang, a night to every day, a pauper to every prince. You get the point. It was childish and best left to feeble minds, to teach lessons of reward and penalty.

At times, after the final bell on Fridays, his friends would offer him a ride to the Khan House and watch him disappear inside without looking back, but at other times Salim waited until the last car exited the school and he snuck out on foot, walked down the Mall Road and hailed a rickshaw puller. This unusual act he conducted in stealth mode, because a Blisschesterson uniform was not stitched for such things and to be caught straddling a rickshaw could jeopardize one's image. Nonetheless, as these weekends approached, an inexorable weight would begin to drag him down, as if gravity had suddenly doubled. Salim treasured evenings spent with General Khan, but Chaku had begun to make his weekends at the Khan House unbearable; his pranks were getting out of hand.

When Prince Azim's gift, the record player, vanished, Salim let it go. But a couple of things set him off. Chaku had shifted his bed outside during the night without him noticing, and to make matters worse, he had pissed on his school uniform. While washing his clothes in the bathroom, anger began to flush his face red. He decided something had to be done. For him, it seemed that the only way out, was in—into the Khan House that is, as a house servant. Because being a house servant meant having spotless eating utensils, new clothes, cash bonuses and, most important, direct access to the family's ears. Indeed, house servants, it went without question, were not to be fucked with. He longed for that. Not just to keep Chaku at bay but to absorb the enigmas of the Khan House. He imagined a lot of things about the house when he heard Bally the hunchback speak about it: the Spanish marble, the ivory banister, and the maniacal color scheme of the living room. Most of all, he dreamt about the mysterious silhouette that danced upon the curtain above the servants' quarters at night. That silhouette summoned his soul. Surely, it was his soul that knew before him that he had to see Laila Khan for the very first time, in the flesh, and confirm that she was truly the angel of his imagination.

Just as that thought arrived, as Salim was pinning his wet shirt on a clothesline, Bally grabbed him by the shoulders.

"By god, come quickly. Khan Saab is asking for you," he said, pulling him into the veranda. Something was up. Panic was making the hunchback's hands shake as he pushed Salim towards the garden.

Khan's ears, it turned out, had fallen upon a rumor.

"Is it true, you little rascal?" Khan asked, sipping tea, slouched in his metal garden chair, "General Ali told me that his son Liber Ali has gone from flunking to miraculously topping the damn class and not only that, everyone at the Garrison Club has been talking about it. They say someone is rescuing the halfwits of Blisschesterson."

"General Saab ... it started with one or two boys but now I tutor fifty or so. They pay me good money. I hope you don't mind, sir. I was going to tell you."

"Mind? Of course I bloody mind. I've been paying tutors through the nose to no avail and here you are starting secret societies around town, you little bugger. From today, you will tutor my children every weekend and on holidays when you're back from school. Is that clear? I will send Chaku to pick you up from the school gates on Fridays."

"Yes, sir. Of course, sir. Why not?"

Why not? It was a ridiculous question; as pathetic and naïve as one he had ever asked himself because he knew very well why not. For there lay a slight encumbrance in his path, one which he had momentarily pushed to the back of his mind. An outside servant could not just waltz into the Khan House like a supplicant among its labyrinth of interconnected rooms, gaudy furniture, and thick carpets. For a servant to be inside the house among Khan's children, one had to either be a eunuch or possibly senile. Only two house servants fell into this category: Bally and Laila's maid, Bilki. Not even the Christian maids were allowed complete access to the staircase that led to the bedrooms. Because from that zone of wicked mirth, one could often hear merciless shrieks which could castrate the manliest of men. The very snake on Salim's ladder of triumph.

No one knew her real name. She was simply known amongst the servants as the Evil Witch. It was hard to describe the fear she had instilled over the years. The hair on Salim's knuckles stood every time her lame foot scraped the marble floor a hundred yards away. As her howls pierced the walls, they sent Jabberwocky meowing like a kitten into his kennel and made the pigeons flutter their wings in agitation. She spewed a dread that encompassed all, even General Khan, which is why he had lodged her in a lurid part of the house. It was on the third floor, where a solitary light bulb flickered in a hallway of nipple-twisting chill. At the end of the hallway was her room. It was about the size of a servant's lair and it had a tiny balcony facing the main garden. From this balcony, all manner of things would fly.

"Anything she doesn't like, she throws out," Bally had once told Salim. "One day, we were in the garden and we heard the Evil Witch scream, 'You call this tea, you whore!'. We froze, by God. Things started to fly out the window. First there were teacups, then saucers, then a fourteen-year-old girl. We don't know what the poor girl had done, but she flew out of there like one of Khan Saab's pigeons, by God. The girl lived, but she still wakes up screaming at night, poor thing. Khan Saab sent her back to Khanpur." Wide-eyed servants shuffled around him reliving the horror. "That part," he pointed. "By God, that part of the lawn, no one steps on. Ask Maali. He refuses to wield his shears there, that's why it's greener than the rest of the garden." Whereupon Maali had breathed slowly, nodding, acknowledging his anxiety induced by the memory of once receiving a flying breakfast tray on the lip.

"We ... just have to be careful my mother doesn't find out," said General Khan as an afterthought. Salim stood frozen until the hunchback yanked him back to consciousness. He returned to his room shivering with anxiety, imagining himself flying from the top floor towards his inevitable death. Shaking his head, he said a prayer, "Oh God, please be kind."

That evening, General Khan led the way as Salim stepped into the house to meet his new students. He hesitated while removing his sandals at the front door, but General Khan pulled him inside. Then, his feet touched the wintry marble and his face caught a breeze from the ceiling fan. Another pull on the arm. This time towards the dining hall, where he was left by himself with no introductions as Khan ran towards a ringing telephone in the hallway. Salim looked down at his toes as they twitched on the carpet.

"So, you're going to be our new tutor? Well, let me tell you something, I don't take orders, I only give them," said Laila, with folded arms as Salim's eyes fixated on her face. He had only seen her silhouette, but the real thing was something else. He had not seen skin so fair before, like the cream that settled on warm milk. She had her father's emerald eyes, but hers were under a roof of the most elegant lashes. What startled him the most though, were her lips; ripened summer fruits tempting him to take a bite, whose corners curled upwards causing the faint illusion of a smile. These were strange oddities he could not come to terms with, small flaws communally merging to create something flawless.

"But this is Salim. He's an outside servant. What's he going to teach us?" asked Khalil, Khan's eldest son.

"No, you silly. He's not a servant. He goes to the boarding house in your school and is one of Daddy's projects," said Laila, as she followed Salim's gaze behind her shoulder.

"You mean like Beema," said Gibran, the four-year-old.

"Not Beema ... Deema Engine," Khalil said.

"Hey, you! What are you staring at?" barked Laila.

"What are you staring at, huh?" Khalil followed.

"Nothing," replied Salim, as he pondered a timely response, "I was just mesmerized by the ... the wall. It's absurdly..."

"Pink," Laila interrupted. "Yes, yes, we know it's shocking-pink and the furniture is golden."

"You don't like this furniture?" roared Khalil.

"No ... I mean..."

"Our grandmother ... she is colorblind, you know. Pink, blue, it's all the same to her. How is she to know, poor woman?"

"No, Madam Laila, I just wanted to say ... that the painting, it's from the ... uh ... expressionist era."

"The what?" she asked, her eyes squinting. "Anyway, you forget that. Just remember to be here after lunch on weekends and we will bring our books. And don't be late! That will be all."

"And bathe before entering the house," Khalil said.

"Yes, sir," he replied, looking downwards as Laila whisked past Bally who had been standing with his head bowed in a corner the whole time, as if he were a piece of furniture himself. Khalil followed his sister out of the dining hall as Salim felt a tiny hand tug on his trousers.

"Pssst ... listen," said Gibran, covering his mouth. "Don't act smart with her. She'll throw you out ... I like you." Salim inclined his head in reply as Gibran skipped towards his sister who had left her scent lingering in the living room amongst the unnerving colors.

After Bally pushed his stunned body through the kitchen door, Salim's fears were shot by a tranquilizer dart and a feeling of satisfaction took over and tucked itself into bed with him that night.

Truly, purpose is a house made from fickle bricks. And his house completely collapsed the first time he took in the beauty of Laila Khan. In place of whatever lay there before, now lay Laila, the foundation. Verily, no love is purer than adolescent love. Yes ... that kind of un-adulterated, unconditional piousness which cannot be replicated; a devotion you feel only once at an early time in your life, in an era governed by passion alone. A weird feeling kept him up that night. Laila's words began to fall like raindrops on his heart. He began talking to his reflection in the mirror.

"I don't take orders, I give them." A smile came to his face as he put his hands on his hips and tilted his head. "Can't you see, it's pink. Our poor grandmother can't tell the difference." Then there was a giggle that turned into a cough that turned back into a giggle. "She can't tell the difference!"

"Shut up, sister-fucker. Go to sleep!" a voice roared from the garden.

"And don't be late ... I'm warning you ... don't be late!" He pointed at himself as he began to dance. Then he fell on his bed and inhaled the tepid silence until his dreams took over.

There are many things we can say about Laila Khan. But, for the sake of our tale, let's examine the elements of a true love saga: two enamored lovers and the enchanted world where they first meet. And let's talk about the first love saga ever told: the story of Adam and Eve, and the garden of paradise that symbolized their union. Of course, in this story, there's a snake, an apple, and an eternity drenched in regret. But there's more to it than that. This story is about Adam's love for Eve but also his desire for the Eden from which they were banished. Eve is Adam's beloved, magically fashioned from his own rib, who becomes the embodiment of a utopia they had once shared. What I'm alluding to is the following: where you fall in love is as essential as who you fall in love with. This is the most vital truth in the story of Salim Agha.

That night, as he giggled in his sleep, Salim had fallen irreversibly in love with the radiant Laila Khan. And, over the years, she became a reminder of his desire for the Pureland of his youth, the country that was eventually snatched away from him.

Yes, it is true that this story is about Pureland, but it is also true that Laila Khan is about this story.

The Evil Witch

Things changed. From that day on, Salim's weekdays turned into a torrid anticipation for Fridays when he would be driven back to the Khan House. When the final bell rang, he waited outside the gates to be picked up. Khan had made sure Chaku, despite his growing annoyance, brought Salim home well before dinner. Chaku was nauseated at the notion of driving a villager to and from school as if he were royalty nauseated him. He would deliver cold stares through the rear-view mirror, but Salim would just look away as though he were in a permanent daydream. He didn't give a fuck anymore. About anything. Anything but Laila Khan.

Thus, for many months, there developed a one-sided love, the most painful kind, the only kind Salim would ever know. He observed and worshipped Laila while seated at the oval dining table. He would sit on the cushioned chairs and, at times, find house servants peeking in to witness this phenomenon with their own eyes. Because they had heard the Evil Witch often claim that there was nothing more repulsive than to have a servant sit on the furniture. So, rumors of this bizarre act made Salim's reputation swell, as if resting his ass on the masters' chairs had injected him with their power.

He nursed the children's curiosity like he had done with the Blisschesterson dullards. Laila showed him he could be their equal even if it was only for two hours a day, three days a week. She did this by asking him questions and responding with satisfaction when he delivered an elaborate answer—she did it with a smile, flicking her hair behind her ears, biting her lip. These were dangerous things to imply to a peasant; the amnesty of your home, the comfort of your chair, then perhaps a sip from your crystal glasses and, before you know it, they think they're you. Laila knew this in the back of her mind. But there was something different about Salim. She could talk to him about anything and he held on to any word she uttered like it was the last drop of water on earth.

"Salim ... have you ever wondered what dolphins sound like?" she asked one day, a casual inquiry which sent Salim on an all-night quest in the library, buried in a leather bound Britannica only to return the next day with a forged dolphin imitation, telling her that the dolphin's lips also curled into a smile like hers. Then she giggled bashfully with her fingers over her mouth. Tempting.

"Liar you are. That's not what they sound like," she said, scrunching her nose. To which Salim stuck out his tongue and crossed his eyes. It made her laugh even more, which tickled his heart. Her laughter was worth anything. To him she was more beautiful than any fifteen-year-old girl could possibly be. With her lustrously taut skin and ripening breasts, and her graceful feet, void of calluses, and her hairless legs that peeked at him from under her long skirts. On some occasions, he masturbated to these assembled visuals of her before he went to bed, and the following morning would carry a sour guilt. After a while, he stopped this foul activity because his love was pure and purity had to be conserved, for it can easily be tainted. And once polluted, it loses its very essence.

Surely Laila Khan must have a flaw like everyone else, no? This was something he had thought about a lot while his mind wandered as she walked around the room, and he imagined what a wonderful existence it would be to become the floor for a day, to be trodden upon by her angelic feet, or how he could become the glass of water kissing her lips at every sip.

Nonetheless, with every ounce of ecstasy she fed him, a menace prowled three stories above them in a dingy hallway, and each time he entered the Khan House, feelings of fear and love tussled in his heart. In the distance, a poisonous serpent slithered quietly towards an upright ladder.

"You should be careful of the Evil Witch. She has the strength of fifteen Zafar Khans. By God, she will chuck you from her window and you won't even know it," Bally said smuggling Salim out from the house one night. Even he recognized the unavoidable truth that it would only be a matter of time until rumors of him penetrating the sanctity of the Khan House would find their way from the servants' quarters to the third floor.

"Oh, Bally Saab ... don't you worry. Laila Madam and Khan Saab won't let anything happen to me."

But Bally was right. Whispers squeezed through lips, drifting upwards like helium-filled balloons, and one Saturday evening, as she did every week, the Evil Witch descended the ivory bannister, heaving and cursing, to dine with her family. She approached the dining hall, which was lit up by two massive chandeliers at each end, and immediately put the fear of God into the children's hearts. They sat upright as though they were pulled by an imaginary string from their heads. A grimace wrinkled her face as she sat down, and General Khan responded to her look with a scorned pout of his own.

"Did you wash your hands, Zafar?" she shrieked, wriggling into her chair at the head of the dining table.

"Of course, Mother. What do you take me for, a peasant?" Khan replied, forking his potatoes with his right hand as he always did in her presence. Because as a child, while eating with his unclean, left hand, he had received a thumping fist on his ear.

"Do you not know it is haram to eat with the left hand? It's impure. Are you a bloody Hindu?" she had yelled, crashing her palm in his face after each word. "The ... left ... is ... for ... cleaning ... bums! It is the devil's hand!"

Those words had haunted Khan ever since, looming over his head as he learned to write and eat with the hand his own body hadn't elected. The Evil Witch had been in control of his life ever since his father, the great General Pasha Khan, died when he was young. There was a saying among the servants—she spent nine months breathing life into him and fifty years sucking it right back out.

"Khalil, line up the fork on your plate when you're done!"

Khalil, staring at his dinner plate, obliged, lining up his utensils parallel to each other.

"Yes Daadi, I forgot, sorry," he said.

"Laila, please put your hair up at dinner."

"Yes Daadi," Laila said, tying her hair in a bun.

"What's this I'm hearing, Zafar?" she began, cutting her carrots into tiny pieces and raising her bushy brow. "I've heard you've let that godless black servant into our home? Without my permission!" Her knife screeched to a halt on her plate as she looked up at the chandelier. "Oh Lord, why did you not take me as well when Pasha died? I had to see this day ... a brown kaffir in my home, in front of my Laila ... and he sits on our chairs!"

"Mother, Salim teaches the children. He's the smartest boy in Blisschesterson and he is not an infidel, he's an Ahmadi from our village. I've brought him in this house! It's *my* decision and it stands." General Khan bound courage into a tight snowball and hurled it down a slope.

"How dare you bring in village boys into my house without asking me? Especially low castes. Ahmadi? Have you completely lost your faith along with your mind? They are the worst of the worst. They're complete heathens. They don't even believe in our Prophet and call themselves Muslims! Bloody heretics! You can become a general, Zafar, but you're still living in *my* house, don't you forget that. You're a disgrace to your father's name." Her long drooping nose pointed at him, and every time she spoke a large black mole danced on her brow.

As abuse was hurled in his direction like unpinned grenades, Khan sat in the quiet shade of his honor. All he could do was vacate the battlefield in silence, something which was against his very nature.

"Little-black-Christian-Hindu boys running around the house! You call yourself a Pashtun man?" she shrieked as her son left the dining room amidst rows of bowed servant heads. Khan had never walked out like this before. Perhaps he had had enough.

It's hard to explain what really happened that night. The best I can describe it as is like this: rebellion took its first yawn after a long hibernation. While she hobbled back to her room, the Evil Witch knew that the last grains of authority had slipped through her clenched fingers, and her son too realized a boundary had been breached—though neither knew who was left holding the reins.

While Laila took her brothers to their rooms, General Khan retired to his study where he sat with Jabberwocky for the rest of the night, sulking in candlelight. Outside, as the loud screams pierced the brick walls, the servants twitched, and each time this happened, Salim recalled Bally's late-night soliloquies.

"It all started with her daughter-in-law you know, Khan Saab's wife, Zohra. By God, she was a compassionate woman; always good to the servants ... the Witch poisoned her after she gave birth to baby Gibran. She gave out her last sigh, like a tortured prisoner, thanking her Lord before she died. The General did not take her death well, because the walls whispered the truth; it was hard to ignore. So he slowly isolated his mother ... first it was the ground floor guest room, followed by the second floor, and finally the top floor with its long hallway that ended in two small rooms: one for her and one for her maid. Truth is, by God, since Zohra Madam's death, Khan Saab has imprisoned himself, sitting in his study at night drinking that piss-water. At times, I can hear his heart breaking over and over again."

No one in the Khan House could digest the Evil Witch's mockery of her son. Not Bally, not Abbas, not Chaku, not the Christian maids, and certainly not Salim. They all shriveled like salted worms that night as the Evil Witch's shrieks tore through the walls and into the foggy Lorr night.

Salim slept uneasy that evening. In the morning, while eating fried rotis just before he left for school, that shrill voice boomed through the garden and into his room, locking his jaw mid-chew. This was followed by the unnerving jangle of shattering glass.

"Salim Baba?" Bally inquired with a gentle knock on his door. "Son, I think you should come outside."

"What is it, Bally Saab?" Salim asked, knowing that that morning, Khan's first-Sunday-of-the month visit to the village had created a brief window of vulnerability for him, leaving him defenseless.

"Son, prepare yourself. The Witch is asking for you." Bally's words sent a gulp of fear down Salim's throat. "Make sure you don't eat or drink anything she gives you. Don't be scared, son, we will be on the lawn. I don't know if we can catch you ... but, by God, we'll try."

He nodded at the old man's noble intentions. He commenced the treacherous walk into the house, kicked his sandals off at the front door, climbed past the second story and waddled towards the hallway of darkness. At the end of the corridor stood a ghost-like maid, hair covering her face, her finger pointing towards his doom. He breathed in slowly, closing his eyes as he felt a swift breeze when she scurried past him like an escaping kitchen rat.

He had not been to the third floor before. In fact, he'd never been this high off the ground. It looked like a sure fall to death from where he stood, his quaking knees were the first to remind him of it. So, with each step he took he tested the floor. *Step ... tap tap ... step ... tap tap.* The hallway went on for miles and everything smelled like dust—dead, Evil Witch skin pluming around his feet. He felt his toes immersed in it; it made his stomach contract as he arrived at the door.

"Can I come..."

"Get inside and shut the door!" the Evil Witch yelled, prayer beads clicking in her crooked fingers. She peered at him as if to spear him with her look. Immediately, his eyes tumbled on to her gruesome hammertoes which curled away from a battered bunion and carted her limping carcass around, inducing nauseating sounds of toenails on marble. Her skin, hanging like loose clothing on her bones, made the hair on Salim's neck dance. She held a long wooden staff, taller than herself, which she used to propel her body at light speed to an inch from his face.

"Tell me, fat boy. How is it that you're in my family's life?"

"I don't know what you mean, Madam. General Saab brought me here from the village. I go to the boarding school..."

"Don't be scared of me, boy," she said, flying in the blink of an eye to the window. Her creased fingers pushed against the glass as a warm breeze blew into the room. Salim pressed his heels against the bedroom door. "Do you know what we do to infidels?"

"But I'm a Muslim. Not an infidel."

"It's bad enough my son has Christian girls running around the house infecting everything. Now I have to deal with a bloody Ahmadi kaffir? Come here, boy. There's something I need you to fix." She walked towards the balcony. "This window's creaking, maybe the screw fell again. My son says you're the smartest boy he knows. Let's see you do something around here for a change."

Salim made a lethargic approach towards her. The balcony was tiny, as if it were an architectural mishap or added as an afterthought. From there, he could see the lawn down below where the staff had gathered. Circling around them was a moaning German Shepherd. "Look closely behind the curtain, the screw must've fallen there. It's this long," she illustrated with her forefinger. Salim's breathing became rapid and tremors invaded his toes, shooting up to his arms, squeezing his heart through his veins.

"Please, Madam. Don't throw me out. I will leave this house and go back to the village immediately," he whimpered, falling at her feet.

"Stop it, you fool! Get off my legs! Bilki! Come here, you bitch. Take this boy off of me!"

"Please Madam, I will not say a word. I'll just leave. Please don't throw me!"

His hands grasped her ankles, and the old woman fell backwards. A seismic quake took over his body. His mind fought to stay in control, and through the corner of his eye he witnessed another quivering body come to a peaceful stillness. Foam dribbled out from the side of his mouth and before his eyes closed shut, he saw something. There it was, under the elevated bed—a metal screw the size of a forefinger.

❖

As Salim's body convulsed to a stop, his soul exited through the Khan House and into the fog. He swept through the clouds, up on his way to space. Looking back from this asphalt emptiness, he saw his planet for the first time; without color codes and labels, different from the map in Mrs. Alam's geography class. Like his city, the planet was surrounded by endless darkness. This was the moment, while his body lay in the VIP section of Mayo Hospital and his soul raced towards the heavens that his heart began to fill with passion as he saw his nation. Had he, like Adam and Eve, succumbed to a venomous serpent, and been banished from his Eden to the Underworld? Had his short-lived dream of being with his beloved, suddenly turned into a nightmare? He couldn't tell. All he knew was that his fondness for his home was making his chest ache.

Then he arrived at an unknown destination. From afar, he heard the sweet chorus of a myna's song. His eyelids fluttered open. His feet now stood on the edge of a celestial floor and, around him, white caped giants tilted their heads towards him. One leaned forward and grabbed him. Salim shook in protest.

"This?" said one beast.

"Yes, I believe he's the one," said another.

"You can't be serious. This one doesn't even have a beard yet."

"Move away you two." Gabriel broke into the huddle. "The little boy's scared can't you see? We meet again, Salim. I first saw you when you were about to be born, believe you me."

"You moron, how can he remember? He was only a babe?"

"We have been waiting for you, Salim. I just wanted to talk to you before you woke up down there." One giant began to smell his armpit, and the other, his hands.

"Just know there is a prophecy of greatness bestowed upon you. It's a foretelling of love. Look," Gabriel said, pointing below at the clouds, "there is your beloved nation and you are its savior. Conquer the rivers of time and attain greatness like the heroes do in the Bombay talkies. I will have you know that I'm fond of these Bombay talkies, believe you me. Anytime you want, I will be here for you." Gabriel started to dance as the others joined him one by one. "Oh, won't you follow the way to my heart, my heart, my heart," he sang as the beasts locked their elbows, swaying like children at a fair.

Salim fought to wake up from this dream as a chant started echoing in his ear.

O when the saints, o when the saints go marching in...

His soul began to fall back into the darkness. He screamed but there was no sound. He sniffed but there was no smell. He breathed but there was no air. Yet his ears heard a familiar voice.

"Salim ... Salim, wake up," Bally said. "By God, doctor, he's back! Tell General Saab!"

This time, there was no confusion between reality and fantasy in his mind as he could smell the hookah smoke on Bally's breath. It was profane, but he was pleased it was there to welcome him.

The General's Vow

Rumors floated amongst the staff, conjoining into a collective nest.

"Did you know the Evil Witch tried to throw Salim from the window? That's what killed her."

"No, I was there. I mean, I heard from Chaku who heard from Maali who heard it from one of the Christian maids who said that the Evil Witch was strangled. Salim killed her!"

"You're both talking shit. You forget that the Evil Witch had the strength of ten Zafar Khans. Bilki could hear them, and she said that Salim grabbed her feet, begging her not to throw him. She fell on her bed ... and it was just her time. Heart attack. One cannot argue with God's will," said Bally as a final verdict, which the surrounding bodies approved with an inclination of the head. "You know, by God, I've never seen General Saab acting this way. When we arrived at the hospital, he was more worried for Salim than his own mother."

"Today, I even saw Saab eating with his left hand."

"Khan Saab has locked the third-floor room, thank God. Now I don't have to clean that filthy place anymore," said Bilki.

It was a peculiar day. The funeral was brisk, the gathering almost jovial. The fog cleared that morning, allowing the sun to kiss the lawn through the banyan tree; the sun rays rode upon plumes of musky, sweet-tasting earth that lifted from the ground. Light had returned to the Khan House. The morning smelled like fresh linen. The pigeons paraded around the lawn, circling one another.

General Khan's strut, too, had altered after returning from his mother's funeral. It was the walk of a newly released inmate. His face showed traces of tears. It was hard to know whether the tears were an upshot of melancholy or bliss. Whatever demon Khan thought possessed his mother had finally released her from her torment, and in the process lifted the latch on a rusty old cage.

Khan took tea in the garden that evening as he thought of his beloved, Zohra, the meticulous arranger of flowers, the carrier of a hundred suns in her heart, whose skin shone golden in the sunlight. A woman who never showed contempt for the Evil Witch, not even during her final suffocating moments, clinging to her bedsheet as she witnessed her executioner savor her asphyxiation. Khan tried removing these grotesque images from his mind, but the walls spoke otherwise, and Zohra's presence lingered in the house long after her death, longer than her actual life. Everything reminded him of her, including Laila's own meticulousness, the way she lined up cutlery at right angles, straightened drapes and reorganized his cupboard from time to time. She, too, felt that settling dust was a reminder of her mother and had servants perpetually polishing, scouring, rearranging.

Khan never married again, never loved again, and only once had the desire for a courtesan's body in the depths of the red-light district. As he lay there on a charpoy in a dingy room reeking of cheap perfume and rose water, he felt as though he were the prostitute. He never repeated this humiliating deed, even though his fellow army men pleaded with him to accompany them during their late-night ventures to Diamond Market, to the corridor-like streets where no diamond was ever traded and where many Mughal bastards were born. For him though, dignity and honor were values that he carried in his shirt pocket like an identification card, because you never know when you need to prove your pedigree. Snaking through the slim raucous roads of the walled city of Lorr among pimps and transvestites was not his idea of fun.

"Khalil Gibran!" he yelled, as his sons rushed to embrace their father. They knew his mood when he would summon them with a single word. Jabberwocky was not to be left out as he too bolted out of his pen to roll with the Khan clan while they lay in the garden, with the servants watching from a distance like doting parents. Khan grabbed his boys and pinned them to the ground every time they tried to get up.

"Daddy, let us go!" Khalil cried. Gibran giggled so hard his eyes began to water.

"Uff, Zafar, please stop. You will get your clothes dirty, na," said cousin Tehzeeb, lingering on in the house after all the guests had left, as she always did.

"Oh, come on, Tezi. They have been through a lot. It's only puppy wrestling." Khan lifted his youngest high in the air with one hand. "You should try it. It will ease the stick up your backside. Your husband not coming to collect you? It's getting late, no?"

Cousin Tehzeeb twitched her nose and twisted in her chair. "Just finishing up my tea, don't get your General Saab panties in a knot."

Salim looked from afar wishing Khan would ask him to join the bear wrestle. Groggy still from his medication, he sat down and began to think. In certain circumstances, the punishment for a servant to even touch a member of the house was a public flogging. Had a servant actually committed murder, he and his family would be extinguished like cigarettes. It was certainly not the case for Salim as he, in Khan's mind, became a hero of sorts. It was a strange thing to think of, but it was a common theme in the Khan House that morning. Salim's innocence was universally accepted. Everyone in the house recognized the naturalness of the Evil Witch's death. Almost as if they had been waiting for her body to finally buckle under seven decades of torture. Nonetheless, it was the happiest day that Salim could recall; one of those memories that endured while others are pushed off a cliff to perish in the valley of broken dolls.

Khan finally did call upon Salim and asked him to accompany him to the terrace. There inside the pigeon pen, Khan held, in his hands, a majestic white creature with fluffy boots.

"See this one is Lat, and that Manat, and that over there is Uzza, the eldest. These are my exalted birds. See how grand they are. They will bring me hundreds of rupees this year." He exposed a pigeon's belly while flinging seeds from his pocket. The fluttering wings startled Salim as he stepped out of the pen. "Don't be scared, boy. They're harmless."

"No, sir, I'm not scared ... maybe just a little."

The General shook his head as he pulled his large body out of the cage and locked the front door. He brushed feathers from his shirt, tightened the twirls of his mustache and headed down with his arm around Salim.

"Come, I think cousin Tezi's gone. We can go downstairs."

Khan's sweat-soaked linen and Old Spice exuded a mustardy smell. Under his arm, Salim felt secure, like the pigeon nestling against his palm. Salim cherished that feeling.

But there was a particular recollection which he treasured most, one that he wanted to preserve eternally. It took place in the study that night. Khan's study had become a sacred office for military men who would congregate at night, muttering under their breaths. At times, Salim heard heated arguments and sinister laughs bleeding through the bolted door. But that night, there were no soldiers in that room. It was just him, the General and an old chessboard.

"Check!" General Khan exclaimed as his knight hooked Salim's king in the arms of peril. "Can't escape me today. I think I've got you!"

"Good move, General Saab. It seems you've trapped me."

"Oh no, Salim!" said Gibran, leaning into his lap. "Will Daddy finally beat you?" General Khan's fingers twitched with excitement as he looked down at the chessboard, seeing a king trudge towards a line of pawns. His face showed a childlike sparkle as four Scotch-and-waters had done a bit of nose painting.

"Ha! Checkmate! Finally, the great Salim Agha loses to a mere soldier!" shouted Khan as Gibran giggled in fits.

"Well played, sir. Today you're unstoppable. Definitely not a mere soldier," said Salim as Laila's commanding cry for her brother invited moans from Gibran and a quiet word in his ear from Salim. "What do we say?"

"Oh, sorry," Gibran said. "Goodnight, Daddy, and well played. And goodnight, Salim, better luck next time!" The boy stuck out his hand to congratulate his father who yanked him towards himself for a kiss. "Aaaah! Daddy your mustache is tickly!"

As Gibran's maid approached to retrieve him, in came Abbas with a squeaking trolley that had just been refreshed with whiskey tumblers of the finest crystal, an ice box, mixed nuts, and a half-devoured bottle of Johnnie Walker, a gentleman whose presence in the Khan House was never questioned.

"Just like you said: two fingers of Scotch, two ice cubes, and water to the top," said Salim, presenting Khan with a drink.

"Are you feeling well now?"

"Much better, sir, much better. I'm taking the medicine the doctor gave me."

"Temporal lobe epilepsy. What a mouthful. I don't even know where these new diseases come from. It's a serious matter and you should be careful not to put yourself under too much pressure. Doctors said emotions can trigger it again. I can call the school, and have you stay an extra week."

"It's fine, sir. I have a lot to do when school starts. I can't afford to take time off."

"Salim," said General Khan, swirling his ice in the tumbler and wiping droplets from his whiskers, "You know we Khans don't back down on our word. I want you to know that you can wish for anything, anything at all, and I will grant it to you. Go ahead, whatever you want, it'll be yours."

"Nothing, General Saab, I don't want..."

"Oh, nonsense! Go on, tell me." After a few moments of silence, he shook his head and said, "Fine, think about it and let me know."

Wavering, and almost chewing his words, Salim said, "Sir, I wanted to ask you something."

"What is it?"

"Sir, before your mother fell onto the bed, she said something." For a second, Salim hesitated, but there was a soothing tenderness in Khan's eyes that granted him a license to say whatever was on his mind. "She called me a kaffir, sir. I know what it means ... I just don't know why she said it."

Khan put his glass down and rubbed his palm with his thumb. Then he took a deep breath and said, "Had your father not spoken to you about this before?"

"Sir, what to expect from a man who uses God's house as a distillery? The painter never spoke to us about religion ... or anything else for that matter, about where we are from, who we are."

"I knew you would ask me this one day," Khan said, letting out a sigh. "Go to that shelf behind the bustard and pick out a brown book. It's in the middle somewhere." Salim headed towards the bird on the mount and bent low, leafing through the stack of old books. "You can't miss it—the cover is missing, and moths have had their way with it ... yes, yes, that one. Bring it over."

Salim held the book out towards General Khan. He felt the pages crumble between his fingers. The binding was coming apart and the tea-stained pages made it seem as though it had been buried underground for years.

"Many years ago, a wise old man, with a flowing beard and a red turban, arrived at our village with a caravan full of people. He had learned that my father, Pasha Khan, was a generous man who had a great love for books, so he brought him this unique gift. He claimed to have written hundreds of volumes that had been burnt in a fire, but this particular one survived. The old man and his people had been driven out of their homes by a furious mob. Their only crime was that they believed in his divinity. These people, banished, homeless, and hungry, had travelled for days just to meet my father." Khan reached for his glass and took a sip, wiping his face with his sleeve. "The old man was a religious preacher of sorts who believed that he was a messiah on a mission to unite the people of the world in service of the Almighty. The man spoke so elegantly, with such immaculate diction that my father became spellbound. Without a moment of hesitation, he embraced the old-timer and told him that he and his people could stay in Khanpur as long as they wanted and that no one would ever harm them."

"Why did he let them stay?" Salim asked, his eyes stretching as far as they could.

"My father could see that these people had done nothing wrong, that they were chased away for what they believed. According to him, some of them also possessed talents that would only add color to our dreary village. The old man's followers included brilliant poets and storytellers, singers and tabla players, and most gifted of them all, painters. Your grandfather was one of them."

"My grandfather was an artist?"

"Oh, indeed. He painted the most beautiful fresco on our haveli ceiling; more elegant than Michelangelo's Sistine Chapel." Khan looked up at an imaginary sky with his hands spreading out like wings. "My father was convinced then that such vibrant, peace-loving people should be sheltered in a time of crisis." He leaned over with his face inches from Salim's nose. "These refugees named themselves after their leader. They were the Ahmedis—your people."

After a few frozen moments, Salim began to feel a surge of devotion rushing up through his chest and into his arms—arms that had the sudden desire to wrap themselves around Khan.

"Salim, one of the reasons why I've never spoken to you about this was because it didn't matter to me. Like my father, I don't judge people for what they believe. The old man who gave my father this book, said that his people were no different than anyone else, that they would blend into the village like sugar in tea." There was a pause. Khan leaned back into his chair. "The Ahmadis believe that their leader was divinely touched. After the old man's death, the followers broke into two groups. Some began to question the finality of the Prophet Mohammed. And you know that some people have a hard time with those who undermine the significance of the Prophet as the ultimate messenger of God."

"That's why your mother called me that word?"

Khan nodded, saying, "Yes. And she won't be the last. Look, there are thousands of people who believe they are divinely touched, and there will be thousands more to come. What's important is that you know that such hate exists in the world, the hatred of ideas. And you yourself should keep to whatever faith you choose ... but in private. Just remember what I told you the first day you went to Blisschesterson. Keep your head down..."

"And focus on your work. I remember." After a long pause, Salim said, "Sir, what is this book about?"

"There's not much left of it now—the pages have withered away, the spine has all but vanished, but, when I was a child, my father read it to me. It is a charming story about a man sent from the heavens to unite people in the name of love and save humanity. Beautiful, isn't it?" Khan looked away for a moment, smiling.

Salim sensed that a childhood memory might have lodged a wedge of silent moments between them. He yearned for Khan's attention again, but before he could utter a word, the General snapped forward on his chair, finished his whiskey with a single gulp, and bellowed, "Right. It's getting late. Run along now, boy. You should get some sleep; it's been a long day."

Salim was slow to stand up. He didn't want to leave. Maybe if I ask him for another game of chess, he thought to himself. What about another story?

Khan leaned back in his chair again, crossed his arms, and tilted his head back. Salim remained standing in silence, watching as Khan's eyes began to close. And only when the sound of snoring echoed off the walls did he begin to pull himself away. As he took off towards the servants' quarters, past the veranda, he saw the staff lined up. They had been waiting for him. No servant had ever spent this much alone-time with General Khan before. Their anticipation was visible on their faces and they all showed him much-earned respect by inclining their heads as he walked by. He accepted their glance with a smile and headed towards his room feeling triumphant, victorious, and loved beyond the limits of his heart.

Pens and Destiny

Sir, let me take your attention away from the Khan House for a moment and further explain the setting we're in. Yes, it is the sixties, and yes, the world is in a state of flux. But let's talk a bit about Pureland for a moment. Surely there was something about that country. What was it that made Salim willing to die for her honor? Salim's love for his lost Eden was soaked in nostalgia, of course, but what if I were to tell you that it was also soaked in guilt? That after the Caliphate had its way with Pureland, he felt responsible for her demise? Because he himself had once played a part in changing her destiny. And he did all that with a pen. Yes, it was that simple. After all, it took just a few strokes of a pen to put Pureland on the map, and a few to wipe her clean off it.

Clearly there was more to it, you say. How can a boy alter the fortune of an entire nation? Sir, I understand your confusion. This all seems far-fetched. But what if it were true? What if creating and destroying empires is as simple as that: a drawing room discussion, a few cups of tea, an unfurled map and, of course, a pen? Sadly, that was exactly how our world was shaped for us. You can imagine how vulnerable these worlds really were and realize how swiftly they crumbled when the Caliphate roared through them.

Speaking of pens, may I borrow yours for a moment? Let me show you exactly where this forgotten empire was. Imagine this as our world. This land here, see? This is now the easternmost part of the Caliphate, where civilization began thousands of years ago. This here was Mesopotamia and down here used to be the Indus Valley. For many centuries, in this region, conquerors came and went, empires rose and fell. Then there came the time of statehood and nations were created. One of these nations was Pureland.

In order to truly understand the birth of Pureland, we must also recognize her anguished mother—Mother India.

We should know that there was once a time before mankind when India thrust itself into Asia creating the Himalayan peaks and the Karakoram valley, a neighborhood of behemoth creatures with hard bodies and soft hearts. It was said that these leviathans succumbed to tragic stories which made them weep. Each time these mountains sobbed, the waters ran down from them, carrying stories. These stories pulsed through the rivers into the Canal of Fables which throbbed across the majestic city of Lorr.

For centuries, under these mighty slopes, Mother India ruled her universe—her secular cities and Ram-governed villages, her sweltering jungles and feudal fiefdoms—where she birthed a civilization and witnessed a thousand wars. We can say that, in a way, she was alive until she died—in childbirth one summer afternoon, when her flesh was carved to create several new nations. One of them was to be the purest of them all.

August,1947: moments from the birth of this new state, a map of Mother India lay on a table while a pen sliced through her. Seemingly, the fate of the new nation hinged on the city of Lorr. We know from history that the determination of the British to flee India overtook things like practicality, logic, reason and what not. We also know that the bloodbath which followed scarred the people for many generations to come. At the time, it was an easy ruling for Sir Cyril Radcliffe, author of the Indian Independence Act who was not a Gandhi man by any means and who loathed the Congress and its loincloth wearing socialism with an undeterred fervor. Sir Cyril didn't have much time to do all this, you see, to carve one nation out of another. He only had two weeks. As he sat one evening to conduct this task the scales of destiny tipped as he granted a favor to a local feudal lord who had earlier whispered a plea into his ear, and who shivered at the thought of relinquishing his hundred-thousand-acre empire to the socialist Indian Republic.

You might have guessed correctly. General Zafar Khan's valiant feats for the British Raj on the battlefields of Abyssinia, aided in guiding Sir Cyril's pen as it cut through Mother India, freeing the city of Lorr and its surrounding towns from the main peninsula, forming a new nation; a nation of India's purest, its finest, the One God'ers, a place where landlords never forfeit heritage, where God himself governs the land.

If that's not purity, I don't know what is.

Salim didn't know at the time, but this purity would become the reason for Pureland's demise. Like I mentioned earlier, there was something else. Something that he did which made him shudder with remorse for years to come. I believe it fueled his compassion for the place. At the tender age of sixteen, his mind was warped with confusion. It was hard to grasp notions like empire, honor, and shame. He was too busy battling his own identity. It wasn't easy. Growing up never is. It's as if an earthquake has split the ground and you have to choose where to stand. One wrong step and you're toast. I can understand that feeling.

I often break into daydreams, thinking of how my own life would've turned out had I known then what I know now. It is important for us, sir, to ponder upon this adolescent confusion since it's the crux of my story. You can see by the fullness of my hair and the tightness of my brow that I myself was a boy not too long ago. Even before my confessed crime, I had committed irreversible sins that led me astray.

Just before the Caliphate arrived with swords held aloft, right before our worlds collided and Pureland was destroyed, my emotions, too, were muddled. Growing up, I was misguided by those who had vowed to protect me. They made me who I am and I let them. You do things like that in a state of passion: believe what you're told, become a weapon. In the end, I guess, we're all weapons of someone else's obsession. I know I was. And Salim, well, he wasn't any different.

For Salim, though, it happened when he was sixteen. In the fetid summer of 1966, soixante-six, the swinging sixties, if you must. It was the year Fidel Castro declared martial law in Cuba and when England beat West Germany by two goals to win the World Cup. It was also the time when Salim unearthed the tools to fulfil his prophecy. Most importantly, it was a time when he discovered love. And who we love ultimately determines who we become.

Over the years, Blisschesterson had begun to leave its footprints in Salim's words. It was difficult to avoid. The English headmaster guaranteed parents precise Victorian accents and shoved marbles into the students' mouths to make sure the words came out polished. If, by accident, local twang ever made it to his ears, a tractable cane walloped naked bottoms. The students were transformed into proper gentlemen. Peaked lapels, sharp ties, polished boots, and the sound of flowery dialect trickled down the hallways of Blisschesterson as the assembly line of post-colonial masters chugged on and sitting on its conveyer belt was a boy who had once made his first pair of shoes from mud.

As his covert tutoring evolved into a powerful organization where teachers themselves became supplicants, Salim's own academic success began to flood columns in the local newspapers. Lorr now waited for summer to arrive and for its youngest ever to pass senior examinations. The legend swelled. An article in the Lorr Times claimed that Salim had also defeated the visiting St. Lawrence School cricket team single-handedly with his left-arm spin bowling. Both Salim and his buddy, Mitti Pao, the cricket captain, laughed at that ridiculous article knowing full well that his sole contribution to that match was polishing off the opposition's lunch in the pavilion while they were fielding.

Apart from all that, there was the boarding school, which was an intimidating neighborhood, where playgrounds were prison yards. Salim's heart ached for the new boarders who would walk into the cricket field quivering like rabbits on the first day of the academic year, while the seniors watched breathlessly, conducting a silent auction. The bidding involved the exchange of money and cigarettes. And in one instance, a cream-skinned, freckled boarder from the North ignited a brawl between three of the heaviest aspirants to settle who would sleep with him first.

It was a carousel of sexuality, one that disturbed its patrons in their sleep. There were some though who did fancy a bit of buggering and traded hand-jobs for favors, but on the whole one had to sleep with both eyes open. Salim stayed clear of the goings-on of other people's dorms and felt cowardly for not standing up for the new boarders who came to the slaughterhouse. After all, he could only protect one identity at a time.

What he did often enjoy was the odd peek over the wall to the other side of the Canal of Fables where he could see the kids from the American Consulate School scampering around half-naked.

"Can you see something? Anything?" said Tariq, Salim's roommate, as he shuffled on his hands and knees while Salim's boots made imprints on his back.

"I can just about make it out. They're all gathering in the pool, girls and boys."

"Girls too? Let me see. My turn!" Tariq pulled out from under him as Salim crashed to the floor.

"What did you do that for? I was coming down!" Salim yelled, which made Mitti Pao snicker as he watched from behind.

"Mitti, Salim, one of you, please, nah. Can you be a doggy so I can get up and see before the guards come? Let me get one glimpse!" Salim, dusting off his shirt, got down on his hands and knees while Tariq stepped on to the small of his back.

"Oh my God, Salim! These people have no shame, girls, boys ... all swimming together. I'm getting a fucking hard on!"

"That's not weird to them. They see it every day. That's what it's like in America, idiot."

"Oh fuck!"

"What is it?"

"They're leaving!"

Salim slipped out from under his feet, making Tariq's belly flop on to the dirt. As he rose back up, he saw his mates already wobbling in a wave of laughter.

"What's so funny, fat fuck! And you, Mitti, you could've told me he was getting out, nah."

Tariq had the facial features of a bulldog and the intellect of a gerbil. From a distance he resembled a lollipop, with his chicken legs and a tummy that indicated the possibility of a third trimester. He told people his family tree went all the way up to the Prophet Mohammed. Truth was, he was switched at birth at Mayo Hospital where his real mother swept toilets.

"Can you imagine this Salim? How these heathens live? Prince Azim told me that in his country heretics are disposed of in public. Hung," Tariq said, as he shook the dirt off from his tie, shuffling away, trying to hide the embarrassment which had begun to protrude from his shorts. "I'm so glad we got rid of all the non-believer fucks during Partition. I've heard there's still an infidel sect who believes in a prophet after Mohammed. Call themselves Ahmadis. Fuck me in the mouth. Can you imagine? What motherfuckers. If I ever see one, I will definitely kill him!"

Salim shuddered. A part of him raised his hand in an explosion of fury, only to be countered by the blocking wrist of Khan's nephew who was an avid refractor of confrontation. For the first time, both detached divisions of his character met face to face.

"Alright, alright ... enough for today. Let's get back before the bell rings," said Mitti Pao, whose attention would often scurry in moments of silence. "I've told the canteen workers to keep a few sandwiches for us."

"Thanks, Mitti. I'm not hungry. I'll see you two at the hostel," Salim said, as he trudged away into the cricket field.

All of a sudden, he felt queasy. He decided he was not going to allow this emotion to upset him. So he took that feeling and tucked it under his bed. Each time it would emerge, he would sweep it right back. It was a talent he had perfected.

At night, he saw from the corner of his eye the result of his roommate's guilt. Tariq would slam his head on a prayer mat—a deterrent he used to override the desires between his legs. Off he went, head to floor, head to floor, the clicking sound of lips and tongue thrashing against each other as he parroted stanzas in a tongue no one had spoken in a century.

❦

"Salim, you're home!"

Gibran torpedoed towards Salim, squeezing him until he pretended to choke.

"Little rascal! How have you been? Ah, let go now."

"Salim, Daddy is calling you."

Salim buttoned his sleeves, pressed down on a lock of hair with his palm and made his way over to Khan's study.

"Come, boy. Come, sit down." General Khan sat behind his desk. He lifted his gaze, breathing through pursed lips. "How's your school year? I heard you will be sitting for your finals with the seniors. Very impressive!"

Khan cleared his throat and tapped his fingers on the desk.

"General Saab, there's something wrong, isn't there? You can tell me."

Fiddling with his glasses, Khan rose from his leather chair, walked around his oak desk and placed a hand on Salim's shoulder.

"I have grave news for you, son. Your father, Jaaji the Painter, has passed."

The air became heavy. Almost as if it were escaping instead of entering Salim's lungs as he inhaled.

"I asked the elders to give him the best funeral possible … in the main cemetery. Your brother Tamboo was in charge and the blind mullah, Unna Huneira, led the prayer. His parting words were to not disturb your studies, especially in this, your final year. If you wish to go for a few days, I can arrange…"

"No, sir. I mean, no thank you, sir. There's no need for me to go to Khanpur. I think the pigeon pen is dirty. I will go clean it."

"Salim, that's not necessary. You should take the bus to Khanpur. Some time off will be…"

"No, sir. He's in his resting place, there's no point. What good will my presence do there? Besides, no one's cared to look at the birds while I was gone. I will go now."

Salim left the study and climbed on to the terrace while, for the second time that week, that indigestible feeling returned. For a moment, he sat quietly as the exalted birds strutted around him.

"I buried him a long time ago, did you know that, Uzza?" he said. "All those memories I have of him are gone. Of times when we rode on a bicycle to the city, and how his fingers smelled after he smoked hookah. And Lat, did you know he would eat kinos with the peel on, straight from the tree?" A small tear curled down and hung upon a forced smile. Then it fell to the floor. "Uff! Manat," he laughed, "do you know I wanted to invite him to the city. Why? To flaunt my success, of course. Show the fucker that while he marinated in ale, lying face down behind the mosque, lamenting a fortune he did not have, stashed away in his home was a lottery ticket that he gifted to another man." His hands swabbed his tears from his face as he sat on his heels. "You're right, Lat, Manat. You're both right. Fuck him. I don't need him. He never once came to see me. What was this man but a painter of signs who blithered away in a mud hut, pickling his liver? You're all right!" He rose from the pigeon pen and took a deep breath. When he exhaled, Jaaji's demise became an instant memory, one that didn't need revisiting.

As she came outside that day to condole his father's death, Laila put a hand on Salim's arm. It was the first time she had ever touched him. Her profile, only inches from his face, sent electricity through his veins.

"Salim, Daddy needs some time alone, and I've convinced him that we will all go to the summer house for a week. I want you to come with us. It will be good for you too. I told him I needed your help with my mathematics. And, after all," she paused to smile, "you are the math guru, as they say."

He clasped his hand around his heart and said, "Of course, Laila Madam, of course."

She headed back into the house before Khan could see her pottering around the garden in front of the servants. Under the white arches of the veranda, she turned to say, "Can you stop bloody calling me madam? I don't like it."

As she closed the main door behind her, the strain of his longing for her multiplied, as if he had just been stabbed with adrenaline. The thought of his hand brushing against her goose-bump ridden thigh as nonchalantly as possible sent a tremor down his own thighs. Amidst the splendid backdrop of the mountain ranges and menthol crisp air, would he have an entire week with his beloved? Solo, unsupervised, and no limping witches either? Oh, anything was possible.

St. Mary Hill Station was no ordinary destination. Set under the Himalayan valley, it was the Goldilocks of peaks. The British became fond of it when they learned of a provincial myth. It was said that Jesus of Nazareth had chosen the foothills as his final resting ground. Of course, in this version of the apostolic narrative, Jesus eludes crucifixion and flees eastward to a town nestled in the armpit of the Himalayas where he spends the rest of his life. The locals offered their reverences at a pale olive shrine carved under a hill, where they would lay garlands at a tomb which may or may not have been Jesus's; it was hard to tell. No one really knew, which only added to the mystery. The British tailored the place by constructing missionary schools, winding roads, and lavish vacation homes. General Khan procured one such villa after Partition from its previous owner, the commander of the thirty-fourth regiment of Lucknow, who had been its patron for twenty years. Sir Edward Pigglesworth had only one condition—that Khan continue the ritual of cocktail hour every evening at sunset. It was a demand that Khan met whenever he was at the house by tilting his Scotch-and-water on the porch as a tribute to Sir Pigglesworth. Out of all the houses owned by Zafar Khan, the summer house was the most exquisite: a tiny castle atop a hill, overlooking a thousand-foot drop into a green valley where the air had a perpetual nip.

One immortal week, sniffing at chestnut hair, breathing the inviting sight of her smile, her laugh. This was too much to handle. Salim was now suspended on the cliff of this dreamy abyss and desperately needed the blessing of his dear leader to make the fantasy come to life.

"And where do you think you're going with such urgency?" Bilki asked, as she ambushed Salim behind the veranda, pinching his cheek with tremendous force.

"Aaaah! Bilki, let me go!"

"Smiling for no reason, Potato? Wah jee wah! What's making you so happy, huh?"

"I ... I have to see Khan Saab for something important."

"Oh really? Look here! Look what you've done," she pointed behind him. "I just brushed the floor and you, with your fat muddy feet, just walk all over it like you own the place? No, baba, no. Not getting away that easily. You may be a big Saab in school, but not here and certainly not with me!"

"Bilki, I swear I will help you clean it up, please let go of me!"

Bilki, in a flash of slyness, let her eyes scan the corridor that led to the study. "Fine. I'll let you go. Only if you give this to General Ali." Her hands disappeared into the valley of her cleavage and out came a letter. Salim held it in his fingers. It was still warm to the touch. He wondered about its contents and tried guessing whom Bilki had bribed to write "Ali" in cursive.

"But why..."

"Don't ask questions, Potato!" she shouted, as her fingers twisted Salim's ear until he began to scream again. "Do as I say!"

"Fine ... fine. Now let go please, Bilki. It hurts!"

"You give it directly to him and no one else, you understand?" she said, releasing his ears.

Salim nodded with an annoyed look, rubbing his reddened ear with his palms as he made his way to the study.

Something was surely up with Bilki. He yearned to tear the letter open, but he knew better than to cross the toughest nail to have ever walked the halls of the Khan House. He needed Bilki to be on his side, especially if they were to be in the summer house together. So, he kept the folded letter in his pocket. Surely, something was up with the whole Khan House though, not just Bilki. Four-wheel-drives crowded the garage and there were army boot-prints all over the cobble stones, and even more along the corridor towards the library. It was one of those nights, uniforms were everywhere. The door of the study was left ajar, and through it, the sounds of a distinct clamor crept out. Two captains stood outside. He approached one and inquired to see General Khan but was asked to leave, when a clicking of the fingers brought both soldiers to full attention.

"Let him in, Captain," Khan yelled. Salim walked into a room that hadn't noticed his arrival. Khan sat at his desk, while General Ali and a younger uniform leaned over a map. He could tell from the stars on his shoulder that he was a brigadier. He walked over to Khan and stood silently by his side as General Ali's voice almost pushed him up against the wall.

"Brigadier Zaid, you're one bloody imbecile! You can't force a barricade in Sector A without the local police knowing."

"But sir, we have only thirty-five men. Only thirty-five. We have to act with caution. If they suspect anything, we'll all be caught."

"General Ali," another spoke from a sofa in the corner. "Thirty-five isn't enough to cordon off the sector and barricade the civilians. Don't forget, we need ten men to surround the courtyard."

Salim looked around the study. There were five people in total, three hunched over the map and two on the sofa. The map wasn't a map; it was a blueprint with angular lines. Brigadier Zaid tilted his head closer to the desk and his cigarette dropped ash onto its white corners. He rubbed his thumb over it, smudging a grey color over the printed letters.

"Are you a bloody junglee, or what? Fucking monkey!"

"Sorry! Sorry, General Ali." Zaid took a handkerchief and began to wipe away the ash.

"Don't mind him, sir," the one on the sofa said. "A village idiot in uniform is still a village idiot." They all began to laugh.

"I'll show you what village idiots can do. Come outside, I'll show you!"

A squabble broke out as Salim's eyes turned to the blueprint. Three words began to fall before his eyes over and over. Sector A, courtyard, barricade ... Sector A, courtyard, barricade. Then, from the convoluted lines that crisscrossed the indigo canvas, shapes emerged in front of him. Nested triangles.

Salim moved towards the desk. From a pencil holder, he pulled out a pen.

"Sir, may I show you something?" he asked, moving the pen towards the blueprint.

"Get your hands off the bloody map!" General Ali grabbed Salim's collar in anger.

"Oh God! Leave him, Ali," General Khan said. "He's only a boy."

"But sir," Zaid began, "he's going to ruin our blueprint."

"How many yards can one man cover, sir?" Salim asked.

"Brigadier," Ali said calmly, "bring me my baton."

"No need, sir. My baton will do just fine for this one."

"Stop it! Stop it, both of you!" Khan yelled. "Go on, boy. What did you say?"

"How many yards does one soldier cover, Khan Saab?"

"I'd say about fifty. Why?"

"Sir, then you need only twenty men to cover Sector A, forming a corner, like so." Pen in hand, Salim traced the outer triangle over the bridges, streets and buildings. "And the other ten can surround the courtyard, which is about five hundred yards across, at a forty-degree angle. If you see from a distance, these are triangles embedded within one another. And this main one surrounds all the others." A visible silence fell upon the room. Everyone turned to see. The lighting brightened, and Salim could have sworn the bustard on the mount flipped his head around to take a look. Khan, mumbling to himself, brought his eyes to the map. "All angles in a triangle must equal 180 degrees. So, if we group the men in such a way, we can cover the map. Two men cover forty degrees each, and one can span the remaining hundred. That means we need..."

"Thirty men..."

"Yes, Khan Saab. Thirty should do it."

Khan puffed his cheeks and his eyes opened wide.

General Ali made his way to the desk. "Triangles? Bloody genius," he whispered, bending over the map.

"What did I tell you, General? This boy is..."

"Bloody fantastic."

"This will give enough time for the brigadiers to surround the guards and make the arrests. After that, General Ali will make the radio announcement." Khan took a moment to look each soldier in the room in the eye. "We've got it, gentlemen, we've got it! Captain, call the hunchback and tell him to bring some champagne from the cellar!"

Bottles arrived. Cigars were slipped under twirled mustaches. The room became drenched in laughter and boisterous cheer. One by one, they all patted Salim's backside as he quietly took to the corner and sat down on his heels. Brigadier Zaid examined the map, scratching his chin, trying to see the nested triangles through the mesh of zigzagging roads. A crease appeared on his forehead. How could a servant-boy see what the professionals could not, he asked himself? Then, he looked over at Salim with vicious, sunken eyes. Salim looked away, disregarding the excitement that bubbled around him. He was on a whole other mission. After Khan had downed his third champagne, he rose from the floor and made his move.

"General Saab, I wanted to ask you for a favor," he whispered, pulling at his elbow.

"Come, Mr. Agha. Brigadier Zaid was telling us all about George Orwell earlier." Khan turned to Zaid and said, "He says that even Orwell despises pigs. What do you have to say to that?" A cheeky smile appeared on Khan's face.

"Yes yes," Zaid replied. "Pigs are worthless according to Orwell. They're evil. We also know this from Islam's teachings thousands of years ago."

Salim, without hesitation, answered, "Sir, actually in *Animal Farm*, the pigs are not worthless. They start the revolution."

"*Abey*! This bloody *bargaydiar* can't even spell Orwell, hahaha!" bellowed General Ali.

"Haha, can you even read English, Zaid Saab?" asked another.

"Did they have schools in your village?"

Through the cloud of ridicule, Zaid sharpened his eyes on Salim as he pressed down on his greasy hair. One after another, jokes were thrown in the air. Knees were slapped, palms met palms, and the brigadier cowered. Before another pun penetrated through the orchestra of laughter, Salim pulled on Khan's arm and spoke gently in his ear. "General Saab, I wanted to know if I could borrow some money to buy books for Madam Laila. For our trip to the summer house."

"Of course, you silly boy! You're the guru. Only you can prepare her. I want her to be like you and come in first place. Getting second place is something we Khans haven't learned." He slurred his last few words as the champagne had begun to do its thing. He reached for his pocket, shuffled his fingers and brought out five rupees.

"But, Saab ... this is too much money. I only need..."

"Shut your mouth and take it. You dare disobey my order, soldier?"

"No, sir. Never," replied Salim, as his hand shot to his brow.

"Then take this. You've done well. You don't even know it, but you've changed Pureland's destiny."

General Khan smiled at Salim and patted him on the backside, a signal for him to leave. Change destiny, he asked himself. Khan Saab must be drunk, surely. How can I change destiny? He walked over to General Ali who had just bitten into a cigar.

"This is for you, sir." He handed him Bilki's letter and, before Ali could look at it, he made for the door.

As he stepped out, he heard Ali say, "What can they bloody do? Shoot us with peas?"

Salim raised his hand to his forehead to salute the captains at the door as Zaid followed him outside and suddenly grabbed the back of his shirt. He closed the study door behind him with a loud thud. It was so loud that Jabberwocky, who had been sleeping nearby, woke up and walked towards Salim, sniffed his leg and sat back down again. Zaid looked at the dog and then back at Salim as his hand tightened around his collar.

"It took years of selective breeding to arrive at this fine specimen, did you know?" he began, pointing at the dog with his boot. "It's in his genes to be servile. For generations, his ancestors were bred this way and those with the slightest objection were considered mad—they were killed." He bent down to examine the dog's ears. "Perfect ears he has, perfect pedigree. Will always show loyalty, no matter what." He looked into Salim's eyes with so much force, he almost toppled him over. Letting go of his collar, he whispered, "And if he begins to show hints of rebellion, sadly he will be put to sleep."

"Some dogs, Brigadier Saab, are not considered dogs but family." Salim pulled himself away.

"Don't be too sure of that, son. You'll be making a big mistake."

Salim did not wince at the foul scent of his breath nor did he seem hurt by the words that travelled within it. He simply walked away towards his room. But while asleep that night, something rattled around in his heart, something he thought he had pacified, something that reappeared without a warning. It was not ridicule; he couldn't care less for the brigadier whom he had belittled in front of his comrades. It was another kind of pain, one that only travels in waves, lashing against the banks of aching hearts.

It was the anguish of losing something forever.

Nautilus

Salim left early next morning to avoid the afternoon sun. Out on the main road, he hailed a rickshaw puller. The old man, with a chiseled and wiry frame, climbed off the bicycle and adjusted the carriage attached to it. He had been working the night shift. His eyes were tired, but when he saw Salim his face lit up.

"Come, Saab. Where do you need to go?" It was a polite plea that Salim couldn't refuse. He leapt onto the bench of the rickshaw and away they went.

Up the Cantonment and towards the Mall Road, the city began to stretch her limbs. Lorr was unhurried in the morning and took a while to wrestle her way out of bed. Unlike other cities, which are at full bustle by morning, Lorr trudged, hungover from her late endeavors. Mornings were not her thing, for she was the queen of the night, the Mughal mistress, the crimson-bricked harlot of the conquerors. She was a city where he'd lived for eight years, mostly confined within the walls of the boarding school or the Khan House, but Salim had always felt her presence. Now he was out to fully devour her magnificence. Lorr spoke to him as he bobbled on the rickshaw; she told him tales of her schizophrenic past. From the Ghaznavids in the eleventh century, to the Mughals, then the Sikhs, and finally the British, she had many lovers, each engraving their impression upon her. Her people, too, endured this. For why should they not absorb the impulsiveness of the Sikhs, the laziness of the Mughals, and the snobbery of the British?

The Mall Road took them towards the rows of hotels where only a couple of decades ago, on jazz nights, Englishmen could dance freely without brushing up against brown skin. Those were simpler times: 'No dogs or Indians allowed.' Since then, the signs outside had changed a bit. There were more imminent threats. "No Servants," it now said at the gates of the Gymkhana.

At a bookstore upon the Mall, opposite the Lorr museum, Salim examined the shelf in the mathematics section. Imported books that had arrived on a recent shipment, their covers still glistening in the florescent light. He pulled the usual Junior Year syllabus materials as he had their appearance memorized. One book, in particular, grabbed his awareness as he licked his forefinger and swiped through its pages. The cover excited him; the colorful image of the nautilus shell with its spiral snaking into itself. Instantly, a bolt of lightning struck in his mind. He had first felt this sensation when he first came to Lorr, sat in front of a lamp in Khan's library, switching the bulb on and off, blinking at electricity for the first time. Then another feeling arrived. As he flicked page after page, his brow crumpled. Confusion irked him and he slammed the book shut. He hated not knowing. It made him feel at a loss. He knew that he had to conquer this, whatever this was. He was reminded of Khan's words: "A book is a revolution bound in paper. It takes one reader to open it and change the world."

He shook his head, put the book back on the shelf, paid for the others and headed out. Walking outside the store, he saw the rickshaw puller with his twiggy legs and bony arms and thick veins on his arms. He was an old man with calves that were shaped into firm domes by years of pedaling Saabs around the city. Salim felt guilty. He walked to a tea stand and bought two cups of milky tea along with fried eggs and rotis.

"Thank you, Saab. This is not necessary."

"Oh yes, it is. I'm a big boy as you can see. It's not easy to pedal around the city with me on your bench, old man."

As they ate, the rickshaw puller eyed Salim's food, and noticing the hunger pouring from his eyes, Salim slid his plate over. His gummy eyelids opened large when Salim said, "Here, you can have mine. I'm done."

He responded with a smile.

"Old man, how do you manage to do all this work in this heat?"

"I'm used to it now. I used to feel very hot when I was young. You know where I went?"

"Where?"

"The Canal of Fables, of course. My friends and I would take our shoes off under the mulberry tree, remove our shirts and jump in. If you're lucky, you get to hear stories in the water."

A short silence hummed in Salim's ear. Then he spoke.

"I haven't heard anyone talk about the canal in years. Will you take me there?"

"Of course, Saab."

They arrived at the Canal of Fables. The caramel water swept through swiftly. As he looked around, he saw giggling children with their single strips of clothing. They were not Blisschestersonians for sure. No boarder would dare touch this filth, he thought. Instead, they would drive by in their cars with confused looks, shaking their heads. The saying was: to hear the ancient legends one had to have the curse of misfortune. Who would listen to the unfortunate except the unfortunate? It's a secret only they knew. It's why Rudyard Kipling had his servants dip in the water and relay folklore to him—ludicrous tales of talking monkeys and misplaced man cubs. The canal was a time machine and what better way to travel for a story than in a stream of water?

Under the shade of the mulberry trees, Salim took off his shoes. He felt the cool earth under his feet. Then he jumped. Children with paper-thin skin laughed as they saw Salim floating like a beach ball on the water with all his clothes still on. Salim rolled his eyes at them and tried hard to listen but there was nothing in the water except silence.

Returning home drenched and furious, he vowed never to engage in such nonsense again, but the next day he went back to the same spot. He didn't quite know why but he did. He did feel remorse for rolling his eyes at the children. He knew it was wrong to do so even as he was doing it. With his eyes closed, he jumped.

He floated on his back for a while and let his imagination take over. He imagined the converging wings on Jaaji's wrist, the reflection of the crows in the water, and he saw Tamboo the Camel. He smelt buffalo-dung cakes, he saw the other villagers, Khassi Kasai, Cut-Two Naii, and, far in the distance, there he was, Potato, the painter's son.

It was there, in those currents, that things started to happen. Stories entered his ears in tranquil whispers. The canal whispered to him the love story of Layla and Majnun, the torrid tale of the Emperor Akbar, the valiant story of Raja Ranbir Singh and, most enthralling of all, the legend of the peasant boy Raavi. So strong was Raavi's power of wisdom that he convinced the world he was a prince, all for the love of Laaj, the princess of Shalm. However, to attain her, he had to conquer the ocean of knowledge and, once he did, the princess Laaj could do nothing but fall into his arms.

These stories ignited within him a bonfire of realization. The journey of love, he said to himself, is built on the supremacy of pilgrimage. The further you swim for love, the closer you get to attaining it. With this thought, he could hear electricity crackle all around him. There is no ocean I cannot conquer for her. None.

Salim went back to the bookstore that morning, in search of the book with the shell on its cover. He bought it and rushed home with passionate, bloodshot eyes. Sitting on the floor of his room flipping page after page, he bit hard on his lips. It didn't make sense, any of it. But why? Answers came easily to him. Always. He had been able to see them ever since he was a child. The workings of the universe came naturally to him. The wings of a crow, the changing of seasons, the oneness of it all, he could see it all in equations. But what infuriated him was that this wasn't how everyone else saw things and certainly not what he was reading. This book wasn't showing the answers but explaining how to revert to the questions through a series of proofs. How stupid, he said out loud, and flung the book against the wall.

It's difficult for me to describe what took place in the aftermath of the storm brewing in his mind, but it was at that moment that he abandoned the system of proofs altogether. He persuaded himself that there had to be a simpler way. But simple is a relative thing. His geography teacher, Mrs. Alam, with her jaw expanding, bore witness to this simplicity when she first witnessed Salim shutting one eye, measuring a map from the back of the classroom. She started to visualize the invisible numbers that were hovering around his eyes: $(forefinger\ to\ thumb) \times scale = length\ of\ Africa = 80,000\ km$.

And after Salim was bombarded with questions in the staff room and tears of panic rolled out from his eyes, Mrs. Alam tried to soothe the boy.

"It's alright, Salim. You can speak a language no one else can," she whispered, with her hand on his shoulder.

It was this language, Salim thought, sitting cross-legged on his charpoy, which held the key to his destiny, the pilgrimage to attain his love. If he were to conquer this ocean, he had to make the world speak this language of his. Then, with a freshly sharpened pencil he began writing equations of his own. Without proofs.

I am not a man of mathematics, but I can imagine those innocent equations giving birth to what he discovered later in life. He began to explain it all. How his world worked or how the world worked around him. The laws of nature spiraling towards each other, coinciding into a universal singularity like the nautilus shell. Yes, this was the power of the true law of the land, the dialect of nature and God himself. Like the pauper Raavi, he swam through the vast oceans of knowledge.

Salim felt that this vision, this divine apparatus he was given, was a gift from the cosmos. Like the old wise man who appeared before Pasha Khan with his caravan, Salim felt aware of a reckoning that was delivered to him by the Almighty, a divine message. There was no other explanation except that the worlds of faith and evidence could actually coincide. He could see it clearly.

And as he fell into a disturbed slumber that night, a voice rushed out to him suddenly.

Eat all the books you can eat.

The painter's words brushed against his face with such force, he rose suddenly from his pillow to see if he were actually there.

Don't you dare come back to this town, there is nothing for you here.

Salim began to sob in his sleep. The early morning rays then crept into his room and brought with them an unwelcome intruder.

"Wake up, Potato! Get up, sister-fucker. The bus is here, we need to leave," Chaku said, with his toe pushing hard against Salim's ribs. Salim leapt up and peered outside at the army bus parked near the veranda. In its shadow, tapping her feet, was Laila Khan.

Here's to Sir Pigglesworth

Chaku steered the army bus to the top of a slope, pulling hard on the handbrake. Inside, from behind the barred windows, Salim saw the summer house, with its dropped porch, for the first time. It was chiseled into a steep mountain, facing the foothills of the Himalayas, in a cul-de-sac around the corner from paradise itself. It had layers like a cake, each tier with a different incandescent color—oranges, lilacs, and pinks, all cached in angles, creating an optical illusion. It was a lasting colorful reminder of the Evil Witch's colorless life. The locals, both animals and humans, had rigid calves and an acute sense of balance. Salim had noticed this from his window on the drive up as his gaze floated towards a mountain goat perched dangerously upon the edge of the hill, a hoof's length from calamity and yet as serene as if the valley below were a photograph.

As he exited the bus, St. Mary's air cracked at his nose. He looked over to the small dwellings that clutched onto the side of the mountains, and beyond, he could see the beautiful Karakoram Valley. The summer house was cordoned off by a picket fence overlooking a thousand-foot drop. A short walk away was the bazaar. If you closed your eyes and listened, you could almost feel the murmurs of tourists bargaining for shawls and hand-knitted hats.

The bus was unloaded and the children were guided down the slope by their maids. The caretaker of the house, Talib the Bear, Chaku's cousin, a man of bristly, red hair and shrub-like eyebrows, scooped the luggage into his arms. Atop the hill, two military guards stood at attention, just as they were instructed to do according to the telegraph they'd received that morning at the St. Mary Hill Station Cantonment. As Salim looked up at them, Chaku's hand slammed into his neck from behind.

"You sister-fucker! Don't think I don't know what you're doing," he said, grabbing Salim's butt. "I will make another hole in this, understand."

Salim shoved Chaku's hand away and said, "Shut up! What are you talking about?"

"You think I'm blind, sister-fucker? I saw you sitting next to Saab's daughter, whispering like a girl in her ear."

Talib put down the luggage and approached his cousin. "Chaku, is this fatty giving you trouble?" He loomed over Salim with his rust colored hair corkscrewing out from his face. Salim cringed as wafts of methane erupted from his open mouth. It was as though Talib secretly curdled this rancid gas inside, waiting to ambush innocent bystanders.

"Talib Jaan ... trouble is all this little shit knows. Don't you know he is the famous Evil Witch Slayer? Asshole, bring your own bags down to the servant's room." Salim gulped as he felt the hair on his arms saluting the air. He recalled the ride, Chaku's eager eyes peering through the rear-view mirror at two innocent souls. Surely, he had done nothing wrong. No servant had ever sat close to Laila before, and Salim had been bordering the forbidden terrains of decency. In his mind, they were just two children sharing a laugh in the back of a bus. Then he thought: if news of this reached General Khan who had, in a way, appointed him, along with the two guards, as caretaker of his most cherished belongings, what would happen to him then? No, surely that wasn't the end he desired. So here he was, like the goat he had seen earlier, on the lip of a precarious cliff.

"Listen, you're talking rubbish," he retorted. "I haven't done anything, and don't you dare accuse me. I'm only here because Khan Saab asked me to be. I'm not here to deal with your pranks."

Chaku approached Salim with the intent of flattening his nose, but his rising hand was intercepted by Talib's wrist. He backed off. Salim ignored them, grabbed his bag and descended the slope towards the garden.

That was Salim's first encounter with Talib the Bear. He recalled Bally's story: "Both cousins worked at a small tire shop outside the city twelve years ago. To increase business, the sister-fuckers would lay three-pronged nails on the road near their shop. So, one morning, fate brought General Zafar Khan's car to a conveniently laid ambush. And that was it, by God. Chaku convinced Khan of his brilliant driving skills and solidified a position for his cousin as caretaker of the summer house."

Both of them could become obstacles in his path, Salim knew that. But all precursory jitters of having to share a room with them were abruptly put to rest by Laila's sweet instructions.

"Salim, you're going to stay in the guest room inside. Gibran can sleep in my room and the maids get the living room," she said as they entered the main veranda. Talib the Bear slipped off his shoes and stood near Laila, looking straight at her feet.

"Laila Madam, Salim can sleep in my room."

"Did I ask for your opinion, guard?"

"No Madam ... but, I was just..."

"You were just about to take all our bags inside. And what in the name of God is that smell? Have you been smoking hashish again? Don't you remember last year when Daddy had you thrashed in the garden? Take a bath before entering the house next time. You're making the whole place stink!"

Talib gathered every atom of obedience floating in his body and held them together. Because he dared not jeopardize his expedient arrangement, which allowed him complete carnal indulgence in the empty house, eleven months out of twelve, unregimented, spreading his stench, sleeping balls out in the Saabs' beds whenever he pleased.

Chaku lent his cousin a hand with the bags. Salim looked at them with a tilted head and smiled, oblivious to the fact that he was on thin ice and there were two behemoths waiting under it when it broke.

The summer house awoke from its hibernation as Gibran played juvenile pranks on the maids, jumping on suitcases, running in the living room in his underwear.

"Gibran, you will catch a cold!" Khalil cried.

The air had begun to chill the house, and a desolate fireplace in the corner of the living room yearned to be touched. Talib the Bear re-emerged through the kitchen door, wrapped in a brown shawl, clean-shaven, with his hair slicked back into neat lines. He carried an urgent look of confusion—the kind a man would give if a lit dynamite stick were glued to his hands.

Pointing to the housekeeper, Laila said, "Khalil, can you ask this moron to light up the fireplace, something His Highness should have done prior to our arrival? Also, help your brother change—the maids are busy with dinner. We'll play a game later."

"Guard! Light the fire!" Khalil shouted.

The coiled red hair on Talib's arms stood up in alarm. But he calmed himself and fired up the logs with a match. The orange flames lit up his face, revealing a look of antagonism. If it were not for the patrolling officers of the twelfth regiment of St. Mary's Hill Station, surely the Bear would've taught the prissy girl and her brat brother a lesson.

"Anything else, madam?"

"No, you fool. Now stay outside. And make sure you give the soldiers breakfast in the morning."

Talib wrapped his shawl around his shoulders and whizzed out through the kitchen door.

The fireplace warmed the air and Salim's belly began to throb. After dinner, the children, Laila, and Salim sat in a circle in front of the fireplace. Dusk deepened into an ardent darkness, where a flickering flame shining on a rosy cheek sent Salim's excitement spiraling skyward. They all had with them cups of steaming cocoa.

"Cheers to Sir Biggleworthy," said Gibran, raising his mug.

"It's Sir Pigglesworth," said Khalil.

"Fine then, here is to you, Sir Pigglesworth, wherever you may be piggly-wigglying around," Laila said, as her giggling brothers clinked their mugs with hers.

Cheers indeed, thought Salim as his mug touched Laila's, electricity transmitting from her fingers to his. Was this deliberate? Did she want him to touch her? He wasn't sure. As he shuffled a deck of cards, he reached out towards her ankle which had dimly come into view and brushed his hand across her shin. The ecstasy which followed pushed his elation to the brink of insanity, to the lip of a cliff, one hoof-length from disaster. And she lit up in the dancing fire like a surrealist painting.

"I need to go to the bathroom," Khalil said as he left the living room.

"No need to make an announcement," said Laila, wincing. There was a cramp in her calf.

"Careful, Laila Madam, careful, careful. You should stretch it out," Salim said, as his hand reached out to caress her leg beyond, far beyond, the realm of decency. Immediately, gasps emerged from the maids sitting far away in the dark.

Salim retracted his hand. The game went on as if nothing had happened, and Laila smirked. In such stealthy moves, masking his lust, he attempted again to achieve the mysterious friction caused between her supple skin and his fingers. Indeed, she was tinkering with his capacity to contain himself. While the silhouette of her breasts, peeking through her cotton night shirt, caused a throbbing in his crotch, he reached out again only to have his wrist locked in an ambush by her heel. He looked right at her as she widened her eyes and spoke the words that poured kerosene over his burning desire.

"*Not now.*"

Not ... now, he thought. Two words which could reflect warning. Said in such an erogenous manner though, the words translated to yes ... the door is ajar, take me, o valiant knight!

Tired heads indicated that it was bedtime. The maids appeared from the darkness. One carried Gibran to bed, the other disappeared into the kitchen with Bilki. When they were alone, Laila turned to Salim and said, "You can never beat me in cards. Tomorrow we will go hiking."

She entangled her fingers with his and looked down, grinning. "Looks like the vanilla-chocolate ice creams. The ones you get in a cone."

They both shared a giggle as Salim looked at his brown fingers entrapped in her buttery skin. Before Bilki could walk back into the living room, Salim withdrew his hand and hurried off to bed.

The summer house brimmed with sensual banter while two livid servants plotted their revenge.

The Faith of an Infidel

The days went by swiftly and the week came to an end. For Salim, one week wasn't enough because he'd begun to spend considerable time alone with Laila—he wanted more. They would meet in the garden at night after everyone had gone to bed and talk for hours.

The day before they were to return, the morning brought with it a strange mist, as if the clouds, which had been looming in the distance, had suddenly fallen to the ground. The air became cooler. Lying in his bed, Salim crawled into a fetal position under his blanket. As he shivered, he became aware of a change within his soul. There was a will within him which was stronger than his own. Perhaps it was not his will to begin with. Was he really that powerful? Could he conquer anything? Indeed, the nautilus-cover book was daunting. But had he not begun to master its complex notions? And that too in his own words, in the language he knew so well. He danced towards his beloved in this Eden of his, and she—the most forbidden fruit a servant could imagine—was at his fingertips.

He smiled under his blanket; it was a smile of vanity. He was proud of himself. He felt that he and his lover were both safe, safe from prying eyes and wagging chins. No servant could dare snitch on him now—he was invincible.

Salim was not a very musical person but that morning he attempted to sing the Lata Mangeshkar tune he had heard on the All India Radio:

> *Oh my naive heart, what has befallen you?*
> *After all, what's the remedy for this pain?*
> *I too have a tongue in my mouth...*
> *If only I was asked about my view.*
> *I have hopes of fidelity from her,*
> *An infidel who knows not what faith is.*

The poet, Mirza Ghalib, surely must have had the deviant fingers of a seductress tugging at the chords of his heart when he penned those words. The pathetic longing of expecting devotion from an infidel, knowing full well that fidelity is but an illusion, a mirage that one sees through the curled lips of an enchantress. He imagined Ghalib struggling in the grip of this fever, spilling goblet after goblet of wine into his arid soul while his quill stroked the paper.

This version of the poem he had heard, ironically, was not sung in its customary lamenting tone but rather in a buoyant manner.

It was this and other such Indian music that trickled across the border, unrestrained and visa-less, into and out of his self-made transistor radio each morning. Yes, the All India Radio station was an empathetic indulgence for a teenage heart in the shackles of desire.

As he sang in the bathroom, he now imagined himself as the protagonist of a Lorr talkie. Scampering through the trees of Lawrence Gardens in Technicolor, with a woolly sweater around his shoulders, he and his beloved danced and sang to the score of the 1966 film of the year, *Aina*.

You are alas my darling, true?
Why then can I not love you?

In this meretricious fantasy, he became the pauper Raavi and swiveling in his arms was the princess of Shalm. This rather bizarre musing, unlike the black-and-white film to which the song belonged, had a plot of its own. The characters, too, differed from the original tale told to him by the whisperings of the Canal. The princess was the most implausible; a fanciful beloved, having no will or consciousness of her own.

After bathing and sprinkling scented talcum under his arms, he tiptoed to the kitchen. Glancing through the diamond-shaped window in the door, he saw that the fireplace which had illuminated Laila's face the night before had gone cold. Surrounding it, the two Christian maids and Bilki lay sleeping wrapped in coarse brown blankets, looking like cocoons. This arrangement struck him as slightly odd since Bilki usually slept in Laila's room, but why should this be of concern to him? After all, he slept in a Saab's bed and those who sleep in Saabs' beds seldom have a fuck to give about servants.

After fishing around the cabinets, he made himself a cup of tea. Before he took his first sip, he felt a warm breath upon his neck.

"No tea for me, lover?"

With the most vehement power of foresight, Salim felt an advancing hand appear in the corner of his vision. Spinning on his heels like a ballerina, he slipped through Chaku's closing arms. He blew out of the kitchen. The door swung back onto Chaku's face. And, like a dog cognizant of his boundaries, he stayed in the kitchen signaling to his target through the window: a forefinger across the neck. Salim replied with a fist under his forearm. *Fuck off.*

Salim sat down on the dining table catching his breath. The back door opened and shut. Chaku had left the house. Salim sighed in relief. He sat quietly observing the living room where Bilki and the maids lay like matchsticks near the fireplace. Shortly after, the boys ran into the room and kicked their maids awake. The brown blankets unfolded and the maids jumped to attention and, like robots, marched mechanically towards the kitchen, scrambling eggs, toasting bread, brewing tea, doing maid things. Talib the Bear entered the house through the front door to replace the blackened logs in the fireplace.

"This boy really smells," said Khalil.

"He smells," Gibran said.

"Oh God, can you tell this idiot to quickly light the fire and get out? I can't breathe," said Laila, pinching her nose at the dining table while the Bear quietly shoved wood into a stack. He seemed like an ape at a zoo, ignoring the jeering onlookers.

"The maids want to go to St. Mary's church for Sunday mass, so we'll go with them." Salim found arousal in her authority; he found arousal in anything she did. While Bilki stood behind her, brush in hand, caressing her hair, Laila had her breakfast and ordered servants around. It was magnificent.

"I want to ride the white horses," said Khalil.

"Me too! White horses," Gibran echoed.

Salim sat across from Laila at the breakfast table. A hand pushed a boat of butter, fingers crept towards fingers. With his jagged toes, he stretched as far as he could to touch her ankle. Just as he was about to venture off again into prohibited areas, he caught Bilki's eyes ... his talon like toes returned to his side of the table. Bilki resumed tying Laila's hair with a peculiar scowl on her face.

The night before, while looking at Laila through the mirror, Bilki had finally found the courage to utter the words every servant had wished to speak, "Laila Madam, this Salim ... you should keep some distance from him."

"What do you mean keep some distance? Has he got a disease?"

"No, madam. You're like my daughter. I just want to say ... if General Saab finds out that..."

"If General Saab finds out what, Bilki?" she yelled, noticing through the mirror that Bilki's mouth almost wished to retract the words it had spilled. "How dare you tell me what to do or not to do? Have you forgotten what my father has done for you? He saved you from a pack of wild animals. He should've let you die with the others during the Partition riots. Don't you for one second forget where you come from. I can have Daddy send you back to Khanpur. Oh yes, my dear. There are no ceiling fans there. Your newfound love for sitting in front of the radio in my fan-cooled room will soon vanish. So, before you complete your sentence, let me finish it for you." Laila turned around in her chair. "General Saab will find out nothing. We came here for a vacation. Salim's preparing me for my school year. That's it. Now get your worthless face out of my room. Tonight, you can sleep outside with the maids."

"Laila Madam, you've misunderstood me. I won't open my mouth again, I promise. Please, not near the Christians!"

"Get out of my room, Bilki. You should learn your worth. This is for your own good. Now take your blanket and get out."

Salim did not know of the night before, but Bilki's face professed a sleepless and turbulent time on the floor next to maids much younger than her and much further down the chain of command. It must have felt like a perturbing demotion for such a seasoned veteran. However, Bilki had it coming. After the demise of the Evil Witch, there was a visible bounce in her strut. She had begun to purposely neglect certain chores and initiated a series of her own orders to the outside servants. Perhaps she thought this was a retirement benefit of sorts for bearing the Evil Witch's torture for a decade, and also because God knew she was well ahead in years, almost catching up with the hunchback Bally himself. Laila had witnessed this change in her behavior for some time but kept silent until now.

Let me clarify a little. There is a code in the feudal world you may not quite be aware of. You see, servants young or old must be kept to their rudimental centers and reminded of the goodwill their master has showered upon them. Like a dog pulling on his chain, wandering, sniffing territories he is prohibited from, servants can, and often will, begin to stray. And sadly, as in Bilki's case, a servant might forget that a leash exists at all. The imminent countermeasure for such divergent symptoms is simple. One must yank the said chain definitively, towing the perpetrator, man or beast, inward towards the straightly aligned path. In case of frequent unresponsive behavior, this action should be repeated with brutal coercion.

It was as if Bilki had also forgotten the one thing all servants feared—the wrath of General Khan's leather whip, which was kept hidden in his study cabinet. The whip's reputation had, over the years, become larger than itself. It was for this very reason that, for decades, the servant-master discipline had remained intact and the leash forever taut.

Salim felt sorry for Bilki, watching her go through the motions, brushing hair, lifting empty teacups.

As the day drifted into night, the trees in the garden whistled with the wind as if they knew what was stirring below. Salim and Laila snuck out of the house and tiptoed towards the orange picket fence overlooking the drop into the valley. The clouds had wrapped around the hills and the garden became invisible. Hidden from the patrolling officers of the St. Mary Hill Station Cantonment and the other occupants of the house, they sat hand in hand as the moon illuminated the canyon. There were tiny houses that could only be made out by the occasional flicker of light and seemed like small insect dwellings.

"If the General finds out that my brown skin has touched your snow-like face, he will cut me into pieces and feed me to Jabberwocky," said Salim, as Laila burst into a wicked laugh while resting her head on his shoulder.

"Oh, come on now, Salim. He'll only put your pieces on the roof for vultures. Jabberwocky doesn't eat Khanpur villagers." He smiled.

"Do you want to go back in time, Laila?"

"Don't talk rubbish, now."

"I mean it. What if I could take you back in time right now? Sixty ... maybe a hundred million years back. Would you want to go?"

"Alright then. Take me, mister time traveler."

He grabbed her fingers and raised them to the sky.

"Do you see that, right there?" he said. "The light from this star has taken a hundred million years to get to us. To your beautiful eyes. I don't know how. But I can sense that that star isn't there anymore. Dinosaurs roamed this earth when the light began to travel from there, and here you are receiving it centuries later."

"You're lying!"

"Have I ever lied before?"

"No, but it seems a little crazy."

"Of course, it does. But it's true. You don't understand. It's like I've found the only pattern in this world that makes sense. What binds us all together, the stars, the moon, you, me. We're all connected through a series of equations. Time and space is nothing but a piece of bendable cloth. One day ... you shall see, I will travel through time—I will conquer it."

It was then, at that precise moment, as his eyes sparkled against the backdrop of the sky that the boundaries between two distinct worlds broke, the dams burst open, and the cosmos flooded with love. Laila lifted her head from his shoulder, parted her lips, and kissed him. Salim's body froze like it had been plunged into the Arctic waters as she thrust her tongue into his mouth, deeper than she had read about in her romance novels.

Salim reached behind her to caress her neck. At that moment, the garden in which they sat, under a tree of immortality, transformed into an element of his love for her. The universe around him came to a standstill.

Then he shuddered when her hand touched his thigh and slowly arrived at the seam of his trousers.

"Can I see it?"

Eyeing her gooseflesh arms, he responded, "Yes," because what else is one to say? He unzipped his trousers. Laila reached inside and pulled out a clammy, unknown object. To her surprise, her novels had not done justice to such a thing. It fascinated her and she was in two minds, whether to put an end to proceedings abruptly or to give in to her fantasies. She chose the latter and plopped her head in his lap, closed her eyes and opened her mouth.

The interaction was brief. It lasted for a few seconds. Suddenly, the sound of footsteps made Salim pull her off. She froze.

"It's Chaku and the Bear. You should go inside through the kitchen, I will keep them busy," Salim whispered. So, she did, fixing her dress, in a sudden burst of realization as if waking up from a prolonged daydream, rushing towards the porch, slipping behind a lonely hanging light bulb, into the kitchen. The swiveling door creaked as she entered. Salim walked up the hill towards the two moving bodies in the dark. They were wrapped in brown shawls and strode sluggishly, like irate zombies. There was a heavy mist that hung around their ankles, making it seem like they were floating.

An impish face emerged from one shawl to say, "Talib Jaan, have you heard of the story of the villager that once had romance with a General's daughter? Very nice story, don't you think? How do you think it should end?" Chaku shuffled towards Salim. "The scum of Khanpur must be so proud of this little sister-fucker." He tightened the shawl around his shoulders to free up his arms, while Talib blocked Salim's advance with his legs. In the brooding mist which had descended upon the summer house, the soldiers on top of the hill became invisible, leaving Salim with two options. One was to leap towards the village a thousand feet below and the other, to whiz past the two beasts who stood in front of him like a wall. He couldn't outrun them, surely. Not at that vulnerable moment, not at any moment.

"Chaku Jaan, can you see he was playing with his small dick?" Talib said, pointing his hashish-stained fingers at Salim's zipper, where a gaping hole pushed out the ends of his shirt. Instantly, Salim's hand went between his legs, but Chaku's fingers snapped at his wrist.

"What's the hurry, buffalo boy? You make a sound, and I will throw you down this mountain."

"I think he needs to be taught a lesson. I'm sure Khan Saab would want just that. What do you think?"

"You've spoken my heart's desire, Chaku Jaan."

Salim's heart fought to stay inside his chest. It wrestled out of every throbbing vein. "Just keep your filthy mouth shut and don't talk about Laila Madam. I'm not scared of you."

"Not scared? I see." Talib reached around the back of Salim's head and put him in a headlock, muffling his yelps while Chaku grabbed his ankles. The two of them hauled him towards the servant's quarters.

The room was dim and reeked of an unpleasantly dense body odor.

"Let me go, you sons of bitches!" he cried into the charpoy frame, the coarse ropes scratching at his face.

Chaku sucked his teeth. "We will let you go, buffalo boy. But not before you learn an important lesson. Maybe you've heard of Pashtuns, but tonight you will feel two of them and will never think about disgracing their honor again."

Talib removed his shirt and stuffed it down Salim's throat. It smelled foul like onions and carried the rancid gas that gurgled out from his insides when he spoke. Salim struggled and kicked. O leader of the cosmos! O Floating Pir! O Lord, please save me, he said to himself. Talib yanked down Salim's pants, jumped on to his back and pushed his face into the charpoy ropes. Then, the Bear thrust himself inside.

He let out another grunt and pushed a second time and then a third.

"Look Talib Jaan, how he lies still. He likes big Pathan dick."

"Hurry up. It's my turn now."

And then came the other, the one with more purpose in his breath. With the clapping sound of torso against torso, Salim bit hard and swallowed whatever taste came to his mouth. He counted the number of thrusts in agony.

Ten, eleven, twelve...

Within minutes, his life had swung from the cusp of heaven to the bowels of hell. The chasm between two distinct worlds shut close. And with the thirteenth and final stab, Chaku let out a grunt and his henna tinted locks fell on Salim's face.

As the two savages stood and wiped themselves, Chaku said, "Talib Jaan, I think this dung-eater has learned his lesson."

"What happens if he says anything to General Saab?"

"Oh ho, Talib Jaan," Chaku said as he threw Salim's trousers at him. "If General Khan finds out, we will have to tell him of that love story, of the villager and a General's daughter. After that, the leather whip will surely stripe that ass as well."

"You're right. Hey Buffalo Boy, stop your crying and go back into the house with the rest of the babies."

Salim sobbed uncontrollably. His legs shook as he pulled himself upright. He tried to breathe but he couldn't. He tried to run but his legs wouldn't move. It was as if every inch of him had submitted itself and he was left imprisoned in his own body. Like a horrible nightmare where you try to run but your legs turn to jelly.

"I can't breathe, I can't breathe," he cried as his torturers, in an almost disgusting show of respect, began to wipe his tears and help him with his clothes.

"Don't worry, fat boy. You'll be fine. Take this as a lesson," Chaku said, giving him a glass of rusty water from the tap.

So, this was a lesson, he thought as his body was dragged towards the kitchen door. A lesson which he should have learned a long time ago. The most important lesson of his life—the one all servants should keep at the back of their minds. The leash around Salim's neck tightened, now tauter than it had ever been, sealing the master-slave relationship. The kitchen door swung open, the naked bulb sputtered, and he was dropped inside. As if to awaken a stray dog, Chaku kicked his ribs.

"Get up now and go to your bed."

Salim crawled on all fours. His legs ached. His face hurt. He could almost taste the smell of sandalwood and sweat as he breathed. It made him gag. He trembled like a flame as he hurried to his room, pushed his face deep into the pillow, and howled, begging for forgiveness. From whom, you ask? From himself, I believe.

"I'm sorry. I'm sorry." The words fell out of his mouth over and over again as his tears soaked the pillow.

Undeniably, this was the gruesome result of his negligence. All they had done was remind him of that; remind him that even dreaming was forbidden.

That night, as Salim wept, he finally understood Mirza Ghalib's couplet. It was an ode to one's careless self: *why seek fidelity from an infidel who knows not what faith is?*

The following morning, he refused to speak with Laila. And to her angered inquiries, he simply responded with a sullen, downcast face. It infuriated her. But before she could tell him, he had disappeared. When they returned to Lorr, as soon as the buss rolled up the driveway of the Khan House, Salim slipped out from the gate an onto the main road. He told no one where he was going. He let the rumors do the talking. Many thought he wasn't going to return, because seldom do servants come back after leaving in such a way.

You might want to believe that Salim recovered from that night. Perhaps became a stronger person. The truth is, he never did. He shuddered in his sleep for many years. Even at the moment the bullet left my gun, just before I ended his life, that night's defilement flashed before his eyes.

You can tell by the shortness of my breath that I find this extremely difficult to talk about. It wasn't easy for me to tell you, but you had to hear it. How, you ask, did Salim end up in this inferno? I am disturbed too. Disturbed but not shocked. People in our part of the world have often described this barbarism as a rite of passage—disgusting, I know. I wish I could tell you otherwise, that this instance was rare, but I can't. Growing up, I knew of many such cases, some too horrific to spell out in words. When it comes to rape, silence is golden. And the citizens of serfdom know this silence better than anyone. It is their first language. What drove those men to do what they did can only be described as an act of retribution—justice had to be served, equilibrium had to be restored. How dare Salim do what he did? How dare he try and escape who he really was? How dare he love someone with such blindness?

I mentioned to you before: who we choose to love defines what we become. As for me, my destiny was merged with Salim's from the very beginning. His love for Laila and the Eden to which they belonged, defined who he became and unfortunately, carved out a predestined path for me. In a way, his fervor spawned mine and I became the monster I am today. Audacious, you might think. Sadly, sometimes, that was love in Pureland: loathed and forbidden. Everyone condemned Salim for having this love. It was considered a heresy. This infuriating heresy nauseated us all until the day I, the alleged Scimitar, Sword of the Caliphate, put an end to this love forever.

I'm not a terrorist, sir. Just someone who happened to be blinded by vengeance.

Home

───・🪷・───

I shouldn't let my emotions get the better of me. This story deserves better than that. Especially at this juncture when something inside Salim has begun to turn. Because, when your soul loses its sense of self and the city coils around you like a serpent, everything becomes a grotesque carnival of misery. Then you are hit with the sudden realization, that you are lost. And when you're lost is when you truly yearn for home. At this point in our story, that's exactly what Salim was—lost.

After that night at the summer house, everything and everyone Salim knew had developed an alter ego, an evil side. The city of Lorr, which once embraced him with open arms, started to frighten him. Especially on the morning he returned from St. Mary's Hill Station, sitting folded against the window at the back of the bus. Around him, Lorr's streets were erupting in a unique celebration, a collaborative declaration of relief. It was a strange occurrence that had all the others on the bus muttering to each other, but he ignored it all. It was as if he were moving slower than everything around him. The swaying trees, the rejoicing children in the streets, the sounds of the drums, the whistling motorcyclists, all whizzed past him. He was also in slow motion when he packed his things that morning and walked out of the Khan House. Something had taken control of his body, a sudden yearning. He didn't like the word 'home'. It confused him. Yet, at that lonely hour, he wished to know what it meant. This longing took over his feet and carried him out on to the Mall Road to hitch a ride in the back of a cattle truck. He was out to look for it. He was going to find this home.

The Canal of Fables, in the quiet of the morning, could be heard rippling through, guiding the road away from the frenzy of the old city towards open spaces. This early in the day, crows settled on the banks of the canal and called out to each other. The grassy green strips of Lorr were slowly replaced with empty fields and an uneven dirt path ran parallel to the water. Motor vehicles were as scarce as people. Nothing grew on the fields except footprints, and this vast nothingness stretched for miles. The road circled away from the canal towards the countryside. As the city disappeared from view, square blue road signs emerged at regular intervals indicating towns and their distance. He recognized the style with which the paintbrush had kissed the metal plates to form the words, "Khanpur 5 km". He knew how the smell of paint and metal could linger on one's fingers for days. At times, mixed with hookah smoke, those fingers could smell like they were decaying. He missed that scent. He craved that aroma.

On either side of the road now were barren pastures of wild grass mixed with fields of sugar cane. In the distance, women dressed in bright colors, headed towards a well with clay pots atop their heads and babies in their arms. Before his imposing weight disallowed it, he too had travelled each morning in such a manner. He remembered how his stepmother's sweat, seeping through her clothes, darkened the red fabric of her shirt. He recalled how he felt: protected, guarded.

Something else reminded him of her as he sat in the back of a truck along with two buffaloes and a newborn calf. The stench of their droppings took him to a time when she would gather dung in a metal bowl, pack it together with hay and slap it on the walls of their home. He examined the buffalo and the calf, holding their ears in his hands; they were thirsty and drowsy. They looked like they were drugged. Outside, dirt from the truck tires left a pluming trail, and on one side of the dust cloud he saw a shimmering ravine which softly spoke words of welcome into his ear.

He had never liked the village. The absence of light at night used to depress him. When you walked at night, you could hear yourself as if you were your own stalker. This time, somehow, he felt like an intruder creeping upon an ancient existence that had been there before he was even born—he felt gravity guiding the way. After all, he had taken his first breath here. It was where he had his first kiss.

The truck halted, thrusting its passengers, man and cattle, outward as the driver approached Salim.

"Listen, boy! This is as far as I can take you. I'm headed towards Kidney Town. You can walk from here."

"Thank you, sir. You should make sure your buffalo sits in water every day. She is thirsty. If you want her to give you lots of milk that is." Salim turned away from the truck as it drove by, its driver responding to his suggestion with a skeptical shrug. I would have liked it better if you had dropped me closer, he thought. Slowly, clutching his bundle of clothing and books, he ambled towards the bending slope that led towards the village where a shirtless child rolled a bicycle tire with a stick. His arms were skinny and his face held a pleasant eagerness.

And what kind of face would I show my family, Salim wondered. Where was I when the painter struggled through his agonizing malady? Was I so shameless that I couldn't even attend my own father's funeral? Were the devious caresses of my lover's fingers of more value to me? Am I even going to be welcomed by my brother? What about Maa? Would she even care? They have to. They must.

Salim strolled along the snaking road towards a congregation of mud huts. As he passed the children with sticks in their hands on their morning walks with buffaloes, he painfully managed a smile. Their innocence charmed him.

The huts appeared smaller than he remembered. He recognized the circular dung cakes which were slapped along the walls. There, among the shacks, was the palace, the first of the three Khan Houses, Gulliver-like amidst minuscule dwellings. It too remained unoccupied all year, except for visiting weekend caravans of drunk generals and their concubines. As he passed the giant walls of the house towards the huts, he noticed that his presence had stirred excitement and children had begun to trail behind him.

"You mean Potato? The one that the General took home?"

"Yes it's him, Potato, the painter's son. He's a big man already. Billa Cycle says he makes almost five rupees a month!"

"Khassi Kasai says he taught him how to read."

Salim turned and smiled at them and headed towards the dera. It was early in the morning; the dera was still vacant, except for a stray dog who sniffed the metal chairs hungrily. The dog looked weak and not of any distinct pedigree. His ears were too angular and his tail coiled more than it should have.

As he approached the two wooden doors of his father's home, he questioned his return to Khanpur. Summoning a little courage, he pulled upward on the metal hook and pushed forward. A wave of calm came over him as he saw his stepmother in a corner of the house, blowing life into a tiny fire. A flowing white cloth covered her head and ran down to the floor.

"Maa, it's me, Potato, your son. I'm home."

She turned.

"Maa, are you not going to say anything? It is me, Potato. I'm home," he repeated, more to himself than anyone else, as he looked into his stepmother's eyes. They had grown weary and helpless. Eight summers had dug rivers into her forehead. Her hair now had salted streaks and her face was held together by a frown. Her eyes were the only luggage she still carried with her after all these years. He knew them. A sigh escaped from her mouth as it opened and applied a balm to the wounds he had been carrying.

"I'm making breakfast, Potato. You look hungry. Come let me feed you."

Charm

———•◆•———

Before we continue, sir, I want to shift our focus away from Salim for a moment and touch upon something important. You should know something about villages, especially the feudal kind. Until you've actually seen one, you can't truly comprehend them, because these villages are a planet unto themselves. They are unique tiny worlds with their own gods and demons, heaven and hell. They have many oddities which we city folk would find peculiar. For instance, names in the village are earned not given at birth. Which is where Salim's brother Tamboo enters our story. As far as names go, floppy eyelashes and protruding teeth earned him his. For as long as anyone could remember, he was simply referred to as Tamboo the Camel.

Nakku was the second name that fell upon him. That too was a gift from his stepmother when she had first arrived in Jaaji's home and stood, hands clasped over her mouth upon seeing the beast for the first time. But Nakku, as in 'nosey', was an accurate appellation because of the enormous snout that covered most of his face. This gargantuan pyramid was useless as he couldn't smell a damn thing. In fact, even breathing was difficult because of the crooked bones and cartilage that created a valley of twisted labyrinths from which air wheezed in and out. It was as though his nose was God's practical joke, useful only as scaffolding, protecting, depending on which way he was facing, sides of his face from sunlight. So, for many years, Nakku took every abuse hurled his way with a lowered, bashful gaze as the villagers pointed at him, chuckling amongst themselves.

As if his plagued appearance was not enough, for the longest part of his life, havoc followed him wherever he went and Tamboo Nakku the Camel was one person you'd avoid in Khanpur. Let's put it this way, if chaos were iron shavings, he was a magnetized rod, forever cursed by his innate ability to attract pandemonium.

To give you an example: Tamboo Nakku's first wife left him on their wedding night after he poked her in the eye in an attempted kiss. One can understand such vigor given that he'd never touched a woman before. It was as if he was oblivious to the fact that his nose was a potent weapon of destruction. Blinded in one eye, his wife left the painter's home cursing out loud. Word spread. Tamboo was alone once more.

Jaaji never quit though. He found his son another bride. This time from Kidney Town where no one knew of Tamboo's misfortunes. But during his second wedding night, as he was about to consummate his marriage, a wailing intruder bolted into the painter's house with horrifying news. Tamboo's bride leapt to her feet and ran out the door. Woefully, two tragic mishaps unfolded that night. According to the informant, the bride's brother died in a freak accident: a donkey's rear kick in the chest. To make matters worse, her father choked to death when a gecko fell in his mouth while he was sleeping. Even though Tamboo had no association with these bizarre incidents, and despite the fact that he'd managed to get to third base that night, his adamant curse convinced wife number two to stay clear. When she left, dowry and baggage in tow, a new terror descended upon the town. Tamboo's presence became a forecast for disaster. As mothers yanked their children out of his path while he walked around the village, the thought of ending his life entered his mind. However, Jaaji had big aspirations for his son; which brings us to wife number three.

The painter conjured up a plan to save his son's life and bribed the blind imam, Unna Huneira, with two buffaloes and the proceeds from his illicit liquor business. The cleric had two elder daughters whose weddings had left him penniless. He had no choice but to wed his youngest to Tamboo. Had fate not dragged him through the turmoil of failure, Tamboo wouldn't have become the professional he did on the night of his third wedding. This time, he decided to go all out. In an accidental yet furious attempt to oblige his new bride, he perfected the art of cunnilingus. Like a worshipper he fell between her legs in a desperate plea during which his once useless nose became a natural pleasure-inducing contraption. Combine this, in your lucid imagination if you may, with his artful ability to oscillate his tongue at great speeds and you could well envision why he became a pioneer, a forerunner in the art of gratification. Eventually, he became a master of the trade, a qualified practitioner whose legend earned him his most celebrated name: Charming.

Shedding all previous names and reputations like snakeskin, Tamboo Charming was born. Wherever he walked, he enticed lusty smirks and lip-licking glances from his growing legion of fans. Women threw themselves at his mammoth feet, offering to wash his clothes, milk his buffalo, cook his meals, the works. Tales of his craft spread rapidly all the way from the Floating Pir's shrine to Kidney Town. His wife, who had not exactly been a shriveling sunflower when it came to sex, recognized that there existed an untapped market and became Tamboo's manager in a rather unique business venture—they conducted personalized love seminars and pleasure sessions with female clients and introduced a new sexual horizon which disgusted and simultaneously aroused their audiences, sending them back into their bedrooms. They pushed the frontier of desire outwards. This made Tamboo Charming, the love doctor, the best kept secret among women. They all vowed to protect him from possible jealous men who might shatter his prized muzzle if they knew where it had been.

To the men of Khanpur, however, Tamboo Charming, the lanky camel with a preposterous beak and hideous tusks, suddenly became an exquisite dazzler, the premier feminist, and a connoisseur of the female body. While he snickered shyly and giggled at their attempts to make him reveal his clandestine talents, his reputation began to change. No longer was he Tamboo Nakku the Camel, the mayhem magnet. He now possessed a gravity of a different kind, the kind all men craved, the kind that could start wars. He shared the art of lovemaking and began a sexual revolution in the village of darkness. No longer was sex a quick relief of urges, but a drawn-out endeavor. Sex became fun.

Life continued on in this way for Tamboo Charming. After Jaaji's death, he partnered up with Pappu Pipewalla in their secret distillery. Further, he had a son. Tamboo's family was complete; he didn't need anyone else. He never thought Salim would ever return to Khanpur. They all had, as a family, bought into the idea that he was gone for good. And when Salim failed to show up at his father's funeral, Tamboo thought that greed had made his brother heartless. That is why, that morning when he returned from the field, he was startled to find Salim sleeping on the clay floor near the stove. A wet cloth cooled the tepid air on his face. He looked peaceful. Tamboo watched as his three-year-old son pushed his fingers into Salim's nostrils.

Salim coughed and sat up immediately.

"Oh ... Maa didn't tell me we had royalty in the house. I would've brought the band *baja* to welcome His Highness," said Tamboo in his heavy, nasal voice as he walked over to a charpoy in the corner and reached under it to pull out a metal canister.

"How are you, brother?" he said, rising to his feet. "Sorry, I fell asleep. I was..."

"Shut up and grab the other can from Maa's room and come with me."

Salim took a deep breath and followed his brother's command, carefully avoiding waking their mother. The house remained the same as he had left it. In the house, curtains acted as doors separating the rooms.

Salim pulled the can from underneath his mother's charpoy and followed his brother outside. The air was warm and the earth moist from the early morning dew. In the distance, people could be seen trekking eastwards, empty water canisters in hand, all on the same mission. The village of Khanpur had three water-pumps located at varying distances along the main road. General Khan's father, Pasha Khan, had built one for the Sikhs, one for the Hindus, and one for the Muslims so the villagers could avoid sharing morning pleasantries with each other and shit in peace. After the Partition in '47, however, more granular divisions were made. The Sunnis congregated at the pump near the houses, the Shias to the one slightly further. And the Ahmadis, the Christians, and the Untouchables inherited the pump at the perimeter of the village almost a kilometer away from the housing compound. Even though at times the villagers worked the same fields, drank the same hooch, and attended each other's weddings, they would never in any circumstance shit together.

Tamboo walked in front of Salim, his large flipper-like feet expelling dust around his heels. His upper back curved inwards as his head sank like a vulture's. The two brothers stood in line at the water pump.

"Did you get fired from the Khan House?"

"No," Salim replied, staring at his own feet, noticing that he was the only one in the queue with shoes. Other eyes also drifted towards the boarding-school-shine that bounced off his Oxfords.

"Did your big mouth get you thrown out of school then?"

"No, nothing like that." Tamboo's nose, like a sun dial, cast a shadow over his cheek as he twisted his face.

"Have you lost your way then, sister-fucker? What shame have you brought with you? Have you no respect for our father? Do you even know that he is dead, you piece of cow dung?"

Salim's hand burst upward to hold his brother, but he shrugged him off. His breathing became heavy and he tried to hold back his tears and quietly pumped water into his can.

Salim tried once more, this time pulling his brother's arm. His can fell to the ground. Tamboo looked into his eyes and before he could open his mouth, tears spilled down Salim's cheek. He launched into Tamboo's arms and held on to his bewildered embrace, taking his pain-filled heart and tipping it over into his chest. With each sob, he begged for forgiveness. Tamboo held him close and pushed his shoulders back, looking into his eyes. There was little resemblance to the cheeky boy that he used to know as a child. Fluff had gathered on his upper lip and chin. With his thumbs, he wiped Salim's tears from his face and said, "You little shit, you dropped my water! Now am I supposed to wipe my ass with your tears?"

Salim's sniffle transformed itself into a snicker as he wiped his nose with his sleeve. Tamboo squeezed him one more time.

"Whatever it is, we can fix it. Everything will be fine."

Those were the words he had wanted to hear all along, and he found them in the most unexpected place of all, in the arms of his brother, the woman whisperer.

With his head still buried in Tamboo's chest, he responded, "I wouldn't waste my tears on your ass!"

They refilled their watering cans and headed for the sugarcane field nearby where a gaunt ox plodded away, pulling a wooden plank, making small channels in the ground while his proprietor, a ten-year-old boy, slept under a kino tree.

There was something fun about shitting with Tamboo and Jaaji that Salim remembered from his childhood, as he found a clean spot and dug a ditch with his Oxfords. Shitting was the only time he felt that his family did anything together. Toilets were only for the Saabs and rarely did anyone get to see one, let alone crap in one. Toilets were myths. To the villagers, shitting was a communal thing; it had been for centuries. There was nothing shameful about it, it was a bonding experience conducted away from the sanctity of home. At times it became a sport, as competing farts and turds were submitted for approval and shared with loved ones. Jaaji would often lay black turds and yell in excitement, "Look, look! Can you get your shit to be this black?" as his sons would hold their nose in disgust and try not to gag. It was the only time Tamboo claimed he could smell anything.

Salim, however, had forgotten how to crap in the open. He felt uneasy and missed his toilet. He carefully managed not to shit on his clothes while he squatted. As he lay last night's dinner on the earth in a neat banana shape, he tiptoed over it to find another clean patch of ground where he could pour the water and cleanse himself. It was a daunting task, one that could only be performed by experienced shitters. As he splashed water on to his bottom, he carried on a conversation with his brother as one would over a cup of tea.

"Do you know what they did to Baa's grave?" Tamboo asked.

"All I know is that he was sick. General Saab told me that he didn't want me to come here and wanted me to stay in Lorr ... and so I did. He never loved me like he did you Tamboo. You were his special son."

"Baa was sick, that's true. The old man drank more ale than he did water. The General came one day, asking about him. 'Where is Salim's father? I want to see him'. We all gathered around at the dera waiting for him. And then he emerged as he always did, from under a tree somewhere. Baa was weaker than a Kidney Town dog and Khan Saab could see that. The clothes fell loosely over his body. Khan felt bad for him and ordered all the elders of the village from all castes to make sure that Jaaji the Painter be taken care of. He even gave Unna Huneria money to hire a caregiver. Everyone at the time said, 'Yes, sir, General Saab. Of course, General Saab'. Baa was so pleased; he thanked the General and said to send you his love. But he made General Zafar promise that your studies shouldn't be affected. He begged him to keep you away from Khanpur in any way possible. And you know promises are everything for these Khans." Tamboo waited behind the sugarcane for his brother. Salim finally emerged, fiddling with his clothes.

"And when Baa died, the General ordered the elders to bury him in the same cemetery as the other Muslims."

"You mean Baa is in a different cemetery from our grandfather? Why didn't you send him there?"

"Baa was a fool, as you know. He didn't care. When Maa asked him one day, 'Jaaji, where would you like to be buried,' you know what he said? 'Surprise me'," Tamboo managed to crack a painful smile as he continued, "He died peacefully in his sleep. Me and Billa Cycle, we took him to the main cemetery where we buried Wannu the Weasel's father. I'd already picked out a corner near the kino trees. He loved kinos, that bastard. We placed him and prayed for him. I covered him with a handful of dirt, I remember." He paused momentarily. "The next day I brought Maa. I shouldn't have. Potato, that day I knew that wherever you were it was best for you to stay away, like Baa had said..."

"What happened, Tamboo? Tell me the whole thing and don't treat me like a child!" Salim yelled, as his brother's voice became more nasal than usual.

"When we went to pay our respects, Baa was lying outside his grave, naked, with nothing but the sky as his blanket. The sons of bitches didn't even respect his corpse."

Tamboo's words stabbed Salim in the chest. His legs weakened.

"What do you mean he lay there? What are you talking about?" Salim's eyes began to redden. "Tell me, Tamboo. What happened!"

"Are you really that clueless, city boy? They left him there like a dog's carcass. Maa cried and cried for days. She broke into tiny pieces. I raised fucking havoc in this village, asking everyone for answers. No one spit out a word—these sister-fuckers. Even in death our people are not spared."

"Did you ask Billa Cycle? Or Cut-Two Naii? He knows everyone in this town. What about Wannu the Weasel? Nothing gets past him."

"No one said a damn word. Billa was the only one who helped me wrap his body in a cloth and we took him to the Ahmadi cemetery. I made a pact to find out who did this deed." Tamboo turned his gaze skyward to stop the tears falling from his eyes. "I told myself I would only cry again after I put the bastards in the ground. It has been so long now, and here we are standing, talking about it. Nothing has happened, nothing will happen. We will go on living our lives under everyone's heels. It's our destiny."

Salim sat down on the dew-soaked earth wordlessly. With his hands gripping his knees, he began to sway. In that moment he forgot about himself, about Laila, the Khan House, his life, his dreams, and the soft whispers of the canal. He had been so strangled all these years by his persona that he hadn't seen his father's sacrifice.

"Oh Potato, he wanted you to stay away not because you were useless but so he could shield you from this place. You waved him farewell as you flew away in your Saab's car, and he swallowed his pride over and over so that you could sleep on a bed, shit in a toilet, and eat all the books you could eat."

"I will kill them all, Tamboo! All of them!" Salim's hand tightened into a fist as he rose from the ground. His fingernails dug into his own palm preparing to defend an honor which he himself had once besieged.

"Potato, you need to calm down. You want Baa's death to mean something? Then become a Saab in the city with a big job. Then we will look back at these mongrels and pity them. Baa is dead and he's not coming back. For his sake, for our sake ... for the sake of the prophecy he believed in so much. Grant him his wish. Rise above them all."

A frozen silence came over Salim.

"We have all been blinded by the prophecy of the Floating Pir. Can't you see, Potato? You're a treasure here. Our very own Lorr Museum piece. Ask any child and they will tell you stories of Potato, the painter's son. Many don't even think you're real."

Tamboo pulled his brother up into his arms as they walked home.

Salim's heart changed direction that night. He slept on the hardened clay upon which he was born. In the broken assembly of fragments, the cracked door, the mud walls, the buffalo dung, he somehow found himself. He knew that his soul could rest there, in the comforting solace, amongst his kin. In his family's destitution he found a wealth far greater than that of any general of any army. In the gloom of the village there lived a besieged light and for the first time in his life, he was happy to bask in it.

———◆———

The following morning, just after sunrise, Salim awoke again to the sound of a child's laughter. A poke in the eye, then one in the nose and he was awake. This time Tamboo was there with their stepmother. They had made breakfast for him. He yawned and leapt onto his feet like a lion sending Tamboo's little boy in screaming giggles.

"I didn't mean to scare him."

"It's fine Potato, I think he got scared of your tits. He's used to seeing them on women." Salim ran towards his brother and wrestled him to the ground. "Stop it you buffalo, you will squash my insides!"

"You like these, Tamboo Charming? Isn't that what they call you now? I thought you're the master of tits?"

"Stop it, both of you! Come, Potato, your breakfast is getting cold," yelled their mother as the family squatted around an imaginary table eating fried bread and sipping milky tea. The others made sure to curb their hunger; Salim on the other hand was oblivious to this gesture and gobbled away at his normal pace.

If pressed to decide on one, Salim would choose that day to relive repeatedly. It was the happiest day he could remember. He laughed harder than he had ever done before upon hearing of Tamboo's tales. So much so that he had to stop and wipe his tears. He stayed on in the village for more nights than he could count. It was hard to keep track of time in a timeless place.

During these days, it was as though the people of the Khan House had begun to hibernate in the back of Salim's mind. He had blunted the nausea of what had happened to him with his family's laughter. But his brother had sensed something from the very moment Salim returned to the village. Tamboo knew that the hurdles of serfdom must have tripped him up along the way, making him stumble over to the village. There was no other reason for a servant to abandon his master and return home sobbing with unspoken regret. And yet he realized that he didn't belong in this environment; the way he shuffled on the floor at night, how he sweat enough to drench his clothes, and how he would burst outside clutching his tummy because he couldn't handle raw buffalo milk. A Khan House servant he may be, but Salim was anything but a villager.

Tamboo's realization made him ponder the years of Salim's absence. And his father's pain, which the painter quashed with ale every night, had begun to release images of a brandishing promise in his mind—a promise that carried the burden of a hopeful village.

So, one morning, Tamboo walked over to Salim as he was sleeping and shook him awake.

"Get up, grab all your things and come with me," Tamboo said.

"Where are we going?"

"Don't ask questions, Potato. Just do as I say and come outside."

Yawning, Salim turned over on his side and tried to go back to sleep until a large foot jammed into his ribs.

"Fine," he whispered. "I'm getting up."

The morning had not begun yet and the day fought with the night to take control of the sky. The fields were quiet and only the crows were awake. From the compound of houses, the road snaked out of Khanpur through the fields towards a turquoise sign that bore the village's name. It could barely be seen through the coats of dust. Its original indigo color had faded, and it stood at an angle tilting the words towards the ground making the letters look as if they would slide right off. Salim, with his clothes rolled up under his arm, walked down the path with Tamboo, gazing out at the horizon. The harvest had just begun and sugarcane was piled up into stacks, ready to be shipped to the factories. Tamboo pulled his brother to the side of the road and sat down on his haunches.

"You need to go back, Potato," he said, letting out a sigh. "Look around you. Nothing changes in this world of ours. That sugarcane will be gone, the field will be torched, and a few months later, another crop will grow. But us ... we stay here."

"Look, Tamboo. I know..."

"You don't know shit, little brother. You don't know anything. We have not seen you in years and have learned to live with nothing but a promise that you would come free us from all this one day. Baa sacrificed a lot for you, Potato. And Khan Saab has given you a chance people here can only dream of. You think your life in the city is demanding? You won't last a single day out on these fields. Look how much you sweat without your ceiling fan. And how much bloody water you guzzle; like a panting buffalo."

Salim crossed his legs and sat on the dusty road hugging his clothes.

"Maybe ... maybe you are right," Salim said, looking up at Tamboo. "I shall return, if not for me then for the ones I love." He looked away for a moment. "But I want more. My dreams have revealed things to me that might not make sense to you right now. But all I can say is, I've found a way to escape."

"Have you lost your mind? What do you want to escape from?"

"The General's generosity can become a trap, Tamboo, and I don't want to be wrapped in his charity forever. Yes, I will return but only to leave on my own terms. You might think I'm crazy, but I've dreamt of things that are far bigger than the Khan House, than Blisschesterson. There's another world I must conquer and for that I must go to a faraway land ... yes, that's it. That's what I'll do." He paused for a few breaths. "I've lived a lie all these years, Tamboo. I must make things right again."

Tamboo shook his head, stood up and pulled on his brother's arm. They began walking again towards the blue sign. "There's always surprises from you, Potato," he said, throwing a pebble into the rice field.

When they arrived at the junction of the road that led towards the city, Tamboo pushed the tilted blue sign upright with his foot. With his hand, he wiped the plate clean until the white brush strokes stood out from its faded blue background. He folded his body in half, bent down, and kissed the plate as if it were a holy stone.

Salim looked to his brother and said, "You know ... in the city, it's not normal to discuss family matters while taking a shit."

"Really? They're such deprived souls, those city people."

Exalted Birds

Salim stood outside the Khan House, admiring the gold spears on top of the iron gate. Only fools would mistake its needle-sharp tips for ornaments. It was a deterrent to intruders: climb at your own peril. He'd been waiting for a while and became irritated. He took a rock from the street and began tapping on the gate as loud as he could. Finally, the iron rods parted to reveal a man in khaki uniform. His mustache was twirled in a half-crescent at either end and his wide shoulders bore the embellishments of the Military Police: 'MP' in block letters. He asked Salim for identification and when he gave his name, the MP approached General Khan in the garden and immediately spun on his heels scurrying back to the gate. Slapping a salute on his head, he welcomed Salim inside.

A floating ring of exalted birds were on their morning flight, and as they landed in succession into their pens, their patron admired them from the garden using his palm as a visor.

Salim couldn't remember how long he'd been away. It might have been just the two weeks servants were allowed annually or maybe longer. Either way, things were different in the house. That morning, the lawn had been freshly cut. It smelled like the sweet mint lemonade Laila would make during summer evenings.

Khan was seated in the middle of the garden having tea and sandwiches with Cousin Tezi. A strange commotion had begun to erupt around the place. Salim stood behind Khan's chair, as an abnormal feeling quivered in his spine. He felt as if he were a different person. Like a stranger, he started sniffing the grass, admiring the arching veranda and the white pillars of the house, as though seeing them for the first time.

"Salam, General Saab," he said with a smile as Jabberwocky, who had been sleeping near Khan's feet, lifted his head.

General Khan turned around and erupted, "And where the bloody hell have you been?"

"Saab, I went to…"

"Khanpur. Yes, I know. And you know how I know? The butcher, Khassi, told me he spotted you loitering around the village with your brother. Do you have no respect for me anymore that you don't tell me before leaving?" Khan's voice, though loud, sounded muffled by the turmoil around him. "I was looking everywhere for you."

"I am really sorry, Saab," Salim said, as the noise level grew.

"Abbas, put up that bloody tent up! I've told you five times!"

"Yes, sir, General Saab!"

Salim tried to speak again, his voice cracking. "Saab, I wanted to tell you that morning but … but, I don't know, sir. I was really emotional and…"

Before he could finish that sentence, his unsettling voice made the General's eyes soften. They looked at each other for uncountable moments. An exchange occurred in that silence; an apology, reasoning, and finally, a hesitant acceptance. The pain that Salim had been carrying for days could be seen on his face. When he noticed that, Khan's anger began to melt and he cleared his throat, shaking his head.

"You can't just disappear like that, Salim … Abbas, you bald bastard, not that one, the other one…"

"Yes, sir!"

"What was I saying? Yes, you tell me next time. Understand?" Salim nodded. "Abbas, get one of the guards to help you lift it, you lazy swine!"

From the obscurity of Khan's shadow emerged cousin Tehzeeb, bouncing on the balls of her feet.

"Zafar don't get your blood pressure rising now. Look, at least Salim is back. Why don't you tell him what happened? Tell him, nah!" she clamored in her unique mousy voice, throwing her ochre clothing over her bare knees, "Uff, so exciting! Salim, do you know what's happened?"

"Tezi, I was going to…"

"I'll tell him, then. We're finally free from that wretched and corrupt government. And it was all your doing, Salim. What was it that General

Ali called it? A mathematical, trapezoidal, algebraic problem ... yes, that's it! Pureland should salute you."

"What?"

"... name a street after you, or something else maybe."

"I don't understand."

"... at least let you be part of the parade. No, Zafar?"

General Khan shook his head and took a deep breath. "It's true, Salim. That night, with your help, our plan was complete. The army has taken control of the government and we did it all without shedding a drop of blood. Something had to be done. Things were getting so out of hand. So much corruption. Someone had to do something. Pureland is headed upwards and no one can stop it now."

In a hostile takeover of her own, in came Cousin Tehzeeb again. "... And ... and did you know? You're looking at the soon-to-be-announced, I don't want to jinx it, but I'm so excited ... Minister of Education! This country was just not ready for democracy. Pureland is like a buffalo, nah? You need a strong stick to show it the right path. Isn't that right, Zafar?" Khan put his hand on her knee as they began to engage in a familiar battle like they always did.

"Tezi, don't you have to go back to your husband?"

"Don't be so mean, nah. I'm just..."

But to Salim, their words began to float away as if they were bobbing upon a tide in the distance. They were suddenly blunted by his thoughts. Cousin Tezi's voice became a silent murmur, which was a unique occurrence to say the least.

"I don't know what to say, sir. I wasn't aware of what I was doing," he began, as images of a rejoicing Lorr came to mind. It was ... not my intention, he said to himself. What have I done? The smiles on the people's faces as they danced around drums on the streets of Lorr—had I done that? Had I been acting upon a dream?

At that moment, his confusion led him to believe the General's words, that his nation was, in some way, better off. But I believe, as he stood there rubbing his shoulders, oddly shivering in the morning heat, he harbored some guilt, however little it might have been. He knew that when the sun rose on the morning he returned to Lorr, the world had changed. People don't just take to the streets, expressing their pleasure in the form of firecrackers and trumpets. The Lorr Jazz Ensemble, the marching band of Davis Road, they were all there in celebration. Though he wanted to believe that this change was good, he couldn't. The tremors that ran down his arms didn't allow for it. Better off, he repeated to himself. Better off.

But what about the people of the village? Khanpur hadn't altered one bit. How could it? It was stuck in a space and time of its own; its people, in their own galaxy, with their own gravity and solar system. None of it mattered: who was at the helm of the nation, or whether there was a nation at all. In that moment, the gulf between the village and the city widened and he felt more a part of his kin than ever before.

Where did General Khan fit into all of this? Were all the thirty renegades who stormed the parliament building, handed out ministries? Salim didn't know the answer to that but he could imagine that Khan's gilded profile might have helped with the Ministry of Education sliding his way on the carving table.

Khan, spirited, continued, "We can change the way every child thinks. We can shape a better future for Pureland." He paused. "Salim, I think you should go have some breakfast, you look like you've lost half your weight." He looked over his shoulder, muttering, "Where has this moron disappeared to now? Driver! Driver!"

Even the stifled yelp of a, "Yes, sir!" from behind the banyan tree followed by the unsettling footsteps of his aggressor couldn't interrupt Salim's thoughts. He was still bewildered, standing silently with his brow in a state of confusion as Chaku dragged his feet on the cobblestone driveway.

"Where do you people disappear to? Can't you hear me calling? Wipe down the car. I need to head to the headquarters. And take Salim to the kitchen, you hear?"

"Yes, sir," Chaku replied behind Khan's chair, with a squint of the eye towards Salim and a smile which sent a shudder down his neck.

"I know where the kitchen is. You don't need to escort me," Salim whispered as he walked past him.

"Oh! I'll escort you into my room tonight but it looks like the village sun has made you black, so perhaps you're safe. I don't like you black village puppies." Salim ignored him as he rushed to the kitchen.

As he ducked under the banyan canopy, staring out past the veranda, he noticed something different about the house. He could feel the roar of an army truck in his belly as it approached from the gate. In rolled General Ali's motorcade, pushing more boots and cars into the packed driveway than he'd ever seen before. The servants seemed to be expecting this as they rushed out of their quarters. They all knew General Ali had a thing for Cousin Tezi. His was a unique desire; he found irresistible what others deemed infuriating. While most men winced, covering their ears at her glass-shattering voice, he'd listen mesmerized, hand on chin, as though she were a nightingale. This came as no surprise to the Raja of Bill-Qul, Cousin Tezi's husband, who himself had a strange courtship with his wife. It was well known that Raja Saab, all three hundred and twenty-five pounds of him, was a compassionate individual who had inherited the entire town of Bill-Qul at a very early age. His parents, coincidentally, were on the same airplane as the late Lord Thompson when it crashed into a hill after losing altitude in the ill-famed rainstorms of 1930. Rumors later surfaced that the plane was severely overloaded—some two hundred crates of Bill-Qul mangoes were piled up in the cargo deck underneath, causing the untimely descent.

Nonetheless, the Raja of Bill-Qul was no ordinary landlord. Among the typical feudal desires for imported cars and polo soirees, the Raja admired the game of tennis and had constructed hundreds of grass courts around Lorr city. Moreover, despite his size, he was known to move around the court with great agility and speed and possessed a serve-and-volley which, many claimed, was better than that of the Australian champion, Roy Emerson. But, the Raja of Bill-Qul was short-handed in the love department. He had been impotent ever since a low half-volley struck his Bill-Qul family jewels a short time after his marriage to Tezi Khan. The Raja and Tezi had developed an open relationship since then, one in which she was allowed to bring home lovers as long as he could watch. Mixed-doubles they called it.

Salim sat on his haunches in the kitchen as Bally pushed a plate of curry in front of him. Outside, he could hear excitement buzzing amongst the servants. They sat laughing in the distance, watching as Tezi and General Ali greeted each other on the steps of the lawn. It was entertainment for them. They claimed responsibility for the affair since they were the ones relaying secret messages, setting up covert meetings in Khan's study, away from prying eyes. They also delivered flowers at the Bill-Qul Mahal via courier. He recalled the mysterious letter that Bilki had pulled from her bosom, the one with the cursive, 'Ali', on the envelope. It all began to make sense to him.

The Khan House had become more than an amphitheater for illicit affairs; it was now a retreat for the commanders of the new regime. Generals, brigadiers and the lot began loitering around the lawn during the day and the library at night. They began demanding refreshments while sitting under the canopy playing cards and even started requesting Bally to cook their favorite meals. Khassi Kassai started a daily delivery of fresh meat: goat, lamb, and the occasional buffalo. Fresh from the village—all pre-neutered, of course. A feast was prepared every night, which explained the growing throng of servants. All this was evident as General Khan was escorted into his shiny new car by an MP and driven off under an arch of salutes outside the main gate.

Salim waited until Khan's car left the compound and the large metal bolt squeezed the gate shut. Then with a sudden jerk, he shot up from his heels and began to wash his hands at the sink.

"Finish your breakfast. Where are you off to now?" said Bally, as Salim wiped his mouth with his sleeve.

"Sorry, Bally Saab. I need to rush indoors for a few minutes. Please keep watch. I won't be long."

"By God, you're out of your mind. Wait, don't go in there!"

But before the hunchback could utter another word, Salim slipped off his shoes at the kitchen door and bolted indoors. He tiptoed up the stairs to the second floor. The inside of the house was not how he remembered it. It, too, had changed. The Evil Witch's obnoxious paintings, which resembled the work of two chimpanzees in a paint war, had been removed. General Khan had replaced them with contemporary Turkish miniatures. The yellow tapestries which could hurt a blind man's eyes were also gone. And the horrid carpeting which reminded General Khan of his mother's inability to tell apart bright pink from mellow green was now replaced with white marble. After his mother's death, Khan had quietly wiped away her footprints from the house. It seemed like, while Salim was away, these changes had picked up pace.

As he peered up at the empty hall that led to the Evil Witch's room, Salim shuddered. He didn't need to venture to the third floor to know it had been abandoned for quite some time, and that dust had settled upon dust. He pulled himself up the banister and swung around in front of Laila's room, waited momentarily, then tapped the door.

"Come in, Bilki. What's taken you so long with my breakfast!" Laila's voice aroused him as he walked in and closed the door behind him.

"What are you doing here? Get out right now or I'll scream."

"You won't do anything until you hear me out," he said, walking towards her and grabbing her hands. She wriggled free.

"Do you know how angry Daddy was when you left?"

"I know, I know."

"You know what everyone thought? That you had gone for good."

"I'm sorry I had to leave that way but I'm back now."

Laila's eyes narrowed to the point where it looked that she was asleep. Scattered around her bed was her nightgown, an issue of the raunchy *Clandestine* magazine, and a collection of romance novels which had shirtless men on their covers. Salim's wandering eyes imagined himself tucked in her large bed alongside her, shielded by the beautiful lace that fell from the ceiling to the floor. He put his finger on her lips. "Please listen, and then if you don't like what you're hearing, you call those MPs and tell them to shoot me in the lawn." He walked a step closer. "I was hurt," he said, taking in a deep breath. "Something awful happened to me that I may never be able to tell you. I had a lot of pain inside me when I left." He paused again, sifting through his mind for the right words. "What I am trying to say is, Laila, your world and mine is divided. But I came back for you. I know there will come a time where this divide will be no more. I have found a way to do just that. I have been touched by something magical."

"Magical? What a load of shit. Is this what you came here to tell me?"

"No ... I came to tell you that I'm sorry about how I caused you and Khan Saab a lot of pain." He paused, noticing Laila's eyes on the door behind them. She began fidgeting.

"Get up on that chair and pretend you're fixing my curtains." Salim didn't hesitate and hopped onto the chair near the balcony. Then she turned back to him with folded arms and said, "Sorry, is just not good enough for me."

Salim's extended silence began to cut through Laila like a blade. What else was he meant to say? His confused look only added to her fury.

"I was in a complete state of ... of denial ... about..."

"You're only making it worse!"

Salim, oblivious still, inhaled her morning aroma as she spoke, it was warm and comforting. He bent closer to her and tried to hold her hand. She yanked herself away from him hastily, her heart pounding hard against her chest. She never had a male servant inside her room before. The idea of being caught repulsed and excited her at the same time. And just as the words left her mouth, Khalil pushed her door open. With a sly haste, Khalil looked at his sister, filling her legs with concrete. "Khalil! Salim was just fixing my curtains. Get your brother and go downstairs for breakfast with Aunty Tezi."

Salim jumped off the chair and without saying a word made for the stairs.

Khalil, venomously, eyed Salim from the door and said, "Servants are not allowed up here! Have you forgotten your boundaries?"

"Khalil Saab, I may be a servant, but you should know that I'll die before I let anything happen to this family. I will go now." Salim leapt down the stairs as Khalil stood for a moment until he heard the front door close and stared back disconcertingly at his sister.

"What will Daddy do when he finds out?"

"Find out what, Khalil? I asked him to fix my curtain rod and to say sorry for his father's death. What? You want me to go outside in front of the outside servants in my nightie? Don't be foolish now. Head to the dining room. I'll see you there," she replied with firmness.

Laila's greatest error was thinking that Khalil's fledgling mind was too tender to comprehend treachery. She couldn't have been more wrong. For Khalil knew what all children at the age of twelve know: what's right, what's wrong, the difference between honor and shame, servant and master. He knew that in this world there were rules, and an intruder was about to trespass upon a sanctity which was his to protect. Yet, at that moment he had no choice but to believe her and put his dignity at ease because, indeed, the image of his sister in a nightgown in the garden was a far more terrifying thought.

As Khalil left his sister's room, Laila locked the door. She went over to her dresser and sat down on the velvety bench. Looking at her reflection, she saw her cheeks flushing red. An unsettling thorn in her side had been fortified with Salim's return to the Khan House. And his lame refusal to bring up that night ... who did he think he was? In her mind, there was an alternative version of how things unfolded. That evening was more than an expression of her muzzled sensuality. She had orchestrated her plan of attack with grand visions of how she would finally enter the sexual arena. But Salim forced his own conclusion on that fantasy. As if it were him who was in charge. How dare he dismiss her like that?

That night at St. Mary's house, Laila had tossed and turned under her quilt with a needling sensation throbbing through her veins. And when Salim left the next day without saying a word, she felt as though her body was being raked over burning embers. What kind of vindication was she seeking? A reasoning for his rejection, or maybe, another go at it, as it were, to make things right? Maybe she wasn't quite sure herself.

Laila closed her eyes imagining that night as it should have been, with a plot of her own. And as she did, she squeezed her thighs together, let out a series of winded heaves, and felt her heart thump in her chest until her passion spilled out in the form of wetness between her legs. And when it all was over, she opened her eyes to behold her reflection biting her lip.

It can be assumed by now that Laila Khan was a creature of immense complexity. I can't even begin to rationalize her thoughts as she let out those passionate sighs. But I imagine that foggy night on the hill of the summer house was an unforeseen disaster for her, a reminder of a bewildering rejection from this obedient figurine she thought she owned in every way imaginable. As she stared at her eyes in the mirror, she vowed to never allow anyone control over her emotions again. And she was not going to be ashamed of this sexuality of hers either. Unlike what she had been told by her elders, her sensuality was not a curse, it was a secret weapon. No man would dare take this from her ever again.

"This ... is my power," she said to herself, raising her chin.

When Laila rose from that dresser bench, poised and convinced, she had a new resolve about herself. The world around her had become an endless celebration of broken boundaries. She wasn't going to stay lodged in her ivory tower any longer. It was her time now. That's because in her enchanted universe, Laila Khan was neither the beloved Eve, nor a symbol for Adam's lost paradise—she was God.

That evening, the servants sat in a circle around a solitary light bulb behind the kitchen. They dipped their rotis one by one into a bowl of meatless curry. The house servants ate first followed by the guards and then the *velas*.

"So, where are you little puppies from," asked Abbas, rubbing his bald head, as he elbowed Chaku in the ribs.

A dark skeletal boy of barely fourteen stared back with forbidding eyes and a counterfeit smile. "General Saab brought me and my cousin from Kidney Town. We served him tea at the roti stand," he said, still under a spell from seeing a light bulb for the first time. The whites of his eyes stood out from the blackness of his skin as he blinked.

"Oh ... Kidney Town," said Chaku. "I hear that you can sell anything there. Listen, did you know that to become an outside servant you have to first serve us? You can't just skip into the Khan House and expect to become part of the staff so easily," he chuckled, slapping his knee and looking over his shoulder. "Where is our tea, Bally?"

"It's Salim's turn to bring the tea," said Abbas, as he caressed the boy's hair and watched it flop back down. "I used to have a full head of hair like this once."

"Yes, that was before he started working for General Khan, polishing his shoes, brushing his coat. You boys don't have to end up like him: bald and useless—without a shred of a purpose in life. Hahaha! Tell me, where are you sleeping tonight?" asked Chaku.

"Nowhere, sir. We were not told," said the other boy as they both began to twitch while trying to maintain a courteous smile.

"Oh, don't worry. You can sleep on my charpoy tonight. The spirit of an evil witch walks the garden at night."

"Tea's here ... enjoy," interrupted Salim as he lay a tray of steaming porcelain cups on the floor.

The electricity went out.

Bally brought out a kerosene lamp from the kitchen. The flickering flame lit everyone's chins as they sat clutching their cups of tea. The two Kidney Town boys remained quiet and managed a giggle at each joke, each historic recollection, thinking one day they too might become worthy of recalling a tale with the others, become part of the outside servants. As the last sips of tea vanished, all the servants dissipated ... all but one. Chaku crouched over his knees gawking at the kerosene lamp.

"Chaku, I think you should go to your quarters," Salim said. "Khan Saab will be coming around any minute. You know how he doesn't like drivers roaming around at night."

With his chin stuck to his chest he said, "I feel like I'm falling into a ditch. Help me! Help me back to my room!" Salim grabbed him by his shoulders, dragging him into the outside-servant quarters.

Chaku's breathing quickened. He began heaving like oxygen was running out. Then he lay on his charpoy and put a pillow over his head.

"Get out of here!" he yelled.

Salim jumped out of his room towards the garden. In the center of the lawn, near the flowerbeds he saw the two Kidney Town boys huddled under a single bed sheet. He approached them as they looked back at him quivering like abandoned kittens. He touched one on the shoulder and said, "You boys come sleep in my room. The morning dew is brutal. You'll get sick. Don't worry, there are no ghosts around here, only wicked servants."

◆◆

What transpired over the next couple of days is something I can only describe as bizarre. If medical professionals were to examine the subject, they would declare that his symptoms reflected paranoid schizophrenia and acute hallucinosis. Believers of the supernatural would claim that an ancient Jinni, a desert demon from Arabia, had slipped into our world from another dimension and entered the victim's body, causing it to act in strange ways. According to rumors from the servants though, Salim had something to do with the whole thing, as he sat wringing his hands with a smile on his face when it became apparent that Chaku had hit a psychological reef and sunk into the waters of madness.

First, Chaku began roaming the garden half-naked, squawking, flapping his arms. He followed this up by getting down on all fours and chasing Jabberwocky around the veranda. Abbas tried putting a lid on things by locking him in his quarters. Everyone heard cat noises from his room all night. Initially, they just laughed thinking that he'd had too much hashish and needed to sleep it off. But on the second day of this lunacy, everyone stopped laughing altogether.

It was a sunny day. Everyone but General Khan was out on the lawn. Laila sat reading in a garden chair, Salim was chasing Gibran around the banyan tree, the Christian maids were braiding each other's hair, and Bally was hobbling through the driveway with a silver tray piled with cucumber sandwiches. That's when everyone's eyes went skyward. From the roof, a black angel emerged. He rose into the sky, above the pigeon pen, blocking out the sun completely, with his shadow covering the garden below. For that split moment, as Bilki put her palms over her mouth, and Abbas covered his head with his, and Bally's tray hit the cobblestone driveway, the same reckoning ran through everyone's mind: the apocalypse has arrived.

A split second later, the angel's wings collapsed into tiny branches, the silhouette flushed with color, and a wiry torso descended towards the garden. Sunlight returned—a naked body made a wet sound as it thudded into the grass and feathers flew up in the air. Immediately, Salim covered Gibran's eyes and Abbas ran towards the body as the others were still frozen with disbelief.

Chaku lay face down on the grass, covered in blood and pigeon feathers with his bare ass smiling back at his gazers. He looked like one of the provocative Turkish miniatures that Khan had mounted in the living room: part man, part bird. Jabberwocky broke the silence as he ran around in circles barking.

From the veranda, a thundering roar approached the garden. The servants scattered like bowling pins. "What the hell is going on? What's this imbecile doing in my garden?" Khan growled as heads bowed and arms tied themselves behind backs. "Abbas! Bally! Why is this swine naked and ... what happened to my birds? My birds! What did you do to my birds?"

Ambushed

It wasn't until a couple of days later that Salim's worst fear had come true. He was in the garden playing cricket with Khalil and Gibran when the gate creaked open. Chaku, on a shiny wheelchair, held together with gauze and plaster, was rolled into the driveway by Talib the Bear. Servants greeted him as though he had won an award. Through a huddle, with his head cocked to the side, Chaku smiled at Salim, revealing several gaps in his mouth where his teeth had kissed the lawn.

Rage began to pour into every crevice of Salim's body. He grabbed the cricket bat from Khalil's hands, took it to his room, and smashed it to splinters against the floor. He couldn't believe what he'd just seen. After the pigeon incident, Chaku was back in the house. But Salim should have seen it coming. He should have known from Khan's reaction that morning when he first laid eyes on Chaku's body in the lawn. After storming with rage out of the house and cursing at every bystander on his way, Khan froze in astonishment when he entered the huddle in the garden. His emotions took a U-turn. Salim should have known then that the General was convinced that Chaku's soul had been possessed by demons. And those who are possessed, according to religious teachings, cannot be held accountable for their actions.

"Should I bring the whip, sir?" Salim had asked as General Khan stared motionlessly at Chaku.

"Huh?"

"The whip, sir. Should I bring it? This madman bit off the heads of all your pigeons, drank their blood, and stuck their wings to his arms. He deserves the whip, sir."

At that point, a single vertical crease had deepened in Khan's brow as his lips moistened.

"No," he had replied.

"No what, sir?"

"We should take him to the hospital."

And before Salim could utter another word, Abbas radioed for a military ambulance and, shortly after, Chaku was carted away on a stretcher. And when he returned later that same afternoon, Salim's fury could be seen through reddening eyes. He needed answers, which is why that afternoon, as soon as he smashed the cricket bat into smithereens, he marched right into the study.

"Khan Saab, this Chaku's back in the house," he said, as Khan was making his way towards his desk.

"Yes, I know. I've arranged another position for him. He will guard the gate at night now," Khan said. His speech was watery and revealed the workings of a certain Mr. Walker. Perhaps, several Mr. Walkers.

"But, sir, you're not going to punish him? What example would that set for the others? He killed Lat, Manat, and Uzza."

"Poor boy had been possessed by Jinns, Salim. What should I do? Kill the bastard? No ... I can't do that."

"But, Khan Saab..."

"But what? He may never walk again and you want me to whip him in public? What is that going to prove?"

"But, sir, he is a..."

"Is a what? A druggie? A bhang drinker? So what? Now you're going to tell me how to run my house?" He leaned forward in his chair. Their gazes fixed onto each other and for the first time since they had met, a never before seen discontent spilled from Khan's green eyes. He lifted his finger towards the door and hissed, "Get out and leave me alone."

Salim nodded ever so slowly, turned on his heels, and stormed towards the veranda.

Thunder struck in the clouds above and the monsoon's first droplets pelted the driveway as Salim stood outside breathing as if he were running out of air. It's true, he thought, there is no bloody whip. Despite the false tales of his ambushes in the war in Abyssinia, and despite the elaborate muskets that lined his study, Khan never hurt a soul, man or beast.

In the soul of Salim's soul, mutiny had been put on the stove to boil. The man who had bequeathed him a new life was, after all, a master and he his slave. That had now been made clear to him. The Khan House, the enigma under which he once stood blinking foolishly as a child, seemed like it had no windows and its walls seemed very high. At times it was difficult to know whether it was his home or a prison. He felt no different from the General's exalted birds which used to fly with audacity during the day and returned with humility at dusk. They, too, had convinced themselves of their freedom and a personality which was not their own, reminding one another of their fortune compared to that of their ill-fated cousins who scavenged the Lawrence Gardens for measly crumbs and carpet-bombed the minarets of the Badshahi Mosque.

Salim knew that his fate was no secret to the staff. Since the moment he arrived at the Khan House, everyone had bought into the same notion: with his education complete, Salim Agha would become Khan's greatest asset. Perhaps he could even obtain the trustworthy position of chief auditor of the feudal dynasty which was currently under the lonesome watchful eye of Kaana Munshi, who had not only lost his right eye in a drunken duel with his own reflection but also his credibility as Khanpur's bookkeeper. Whip in hand, Salim could stand watch over each bushel of wheat, each sack of kinos, and each truckload of sugarcane that was harvested. Unlike Kaana Munshi, he wouldn't embezzle. He would bring to his master every loose coin, keep in check every wandering dweller. He would be, depending on how one looked at it, the greatest villager of them all. How dare Salim think that this gift was for him to keep? Like everything else, it was a debt he had to repay. Similar to the debt his ancestors were bound with for centuries. Perhaps that's why Deema Engine had fled the shackles of Khan's stifling benevolence. Maybe that was the reason for General Khan's abhorrence every time Deema's name was mentioned. Either way, as the rain fell that night, he felt the walls of the servants' quarters beginning to choke him, closing in on him while he slept. The next morning, before he left for the hostel, he met Khan in his study.

A mysterious letter had arrived and with it a reminder of a captive promise that needed to be unshackled.

The opened letter lay on General Khan's desk. Salim stood with his hands behind his back. The General's figure was dark against the morning sun and, for some reason, the drinks trolley from the previous night had not been cleared from the study. Khan had been alone the night before and had polished off an entire bottle of whiskey by himself.

"First you have the audacity to question my authority and now this?" Khan, with his back towards Salim asked politely. "So, you want to further your education, then?"

"That's correct, General Saab. I thought you would be happy; is that not what you wanted for me?"

"And just like that you will leave for this university, without having to pay them a penny? Use them, like you did me?" His voice bounced off the walls as he turned to face Salim.

Salim's gaze refused to fall as he swallowed. The taste of his newfound courage was bitter. In the background, the bustard shed a feather in the echo.

"You said once that I could demand anything from you. It was a promise you had made..."

"I know what I said. I'm not a fool. This is what you choose to use my promise on? How dare you!"

"Then help me, General Saab. Like you had helped the son of a painter once before." He approached the General's desk. "Grant me this one last wish. Let me go, sir, please. You have read what they say. I have what it takes. I want to change my destiny."

"You have some nerve, telling me about destiny. Going behind my back, writing letters to these universities, begging bowl in hand. And what about me?" he pounded his chest. "Who gave you all this? Tell me, who? Am I to sit here and watch as you leave me in my old age when I need you the most?" He dropped on to his chair and flung the letter across the desk. Salim watched it fall off the edge before picking it up. "Leave now. You can take the bus to Blisschesterson."

Salim was going to take a bus back regardless, that day. It was one simple step towards his self-demolition, his emancipation. General Khan's words flowed through his veins like ice water as he held on to the letter. Attempting to embalm his master in his own promise was a risk no servant would dare take. It was a ruthless ambush, worse than Khan had encountered on the battlefield in Abyssinia. He felt guilty, but there was an excitement enclosed in that envelope; letters are like gifts in that way, even opened ones. This gift arrived at just the right moment.

Earlier, when Salim's application for an undergraduate degree reached the offices of Columbia University, the dean and faculty members sat up in their chairs. Along with the usual transcripts and essays, he had submitted a paper. Now, some might say that the layout was incorrect, and the language might have been primitive, or that mathematical protocol was not obeyed. But what was startling was the conclusion. In this paper, Fermat's Theorem, which was up until that point deemed impossible to prove, was solved in a simple three-step approach. Of course, Salim could only partially establish that the theorem held true for certain integers and his proofs were incomplete, but the point I'm trying to make is that the faculty members could see that the boy had a gift which only came about once in a lifetime. Immediately, the university issued a full scholarship and sent along their acceptance package in a special envelope with a wax seal. Because they knew if they didn't, some other place would. They didn't want to lose out. At night, Salim rubbed his fingers over that wax seal over and over again. It felt like it gave him mystical powers.

———◆———

At this junction in our story, some things are beginning to weave together while others seem to be reeling out of control. Salim, though elated, felt compassion evaporating from his body. General Khan's reaction to his admission into university was something he didn't see coming. His love for the General slowly started to churn into uncertainty. I think it was that admissions letter and Khan's bitter retort that planted several seeds in Salim's heart and when he returned to Blisschesterson, one of those seeds had begun to sprout.

That semester at Blisschesterson was unique. It had begun as every other had and Salim fell into the grooves of routine. But a couple of months in, something strange began to keep him up at night. He started acting peculiar. The other students picked up on his reclusive behavior, as one day they witnessed him sitting on the boundary of the cricket pavilion throwing stones at an imaginary target. I want to take us to that exact moment and draw our attention to that troubled boy in his navy-blue autumn blazer, sitting on the steps of the pavilion, pebbles in hand...

It's Friday, the final bell has sounded, the sun is setting behind him, and the pipal trees are perfuming the air. He hears the sounds of students running towards the gates but he shuts it out by throwing a stone as far as possible into an empty field. He's not going to the Khan House this weekend. He hasn't been since the school year began. He just wants to be left alone with his thoughts. If you look closely, a particular recollection has moistened his eyes. A single tear begins to fall down his face. But there is more. If you look closely, you can see the slightest of smiles spreading across his face. And there is only one thing that can induce such a smile: Tamboo Charming.

In the village, when the two brothers had visited their father in his final resting ground, Salim had turned to Charming and said, "Should we pour his favorite ale over his grave."

Tamboo laughed and said, "Already did it, brother ... the first thing I did when I brought him here."

"I want to go inside Khan's haveli," Salim said.

"What do you want to see there? It's been empty all year. It's not like the other Khan Houses. Its full of dust and cobwebs."

"Come on, Tamboo. We can sneak in, please. Who's the guard these days?"

Tamboo raised his eyebrows and said, "Pappu Pipewala."

"So, what's the big deal? He'll let us in."

"That donkey-dicked fucker is a slippery one. We're going to have to bribe him."

Back on the steps of the pavilion, Salim's broadening smile turned into a chuckle, then a full-blown laughter as he recalled what happened next. Holding his belly, he fell over thinking about the time when both brothers had found Pappu sleeping on a charpoy outside the haveli. His mouth was open and flies buzzed around his face. Then, despite Salim's warning, Tamboo stuck two fingers down Pappu's throat until he started choking. When Pappu leapt from the charpoy, grabbing his stick, he chased after them. They ran towards the house, laughing, as Pipewala shouted curse after curse behind them. Through the arches of the veranda they went, weaving through the hallway and on towards the round living room. Then, all of a sudden, they became stunned; their eyes rising upward. As sunlight from the high circular windows illuminated the dome ceiling, their jaws fell open.

Every inch of the ceiling, doused in color, pulsated with figures, human and animal, gods and demons, heroes and villains—a single red thread weaving through weeping mountains, dripping into rivers and canals, men on horseback leading a caravan to the promise land, throngs of ogres with talons and long tongues chasing behind them; there leading the pack, a messiah with a red turban and a green flowing beard held, in his hands, a tattered book. And there in the center, a god-like shepheard, scepter in hand, stood tall, opening the doors to his kingdom. As Salim's eyes closed, that image became sharper in his memory—that ceiling, a revealed universe, was history retold through the hands of a master, the most remarkable fresco that could rival any renaissance painting.

As Salim stood up from the pavilion steps, his feet were energized with a vigor they hadn't felt before. It was as though the image of his grandfather's fresco had injected him with adrenaline. He could feel it throbbing through his body. This was no mere painting. It was an endless imagery of humanity with all its flaws and all its potencies, raptures and torment, laughter and grief. He recalled that the closer he got to it, the denser the images became. Intricate subtexts emerged in the form of calligraphy; letters transforming into human form, people turning into scripture. The outpouring of his grandfather's virtuosity was nothing but the story of his people—an immortal tale of triumph in the face of calamity. So powerful was that ceiling that when they first saw it, both brothers held each other and wept. But he knew why that memory came to him at that moment—at a time when he swam through an endless river of abandonment. It was a generous gift from a time long ago, reminding him that there was no reason to be afraid any longer.

That weekend Salim sat, as he had done for the last several weekends, alone in his hostel. That night was so quiet, he could hear himself breathe. Many of the boarders had left to attend Mitti Pao's birthday party in his farmhouse. Usually, he would have gone with his friends but, like I said before, his unique aloofness had kept him isolated. He also hadn't informed Khan of his whereabouts and the General himself hadn't cared to check on him. He never went a single weekend without informing Khan where he was. But he didn't care. His earlier uncertainty, about his true rank-and-file in Khan's dominion, had begun to melt like wax. He knew that what he would do next would have a wave of undesirable consequences. He knew it all. And for a brief moment, he thought of Laila Khan—the only thing left binding him to the Khan House—of what she would think of him. He also wondered why she hadn't replied to a single one of his letters, about how she could become so cold after they had kissed. And after the brief moment of contemplation, he knew that what he was about to do would answer all those questions and his world would finally begin to make sense again.

What I am alluding to is what took place when that weekend came to a close. As Salim walked into the crimson walls of Blisschesterson on Monday morning, he removed his stifling veil, revealing a servant boy from a feudal village. He decided to expose himself—who he was, where he came from, and who owned him. He started with his friends, then his teachers, then the cafeteria staff, the cleaners, the stable boys, and finally, the headmaster.

"I have lied to you all this whole time," he claimed, over and over again. He felt that by confessing to his reality he would finally emancipate himself from the chains of his own falsehood. But that wasn't what happened. In his modesty, the Blisschestersonians saw their own humiliation. In his claimed poverty they saw disgust and in his creed they saw betrayal.

I must warn you. Boarding school machismo cannot be underestimated. A throng of teenage boys, caged together with no female in sight, can become as vicious and cruel as the deadliest predators on earth. They display the kind of masculinity that enabled our ancestors to survive harsh climates: isolate the dissimilar; appease the tenacious and disparage the weak. Fight. Destroy. Celebrate.

In the cafeteria, where people once wrestled to seat themselves near him, Salim now sat alone in a forest of evil stares. In the hallways, brash shoulders impeded his path. Things of this nature went on the entire week. Then the real bullying began. Some seniors went as far as to bribe the cafeteria workers to only serve him from the sweepers' plates. No servant, the prefects announced at lunchtime, is to use our plates. A roar of fists on table followed that statement. Salim began skipping meals altogether.

Then one day, as the seniors were taking their exams, the proctor, sat at the head of the class, stood up abruptly and chanted, "Enemy of Mohammed, friend of Shaitaan?"

Instantly, a reply echoed, "Ahmadi, Shaitaan, Ahmadi Shaitaan!"

This disgusting slogan boomed through the hall until Salim got up from his desk, submitted an unfinished paper and left the room.

He didn't know how it happened but this fire caught on quick. There weren't many places left for Salim to hide.

"I'm sorry, champ. I have to take you off the team roster this year," said Mitti Pao, as he stood with Salim near the horse stables.

"But, Mitti, this is my final year. I need that credit to graduate," Salim pleaded, noticing that Mitti's eyes spoke of a fear which had become common among the boarders. Standing up for a heretic was almost as bad as heresy itself.

"Champ, you know I would. I've put you on the team for so many years. But things are a little different now, as you know. You can't just go around telling people you're a kaffir and a servant. What were you thinking?" he said, looking over his shoulder towards the cricket pavilion. "I'm the captain and I'm applying to Oxford this year. The team will refuse to play for me if you're in the line-up, there will be bloody mutiny and I'll get voted out. I have to go now. You take care now, champ." And with those last words, as fast as he could bowl a screaming, in-swinging ball, Mitti Pao sprinted towards the hostel.

Salim hadn't expected this from Mitti Pao. His face turned cold with the thought of swimming laps in the pool or wielding a polo stick while trying to stay on a horse and he knew he didn't possess the talent, like the Raja of Bill-Qul, to play an inside-out forehand.

Crestfallen, he trudged to his room where he had begun to spend most of his time alone. His roommate, Tariq, had submitted a request to switch rooms, which was denied. So, he spent nights next door at Rasheed's. But that night, when Salim opened the door to his dorm, he found his clothes, bedding, and other belongings flung everywhere as if a wild Khanpur boar had torn through his room. On the concrete wall above his bed sat a welcoming slogan written in black charcoal:

All infidels should die! Go home kaffir!

Tariq stood in the corner of the room with his bulldog face crumpled more than usual and his blackened fingers exposing him. To Salim, ridicule had become an unwanted companion which he had managed to accept. But that phrase, scrawled above the place he slept, was too perverse for him to consume. His books dropped from his hands as he took a bottomless breath and bolted towards Tariq, who responded with the look of a stray dog that had aimlessly walked into traffic. Salim wrapped both hands around his neck and lifted him clean off the ground.

"Let me ... go ... you crazy bastard!" Tariq's voice choked in his throat. Salim's grip tightened as he dug his nails into his victim like a wild jungle cat.

"Stop it! Just stop it! What are you doing, you're going to kill him!" yelled Rasheed, their next door neighbor, as he rushed into the room.

Six hands were in a mesh: four trying to free Tariq's neck and two attempting to rip it off. His lips began to look like blackberries.

Salim let go and Tariq's body fell to the ground. Rasheed fanned him with his palms as Tariq chugged the air in painful heaves until the purple floated away from his face. Salim stared at the charcoal message on the wall once more. He picked his books up from the floor and stacked them in the corner.

Behind him, Tariq rose to his feet, his round belly jerking with each rapid breath.

"You've gone too far, you scum! Watch what happens to you now!" he wheezed.

"Tariq, go tell the headmaster, let's get this infidel suspended," Rasheed said. "We will see how the boy genius goes to America."

"No, Rasheed, no. We will make sure he asks the headmaster for his own suspension. This little sister-fucker thinks he can come to this school and put his filthy servant hands on us? Now you watch what I do to this Ahmadi heathen," Tariq said, pulling his friend's arm out of the room. "Come with me." And they left.

Salim's body refused to move and his arms ached from adrenaline. Chills ran down his face, stretching to his chest. Behind the boarding house and across from the football pitch, Salim's chastisement loomed. Tariq and Rasheed knocked on doors and soon they found whom they were looking for. The Iron Gang, grinning with excitement, popped their shirt collars and followed Tariq to his dorm. These lowbrow goons, sons of corrupt politicians and drug lords, were not to be fucked with. They were the ones who made you warm the toilet seats in winter and hand over your breakfast. They hazed newbies into dressing like Diamond Market hookers and dancing on top of cafeteria tables. As a junior, you obeyed these brutes. If you didn't, they would burn their initials right onto your ass with a hot iron. Salim was well aware of them. He took a deep breath, wrapped his fists with a pillow cover and gripped the sharp remains of a broken teacup. As Rasheed, Tariq, and the Iron Gang approached the dorm room door, he could see the remains of a dark blue dusk welcoming the night outside.

He rose to his feet as they walked in. Rasheed locked the door behind him. Salim tried to pick the crowd into individuals.

"Wali, I see you've fallen for this asshole's lies. Don't forget, it was I who helped you through your exams last year. And you?" Salim's eyes moved towards the tallest one, "Romi the Romeo. You want to hurt me? I thought we had an understanding. You want to believe what this fucker says? He thinks you're big and stupid. I know you're not ... you..."

"Shut up, you swine!" cried Tariq, his voice still caught his throat. "Don't you lads fall for his emotional shit. He's trying to talk his way out of this, as he always does. He's a heathen who's been posing as a Muslim. Do I need to remind you what our religion says about heretics? Boys, take his arms and legs, let's teach this kaffir a lesson."

Salim held up the broken teacup.

"Come on, Iron Gang!" Rasheed's voice ignited a final push as he advanced first, but Tariq broke through the thugs and bolted towards Salim, who stepped aside and took a wild swipe at his bulldog face with the teacup. Tariq's hand shot up to his chin. He fell to the floor and Salim leapt on top of him.

"Aaaaaaah! You sister-fucker! Help me, you assholes!"

"Get him off now!" Rasheed cried, as the Iron Gang stood in disbelief. "Look what you've done!"

Tariq's screams reduced to soft hisses, like a punctured bicycle tire.

Salim's hands trembled as he pulled himself away.

The Iron Gang scuttled from the scene of the crime like wild partridge. The hostel halls began to echo with Tariq's repeated inquiry.

"My nose! My nose! Where's my nose?"

Exile from Eden

Celestial seraphs gathered around and looked down from the heavens. They threw their heads back and slapped their foreheads as their final savior, the last clairvoyant of a dwindling cosmos, began his explanation. The headmaster didn't buy it. Neither did General Khan, who sat hunched over his scepter.

"An accident," Salim kept saying. An accident, the angels repeated. In the hostel, an intense search had commenced. The sweepers, the stable boys, and the cafeteria staff were kept busy hunting for a missing nose. But no matter how hard they looked, it was nowhere to be found. Tariq's nose had dislodged from his face and disappeared.

The angels muttered amongst themselves as they saw General Khan standing up, tapping his scepter on the headmaster's floor and escorting Salim out onto the main lawn. The Blisschesterson boys mockingly waved him farewell as they knew Salim's time in the hostel had come to an end.

Khan, after negotiating a deal with the headmaster, had not said a word to Salim that day as they headed back to the Khan House. The shock of his behavior swiped a jagged sword into his heart. Salim should have been grateful, for he could have easily found himself in handcuffs, heading for prison. But he was tired of being grateful for this compassion—it suffocated him. Khan's generosity had become a curse that hung around his neck like a noose and he could feel it tightening with every minute that passed.

When Salim returned from the boarding school, news had already spread of his expulsion. The servants greeted him with squinted eyes as he walked past them. Chaku giggled toothlessly and gave him a salute as he retired to his room for the rest of the day. Nobody said a word. They all felt his shame as if it were their own.

That night, it occurred to him, in a spit of fury: what is this General but a hoarder of downtrodden outcasts? He stood in front of his mirror and, one by one, began to interrogate the members of the Khan House staff.

"Let's start with you, Bally. Hobble on over, hunchback. What was your real name again? Oh, I remember. Bhaskar Bhiswas, a Hindu Brahmin from the old city. General Khan saved you during the Partition riots of 1947. Remember when Muslim mobs came to lynch the Hindus of Shalmi Bazaar? You deserted your famous samosa shop and ran straight into the waiting arms of your most ardent customer. Your false identity: a wise old Pashtun from the North. Your reality: a hand-crafted-idol worshipper. Shame on you, Bally. Shame on you." He clicked his tongue at his reflection, looked down at the floor, then back into his own eyes, "And you two. Khan adopted you both off the streets after you had slashed his tires, you bastards! Your identity: chauffeur and guard of that exclusive hill station summer home. But your reality: hashish-mongering rapists. Fuck you. Next: you don't hide from me. Come here girls, you're the most important. The caretakers of Khan's children, though you're children yourselves ... orphaned teenagers to be exact, adopted by Khan upon his visit to Lorr's St. Andrew's Church. You must feel real safe here, don't you? You prance around in your Sunday dresses, completely ignorant of the fact that the dangling cross on your chest makes everyone steer clear of you. I pity you two. Then there's Madam Bilki. How could I leave you out, Bilki ji? Or should I use your birth name, Bilkis Kaur, daughter of the Sikh kino farmer, Paramjit Kaur. You refused to jump into the Khanpur well when ordered by your father, while Muslim hoards raped your sisters during the Partition. Coward. Your false identity: specialist warden of malevolent witches, stewardess of princesses." Salim paused for a moment and wiped his tears. "Batman Abbas. Come here you fat, bald fuck! Where are you hiding? Khan found you collecting litter in the army barracks as a child. Come, let's talk about you: a reconstructed soldier of servitude, commissioned officer of personal errands. Oh, and what of the countless *velas* who come and go with regular frequency, occupying empty spaces and lending a hand here and there until they find more credible pursuits in the city? And wait, wait. There is, of course, Salim Agha." He pushed his face closer to his reflection until he could feel the coolness of the mirror against his nose. "What did you say you were? I can't hear you. Khan's nephew? Attendee of colonial private school? Wearer of Oxford boots? Really? I'll tell you who you really are. The son of a drunken sign painter, equestrian of cattle, curator of buffalo dung. Yes, it's true; General Khan is no fucking savior. He's a collector of unfortunates, a connoisseur of forsaken souls, and you, Salim Agha, are his prized possession, an exalted bird that he can show off to his friends like he had done with Brigadier Zaid. You are a show pony. And you have breached the most sacred barrier—you began thinking you're in charge of your own destiny. You think you're different? You're just like the rest of them, brown of skin, bleak in fortune, with your future firmly attached to the strings controlled by the master puppeteer himself. Fuck you, Salim Agha, fuck you." He slapped the mirror until it broke into three even pieces. A trickle of blood fell down his elbow onto a shard of mirror. He watched his shadowy reflection turn red.

As the night ran through the windows of the Khan House, the early winter chill frosted the glass. Dew settled on the cobblestones making them glow in the moonlight. During this playful time in the city, the air licks your ears and kisses your nose just enough to make you blush. The chill creeps up on you slyly. If you take it for granted, it makes you pay by weakening your body and crippling your lungs.

Outside, a car hummed near the garden. Laila, in her high heels, stepped out and onto the cobblestone driveway. Salim could hear her footsteps as she made for the main door. He leapt up from his charpoy and ran towards her. She was speeding towards the veranda, rubbing her shoulders, when he approached.

"Let go," she whispered, as Salim took hold of her hand.
"I have finally done it, Laila."
"Done what?"
"I will leave for America. And when I return, our worlds won't be divided any longer. I did all this for you. Because I love you more than anything I can imagine." A prolonged silence followed.

Laila stopped rubbing her shoulders as her eyes opened wide. "Are you out of your bloody mind?"

"When I come back, I can be anyone. I'll be one of you Saabs. What did you think I was doing all this time? Fighting against the world, putting up with ridicule about my religion, my family, and this cursed poverty? The only thing that kept me going was you."

"I'm going inside now, Salim," she whispered. "Don't try and stir something else. You're lucky Daddy hasn't killed you for getting kicked out of Blisschesterson. Do you know all the people he had to bribe to keep you alive? Now go, before you get us both killed."

She sped away from him as though he were contaminated.

Salim, stunned, wrapped his shawl around him and stood frozen in the garden. For the first time ever, Laila had ignited a flame of anger inside him. He couldn't believe how quickly she had dismissed him. After what they had, after what he went through. How could she treat him as though he were not real, as though he were just another servant?

"No," he said out loud as mist formed around his words. "I will get an answer out of you."

Salim trudged back to his room. Outside, there was nothing but moonlight and the muted shadow of banyan leaves. He slowed down to a waltz, his teeth clanging against each other in the cold. Through the floating mist, he could barely make out the shape of his door. As he approached it, a hand reached out and patted him on the shoulder.

"Get inside. I want to tell you something," Bally said, as he walked Salim into his room and closed the door. "Sit down, shut up, and listen."

"What is it, Bally Saab?"

"I'll tell you because no one else will." He shuffled towards the charpoy and sat down with him. "You can try all you want, son, but you will never be one of them."

"I don't understand."

"I've seen you both grow up in front of my eyes. I've seen you, time and time again, on that balcony of hers. By God, you're as good at lying as you are at climbing rope. Just remember, at the end of the day, they are Saabs and we're mere dirt on their shoes. Have you ever sat down to speak to the dirt on your shoes? We all believe, even after what happened today, that you will succeed. If you succeed, in some way, we all will."

"Bally, I..."

"Let me tell you one thing—and never forget it. Dream to your heart's content but know that no dream is worse than the fantasy of escaping who you are. I know that more than anyone. By God, dream all you want. But when you awaken, slap yourself with reality. You will be as rich as they are one day. I know it, we all know it. But never their equal. They're not made from the clay of serfdom like we are. Let that girl go and don't throw away what you have. She's changed—she's a young woman now. See for yourself tomorrow. What you thought you two had when you were young was just a childish game. I'm only showing you what you can't see for yourself."

Bally dimmed the kerosene lamp and walked out of the room, leaving Salim with his words.

The hunchback was right. By the time the summer had come to a close and the seasons changed, Laila had completed her evolution. She'd begun to rebel in her own way. The boundaries limiting her earlier had been breached. She would be out late with boys and would sneak back in through the kitchen at night. She had begun to see a world outside the Khan House. And for her, Salim's musky odor had begun to stand out. He seemed so different now from the fair-skinned, cologne-slathered boys she had met at wedding parties and Sunday polo matches. She had completely erased that incident from the summer-house garden from her mind. She had been desperate for a boy's touch, she had told herself, and he was simply a practice tool.

Winter mornings in the city of Lorr were something special. The anticipation of school coming to a close, holidays around the corner, and of course the wedding season; a season rejoiced by all: rich, poor, mainstream Muslims, Ahmadis, Shias, Christians, Untouchables, generals, politicians, and sweepers of human feces. No matter who you were, you could not escape it. Weddings were a platform for celebration.

That day, there was a wedding yawning at the Khan House gates in the early morning chill.

It was no secret that General Khan's ascent in the military government was because of his lavish parties, his open-heartedness, and because he had the most astounding home in all of Lorr where Johnnie Walker flowed like water and where there were more servants than Saabs.

As Salim awoke, people outside had already erupted into morning rituals, children were being dressed by maids, breakfast meats were sizzling, and clothes were being ironed. Laila's voice could be heard in the distance, demanding a timely presentation of that morning's breakfast on the lawn, where Khan's radio had been brought out trailing a long wire.

General Khan was unusually late for breakfast. This was odd because breakfast outdoors was something he looked forward to in winter. When he did arrive, he sat down without a word, ignoring Salim who was standing behind his chair. Then he opened his newspaper as Abbas poured tea into his cup. Salim made a coughing sound, clearing his throat. The General ignored him still. In the background, tents were being slammed into the lawn with large wooden pegs.

"Daddy, are the guests going to stay here the whole night?" asked Gibran looking worried as his tricycle was ushered from the garden into the veranda by a *vela*.

"No, dear. They're only coming for the wedding, then they will leave. Now finish your eggs and your sister will take you to get your haircut. Don't forget to pick up Aunty Tezi on your way back," General Khan said. The children were swiftly removed from the breakfast table and, when he was alone with Khan, Salim finally spoke.

"General Saab, you can ignore me if you like but you have to hear my story."

"Did you do it?"

"What, sir?"

"Did you do what they said, dammit! Do you want me to repeat it?"

"Yes, sir, I did. I did exactly what the headmaster described," Salim said, his confidence wilting. A hammer slammed a bamboo pole. Bang ... bang ... it went, driven deep into the lawn. He quivered. Another pole-like silhouette floated in from the corner of his eyes.

"What have I not given you?" the General turned around to face him.

"General Saab, I was being abused time and time again. They ridiculed me and kept pushing me into a corner."

"So, you sliced off a boy's nose? Is that how it works? What have you done with my legacy? The whole of Lorr will hear this story," General Khan said, reaching a feverish note. The lanky silhouette now stood behind them.

"Sir, you have to believe me. It was a mistake. He came for me, my eyes closed and I just swung. I don't know what happened, Khan Saab, honestly. I was scared. There were many of them."

Then the shadow startled him with his nasal voice.

"You should've let them beat you," said Tamboo Charming, emerging like a ghost, his flipper-like feet tapping on the grass.

"Tamboo?"

"You've disgraced us, Salim. You've brought shame to General Saab."

"I'm holding General Ali's daughter's wedding at the house," Khan said. "You two can stay the night. Tomorrow, I want you both out. Today, you have proven to me ... that you are truly a low-caste servant."

Khan's words sliced through Salim's heart. And just like that, with the same swiftness as he had become part of his kingdom, he was dethroned. Bang ... bang! The noise grew louder.

"General Saab," sobbed Salim, his heart sinking into his chest. "You can't just throw me out after all these years? What about the children?"

"Don't mention my children. I know how to care for them. There's no shortage of tutors in this city. Besides you've found your own future, haven't you? Who am I to keep you from fulfilling your destiny? I'm a man of my word. I will honor my promise to you. I've struck a deal with the headmaster. You will finish your exams in private and take up your university offer. After that, you leave and never come back," he paused as a final bamboo pole was pushed into the ground. "I knew this day would come ... I just didn't know how soon. Empty your servant quarters by tomorrow."

Salim turned to Tamboo Charming as he nodded back at him, noticing a face on the verge of melting into tears.

"Come, brother. Let's not stay a single minute. We don't need to wait till the morning," said Tamboo as he hugged his brother. He could see that Salim had been crushed. But he also believed that it was only a matter of time until he saw the side of Khan everyone else saw. Tamboo had kept a lot of things from his brother. Things about Khan and the village. How the General had charged the farmers a tax even when wild boars had destroyed the kino trees, and how he would turn a blind eye to his army men having their way with young village girls. The General knew all along about Jaaji's grave but refused to do anything about it. Why would he? To Tamboo and the rest of the villagers, Khan's actions didn't come as a surprise; he was, after all, their king. Tamboo had kept all this from Salim so it wouldn't break him.

Salim followed Tamboo to his room to collect the broken remains of his childhood and roll them up in a bed sheet. To leave as he had once arrived, with the threadbare belongings of his village. It was the first time he would be excommunicated, but it wouldn't be his last. As he lifted up his transistor radio, a Ghalib couplet came to his mind.

We have known of Adam's exile from Eden,
but painful yet was my exit from your door.

"Charming, I won't leave until I speak to Laila," said Salim through hiccupping sobs.

"After all the books you've read, you fail to understand one thing, Potato. Even our dreams are not ours to keep," said Tamboo Charming as he emptied Salim's cupboard. "Fine. We will stay until you speak to her. Talk to her but expect nothing. Because you are nothing. To them we were always nothing." Salim put his palm to his eyes and wiped away at the endless stream of tears. Both brothers sat on his charpoy and waited patiently for the evening to arrive.

When the night finally came, the festivities engulfed the Khan House like wildfire. General Ali's daughter was to wed a Pureland Air Force captain. The Khan House shone with gallant audacity. Outside, swarms of beggars gathered their nestling babes in flaky blankets staring through the slits of the iron rods until they were shooed away like flies. Bicycles and cars alike made start-stop movements on the street as they passed. The Khan House was the bride at this event, dressed to be courted.

That evening, under the sparkle of Lorr's most decorated ornament, Salim sat breathing in the words of the general; the ones that he firmly slapped on his face as a reminder. All this time he had wanted Khan to man up; with Chaku, with the other servants, with anyone who dared to question his authority. And he thought that the General had been softened over the years by the Evil Witch's torture to the point of no retreat. But he was wrong. Because, in the end of it all, Khan had taken his most favored subject, the envy of all servants, and transformed him into a chilling archetype of disobedience. As soon as he realized this, he felt the gap between himself and the General widen into an unassailable chasm.

Salim sat outside the kitchen with Tamboo and the other servants that night. He peered through the wedding tent as his eyes fell on the glowing face that captivated everyone in attendance. The Majors, the Generals, the gate openers, and toilet wardens all marveled at her beauty. Laila's skin shone brighter than the towering lights of the Khan House. He saw her break from her cocoon and flap her wings. He felt he didn't know her anymore. His blood simmered as he saw one man after another trying to engage his beloved in banal banter as she responded with a counterfeit laugh, touching their arms, kissing their cheeks slyly like she had once done with him. The Lorr Jazz Ensemble played Bombay Talkies music, the champagne spilled from goblets, and drunken soldiers rejoiced with each other's wives. It was a kind of celebration Lorr had not seen before and certainly not the servants who watched with wide eyes, blinking in the sparkling lights. And despite everything that had occurred, all Salim could do was long to be part of it all.

As soon as Laila exited the tent to take Gibran to bed, Salim pounced. From out of the dark, his hand snatched at hers.

"What are you doing, Salim? Let go of me!"

"No! You have to answer one question first. Your father has thrown me out of his life. I am banished forever. All I want to know is whether you ever loved me. Was there anything ever there in your heart?" Khalil had entered the veranda and approached him menacingly.

"Let go of my sister!" he cried.

"Salim, why are you crying? Come tell me a story before bed," Gibran pleaded.

"No stories tonight, Gibran. Go inside with your brother!" Laila yelled. The boys obeyed and the main door slammed shut.

"Laila, I'm not leaving until you answer my question."

"You want an answer? Look around you Salim, what do you see? This is what our life is like ... and you? You're a bloody servant. Always were and always will be. There will be no 'you and me'. Remove this fantasy from your mind. Whatever you think we had was a mistake, it never happened. Thank God for what you've received all these years. If it wasn't for Daddy, you would be patting buffalo dung on to the walls of your stupid little hut," Salim's head fell, his chin touching his chest. "My grandmother was right. Give servants an inch and they forget their limits. They begin to think they're you." He opened his mouth but words had evacuated his body. From the corner of his eye, he saw Khan's shadow approaching.

"What's going on? What's happening?" he yelled as a half-full goblet of Scotch emerged from under his shawl.

"Nothing, Daddy ... Salim just came to say goodbye. Let me take you to your room," said Laila as she took her father inside towards the study where he would sit alone through the night. Salim pedaled backwards towards the darkness of the servants' quarters, to the shadows that remained loyal to him no matter how many times he tried to escape them. It was where you're born into a bottomless ditch and those who try and escape are pulled down by the ankles. His feet still carried him there while, in the distance, among the festive lights, Laila disappeared from his life.

Part II

*The achievements of exile are permanently undermined by
the loss of something left behind forever*

— Edward Said

The New World

This hasn't been easy, but you and I have progressed nicely towards this juncture. You pace about the room, rubbing your temples, untangling the nature of my testimony, realizing the great love I have displayed for the man who died by these very hands. You long to understand my motive. Moreover, you ask about the fatwa: the holy decree that sanctioned Salim's execution and brought about my involvement in the whole matter. If you don't mind me saying, sir, your knowledge of fatwas remains simple: maniacal dictator issues, the Scimitar executes. There's more to it than that. Salim's fatwa was issued decades before anyone ever heard of words like 'Caliphate' or 'Scimitar' or even, dare I say, 'terrorist'. Such pious orders don't just fade away, they swell into an avalanche that sweeps everything in its wake.

Nonetheless, it is love that creates infidels, not confusion. Since love exists in triangles—the self, the desired, and the one you end up with. A similar love triangle gripped Salim when he first arrived in the US. America loved him. Yet, like a lover who kisses with open eyes, his devotion belonged elsewhere, to a beloved that continued to betray him.

As we find equilibrium in this narrative, I shall place us on familiar ground: New York City. We'll put aside Salim's childhood and the city of Lorr for a moment. Time has passed and Salim has come a long way from the day he left the Khan House. At this junction, it is imperative that I tell you about the fall of Potato, the painter's son, and the birth of Dr. Salim Agha. We might take sudden leaps in time, so bear with me, sir. Not everything is linear. Prophecies are like treasure hunts that way.

1968. Salim arrived in New York as he had at the gates of the Khan House once, clutching his tattered belongings, dazed and motionlessness amongst the bustling streets. There, upon the horizon, emerging from the water, a copper goddess welcomed him to the land of liberty. Yet, he felt everyone around him was struggling with this freedom. It was a different time back then; a time when people like Salim hardly made it past the loading docks of the Port Authority, let alone a university campus. Harlem was where he would spend his student life, tucked away between the streets where mayhem had broken loose, in a honeycomb of cinder-block rooms. That summer, months after Martin Luther King Jr. fell to the ground clutching his chest, Harlem was set ablaze. Riots and protests left the streets strewn with broken glass and above, in the column-like buildings, students hung from their balconies chanting through megaphones.

All this was too overwhelming. It was as though Salim had slipped through the slits of the universe, from one divided world into another. The dams that separated the haves from the have-nots had begun to crumble and the streets were flooded with havoc. On his first day, before he could make it to the university registrar's office, his luggage was stolen at gunpoint. Not that he carried much with him, but still. I can imagine the pain that the mugging must have caused him: a penniless boy from a feudal village halfway across the world, on the burning sidewalks of West Harlem, kneeling against the university walls, tears falling onto neatly ironed trousers. And we can visualize, too, that feeling of relentless misery which never seemed to leave his side. After the robbery, the only thing he was left clinging onto was a blue colored booklet that revealed his identity. The thief had earlier pulled it from his hands, leafed through it, and threw it back at him.

"This is all I have left, Madam," he stuttered, through pursed lips as he presented his passport at the orientation desk. "I was burgled just outside the building."

The young lady at the admissions office, startled to hear the word "burgled" for the first time, checked his name off a list and said, "You don't have to worry about anything."

"I don't have any money left."

"Here," she pushed a small booklet towards him. "Take these tickets to the cafeteria and you can have something to eat."

Salim's abandoned look exposed his vulnerability.

"Don't worry. We will explain where you are staying, where you have to go, everything. We've been waiting for you."

Salim slapped on his badge and followed the others through the campus. As he shuffled in the cafeteria line, he felt frightened out of his wits. He was never this scared on his first day at Blisschesterson. The vociferous American twang, echoes of laughter, and the alien odors of sizzling pork made him feel as though he were on another planet. The students glared in wonderment at him, talking through their palms. He felt like he had grown horns on his head. It made him want to vomit.

He placed his empty lunch tray back in the pile and left.

That first night in his dorm was the most challenging one of Salim's life—friendless, lonesome, and aching with hunger, he wept staring out of his window at the streets choking on the sounds of pssts and wanna-get-highs. America was not just a new world. It was a universe of bustling galaxies, one more complex than the other. It was impossible to take it all in.

Columbia University was one of those elaborate galaxies. The classrooms were like deep caves carved into the ground. The students, with their bulging sideburns and skinny black ties, stank of cigarettes and rock music. There was a revolution brewing outside, or at least that's what he was told by the long-haired hippies who marched through Morningside armed with placards and catchy lyrics. But Salim wasn't there to participate in an uprising. His purpose, he told himself, was to conquer that ocean of knowledge he'd dreamt about long ago. This, he told himself, was the only way he could feel a part of something. But in his first lecture, as all the students sat chatting to each other, the professor walked in, and without a moment of hesitation, Salim stood up. Immediately, everyone became silent.

"May I help you?" the professor asked. After looking around to see astonishment on everyone's faces, Salim shook his head and sat down. Then, they all laughed.

That laughter, at his expense, didn't harm his ego much. He had seen worse. What really surprised him occurred a couple of months later as he sat in that same lecture hall awaiting his midterm grade. When the professor had slapped his paper on his desk, Salim shook in astonishment.

After class he walked up to the professor and roared in disbelief, "Professor, there must be a misunderstanding. I've never received anything below an A."

"Your attempt was average. You have all the answers but don't show how you derive them," his teacher said, lowering his glasses. Then he tapped Salim on the shoulder, and said, "Listen, son. Look around. You're not the only genius around here."

Those words wounded Salim. Humiliation seared his cheeks red.

At night, he stood in front of a mirror staring at his reflection.

"Not a genius anymore, Salim Agha. Maybe you never were," he said to himself. Then his palm clapped against his cheek over and over as these words became eerie repetitions: "Not a genius. Not a genius." He put his hands to his face and howled.

Salim had resigned to the realization that even his greatest power, the promise he was bequeathed upon his birth, had failed him. He always believed that, if anything, he would be made to feel welcome in this new world if he had just managed to display his talents. Maybe then, he thought, everyone would offer their friendships. But who was he kidding? This place was no Blisschesterson.

Salim fell onto his bed and sighed, looking up at the ceiling. Then he closed his eyes and imagined he was back in Lorr. A smile came across his face as he flew through the streets of Lorr; from the havelis of the old city and on towards the canal. This delightful musing soothed him to sleep.

Over the next few weeks, the people of his old life began building a home in the folds of his memory, growing into enchanted versions of themselves as though in a children's fable. They were all he had—immortalized memories. He missed his stepmother, the old hag who had labelled him, his brother the camel, the painter and his gummy bloodshot eyes, the General, for whom he would have given his life and, most of all, he missed Laila Khan. She, out of all of them, had elevated into a mythical goddess, morphing into a dream that appeared every moment of his waking and sleeping mind.

He would spend countless minutes staring at the telephone on the wall of his dorm hallway and murmuring to himself the only phone number he had memorized, the one that could lead him directly into the Khan House living room. Several times, he picked up the receiver and placed a call with the operator and hung up immediately as the ringtone sounded in his ear. He would remind himself that any voice on the other end would only fortify his banishment from the world he loved most, adding fuel to the flames flickering inside him. There was no one he could share his sorrows with. The people of Khanpur? Well, what can we say? At first sight of a telephone, they would be frightened half to death. Then who else? If he didn't relieve the burden of his wistfulness soon, he felt his loved ones would slowly vanish from his thoughts. His memories were the only things that kept him going. So, he pulled up at his desk, filled his fountain pen, and laid out a clean sheet of paper. But his pen hovered above that desk, unable to move. Whom would he write to? Laila, of course, could never receive letters from him—he dared not cross General Khan's final commandment. Besides, it was too heartbreaking to even write her name. His mind unquestionably turned to the only person who could help him make sense of everything. Even though Tamboo Charming, through no fault of his own, couldn't read so much as a village sign, Salim took a deep breath and began inking letters that he knew would never be delivered. One of them went something like this:

Dear Brother,

I take up this pen in a state of great nostalgia. I'd informed you that leaving for this new world was what I needed, what my dreams asked of me. But nothing about this place makes me believe I've done the right thing. I miss the village, the Khan House, our father, and I miss you. Do you remember when Khan Saab's cousin Tehzeeb was married to the Raja? That fat mango farmer from across the canal? We went to see the tent-pegging ritual in Khanpur: General Khan galloping on his horse, the Raja on his, both marching towards a peg with their lances. They looked like ancient warriors roaring at their steeds, raising the pegs to thousands of cheering villagers. I never forgot how you looked at me with astonishment that day. None of us had seen anything like it.

Remember how Baa and Pappu had bribed the caterers to sneak them a bottle of English whiskey? The painter drank himself silly, clapping like a transvestite at the sound of the dhol. Oh, how we laughed. We watched, peeking through the colored tents as the Saabs danced in the Khan haveli. And when Tezi's brother caught me trying to sneak out a roti, he slapped my face. You grabbed him from behind and shoved him on to the electric light poles. Then you turned to me and said, "Run, Potato. Run for your life!" I remember how you laughed while those Saabs beat you until you couldn't walk. I feel guilty now, but it still makes me smile every time I think about it.

I was five then. I never thanked you for that. So, I just wanted to tell you that I miss you and that I love you, and that, after all of this, I'm glad to have a brother like you.

Nothing here is familiar, Tamboo, nothing. These awful smells, of ground coffee in the libraries, of urine in the subway from both rats and humans, of maple leaves in the parks. It makes my eyes water. What I'd give for just one cup of milky tea, one greasy samosa. I can't eat anything here. Even the oranges taste like cardboard. Oh brother, what I'd do for a bite of a kino ... I don't know how much longer I can survive. Maybe this whole thing was a bad idea. Sometimes, Tamboo, I feel like giving up and coming back to the village. God help me.

Your brother,
Potato

That tear-stained letter, among others, was sealed, dated, and stashed into a drawer where it remained, undelivered. And those melancholic distances between Salim and his homeland began to swell. His fondness for Pureland took on a magical aspect. It felt like a part of him was floating out into the void of space moving away at rapid speed.

As the days progressed, Salim felt like abandoning everything. He longed for things he hadn't thought too much about before. Like the nakedness of the stars at night and the colors of springtime kites that buzzed like flies over Lorr's old havelis. I'm not going to lie. Those first few months in New York were the toughest days of his life. Yes, he was born in a village of darkness to an unworldly painter, but there, in the stirring commotion of this new world, was where he truly felt like a peasant.

That wasn't all. Salim's professors were right about one thing. These Ivy League peers of his were no simpletons, and to rise above them he had to raise his game. So he withdrew, away from the rallying cries, away from where the shields and batons clashed with protestors, away to the library where he spent nights huddled under a heap of books, polishing his craft. It was the only place where he could find peace. Between the struggle to abscond and the yearning to learn, he submerged himself in the world of science. He did whatever he could to veer his mind away from the sadness.

Then Salim prayed. He had done so at Blisschesterson from time to time and had enjoyed being surrounded by his friends, bowing and raising their brow on the football pitch in unison. He missed that. One night, seated around a television set in the dormitory's living room, flashes of an enigmatic man caught his attention.

Salim looked over at his hall-mate and pulled on his sleeve. "Who is that man?" he asked.

"Are you kidding? You don't know Malcom X?" Salim shook his head. "They are playing one of his old sermons from when he was with the Nation. He died a few years ago."

It wasn't the charisma of the man that excited Salim. It was an enchanted phrase that sounded when the handsome minister raised his palms upwards: peace be upon you, my brothers.

Peace be upon you, Salim repeated. Then he burst up from the couch and ran to the library.

He only needed to flip through a few newspaper microfilms to be convinced that he should attend the sermons at the Nation of Islam's Mosque #7 in Harlem. He was unaware that Malcom Little, who had disposed his last name when converting to Islam, had long left the Nation in pursuit of traditional Sunni beliefs. Nor was Salim interested under what circumstances the organization was formed; whether Elijah Muhammad, who had convinced his followers that he was a prophet of Islam, repudiating the finality of Prophet Mohammed, was himself rejected as a divine figure by own his son Warith Deen. Salim just wanted to be a part of a brotherhood. It didn't matter what kind.

Soon, after attending a few sermons, Salim realized that even in Harlem, God's merchants had agendas. Similar to Unna Huneira, the blind imam, who would ask for donations of rice, kino, or even, banknotes after Friday prayers. As the Friday worshippers roared in appreciation at the apex of the sermon, Salim bent his head low and made for the exit.

That was when he ran into Brother Carl.

"Leaving before the sermon ain't what we do here." Brother Carl stood under the exit sign with folded arms. Brother Carl was a petite man with womanly features; handsome, some might even say beautiful, with a nose that looked as though it had been sharpened on a whetting stone. From it sprouted long and equally sharp nose hairs, like a rat's whiskers.

"What's it to you?" Salim replied, with his hands in his pockets.

"You a reporter?"

"No."

"A cop?"

"No. A Muslim."

"A Mexican brother? Never saw one."

"Well, you have now. Let me through." Salim managed to pull away and headed outside with Brother Carl following him hurriedly.

"Wait, brother. That's my diner over there, across the street. Let me get you a coffee."

Salim stood silently for a moment and said, "How about a sandwich?"

"Fine."

At the diner, a dimly lit establishment that smelt of burning butter, they sat folded in a booth. Around them were pimps with lustrous belt buckles and feathered hats, hookers trudging lazily after their nightly shifts. None of them bothered to give Salim that look he had been getting since he'd arrived in New York. Maybe because, unlike at the university, here he wasn't so—how do you say—different. Suddenly, a mysterious blanket of kinship fell over his shoulders and before the waitress ambled towards him with his sandwich, he knew he'd finally found a friend in the chaotic city.

There was something about this man that made his mind slip into memories of his village. He was no feudal servant, Brother Carl, but his ancestors sure knew a thing or two about bondage. In his mind, Carl's generosity emerged from a garden of love, something that Salim could tell by looking at his eyes. He could see that he harbored a unique wisdom too. Carl didn't need to attend lectures to know how it all worked. He'd been ingesting Ivy League talk for years. He also knew immediately, when he first saw Salim, that the boy had a look of abandonment that made him seem like he was shivering.

Hours passed and Coca-Colas turned to beer.

"The only thing I can't give up," Carl said, as the first glass of chilled brew arrived at their table.

Beer was something Salim hadn't had before. It began running warmly through his body. He remembered the St. Mary's Lager billboard on the Mall Road: a frosty glass, golden liquid spilling over the sides. Then he recalled how General Ali, on hot summer nights, would gulp down ten such glasses and relieve himself—with little embarrassment—on the lawn, in full view of the servants. Many times he would just go in his trousers. As Salim put the glass to his lips, he remembered Abbas's annoyance every time that took place, since it was his job to change him out of his wet clothes and then make sure the bastard made it back home in one piece.

Salim snickered to himself. Then he began, with newly found courage, to reveal his story. He told Carl about the faraway country that he so missed and the feudal village where he was born. He didn't mention General Khan, the servants, nor Laila for some reason, as if he were protecting them. He just jumped to the part about his university admission. He spoke of the scholarship that paved the way for a dream he'd once had.

Carl, bewitched, leaning over the table, started to sense that this dream had been a somewhat double-edged knife. But he didn't say anything at the time and sat quietly listening, smoking cigarette after cigarette, until he was asked a question that made him sit upright and reply, "Why the Nation? Why not, Brother Salim? This diner ... it's all mine. It's my establishment and not many Negroes can claim to run their own business. The Nation's the only place that puts us at the top of the food chain, tells us that we're not only equal but better. I believe that. But what I want to know is, why did you leave the sermon today?"

Salim hesitated for a moment. "I thought I could feel at home there, but it felt like I was being lied to. It's like any other church on this street. Besides, I don't think I'll be here that long. I've decided to go home."

"Go home?" Carl asked with a frown and a sideways nod. "They gave you all this money. Money that any brother on this street would give his nuts for. And you decide that this ain't for you."

Infuriated a little beyond his own comprehension, he reached over the table and seized Salim by the collar.

"I thought you were just like us, but you ain't. You're just like them privileged white folks who ain't seen nothin' in this world ... take everythin' for granted."

"Let go of me!" Salim pushed his hand away and stood up. "You don't know me. If I'm privileged, then you're a confused bastard."

"Oh yeah?"

"Yes! Changing last names and calling each other brother doesn't make you Negroes any less confused…"

Just as those words left Salim's mouth, Carl's fist flew towards him. In the diner, a clapping sound brought everyone to attention. The hustlers reached for their pockets. Salim fell into his seat. Sounds of squeaking chairs and shuffling bodies moved towards him.

"It's okay. The boy's just drunk. Leave us alone!" Carl's voice became an echo in Salim's pounding head. Everyone returned to their seats and before his vision could align itself, he was out on the street, being pushed against the wall by Brother Carl. Salim threw him to the ground and sat on top of him. He raised his fist and swung for his face, but his knuckles hit the sidewalk instead. He squealed like a cat.

Brother Carl began to laugh.

Salim rolled over his hand, screaming into his sleeve.

"What are you laughing at?" he cried.

Carl's guffawing became so loud it sounded like gunfire. As Salim panted, raising himself to his feet, he saw Brother Carl howling, hunched over on the sidewalk. And at that instant, Salim's short-lived fury, transformed into a cackling laughter that came out through his nose and dribbled onto his mouth.

Universality

———— ❧ ————

Brother Carl's knuckles did more than knock some much-needed sense into Salim. They established a friendship which was to be the strongest one Salim had had. Carl saw in him something similar to what the Floating Pir had seen all those years ago. He could also see that nostalgia had made the boy soft, and that he needed a bit of tough love.

Carl knew all about tough love. His father, a World War II veteran, had shown him tough love four times a week and sometimes on the occasional fifth. Carl appreciated his father's beatings as he believed they had given him discipline. It was how he had managed to achieve so much in his life, and he believed his young friend could use a bit of it himself.

Salim, on the other hand, returned from the diner that day with a black eye and a contusion to the wrist, laughing like a crazed hyena. In his dorm room, he opened the drawer of undelivered letters and, one by one, began to tear the pages into tiny squares. Then he flushed them down the toilet a handful at a time until they were all gone. All but one. It was the one Laila had written to him back in the summer of 1966 before they had left for the summer house—her last letter. He'd kept it close to his heart. With a red pencil, he had highlighted the words he loved most:

> When you talk about those faraway stars, I see something remarkable in your eyes. It means a great deal to you. Don't stop dreaming about those stars, Salim. One day you'll get to touch them. I'm sure of it.

He cut out that phrase from the creased page and pasted it on the wall above his desk.

The next morning, he returned to Carl's diner and waited for him in the same booth.

"I guess you decided to stay," Carl said, as he sauntered towards him, his sword-like nose leading the way.

"Not only that, I think I am ready to try coffee. May I have a cup?"

Carl raised his eyebrows, ducked into the kitchen, brought out a pot of coffee and sat down.

"Your eye looks like it could use some ice."

Salim took a sip and grimaced. "And this could use some sugar."

Brother Carl chuckled, slapping the table.

The sun came out raging that morning. The clouds had been threatening it for a few days. Winter, Salim's very first in New York, had arrived suddenly and the air became demanding. This sunshine was much needed. Like many times before, it brought reassurance to Salim when he needed it most. He knew he had to overcome these small battles one by one—starting with a cup of coffee. The more he looked at Brother Carl, the more he resembled Pappu Pipewalla. So much so, it seemed as though Pappu had been possessed by a black man. That nose and those piercing eyes became reminders of the couplet children used to tease Pappu with.

Pappu Pipewalla sleeps under the peepli tree
Beware: he's got the biggest pipe you'll ever see

He couldn't help but smile thinking of that every time Carl spoke.

"I was thinkin' about somethin' yesterday ... I mean, you must be the only colored kid in school."

Pappu Pipewalla sleeps under the peepli tree

"Why you smilin'?"

"Nothing. Don't worry about it."

"So, tell me somethin'. These people don't bring in brothers like you if they ain't lookin' for shit."

"What do you mean?"

Carl lit a cigarette and took a big drag. "They gave you a scholarship, paid for everythin'. You think they runnin' a charity? No, brother. They want somethin'."

"What could I possibly have to offer them?"

"Listen, kid, I've been here for so long. I might be on the outside of those buildings but I know exactly what goes on in there. It ain't any different from what happens out on the street. They brought you here so they can buy your future. I ain't gonna say it 'cos you already know. So, tell me. Why do you think they brought you here?"

Salim pouted as though he had bit into a lemon. He fell into his seat and sighed, knowing exactly what it was they were after, but didn't want to say it. "I don't know," he started, then paused. "I guess ... they need me to validate the equations I sent them. Give them proofs ... I'm not just here for a degree, am I?"

"No, you sure ain't, little brother. You're here to help 'em beat the others. This is a goddamn race and you's a winnin' horse. But remember, give 'em what they want and you get yours." He took a sip from his cup, blew out cigarette smoke from his nose and asked, "They hustlers just like everybody else. So, what make you so special? What d'you have that us brothers don't?"

"I guess they saw something in me. I realized that yesterday. That's why I decided against leaving. I can't give up. You see, I don't look at things the way people are taught to. I approached it the way I know how. I don't know how else to put it. Let me ask you something. Did anyone teach you how to speak?"

"No."

"It was the same with me and mathematics. It's a language I knew because it was all around me." He took the salt and pepper shakers from the table and lined them up. Carl put out his cigarette and leaned over. "The gravity between these shakers can be calculated by a formula. The energy from that light bulb, the magnetism from your wristwatch, every kind of energy has an equation, a formula. Nature spoke to me in formulae very early on, probing my senses. It may sound absurd, but once I even heard a body of water talk to me in the most coherent way. It all made sense somehow. It made me realize that there is universality to everything. I can write the equation to it, but I don't know how to derive the proof. And in this world, no one takes you seriously without proofs. That's why I'm here. To learn how they do it, I guess."

No sooner than those words left his lips, Salim accepted his own verdict. This man, this sharp-nosed stranger who had never stepped inside a lecture hall, suddenly exposed the inevitable. On the streets of Harlem, not a dime changed hands without a hustle, and under the shadow of those Roman columns, where he had begun his new life, a bunch of hustlers held his fate in their talons. Hustlers. Just like the tall black men in colorful double-breasted blazers walking down Ninth Avenue with their rosy-cheeked hookers. Hustlers, Salim said to himself. He returned home that day more determined than he had ever been. A bachelor's degree? No. What a banal dream that would be. He needed to rise higher than that.

———◆◆———

A couple of months later, in January 1969, Richard Nixon was sworn in as the thirty-seventh President of the United States. That same summer, Apollo 11 became the first manned mission to successfully land on the moon's surface. That one small step was not only a giant leap for mankind, but also for the new country that Salim called home. Similar to him, science, the discipline which ratifies the rise of empires, officially left its European home and settled stateside.

The next few years passed, and Salim did indeed receive that bachelor's degree and extended his scholarship with the promise that he would complete his doctorate in the discipline of physics. But in the summer of 1971, by the time Nixon ordered the invasion of Cambodia and news of Jim Morrison's death shook students in their bell bottoms, Salim began to struggle. The proofs he sought didn't come easy. In fact, they didn't come at all. Having the answer wasn't enough, he had to pose the questions. That summer, in a fit of anger, Salim threw his epilepsy medication out the window. Paranoia made him blame everything for his incompetence—his medication, coffee, the lack of ventilation in the dorm rooms. But as those pills went out the window, things worsened and his thoughts slipped into the world of the fantastical, where angels reappeared delivering gloomy warnings in dream sequences. One day, sitting on the floor of the library, he had another epileptic fit. The doctors had warned him that taking the drugs was his only way of surviving. Frustrated with all this, he began to pray at night, hoping that the cosmos had something to offer. But no help arrived from the heavens either. So, he decided that he must clear his mind altogether of all enigmatic voices, and direct his sane faculties towards one focal point. In order to seek universality, he thought, he needed to follow a universal decree.

Obsession doesn't have a cause, that's why it's called obsession.

By the time the Pentagon Papers were released and arrests were made over the Watergate scandal, Nixon was re-elected. That summer of 1972, as Apollo 17 became the final manned lunar landing, Salim hit rock bottom. Those proofs remained incomplete. The doctorate committee held their breath, as time and time again, the failure of the boy from Pureland became a regular occurrence. They offered him one final attempt at presenting his thesis, and this time, he was more determined than ever to succeed. In the days before he was to be summoned before the committee, during the time of the Senate Watergate hearings, Salim began to have the same dream every night:

There is a boy in the servant quarters of a large villa. In his hand is a book with a nautilus shell on its cover. He comprehends everything but can't articulate it. He tries to write but, as he does, the ink evaporates from the pages and the numbers begin floating around his head like flies. Then he's under threat. The walls are closing in. He begins to run, but his legs have turned to jelly. He can't move.

He would awake from these nightmares sweating liberally, sometimes crying at the recognition that his dreams were informing him of his worthlessness.

The night before his thesis submission, Jaaji visited him in one of these dreams. He said nothing, and sat silently in a corner, smoking his hookah. When Salim awoke from this, he was shocked. He thought he heard the walls say something:

Eat all the books you can eat.

That morning, as he presented his work yet again, the professors laughed him off campus, mocking him for his outrageous notion: the unification of all known energies through a single formula—a formula with incomplete proofs.

Consequently, the university believed that Salim's lunacy had gone on far too long. It was all fine through the undergraduate years but the doctorate, which at first seemed a promising prospect, was a bit of a stretch. No one had achieved that so quickly before. It was impossible. The two-year window he was granted had expired, and the professors expressed their uneasiness. In staff meetings, they sat muttering amongst themselves. They didn't think he had it in him or, in my opinion, they just thought he was too damn crazy. It wasn't because of the believability of his formula. They'd seen worse, almost pathetic, submissions before. It was because he would show up wearing a different shoe on each foot, unshaven, shirt buttons misaligned, and his hair standing on end as though he had been given electroshock. He looked like a wooden puppet, put together at the last minute by drunken chimps—preposterous and fragile.

After his thesis was rejected, Salim's scholarship was rescinded, and he was forced to drop out. That's when his world came crumbling down.

Crazy

———•❦•———

Pretty soon, Salim was broke. He could have, if he tried, picked up a small-time teaching job, but he was convinced by Brother Carl that a dishwashing job was as good as any. And so, he moved out of his dorm and into the back of Carl's diner, where an old pantry was cleared out for him. He worked the night shift and afterwards would sit with Carl and talk as the sun came up.

"They think I'm crazy, Brother Carl," he said, sitting on the edge of his seat. "Sometimes I myself think the same. I don't know what it is that they can't see. Maybe I'm the blind one."

Carl sighed and came over to sit next to him. "Brother, you still don't get it do you? There ain't nothin' wrong with you. It's them."

"I don't think I can deal with a lecture right now."

"I ain't givin' any lectures. Do you know about that math guy Rama, Rama somethin'?"

"Ramanujan?"

"Yeah, him." Salim looked at him with a half-smile. "What? You think I don't know shit? I know more than you think. That Indian brother had all the answers in the world, but no proofs. That was until he found a mentor, a good ol' white man to make him speak their language. If you ask me, it ain't got to do with proofs and shit. You need one of them on your side."

"What does that mean?"

"Go to the library down on 134th. They have archives of all the journals ever written. I've been hearin' kids talk about the archives for as long as I can remember." He clicked his fingers at a waitress who disappeared behind the counter. "Find out who else was doing what you's doing and ask him for help. These white people ain't gonna listen to a brown brother. But if you's got one of them in your corner..." He shrugged.

At first, Salim put off Carl's comment as another one of his race rants, but as the morning came up, his feet shuffled towards 134th Street on their own.

Failure's an essential element in discovery and others' failures are launching pads. Salim had forgotten this basic fact. What he was about to attempt had to have been attempted before; surely someone had to have come close at least. When he began leafing through old journals, one name kept reappearing: Stanley Weinberg.

You've probably heard of the Weinberg-Witten theorem. I don't really know what it is but apparently it's a big deal. What about the recently discovered Higgs-Boson particle? Yes, I too have come across it. Before coming here today you'd have read a bit about the unification theorem, better known as, the Agha Principle. All these ornate philosophies that I've mentioned have one thing in common: Crazy Stan.

Theoretical physicist, Stanley Weinberg, was exactly whom Salim was looking for. In his youth, Dr. Weinberg of Cornell University had proposed the notion of energy unification but fell short on the proofs. It remained a plausible theory. Salim had heard about it before but hadn't paid too much attention because of the reputation of the man. Crazy Stan, as he was known in the physics world had, after the untimely demise of his beloved wife, become, how can I put it ... crazy. Your mind might wander towards the portrayal of John Nash in the film *A Beautiful Mind* in which Russel Crowe's character is enveloped by paranoid schizophrenia and mutters to figments of his imagination. That's not the kind of crazy I'm getting at. All I can do is tell you what took place and let you decide. I'm talking about the day Salim borrowed twenty dollars from Brother Carl and got on a bus to upstate New York. Ithaca...

———

"Did you bring my lunch!" Weinberg cried. "They said they sent someone, but it hasn't arrived yet. Did you bring it?"

Salim, standing in the doorway of Weinberg's office, took a step back.

"No ... I'm Salim Agha. We talked on the phone. I'm here to..."

"Oh ... I thought you'd be ... never mind." Stanley Weinberg, stout, pot-bellied and bald as a cannonball, stood at a mere five feet off the ground. He walked over to Salim, shook his hand and rushed back to his desk. "What are you waiting for? Close the door behind you and sit down, ol' sport." His accent reminded Salim of the movies—Humphrey Bogart to be exact. It seemed like Weinberg had failed to shake Brooklyn off his tongue in all these years. "I've been getting my lunch delivered for forty years and still the cafeteria is late every time. What're you gonna do, right?" He looked over at Salim, but his eyes were focusing somewhere behind him, as though he were looking right through him.

"Professor Weinberg, I've come all the way from New York and I need your help."

"Yes, yes. I know who you are, ol' sport. The wonder kid from Greenland."

"Pureland."

"Whatever-the-fuck-land. Listen, I read your proofs and they're absolute shit."

"Excuse me?"

"You deaf? Absolute shit! I bet my grandson could do better and he's at Michigan State. Hahahaha!"

Salim shuffled in his chair, feeling a burning sensation in his chest. Stanley Weinberg sat across from him in a swivel chair, rotating from side to side like a child. He had a head shaped like a kino, completely round. The sun shone behind it creating a silhouette. Salim began observing all this in a state of sincere anxiety and questioning having his crazy idea refereed by a lunatic.

"Listen, ol' sport. I'm sorry for being like that. I'll tell you what ... take this, write your equation at the top and work your way backwards." He tossed him a piece of broken chalk.

"Now?"

"No, day after. Of course, now! If we're to do this, we have to act fast. I'm an old man. Can't waste my office hours on every kid with a hunch. You know, Maggie used to say..."

Weinberg's words carried on in the background as, with great hesitation, Salim rose from his chair and walked to the blackboard that faced the window. The office was the largest he'd seen, much more spacious than the rat-holes his professors had back in Columbia. He took a deep breath, shut his eyes and began, ever so cautiously to pen the formula, define the variables: lambda, X, e, M for mass, and the one that gave him the most trouble, Tau for the electromagnetic charge.

"You know, they've got the bastard on tape admitting everything. I dunno what the fuck's taking 'em so long." Salim looked back at Weinberg. "I'm talking about nailing Nixon. He plunges an entire nation into war, lies about it, then destroys the evidence, and now he's fired the people investigating him. Can you believe it?" He shook his round head. "And they call me crazy. Do they have leaders like this back in Swaziland?"

Salim pretended he hadn't heard him and tried to focus. The chalk did what it had been doing over the years, but as soon as the symbol for the electromagnetic charge hit the blackboard, Tau let him down again.

"No! No! No!"

"What's wrong?"

"What's wrong? You can't have an equation longer than a football field and expect people to take you seriously. Reduce! Reduce!"

"I'm trying, but this is as far as it goes."

"Reduce! No wonder they keep rejecting your thesis."

Salim turned on his heels and stared back at him, his eyes avoiding the curve of his head. "Professor Weinberg, with all due respect, you're a rude and obnoxious man. This has been a waste of my time." He buttoned his blazer, placed the chalk back on the desk and began to walk towards the door.

When he put his hand on the door handle something made him freeze.

"The dreams jolting you awake yet?"

"Excuse me?"

"The nightmares, ol' sport. How bad are they? Do you wake up at night, sweating balls?"

A bolt of electricity stunned Salim and he turned to face him.

"They get worse. First the walls cave in, then you begin seeing things in the daytime that aren't there. That's when you know you're fucked." He sighed. "That's when they start calling you names."

Crazy Stan leaned back in his chair and the sunlight began to brighten his face. Salim walked back towards the desk and sat down.

"I had those dreams. Right before I published my theorem in '52. Listen, ol' sport," he stood up and walked towards him, tiptoeing as he sat on the desk. "Maybe I've been a bit harsh on you. You must be hungry. These fools aren't getting me my lunch anytime soon, so what say you and I grab a slice of pie from the diner down the street? Do you like fast cars?"

Outside in the parking lot, Salim followed the professor to his car.

"Buckle up, ol' sport. This here's a '53 Corvette and she gets pretty mean when she's on the highway. Black was Maggie's favorite color. I used to say, 'Honey it ain't really a color'. She hated it when I used to get technical on..."

"Wait. Professor Weinberg, there's no seatbelt," Salim said, as the engine roared under his feet.

"Ah, yes! Been meaning to get that fixed. Don't worry, ol' sport. I may be mad but I'm the best damn driver in the state of New York." He started to laugh as he reversed out of the campus parking lot and screeched out towards the highway. "Although I can't see too well these days."

Salim gulped, grabbing the door handle tight in his fist. His other hand clasped on to the seat as though that would help in a crash. Then, if things weren't already bad enough, Crazy Stan began to sing.

"En route to get a pie. Route to the pie. Yeah, baby!" As he clicked into fifth gear, the car flew along the bend of the road and Salim began to panic.

"Professor Weinberg! Professor Weinberg! You're doing 70 in a 35 zone. Please slow down!"

"What? Can't hear 'ya. I guess the ears are going too. Oh ... en route to get a pie, en route to a pie, route to pie!"

"Stop right now! That's enough! Stop! Please, for the love of God!"

"70 in a 35! With the kid from Swaziland! 70 in a 35, en route with Crazy Stan!"

A swerve to the right and the car began to swerve. Stan lost control and they were sliding like a bar of soap along the road. Salim bit his lip, closed his eyes and howled like it was the end. Stan, well, he kept on laughing as the car spun in circles until it came to a screeching standstill on the dusty shoulder. Salim opened his eyes and bolted out of the car, still trembling with horror. He stood for a moment to gather himself and ran over to the driver's side, pulled the little bastard out of the car and pinned him to the door.

"You want to die? Do it on your own time! Leave me out of it, you madman!"

But the laughter only got louder. "Hahahaha! 70 in a 35. Route to pie!"

"What are you on about? Have you gone insane?"

Salim stood up and began walking down the empty road, checking to see if he'd peed himself.

"Your equation," Weinberg cried from behind. "It's too long, kid. 35 to 70. Root of pi."

Salim's eyebrows met in the middle of his forehead. Now fury made him ponder murder. But, as he fastened himself firmly to the soles of his shoes, his heart slowing itself down to its normal pace, he realized exactly what Crazy Stan was on about. He said it out loud to himself to confirm it, "Two times the root of pi. Root of pie times two."

"That's right, ol' sport. Multiply by two root pi on both sides of the equation and we have lift off. The eagle has landed. Houston, we are a go." He lifted himself and began dusting his pants. "I mean, you still have a lot of work to do. You skip too many steps in your proofs. You have to learn to walk before you can run."

"So, you're saying that my Tau problem..."

"It goes bye-bye." He started waving his hands with one eyebrow raised. "I can help you if you promise to work hard—and just trust me. We can turn it into something great. One, simple, elegant, formula. Universality. It's a good name, I think."

Crazy Stan sat back in the car and stared at his own reflection in the rear-view mirror, checking the gaps between his teeth with his tongue.

"You couldn't tell me that in the office?"

"And miss your scared-to-death look? Not a chance. It was too much fun. Too much."

"You're a maniac. A maniac!"

A car sped by, honking its horn, leaving a plume of dust hanging in the air.

"Fine, fine. I was just messing around. Now let's get that pie. I'm hungry. I promise I won't scare you anymore."

Salim walked back to the car and held his breath for a few seconds before letting his hand grasp the door handle. As the engine started again, Crazy Stan clicked the radio on, pressed the gas pedal, looked over at the passenger seat and asked in the softest, politest of voices, "Do you guys have pies in Newfoundland?"

Prizes

In the spring of 1975, two days after the Fall of Saigon, the Agha-Weinberg Principle was published in the *International Journal of Theoretical Physics*. Much to the excitement of Stanley Weinberg, a few months earlier Richard Nixon had resigned before he was to be impeached and President Ford would begin recalling US troops from Vietnam. Crazy Stan deemed that the world had finally returned to normal and that it was the right time for him to retire. He swapped his '53 Corvette for a Jeep 4x4 and set out to drive around the world.

Weinberg, before his sudden disappearance, did more than just legitimize the unification theorem—he slapped whatever arrogance Salim had right out of him. Some would say he smacked the Blisschestersonian right out of his ears. Brilliant as Salim was, in his own right, he was big-headed and lacked discipline. He'd never bothered to learn the virtue of deriving a step-by-step guide for the very things he was trying to prove. Weinberg taught him a valuable lesson, one that he would never forget.

Things didn't end there. By the time the paper was published in the journal, Salim was still working shifts at Brother Carl's diner. Times of tribulation continued. Just as President Ford survived the second of two assassination attempts, Salim convinced the doctorate committee to let him defend his thesis one last time. He submitted his paper, as he had done many times before, and the professors told him he would be hearing from them. He waited for days but no one called.

"I don't know what I can do, Carl. Without a doctorate, no one will take me seriously," he said one day at the diner, tears welling in his eyes.

"Be patient, brother. They just bein' arrogant. They'll come through. No one likes admittin' they're wrong."

That night, however, after sensing complete abandonment, with his hands immersed in soap-water, Salim began to think that this was indeed the last straw. He cried into his palms at night, believing that America was a grave mistake, that the village was his only refuge, and that his inherited serfdom, from which he'd tried so hard to escape, had finally caught up with him. Just when he thought about falling silently under the E train, something strange occurred. Some say this rumor's just that, a rumor. But I believe what transpired next is something that can only be described as a miracle.

Those Columbia professors, who had reacted with tepid indifference to his theory, letting their egos get the better of them, started receiving phone calls from all over the world inquiring about the Universality Theorem. One phone call in particular was from Princeton University. A professor claimed that his mentor, Professor Einstein, in his final years, had yearned for a theory that supplemented his notion of special relativity. The professor believed Einstein might have been hinting at the underlying tenets of the Agha-Weinberg Principle. When news of that phone call spread in Columbia, the stubborn old fools who had rejected Salim's paper looked sheepishly at each other, shrugging their shoulders in astonishment. They rushed to their respective dens, flattened Salim's crumpled paper and secretly awoke to the possibility that the village boy had been right all along and that science had, in fact, prevailed.

In the world of science, being proven wrong is celebrated. And thus, the professors of the university, in a remarkable change of heart, began championing the principles of universality as their own collective triumph. Salim presented his theory to crammed lecture halls where his peers clapped their hands raw. Under the cloud of their applause, a renewed conviction returned to Salim. He suddenly acquired a position of power. The campus recluse, who was often found mumbling to himself in the hallways, became like one of those guitar heroes whose posters students pasted on the dorm walls.

Those university professors, they were like clay in his hands after that. They gave him permanent tenure: a deal where he would become a faculty member and receive funding for the research of his choosing.

Thus, among the unruly rubble of Harlem, where struggle had become an everyday affair, there emerged Dr. Salim Agha, PhD.

Some might say that the fortuitous events in Salim's life would seem like something out of a fantasy movie. But like I have mentioned time and again, the truth—for most of us, including myself—is rooted deeply in the fantastical; under the brush-strokes of a painted sunset, tucked between the lines of a sonnet, folded between the bars of a melody. If this were a fantasy story, now is where it would conclude. And the words of the levitating clairvoyant would finally come true. The world, in this case the world of science, would finally listen to the boy who was once considered a mute. The truth is stranger than any fiction I can possibly contrive. And what happened next is something even I didn't see coming.

It was how the Agha-Weinberg Principle eventually became known as the Agha Principle or the Universality Theorem.

In the years following the publication of Salim's journal, by the time Jimmy Carter was inaugurated as President, and Margaret Thatcher became the first female leader of a major political party, and, of course, Pureland's long-standing military rule came to an end, Salim had established himself as an academic leader in the world of physics. All this before his thirtieth birthday. Things, depending on how you look at it, were looking good for modernity on the whole. The swinging sixties had given birth to an era of progress. Our imaginations took a leap as well. Superman, Star Wars, Close Encounters of the Third Kind; we as humans began to wonder and push forth into the final frontier: space. The Agha Principle, which enhanced our understanding of the space-time continuum, had become an accepted fact of science. It was used to maximize energy utilization. This gave birth to innovation and industry. And by the year 1978, when President Carter postponed the production of the neutron bomb, people thought that the era of warfare was over. Our species was headed up.

During all of this, Professor Stanley Weinberg's absence became collectively accepted. He vanished from the world completely. One day, in the winter of 1978, Salim finally received a phone call from Crazy Stan.

"Professor Weinberg? Is that really you?" Salim stood up, the telephone cord wrapped around his waist. "I've been trying to find you."

"You can't find someone who doesn't want to be found, ol' sport. But somehow they found me."

"Who found you?"

"They called me first. And I told 'em I got nothin' to do with the whole thing. It was you all along, kid."

"Who's they? What are you on about?"

"Listen, ol' sport. I've had my time in the spotlight and, don't get me wrong, I loved every minute of it. But it's your turn now. I thought they'd call you years ago, but better late than never."

Salim began to rub his temples. Slowly, Weinberg's words began to sink in. "I can't accept this, Professor. I know what you are doing but I can't let you shy away from our achievement."

"It's already done. Listen, I want you to do something for me."

"Wait, didn't you hear what I said? Where are you?"

"I drove through Pureland last month. She's a beauty, ol' sport. Maggie woulda loved that place... I want you to rub it in their faces."

"Rub what?"

"There was this guy at my hotel there, in Lorr. He guarded the door. He was wearing the most elegant outfit—baggy pants, colorless coat, a turban that stuck out in the air. He reminded me of you. I want you to wear that to the banquet. Rub it in their faces. I hope you'll be the first of many."

"Professor Weinberg, please, just tell me where you are."

"And one more thing. When you go there, bring a date. Life is short. Don't forget to have fun. I'm gonna go now. You take care, ol' sport."

Salim held on to the receiver for several minutes in astonishment.

That was the last time he ever heard from Stanley Weinberg. No one truly knew what became of him. But every once in a while, Salim would close his eyes and imagine him speeding down the highway in his open-top car.

When a mysterious message did arrive, a few days after Weinberg had alerted him, Salim was ready for it. The university, too, had been buzzing with excitement. Like Weinberg had said, he would be the first of his kind: a Muslim from a third-world country.

———◆———

Which brings us to Stockholm, 1979.

Salim was at the podium in a starched white turban and a black sherwani—his knees quivering as he delivered his acceptance speech.

"Holding this year's Nobel Prize for physics, I recall a story." He paused and swallowed. "The story of two boys in a village in my home country. One was given a book that eventually changed his life. But for the other, knowledge was as far-fetched an idea as flying to the stars. One of those boys stands before you today while the other represents the millions for whom knowledge is a luxury. The onus is upon us to emancipate everyone from ignorance and allow curiosity to thrive. Let's show them that even flying to the stars is possible."

The applause drummed as he walked back to his seat. As he sat down, a familiar, milky white hand reached out from under the tablecloth and grabbed him. He looked up into her boundless eyes—eyes that had their own light—eyes like an oceanic creature that illuminates the subterranean abyss. Her eyes pulled him towards her and he sank deep into the chasm of her magnificence. Then, squeezing her hand, he said, "Laila, all this feels like a dream."

Laila Khan, regal as ever in her silver ball-gown, reached over to kiss his cheek. Then she whispered in his ear, "You always wanted to touch the stars, Salim Agha. Now you're one of them. Look around you."

"I can't believe it," Salim said. "Somehow, I know this dream will end soon. But tonight... I want you to be mine."

"Tonight... I am all yours."

Salim smiled at her. He knew she wasn't going to stay long and that she would leave a crater in his heart larger than the one that was there before. He looked down at her creamy skin. On her wrist was a bracelet with a key—the key to his heart. She'd said it was a cheesy and juvenile gift. But his love was just that. Hers was a veteran of many lovers and one-night stands. Her love was ruthless.

He recalled how terrified he was the day the Nobel Committee called; days after Weinberg had alerted him. He was scared of how he would do it, how he would convince Laila to come meet him after all those years. Excited, he rehearsed his lines several times in front of the mirror before he made that phone call.

"I know Salim," Laila said, dismissively, when Salim told her. "We get international news here too, you know? But ... I am actually proud of you."

"Then you must come to the banquet with me. As my guest." He wanted to say 'date' but couldn't find the courage.

"I can't."

"Why not? There's nothing that I have yearned for more than the acceptance of my achievements by Pureland and, more importantly, by you. Can't you see? Without you, all this is worthless to me."

"I'm going to get married next week. You expect me to travel across the world for this one night?"

"Yes. I will live a lifetime in this one night. And ... so can you."

Laila's reluctant sigh and the pause that followed made Salim hold his breath.

"Fine," she whispered. "Just one night."

Salim never forgot that evening. He never asked why she'd agreed to come in the first place. He didn't want to. Was it some kind of last-minute hurrah before the curtains fell on her life? Or did she actually yearn for him like he did for her? Was there a love there that they both shared but were afraid to admit to themselves? A shameful love. He didn't want to think of any of those things. All he wanted was her. Just one night.

They spent that magical evening locked in each other's arms, lost in an Eden where the fruit remained uneaten, where time stood still. And in the morning, as she had warned, Laila vanished.

On Salim's return to New York, celebrations erupted at the university. People cheered as he entered the lecture halls, and the department even offered to throw a luncheon in his honor. But he refused. Still reeling from the agony of Laila's departure, he wanted to surround himself with the people he called friends.

Brother Carl decorated the diner with plastic banners and balloons and threw him a party for the ages; where street hustlers, pimps, rock slingers, and every downtrodden hippy that Salim knew turned up to show their support. It seems hard to imagine, but somehow he felt at home with them. They drank cheap champagne and smoked cigars and, when the raucous drunkenness set in, Carl made short-order breakfast.

As the celebrations spilled into the wee hours of morning, when coffee pots were put on the boil, a small black-and-white TV stunned the party guests, Salim in particular. The images left him in a state of burning despair. It all unfolded before him as he stood hunched over a bar stool with a maddening rage singeing his brow. How could it be, he asked himself. How? It was happening all over again and he could do nothing. As Brother Carl hushed everyone up, the broadcaster's words echoed throughout the diner.

General Zaid has ambushed parliament and hanged the Prime Minister.
This is Pureland's second Martial Law.

That face ... the face that was the source of his abhorrence burned through the screen. He could not forget such a face. The greyness of those sunken eyes delivered an ominous warning—he was there to stay.

Salim went home in tears that morning. That night weighed down on him like a boulder on his chest. That scumbag brigadier who'd once taken to his collar like a rabid dog now held his nation in those very hands. I can't be sure of it, but I can imagine that a nameless emotion swirled through Salim's mind all night—love, sympathy, or perhaps, remorse. And with remorse came fury.

What I am about to reveal cannot be found in any history book and its consequences were so powerful I believe it changed the course of

Salim's life forever. If this anger of his was, somehow, curtailed at the time, I believe he could have acted with a bit of diplomacy. But I can imagine the telephonic conversation, through the open door of his office, Salim's eyebrows rising in shock, and General Zaid's voice adding to his anger, making him thump his desk as the receiver hung from his ear.

It was a Friday—a holy day. Zaid had prayed hard. He wanted something and Salim was the one he turned to for help.

"A Muslim bomb? Bombs don't have religions, General Saab ... Nuclear? Do you know the difference between...? And you need my help with that? What if I refuse? Are you threatening ... Excommunicate me? Go ahead, you deranged bastard! Go ahead!"

The phone receiver was then hurled against the wall. Had that conversation gone differently, I believe it is quite possible that Salim would still be alive. But it was those words of disdain that lodged a rock of animosity in Zaid's mind. And ever since he took over Pureland, and for the years that followed, strange things started to occur. After that telephonic outburst from Salim, Zaid marched to the Pureland Television building for a special announcement. A hierarchy of citizenship, an immediate amendment to the constitution of the republic, was to be ratified. Zaid began by defining the criteria to define a true Muslim. Ahmadis, he claimed, do not always believe in Mohammed's finality and, therefore, cannot fall into the Muslim category. Hence, all Ahmadis, it was declared, had to register their identities with the state and carry special identification cards. This was just a precautionary measure, Zaid said. He was acting in the interest of national security.

That's when mayhem began. The state was to decide how to treat its citizens based on creed alone. God had to be handed the reins and the new dictator did just that. A cabinet of mullahs was formed and everything had to attain celestial approval. And I mean everything. Should women vote? Can squash players wear shorts? It became clear that God—Zaid's God, that is—had taken over. That's the problem when you create gods more powerful than yourself. The creation becomes mightier than the creator and they become bloodthirsty, as gods often do. Such was the beast that brought with it the thirst for Salim's blood.

You asked me what it was that inspired the Scimitar to assassinate Salim. Sir, all the while, you've been asking the wrong questions. What you really should ask is why Salim became the heretic we all wanted to slay. All this began with Martial Law, that holy Friday night, the phone call and, years later, the fatwa.

Over the next ten years, the distance between Salim and Pureland had grown to unconquerable depths. His hope of one day returning to his country was crushed by Zaid's regime, one declaration at a time. The longer he stayed in exile, the more his pain grew. He became an android functioning solely in a world of routine. He plunged himself in lectures and research, conferences and academic papers—anything to blunt the pain. And he watched as Pureland started becoming like a Shakespearean tragedy played by clowns. In these ten years, banishment became Zaid's cherished weapon. Ban everything, he'd say: TV channels, radio jockeys, discos, kite flying. Anything his feeble mind felt threatened by, he ended with one swipe of the pen. This maddening tyranny, which began with that phone call, spawned hatred and this hatred grew and grew until the year 1987, when it erupted in the form of a fatwa.

After that—well, after that Salim was never the same again. More importantly, neither was I.

The Fatwa

Sir, before I tell you about the fatwa and the rise of the Caliphate, let me set the scene, by telling you how things were back then. This is crucial, not only to this story, but also to me, the killer who sits before you.

You could feel it, growing up, that Pureland was in some way being set up for the Caliphate to take over. We felt it many years earlier. In fact, way before the turban-clad army blew through our cities with AK-47s slung over their shoulders, we were, in a way, expecting them. By the late 1980s, two decades before the Caliphate arrived, Pureland had already witnessed holy wars, frenzied mullahs, zealous dictators, and, of course, fatwas. We thought we were done with that shit. But our nation was hollowed out from the very beginning. Yes, Zaid was a disaster, but he was given license by the citizens of the state. We had become a rudderless people, ripe for the taking, by Zaid and, later, by the Caliphate. I am talking in particular about the generation before mine. If I am to point fingers now, I would take them to task; ask them why they were sleeping at the wheel. They were meant to guide us. We were ambushed by that post-colonial generation, our elders, the drawing-room class. They were the ones who expunged our heritage. They were victims and, at the same time, agents of their colonial masters, who spoke in foreign tongues and worshipped the West but scoffed at their own culture. They forged a nation out of an idea and then watched that idea devour us all. They were the confused fucks who sold us out.

New York, 1987.

Sorry for that, sir, I got a bit carried away. I get emotional, as you can tell, when it comes to my nation. I love my country too, you know. I have formidable anger for how things turned out. But all that aside, here I shall respond to your earlier inquiry about the fatwa.

Salim's fatwa, in a way, was his own doing. If he'd wanted, he could have decided not to blaspheme in the first place. He could have, like many others, continued to live the life of an exiled intellectual. He could have easily ignored the mounting fortuitous accidents in his life. He could have ignored all the signs that were hurled down by celestial order. But he could most certainly not have ignored Andrea "Chip" Beetlewood. She was pretty and manly at the same time—she was pretty manly. She had the body of a pole-vaulter and the humor of a crass court jester, with arms that could hold open the jaws of a crocodile and yank out a sixty-pound dumbbell. She had stalked him for some time and one afternoon, approached Salim at the 86th Street subway station. As the 6 train screamed into the station, she pulled on Salim's arm like a soliciting pamphlet purveyor.

"Hello, Dr. Agha. Chip Beetlewood, I work for ..." she stopped, extending her thick forearms. "Our agency represents most noteworthy Nobel laureates and I was going through this list and ... frankly, I think you and I can both make money if you just write a book."

As another train whizzed in, her hair flew up. She was quick to tuck it behind her ear. Before the train doors shut, she pulled Salim inside the car. He stared at her as she squeezed in next to him. She smelled like apples.

"I am extremely busy. Thank you for your offer but..."

"Alright then. How about I buy you lunch?"

"Lunch?"

"You have to eat, don't you? I promise to leave you alone after that."

Stand clear of the closing doors please.

They stepped off at Grand Central and pushed through crowds towards the food court below, then sat down with deli sandwiches and iced tea. Salim ate in silence as she spoke in her Long Island drawl.

"... so I told him, you know what, fantasy novels are about as useful to me as tits to a nun. I can't sell that shit. It's 1987 you know. That genre's been dead a *lawng* time." She stopped, biting into her tuna sandwich. With her mouth half full, she mumbled, "Sit in front of a typewriter and bleed, as they say in the industry. You can write just about anything you like, anything that's on your mind. I promise to make it sell."

After much deliberation, Salim spoke. "But I only write research papers."

"And what do you think that is? Writing is writing. Listen Doc ... may I call you that? Look around you. This is the busiest place on earth. Everyone here has a story. You certainly have one. See how these people hustle back to their offices with pastrami sandwiches tucked under their arms, newspapers in their teeth. You think they like to be pushed into train cars every morning, listening to phones ring on top of phones, their bosses yelling over their heads? They do it because they're driven. What is it that drives you? What makes you cry, laugh? What makes you love?" And then as she leaned over with her nose almost touching his, she whispered, "What would you die for?"

Her words settled into the back of Salim's mind. In fact, they did not resurface until later that night when he was trying to sleep, because at that moment, he was thinking of something else. It was clear to him, as Chip ignored the immodest glances from men that fell right on to her demanding cleavage, that she had no interest in them ... men, that is. It became more apparent why, as her tongue swiped her lower lip when a young lady walked by, wearing a tell-tale ensemble.

Had he known that that evening, while perched upon his desk, smelling the freshness of empty white sheets of paper, that he was about to put his life in peril, Salim would have stood up, chucked the bottle of typewriter ink in the trash, and gone about his business as usual. Had he rubbished this idea, in a way, there would be no fatwa, there would be no Scimitar, and I wouldn't be here talking to you. But that night, Chip's words tumbled back into his mind. He knew exactly what it was that he would die for. So, he began to write the story of the city he loved—Lorr—a city held captive by an underworld demon. He could not stomach the idea of her stifling under military curfew each night, when all she really wanted to do was dance. More importantly, he thought about Laila Khan.

A few months later, he was done. His book, *Exile*, hardly made it off the shelf. Salim waited for a good review as one would for the sound of a pin dropping in Grand Central during rush hour. All he received were bad reviews and lots of them. One critic said rather harshly, "Dr. Agha is merely screaming into a pillow when he should be suffocated by it instead." An even harsher criticism drove the book to the international stage. Amidst murmurs of a democratic revolution, and in a hasty attempt to galvanize his dwindling support, the dictator-general Zaid of Pureland issued a death warrant on Salim's head. In 1987, the fatwa was the first of its kind in the literary world. It carried with it a handsome bounty that, if you can imagine, supplemented with martyrdom, could make budding vigilantes take up marksmanship. This added to the growing anti-hero narrative Zaid was building against the Ahmadi's most revered icon. What particularly irked him remains unclear. But I believe, it could be the following words from chapter six:

> No one, not even General Zaid, can claim to know the desires of God let alone try and act as his administrator. He doesn't determine whether anyone can or cannot be Muslim. He barely knows himself. What he is, is an agent of hatred bought by those who know how inexpensive his integrity is.

Tough words, I know. But there it was. One literary appraisal by a maniacal dictator launched Salim onto the front pages of newspapers and gave his book an added bit of naughtiness. The book was banned in all Muslim countries and even some stores in the West refused to sell it. Yet somehow, the publishing house couldn't print enough copies. The world, as we knew it, became divided. Freedom of speech, the only freedom there is, became debatable.

But what exactly was this warning Zaid had delivered? All I can say is that it was a deranged extension of Zaid's persona, one obsessed with infidels. What had started as a precautionary security measure, where Ahmadis were asked to carry special ID cards, turned into a systematic persecution. Salim and the Ahmadi sect were deemed heretics, imposters posing as Muslims, dangerous and sinful people. When Salim's book was released, he was declared their leader who, in exile, promoted blasphemy, tainting the very innocence of Pureland's youth.

All Ahmadis, especially Salim, had to be stopped, Zaid announced on national radio.

Riots broke out. Vigilante gangs were formed. Ahmadis were hunted like wild partridge. Salim's name was ripped out from textbooks and his triumphs were instantly forgotten. Propaganda pamphlets were distributed at Friday sermons in mosques across the country. Salim Agha, the vile infidel, became known far and wide as the villain who had shamed Pureland.

That was the first time, as a child, I heard the name Salim Agha—and it immediately became synonymous with evil.

Why such hatred, you ask. The finality of Mohammed, it goes without question, as the ultimate celestial messenger is as absolute as the existence of God himself. I don't need to explain the sensitivities of people when it comes to things related to the Prophet. Say anything you might about God, and you may get away with it. But sway ever so slightly in your comprehension of His messenger and, well, you know the deal.

Zaid knew this. He knew the manner in which kernels of hatred could germinate overnight, sprouting into mosques in every corner of the city. He knew that the Ahmedi could serve as the perfect warning sign—the infidel that stops all infidels. He knew that teenaged benighted mullahs were perfectly placed to blast more than just the call to prayer through their rambunctious megaphones five times a day. He knew that even at absurd hours of the night hate speech had the ability to echo from the minarets and seep through every window into every home and yank people out of slumber. He knew that the Ahmadi could be manifested into a hellish creature of the underworld which should be dreaded, loathed, and eventually, eliminated at all costs.

Zaid knew all of this and thus, so did we.

At any rate, back to the fatwa.

Zaid had never read Salim's book. In fact, he didn't even know about it until one of his close confidants, a young mullah from his cabinet, ran to him one evening with the book raised above his head. The mullah, shivering with fury, claimed that in order to maintain Islamic order, Zaid must act as the undeniable leader of the Muslim world. He also said that, according to his understanding of the religious texts, Ahmadis were more dangerous than he had previously thought. People who undermine the very finality of the Holy Prophet must be dealt with authoritatively and the only way to do that was through a holy verdict. The fatwa of 1987 was a dual judgement on the Ahmadis and Salim Agha in particular. It pretty much sealed the deal.

So General Zaid, who had first-mover advantage on the fatwa, became a pioneer amongst his peers. Dictators around the world perked up in their beds. Fatwas became fashionable. One after another, fatwas were dealt out like cards at a blackjack table. There were dueling fatwas against other fatwas, and new fatwas on old fatwas. At times, it became difficult to recognize where the fatwas were coming from. They stormed the world like locusts.

What happened to Pureland when the Caliphate arrived there a few years ago was sudden, I must admit. But like I said, the seeds had been sown way back, when I was just a child, when the Salim Agha fatwa was first announced. Months after that announcement an emergency was declared in the republic. It was a time when we would rush indoors at sunset. When the army sirens went off, iron shutters fell down in the bazaars, the streets were plunged into darkness, and our doors were locked shut.

1987. It was a tough year to be in New York, too. The markets nose-dived and hairdos frizzled into coils. There's so much we can say about 1987, but first ... Tamboo Charming.

Salim, after his tenure was solidified, began sending money to keep Tamboo Charming afloat. Their stepmother had passed away after a deathly bout of pneumonia and, some days later, Tamboo's wife ran off with Wannu the Weasel. Heartbroken, Charming moved to Lorr to become a tour guide of the walled city. He enrolled in English classes and bought himself Elvis records which he played on a loop, mimicking his accent. Salim's monthly stipend and his day job kept him afloat, but he was restless to leave Pureland. He was destined for a greater purpose.

One day, Tamboo Charming approached a young lady, Mrs. Delean of the American Consulate School, and convinced her to take her fifth graders out on a tour of the old havelis. Mrs. Delean, a quiet and simple gal from Iowa, fell head over heels for Charming within an hour of that tour. As their bus zipped down the Mall Road, all of Mrs. Delean's midwestern values went out the window.

Charming convinced her to run away to the US before her husband found out. And once he did find out, Mr. Delean, a bareknuckle boxing champion from the streets of Detroit, stormed through the city looking for his wife's camel-like lover. But Tamboo had his shit planned out. Through his new girlfriend of two days, he managed to secure a passport, a visa, and two one-way tickets to JFK. When the new couple arrived at the airport, arm-in-arm, Tamboo asked his lover to watch their bags while he took a piss. Then, he disappeared over the Jamaica Station bridge into the city, leaving Mrs. Delean sobbing at Terminal 4's arrivals section.

"I don't believe this," Salim said, as he opened the door to find his brother standing there with open arms.

"You better believe it, little brother," Tambo said, moving his hips. "Love me tender, love me sweet. Never let me ... go!"

Tamboo jumped on his brother and wrestled him to the ground.

"Ah! Stop! Stop! I'm too old for ... stop!" Salim cried, giggling until his eyes began to water.

"I am finally here!" Tamboo sang, jumping up and pounding the floor with his feet. "I knew I had to be here the moment I heard. No fucking fatwa is going to harm my little brother, no sir. You'll see, no one will dare touch you now!"

"But how did you get here? And why are you speaking that way? Did you swallow old records on your way here?"

"Like a river flows. Gently to the sea..."

"What are you talking about?"

"Shhh..." Tamboo put his fingers over Salim's lips. "A little less conversation, a little more action please." Salim looked at him strangely then bit his finger. "Aaah! You fat fuck!"

Salim wrapped his arms around Tamboo and squeezed him tight.

"O Potato ... You were always on my mind."

"You can stop now."

Tamboo walked over to the window and thumped it. "Wow! This city's better than I'd imagined in my dreams. Full-on sister-fuckery!" A chuckling sound made him turn around and stare at Salim. "It's good to see you laugh like that, little brother."

Salim, shaking his head, said, "Only one absurd thing in the world can make me laugh like that."

Tamboo began rubbing his shoulders. "Why is it so bloody cold in here."

"The air conditioning is on."

"Turn it off!" Tamboo began doing jumping jacks, singing, "Defrost your charms. There's only two of us here." He spread his arms out. "Come in my arms and make yourself comfortable dear."

With Tamboo's arrival came laughter. It impregnated the walls of Salim's apartment, bringing some sense of tranquility into his chaotic life. And the camel took to New York like a buffalo to a pond. Unlike Salim, his talent for embracing renewal allowed him to be blind to his past. The nostalgia of Pureland hadn't strangled him like it did Salim. He never gave in to pathetic dreams of a glorious past. He only had one kind of dream—the American kind. And he walked down the streets like he owned them—speaking to strangers like they were relatives, eating the local grub like he had grown up on it. He wore his hair in a bandana, pulled on tight-fitting jeans; smoked Marlboros and drank beer. Before anyone could tell, Tamboo Charming had transformed himself, replacing Elvis lyrics with street talk. His most peculiar activity was spending countless hours staring into windows of ground-floor yoga studios, perplexed beyond his imagination. One night, he asked Salim about it.

"But how do people fall for this sort of shit?" he asked, sitting on the floor in a lotus pose with his eyes closed.

"In this city, people pay good money to learn new ways to be enlightened." Just as Salim said those words, a lightbulb went off with such force in Tamboo's mind that when he opened his eyes, Salim could have sworn a bell had rung.

Enlightenment, Tamboo whispered to himself.

The next day, Charming borrowed some money from Salim, filled out an application and rented out a studio in the Lower East Side. He bought several electric heaters, a record player, painted signs, dished out flyers and before anyone knew it, Blistering Yoga was born. Charming was out to teach the world a new way to live. It was a forgotten art form from the East, he had told his clients, which required minimal clothing and the only way to reach nirvana was to sweat your way there.

"Your pores are bent out of shape. You New Yorkers have forgotten how to sweat!" he cried, prior to each session, standing shirtless in a ponytail. "You have stifled your bodies with air conditioners. Your body doesn't know how to express itself anymore. How do you expect to find enlightenment?" Then he would stand with his hands on his hips and yell, "Breathe in. Breathe out." And as the class would begin limbering up, he would crank up the heaters and shout out his grand three-word mantra, "Sweat! Smell! Love!"

Blistering Yoga ignited a wildfire in the city. Pretty soon, the best kept secret of Khanpur had acquired a legion of devoted single girls and housewives from all five boroughs because Tamboo's only induction rule was: no men allowed. Men always sexualize everything; he would say with a grimace. Thus, the program's exclusivity propelled Charming to new heights. Before anyone could blink, his distinct methods of enlightenment spread in an emotionless, cold city that had forgotten how to sweat.

As Tamboo gained success and moved into his own apartment, Salim's fretful disquiet returned. The dread of the fatwa lingered over his head wherever he went. Tamboo could feel that his brother was falling off a melancholic cliff, but he was unable to do anything about it. The fatwa began to snatch away any little happiness he was able to bring to him. Salim's mounting paranoia made him isolate himself, forced him into evenings of solitude staring out of his apartment window. Everything frightened him; every loud noise, each slamming door, every unwanted knock on the door, made him jump with anxiety.

Until one summer day, on his way home from the university, Salim was followed by a tall shadow.

Engine

———•❦•———

Salim stopped mid-stride and swiveled around to confront the man who had been on his tail for a while.

"Come closer and you will have it!"

The stalker stood motionless. His eyes opened wide as he said, "Salim? Do you recognize me?"

Peering through his thick eyeglasses, Salim replied, "No."

"Salim, it's me, Nadeem," he said, as Salim delivered a cautious look. "Deema? Deema Engine from Khanpur. From Pureland."

Deema Engine? Could it be, Salim thought? General Khan's exalted bird?

"Deema? How did you find me?"

"I met your bagel vendor. The young boy, Tiger, from Bangladesh ... had to convince him that I wasn't out to kill you."

Salim paused for a moment and thought about when Billa Cycle had first told him about Deema Engine, and how he had marveled at the legend of the boy who escaped Khanpur.

"How do I know you're the real Deema?"

"Ask me anything about Khanpur."

"Name the barber."

"That's easy. Cut-Two Naii."

"Who began brewing ale at the mosque?"

"Pappu Pipewalla and, of course, your father, the painter."

"What's the remedy for every fever, every cough, every scraped knee?"

"Kino juice."

"Okay, tell me, then ... who does every child aspire to become?"

"Simple. They all want to be Deema Engine." Salim smiled then a giggle shook his chin.

"Wrong. They want to be Salim Agha." Tilting his head towards the street, he said, "Come let's take a walk."

As they began to talk, Salim's anxiousness began to flake off his body. He felt his heart slowing down. They both began to fall into a comfortable groove. "You see," Deema began, "I came to you for a specific reason as I feel we are alike, you and I, both sons of Khanpur, children of feudalism. Boss, we both were blessed—blessed to be sieved from the dirt and judged by our talents and not by the brown of our skin. You know..." He paused as they walked past a salivating pit-bull on a rather flimsy leash. "I recently heard about General Khan. He's not well."

"What do you mean?"

"I know what you may think, boss. I know what everyone thinks in that country. That Deema Engine is a good for nothing servant, that he is ungrateful. The truth is, I never once stopped praying for Khan Saab. All I wanted was to be my own man and not a charity case. I tried to contact him but his son, that wretched mongrel, he has imprisoned our beloved Khan Saab, Salim."

"How so?" Salim asked, as an old feeling he had kept in a small corner of his heart returned to him.

"I think you should see for yourself. Let me guess ... you have tried to reach him."

"I tried sending letters but..."

"But no one responded. That bastard, Khalil." Deema said, rolling his eyes. "I don't think Khan Saab has much time, boss. He won't live long trapped like an animal. Look at us now: Me, an engineer and inventor. And you, the great Dr. Agha, pioneer of physics. He lifted us from cow dung and gave us a life. We owe him."

They found a coffee house with outdoor seating and sat down to two steaming cups among the murmurs and distant clanking of plates. Raindrops of laughter mixed in the air, creating an endless buzz. In this honeycomb of soft mumbles, Deema Engine spoke loudly. His was a distinct voice. He plonked a large brick-like object on the table. "Everyone will be begging to have a cell phone one day boss, you'll see," he said in his provincial accent. "I helped make this thing, you know?"

He spoke of the wounds of exile and the desire for belonging. Their words intertwined as the light of dusk began to dwindle behind the skyline and Deema began to scratch his balls. It was an itch of cerebral activity. The more he thought, the harder he scratched, and by the time any meaningful clarity arrived, his genitals had been scraped raw.

"I think I've got it, boss," he said as he lifted his fingers from his crotch and placed them on the mug of coffee that lay between them. "Patents! We get bloody patents. Take the money for all the work and sit on our asses—patents!"

Salim nodded as if he were acknowledging a child's eagerness. "What do you need me for?"

"Dr. Salim, you have the science knowledge and I have done a few patents already. Combined, you and I can do something great. Do you want to swing pendulums your whole life? We can make money like no one has seen and use it for whatever we want. I know you science types. You can use it for your own research, boss."

It was an interesting thought. One that Salim was not paying full attention to at the time as the sunset brought a chocolate glow to the atmosphere. He abruptly stood and said, "It has been great meeting you, Deema Saab. I will keep in touch with you for sure." The two men wrapped their arms around each other. Salim took in a whiff of his scent as he closed his eyes, hoping it would take him back to a place he knew long ago.

Exile can be a painful state, sir, let me tell you. A dreadful punishment that brings with it the crippling sorrow of estrangement. Salim had endured this for years and was imprisoned by it. That day, though, he discovered a souvenir. It opened up a part of him that he had kept locked away. Nostalgia, too, can be agonizing. He hadn't felt it in a while, but an agonizing nostalgia had returned. Deema's voice revealed to him the inconsolability of his past and a perpetual bitterness about the present and the future. He felt the pain of regret and banishment. Nostalgia makes you treasure the simple things of the past because it is the simple things that remind you of who you are. In Deema's breath, Salim could smell the soft earth of his village after rainfall, and in his voice, he could hear the crashing of the Canal of Fables against the shallow bridge. Simple things.

That night, Deema's words settled like winter's first snow on Salim's heart, slowly and gradually drifting into a pile. Those words became a reminder that his life had once been filled with beautiful noises and now there was nothing but silence and loneliness. And there was something about feeling another's loneliness that made him feel loved again. He felt the love Deema had for General Khan. In some weird way, that adoration seeped into Salim's skin as well. The thought of Khan suffering in his old age bothered him. Sleep didn't come easy to him that night. His heart began to ache for Khan. More importantly, it ached for Pureland.

In his mind, strange thoughts arose. A moment arrived from the past, an image burning behind his eyes, of a soundless child, his fingers wrapped around his father's wrist, and there, not too far away, a hovering, silver-haired saint who looks upon the father and declares: 'O foolish Painter, he will change our world forever.'

Salim began to shudder. Change our world, he thought. "All this while, Salim Agha, you thought you had achieved everything, reached your destiny? You're a fool to think that. What if your destiny was to destroy, and not to save?" he asked himself, as a tremor crept up his leg. "What if you were meant to do just that? Or did just that? Destroyed something you loved." Another image appeared without warning: a young boy, he has a pen in his hand, huddled over him are cigar-scented uniforms, and below him a map, and on the map a triangle, and on the triangle a numeric conclusion, and hidden in the numbers a recipe for calamity. Salim's shivers multiplied.

This novel perspective on his prophecy pummeled him with remorse. He couldn't help but give in to the possibility of a cosmic message gone wrong, all wrong. This guilt led to something else. Salim's legs quaked until he fell to the ground, and he trembled in agony until he finally fell asleep.

When he awoke from those strange dreams, he found himself in a hospital. It hadn't happened in a while, but his epilepsy had returned. It was nothing to be too scared about, the doctors had concluded, but nonetheless precaution was prescribed. Take it easy, they said, as Tamboo Charming escorted him out of the ER. But taking it easy was not what Salim had in mind.

"You can't possibly go back there!" said Chip the following morning in his apartment, upon hearing of Salim's decision to return to Pureland. "I do like my job, Doc. If they slay you, I'll go broke! And you just got out of the hospital. You tell him something, Charming! Don't just stand there looking like a stop sign."

"She's right, brother," said Tamboo Charming. "I can't lose you to that hellhole."

"I understand what you are both saying. But after all, this life was a gift. If I do not return it to its rightful owner, it will weigh on me for eternity."

"Gifts are for keeping brother, not returning."

"Tamboo, gifts of honor must be repaid honorably, otherwise they become burdens. This life is on lease and I think it's time to pay the final installment."

The Pact a Soul Makes

Sir, here I shall tell you about the Lorr of 1987, the city of my childhood. Just thinking about it torments me and I can understand the tragic longing that plagued Salim Agha. I can understand why his love for Pureland became an inescapable thing. I want to tell you since there's no other way to know because, like I said, all knowledge of our past has been wiped clean. It goes without saying that the wasteland that exists today is not the Lorr that I recall.

Conquerors have come and gone throughout our history, but we never forgot who we were. This time, when the Caliphate arrived, they hypnotized us and watched as we demolished ourselves. They used the very idea of Pureland and its wholesomeness against us, and we didn't flinch. Burn it all, we chanted.

We should have seen it coming. Like I mentioned before, our world was made fragile a long time ago. For some reason, even amid such brittle instability, we remained hopeful. Even back in 1987, as the dictator General Zaid strangled us with military curfew, I remember looking out of my window at night knowing that revolution was only a whisper away.

I recall this one day, on my way home from school—there was a bonfire. The flames were high, and they kept rising, that is to say, things kept being thrown in—unusual things. That afternoon, up on the Mall near the church, Zaid's Military Police had arrived with a purpose and boy, did they mean business. The fire was a spectacle for all to see, a public warning of sorts. The Lorr Jazz Ensemble, with tears in their eyes, stood by in an airless silence as their livelihoods were set ablaze before them. Then, suddenly, there was this lunatic: the saxophone player. I can't remember his name. Let's just call him Samson. Why? Because I recall he had long untamed hair that swung below his shoulders, golden hoops that dangled from his ears, and a silver crucifix that peered out through his unbuttoned shirt. Most of all, I remember the audacity that shone from his eyes. When his instrument was thrown into the fire, he walked through the crowd in a deliberate canter, right past me, removed his shirt, lunged into the flames, and yanked his sax back out. His hands, I can imagine, scalded immediately, but that didn't stop him. He wrapped his shirt around the sax, put his lips to the mouthpiece and began to play the most remarkable melody I had ever heard. That tone, the silkiness of his breath, the way he made the notes linger in the air with an anticipated magnificence—it continues to echo in my mind to this day. It awakens me from the deepest of sleep. It's why revisiting that memory brings me to tears.

Nothing mattered to Samson. It was as though the world around him had evaporated and there he stood, upon an invisible stage. We, the audience, couldn't help but let our jaws fall to the ground and admire that impudent bravery which blew through the air in the scale of D Minor.

I've listened to "In a Sentimental Mood" thousands of times since that day. I've even heard Johnny Coltrane's live recording from Lincoln Center—pure magic. Let me tell you, sir, nothing—nothing—compares to what Samson delivered that day on the Mall Road. Although it seemed like an eternity, that performance, it only lasted for a minute. In those sixty seconds, as the MPs gathered their comprehension and tightened their fists, Samson had secured victory. He just kept playing, with his palms in blisters, head bombarded with batons, army boots pressing his knees to the floor. That bastard just kept on playing until the rifle butts bludgeoned him into stillness.

I don't know what happened to Samson after that. I don't want to know.

Sorry. I need to compose myself a little before we continue...

As the plane touched the tarmac, Salim's soul fell to the earth as though it had waited all these years to reattach itself, like a droplet of mercury fusing to a puddle. The airplane door opened to let in the sugary fragrance that he knew so well. He stood for a moment among the shuffling crowds, breathing in Lorr.

Just outside the airport, the city assaulted his senses. He stood still among a swarm, taking in the incursion as though it were a gift. The tiniest of tears squeezed out from his eyes and made a streak as it slid down his face. The air was dense with a musky whisper. He stood mesmerized like many travelers had been before him, thousands of years ago when the city was a vivacious caravanserai, where silk traders from the east and gold mongers from the west met at the intersection of the world. This was Lorr. Her most seductive ploy was to make you believe she was yours. The cracking sounds of the rickshaws, the raw body odors, the elbow nudges, and the crass provincial shrieks of street hawkers let Salim know that he was home. Welcome, they said.

"What's your name, sir?" Salim asked the driver of a 1986 Toyota Corolla rental car that Deema Engine had arranged for him.

"Fez," replied the driver.

"Right, Fez Saab. Could you take me all the way into the walled city and drive back up the Mall to the Cantonment?"

"Of course, sir. Please, you can call me just Fez," he said, whizzing out of the airport on towards the old city.

Kissed by the morning rays, Lorr was molten gold. The misty crimson of the colonial homes frolicked with the hue of her morning breath which rose up from the earth with a distinct fragrance. She was divine—her subtle yellow reflection bounced off the Canal of Fables, while in the distant walled city, her cramped havelis towered over each other. If you woke up before she did, you would realize that there was no one more beautiful than her. Salim closed his eyes, tasted her breath and took in the sounds his city made as she awoke.

The car rolled up the Mall Road where eucalyptus trees on either side bowed to embrace each other, sheltering the pavement below. It was where Salim had once sat on top of a bicycle frame while Jaaji pedaled towards St. Andrew's Church. He remembered how the painter often lost his balance while avoiding potholes and shook the handlebars violently. Most of the time, they both fell on to the road with a thud. During those years, he accumulated scars that stained his shins, like permanent post-it notes reminding him of that time. He had become a skilled tumbler, and would sense, with the slightest turbulence, which way the bicycle was headed and would launch himself in the opposite direction, landing like a feline while his father slammed into the sidewalk.

On the Mall across the canal the Governor's House shuffled by, with its unending shrub-encased white columns and gold-plated gates. Then there was Lawrence Gardens upon the hill and shortly after, the Lorr Zoo, where Kipling's father was once the curator and where little Rudyard sat as a child whispering to animals, concocting tales. Up towards the gates of the scarlet brick campus of St. Walter Blisschesterson Boys College, he saw future aristocrats walking in, and he couldn't help wondering if any of them secretly served a master on their day off.

As the car made its way over the Garrison Bridge towards the Cantonment, he felt unwelcome. The last time he rode over this bridge was when he had been banished—dispelled from the Khan House. Now, as he looked through his own reflection in the window, he knew he could own one of these bungalows and perhaps a set of servants himself. Was it that easy? To own property in the Cantonment, sit in air-conditioned rooms on gaudy furniture, hollering at bumbling serfs? But would anyone ever accept him? It was difficult to know the answer to that. He rolled down his window as the car fired past a rickshaw. Burnt diesel-fuel blew onto his face as he smiled, while his driver covered his nose. The car lumbered past villa after villa until it pulled up at the iron gates of the Khan House. The house didn't seem as grand as it once had. There were other buildings its size all over the place. The gates creaked open, revealing a tiny man who approached the car with watchful baby-steps.

"Is General Khan home?" Salim asked, as the bashful guard withdrew inside, emerging moments later like a hare under threat, thrusting open the gate with his tiny body.

Salim saw the busy structures that lay before him. The garden, where flowers once spoke in varied scents and where the foliage waltzed to monsoon winds, had shrunk. The servant quarters had given way to a new house, a bungalow that smothered the spot where a mango tree had played host to hide-and-seek—where he would brush his nose against Laila's hair. The terrace was gone too. The pigeon pen no longer guarded the main house from up top. There was no cobblestone driveway either and the banyan tree, which had a canopy that spread over forty feet, had been murdered. In place of all these memories now stood two houses facing each other with a slim road leading to the back alley.

The guard directed him inside the old Khan House, under the white pillared arches. Salim walked to the living room and sat down, as a reed-thin boy rolled in a trolley of orange sherbet.

Looking around the room, he noticed that the paintings on the wall had vanished. Khan's Turkish miniatures had been swapped with black-and-white calligraphy. The photographs of Laila's mother and of the children that once sat watchfully above the dining table were no longer there. In fact, there were no photographs at all and the room felt bigger than it was with him sitting alone in the middle, like a suspect held for questioning. It was very quiet until he heard a roaring voice. An unfamiliar figure entered. He had a long beard, no mustache, and wore a white skullcap.

"So, the famous Dr. Salim Agha comes back to the Khan House."

Salim stood to greet him. "Don't remember me? It is I, Khalil." Salim shook his hand again and tried to enforce the customary Blisschestorsonian embrace: handshake, hug, handshake.

"Khalil, I'm sorry I didn't recognize you. How've you been?"

"I am good Salim, I am good by the grace of Allah. It's a surprise to see you here after ... how long has it been, almost twenty years?" asked Khalil, pulling up his sleeves, grabbing one of the orange beverages. He sat down, one foot on the sofa. A dark callous sat on his forehead—an indication that he touched his brow to the prayer mat at least five times a day and possibly the optional sixth. It was a nuisance for an onlooker, but for Khalil it was a trophy of his piousness. "I heard the president booted you out of the country. So sad, but it was typical of you to challenge authority, no? And that fatwa against you?" He sucked his teeth. "So sad, no? That too by that rodent Zaid who used to wag his tail around Daddy like a dog."

"The fatwa is Zaid's way of taking revenge," said Salim. "He asked me to help him make the nuclear bomb."

"Nuclear bomb?"

"Yes, a bomb."

"And he wanted you to make it?"

"I think he wanted my help. He called me after I won the Nobel, after he had taken over. But I refused. This whole fatwa thing is just a joke, if you ask me. I bet he hasn't even read my book. Listen, I'm not here to discuss politics. I want to see General Saab. I've written to him many times. How is he? I've heard he's not well."

"Yes, I know you must have heard." Khalil put his glass down on a coffee table and clicked his fingers. The thin servant boy responded with the urgency of a famished dog and refilled the glass. "So you've been talking with that bastard Deema Engine. After all we gave him. Son of a transvestite! You think that sister-fucker would have been anything if Daddy had left him in that village?" He took a large sip and set the glass down again. "So, what do you want now? You used us when it was convenient for you and then left Daddy alone. Now you're back, wanting to see him, showing off your English suit and your English boots."

They're Italian boots, asshole, Salim thought. Out loud he said, "Please Khalil, I just want to see how he is. I've never forgotten for a single day what he did for me. You have to understand, I have something for him. It's important." He could sense where his letters must have ended up—in a pile of burnt rubbish. "I want to see Gibran. Even if it's just once, I want to see..."

"Don't say her name with your filthy mouth, for God as my witness, if you say her name, I will rip your tongue out!" There was a dense silence, rich enough to have a gravity of its own, pulling down everything in the room.

"I know Laila is married, Khalil. You're still part of my childhood and I just wanted to see that you're all well. There's no cause for such anger. We are all adults now."

"Fine," Khalil said, swiping his tongue over his teeth. "What did you bring for Daddy then?"

"That's something I will only share with him, I'm afraid," Salim persisted as Khalil's frown turned into a sly grin and he began to rub the callous on his forehead. Then he yelled for the skeleton boy, "Where did you go, sister-fucker? Do you not hear me calling?"

The boy looked down at the floor. Khalil raised his hand and slammed it into his neck, as a loud echo caused a tremor in Salim's ribs. "Good servants are hard to find these days. Not like they used to be. We have to bring them in from the village, good feudal servants. But they can be such simpletons, like this fellow here. They have to be herded like buffaloes. Of course, you know all about herding, right Salim?"

The boy walked up closer to his master and Khalil gave him a kick in the shins.

"Take our guest to see the old man, I will join you in a minute." Khalil snapped his fingers.

Before he could say another word, Salim left the living room in anger, his nostrils quivering. The boy followed, overtaking him up the steps. From the thin pubescent mustache that lined his upper lip, he could tell that the boy was no older than thirteen, his expressionlessness indeed supporting the claim that he was like cattle: no opinion and no soul.

As he climbed the old staircase with its pearly white banister, Salim felt the velvet carpet against his toes. It was as opulent as he remembered, and he could feel the Spanish marble underneath. The boy led him further up the house to the third floor, to an eerie, dark hallway. His footsteps slowed as he eyed the dim passage that lay before him. The floor was dusty. Salim followed his guide as they approached a closed door. This situation was too familiar, a life reduced to meal trays and newspapers.

The skeleton boy wrapped his bony fingers into a fist and tapped on the door.

"Who is it?"

"General Saab, there's a guest here to see you."

"Send them inside and go get me my lunch. And how many times have I told you to bring marmalade in the morning, not jam?"

The door swung open and Salim's eyes scanned the room. It had shrunk in size since the last time he was there. Nearly unnoticeable, in the corner, was a skinny carcass sitting on the bed, with his elbows propping up his body. A hand swiped at wild silver hair that spread like foliage. The old man was pale. He had not read his morning newspaper in the garden in quite a while. His face was gaunt and deep wrinkles creased the back of his neck. For a moment, Salim imagined the neatly combed, side-parted hair, oiled mustache, and white safari suit from the time he first met him. He tried to see him like that but he could not. He wouldn't have recognized General Khan at all if it weren't for his eyes. They were greener than the ocean and they opened wide to receive him.

"Salim? Salim, is that you?" he asked, sliding his palm over his forehead, fending off an imaginary sun.

"General Saab, it is me ... wait, what are you doing, please keep sitting," he said reaching out to grab his arms. General Khan hung on to him and embraced him. His hands trembled as they enveloped Salim's shoulders. Salim could feel the softness of his skin against his cheek—he shut his eyes, crushing a puddle of tears.

"General Saab, how are you? Why are you locked up in here?"

Khan sighed, managing a painful smile, "What can I say? Tyranny is a funny thing. It approaches from where you least expect it. Besides, I cannot fool my own fate now." He sighed again. "Old age can be harsh. I don't mind anything, just the frailty. You tell me. I was worried about you. So worried. That bastard Zaid. I knew he was a weasel from the start. I saw it in his fake smile every time we joked at his expense. I always felt like he was up to something. I hear he has taken your work out of the schoolbooks my grandchildren read. I get some foreign newspapers from time to time. There's mention of Dr. Agha this and Dr. Agha that. It makes my heart grow ten times in size, you know?" He tapped his chest which was once wide like a barrel and now hung loosely from his bones. His skin was covered with brown blotches that ran down from his face to his hands. The old man emanated a peculiar smell, earthy and rank. Salim absorbed these odors as they spread through the room.

Then a realization crept up on him. He was wrong about Khan's love. The General had never stopped loving him. He could tell from the way his eyes received him, as if they had been waiting for him this whole time. And Salim? Well, the painful exit from the Khan House had hurt him for years, but he had learned to let it go. Deema's words had only brought back a buried fondness.

"It's nothing, General Saab. There's nothing there but the result of the seeds you had sown. And about that Zaid ... it was a vendetta against me from the first time we met in this very house. He cannot help it. He's deranged. Do you remember that night?"

"I remember that, I remember that," he said. "How he tried to show off in front of me. You did put the bastard in his place, though. No one in the army thought this fool would make it further than a one-star brigadier, let alone a general. And when he got his chance, he stabbed us all in the back." He shook his head. Then he looked over his shoulder at the door. "Would you like a drink?" Salim raised his hands in front of his chest. "Oh, come on now, boy. Don't tell me you don't have a drink once in a while. You're old enough now. Grab the glasses over there and go into the closet. There's an old medicine bottle. Pour us one, would you? Like old times."

Walking to the closet, Salim looked up at the ceiling fan that creaked at every revolution, its blades slicing through the warm air, making the room denser. His three-piece suit suddenly felt suffocating. He opened the closet and bent low to find the medicine bottle. Deep in the musky stench of moth balls and old shoes emerged Johnnie Walker as he'd never seen him before—in a misleading outfit: Hydrylin Cough Syrup. 'Two teaspoons twice a day,' it read. Salim recalled another dosage: two fingers Scotch, one water. Like old times indeed, he thought, as he poured the liquid into the iceless tumblers that lay on the dresser. Nearby, a jug with a knitted cloth over its mouth held stale water. He shook it gently as if to freshen up the water, then poured.

Khan began to flutter his fingers like butterfly wings, signaling to bolt the door. Salim did so and sat down. Tumbler kissed tumbler. Cheers.

"I've brought you something, General Saab. I thought you'd like to see."

"You see, this Khalil, since he's become a bloody mullah it's become impossible to even drink in peace. Always buggering someone or another with bloody religion," Khan muttered to himself. "Even his children live and breathe the damn thing—religion that is. Like a bad medicine they drink it. They too will get intoxicated by it. I feel for them. This is child abuse, I tell you. This entire country has gone bonkers. What can I say? I'm just an old man, one foot in the grave, one out." The General put his glass down beside his false teeth, a half-empty leaf of tablets, and a flashlight. His feet, dangling off the bed, began to kick as if he were a toddler on a park bench. The bed was elevated from the ground with bricks and the floor below had not been swept in days. The soles of his feet were smeared with dust. In that very moment, it occurred to Salim how isolation could crush even the strongest of wills.

"General Saab," he said, making eye contact. "I have something for you."

"Oh ... you brought me a gift, have you?"

"We had left on such horrid terms all those years ago. But I want you to know that I never stopped loving you. I never once forgot what you did for this boy from the village." He took a deep breath to stop his tears. "I've launched a scholarship in your name, sir. The Zafar Khan Theoretical Physics Fund. It's for underprivileged children from all over the world. This is the plaque they presented me." Salim pulled out a gold square from his vest. Khan took the plaque between his fingers and raised it to his face. His mouth quivered and tears found their way to his eyes again.

"Salim ... this is really something. I don't have the words ... thank you, Salim. Thank you for your kindness."

"Please, General Saab. It doesn't compare to what you have done."

Khan placed the plaque carefully next to the medication and flashlight on his side table, and even before there was an interruption, the atmosphere in the room immediately began to change.

"Open the damn door!" Khalil's voice made the sliding bolt shiver. Salim leapt from the bed and opened the door. "Why is your door locked, Daddy. What has Salim come to show you now? How rich he's become? Did you ask him where he was all these years?" General Khan's face dimmed along with any lingering joy in the room. He looked at his hands like a child.

"Oh look!" Khalil said, lifting the tumbler in the air. "The professor is giving Daddy his poison to finally kill him off!"

"It was not Salim's idea. I wanted a drink with him," Khan moaned.

"A drink? You're not supposed to have any drinks Daddy—zero. And you ... you come back after all these years and try to poison my father?"

"No, Khalil. I've just come to give General Saab a gift. I've opened a fund in his name and..."

"A fund?" asked Khalil. "What kind of fund? Are you going to give money to General Zafar Khan now?"

"It's a scholarship..."

"So, you're not giving him any money then. What a shame! At least you could have paid your dues. All the years of tuition at Blisschesterson," he said, as he waved his arms. A cloud of stillness settled, and the fan could be heard slicing away in the background. Salim swallowed hard, rose from the bed, took General Khan's hand and kissed it, putting his palms on his forehead. It was not the farewell he had hoped for. He closed his eyes and imagined a safari suit, those tan leather shoes tiptoeing over puddles, and the mighty Khan, scepter in hand, with one arm around his shoulder.

"Goodbye, Khan Saab. I will return again."

Khan's eyes pleaded with him to stay, but his warden's shadow fell over him, stifling his words. "I hope," he said, shaking, "I hope we meet again, my boy."

Salim closed his eyes and pulled himself towards the staircase, then down to the front door. He stopped for a second as a glass shattered in the upstairs bedroom.

"He was trying to kill you, Daddy! Why don't you see that?" Khalil roared.

Salim's breath quickened and his fingers locked into a fist as he looked up the staircase.

"You're the one who's killing him! You have no right to be his son!" he cried as the door flew open.

"You fucking servant, I will have you thrown out like the infidel trash you are!"

Before Khalil could make for the stairs, Salim stormed out of the house in a cloud of fury. The afternoon sun, his jet lag, and anger, all added to a brewing hostility inside him. As he walked out of the house, his feet carried him of their own accord towards where the servant quarters used to be. He wasn't sure why his body reacted in this manner, pulling him towards the back of the kitchen. He probably yearned to see those rooms again, but as he came closer, he could see those small dwellings fading from the mist of his memory, turning into a double-storey bungalow.

"Salim! You're here!" Gibran shouted from the balcony above the gate. Salim looked up to see him—handsome, long-haired, cigarette on the bend of his lip. "Come inside, Salim. It's hot," he said, and Salim obliged. He was welcomed at the door by a tight hug and incessant pats on the back.

"Oh my, how are you Gibran? Looks like you've made quite a bachelor pad for yourself." He was taken to the living room where the house servants had been summoned and, as expected, orange sherbet arrived on a silver tray.

"Bachelor pad. Hardly so Salim. After Daddy's illness, Khalil has been after me to get married. I can't just get married like that, you know?"

"Khan Saab's illness? What is it?"

"You know, old age, liver, heart. A bottle a day can do that to you. Really sad."

"This is all so surreal you know ... I just met your brother. Not too happy to see me, I think."

"Don't mind him. Planning for Daddy's death since he sold Khanpur. Have you been to Khanpur?"

"Khanpur? No, I have no family there anymore. My mother passed and Tamboo lives in New York now."

"Hahaha! Tamboo Charming. How is that fucker? You know, I let him hide in our house when he ran from Khanpur? He fucked every girl in town. What a man! As for my brother, forget him ... Do you know Daddy sleeps under his bed? Doesn't know when it's coming, but he knows his death is in his son's hands. A little paranoid I'd say."

Gibran's mullet fell over a t-shirt that stretched around his biceps. Through the living room door, Salim could see a staircase. There, at the top, were a woman's legs. She bent down to peep through the bannister. The living room was smothered with artwork and family photos. One in particular caught his gaze—a graceful bride with lowered eyes. She looked more beautiful than his memory had permitted him to believe. But it was an obedient new bride, staring down, devoid of emotion, like new brides should be. He convinced himself that she was thinking of him at that exact moment, just as he had thought about her at every moment.

"Laila got married?" he asked as an afterthought, speaking to himself more than anyone else, as if he needed a reminder.

"Hmmm ... a few years ago, I think maybe eight. She married an army man, what a surprise, right? That guy, Liber Ali, General Ali's son. Oh, and guess what? Aunty Tezi ran off with General Ali. They now live in Canada or something. What a circus, no Salim? I wonder what ever happened to the Raja of Bill-Qul. That fat fuck must be beating his head against a wall somewhere. Did you hear about Khanpur?"

Salim was lost, sinking deep into the picture frame. Far away in the cosmos, angels gathered, peeking over each other. He closed his eyes and remembered Stockholm—the scent of her perfume on his pillow, her sly touch under the table. Nothing to him ever felt that good—the angels slapped their foreheads.

"Khalil sold Khanpur to some local businessman and as soon as he did, the property value doubled. We really got fucked. As if that wasn't enough, the moron then put all the money in some Islamic fund with no interest. Lost it all!" Gibran reached into his pocket to extract a pack of Marlboros. The cigarettes had their tips squeezed into triangles. He lit one, breathed in and blew smoke towards the ceiling. The smoldering stick plumed more than Salim anticipated and the room began to smell like ground meat. Khalil offered him one but he refused with a shake of the head. "So, tell me. What are you doing in our humble town?"

"I just had to return. I've always wanted to. My body feels at ease here for some reason. It's as if your soul makes a pact with the earth when you're born."

Salim's gaze landed on Gibran's lips, which were darkened by years of cigarette and hashish smoke. However, his bronze smile was intractable.

"I like that, man. The soul making a pact... It's beautiful. Yes, despite the curfew and everything, you truly feel at ease here."

Salim felt sympathy for the General, who had spent his entire life constructing a world for his boys, a world others could only dream of, only to have them smoke it away on afternoons like this one.

"Very good man, very good. Oh, and don't mind her," he said of the legs that reappeared, tiptoeing on high arches and painted nails. "Stayed over last night." He winked.

Whiskey tumblers, that Salim assumed were inherited from the main house, littered the room, cigarettes dipped into them, overflowing from the edge. The servants had not cleaned up after the party the night before.

A commotion erupted outside. A yelling master and shuffling servants approached Gibran's gate. By the time he realized it, the room was clogged with smoke and it was difficult to see.

"Oh! Don't worry about him. Khalil's always fucking shouting at these poor servants," said Gibran. Salim had caused this. An army had gathered to ambush him. Their sticks could be seen from over the top of the gate. Hands began to creep up the wall followed by a tiny head.

"Gibran, I wanted to meet you all."

Salim swallowed. His mouth had suddenly dried out. "I want to meet Laila before I leave, do you know where I can find her? Is there a number I can call? Please help me, Gibran, I don't have much time."

Gibran's eyes fell on Salim's shoes, then his suit, then back to his shoes.

"Those are damn nice shoes, Professor Saab—all shiny," he paused. "Yes, Laila lives right here in the Cantonment. Do you have a pen?" Salim extracted a pen from his shirt pocket like a fencer. Gibran spilled some numbers from his lips while rubbing his forehead as if to extract the information by force, and Salim jotted ferociously on a piece of newspaper. Outside the living room window, the skeleton boy walked past, stopped, reversed, and pointed directly at his target with his nose pressed flat against the glass. The noise grew louder.

"Gibran, I think I better leave. I will be back soon though," Salim said. Gibran rose up from the sofa and wrapped his arms around him. This hug was different from the one Khalil had given him earlier. It was like the one he used to give him when he was little. An embrace one would give to a loved one.

Before the brigade of scorned servants invaded Gibran's house, Salim jumped the back wall like an alley cat, a place his legs knew from memory. He came out into the lane and ran to the main road. His rental car was gone. He was fucked.

"There he is! On the main street! Quick, he's getting into a rickshaw!"

Salim glanced behind him, maneuvering himself into the rickshaw, patting a hundred rupee note on the driver's shoulder. "Fast!" he cried. The hollering servants were drowned out by the deafening blasts of the rickshaw. He turned his head away from them, breathing calmly; his pounding heart slowed down as the Khan House staff and their master were left coughing in the smoke.

The rickshaw screamed through the streets of the Cantonment and over the bridge. Underneath, the railway tracks cut through the teaming slums and children walked on them as though they were tightropes. The call to prayer boomed from megaphones that clung to minarets. One cry ended and another began like a disjointed children's choir. It was haunting. This was a different Lorr from what he remembered. He pushed through the blue plastic doors of the rickshaw and peered at the people on the street. There was a force that drained their faces. A gravity that pulled their smiles into frowns. It was a fear he had not seen before. And God, well, he was everywhere. On juice boxes, billboards, newspapers, on TV and radio, and hell, even on the inside of the rickshaw, inked in white, there was a propitiating phrase: *Allah de havale*. In God's custody. It seemed that he was here to stay, this God. Salim's worst fears about his nation were coming true before him. He was witnessing Zaid's God firsthand. Because once a god is made, he cannot be unmade—he becomes untouchable, un-debatable—immortal.

The Captive Beloved

———⋆✿⋆———

I struggle with insomnia from time to time. It's worse than any disease I've ever had, sir—the worst. The agony swells as the minutes tick by. Endless thoughts bombard my senses; my heart beats through my ears as the body wilts away under fatigue. In those restless moments, I dream with open eyes—of everything and nothing, of sadness and glee, madness and sanity. I lie awake in a prison of my own thoughts, at times wishing for death to sweep me away.

Something similar happened to Salim that night when he returned to the hotel. He tried to sleep but his mind wouldn't let him. A preposterous exhilaration had overtaken his soul. Somehow, he felt that at every corner he would see a shirtless rickshaw-puller tugging an overweight Saab, or a marching band strutting down Davis Road, or young lovers in bellbottoms, tugging at each other's elbows at the Regal as they walked in for a matinee, or maybe tiptoeing past the cigar lounge where Khan would meet his friends for a drink and listen to jazz. Perhaps he thought that if he looked hard enough, he would find his Lorr. But lovers can have a heartless way about them sometimes. Lorr had changed. But he could not come to terms with that just yet. So he stepped out again, to discover his beloved as he remembered her.

"Sir, please be aware there's curfew at eight, we have to warn our guests," the concierge pleaded, as Salim waited for his rental car in the hotel driveway.

The word curfew infuriated him. He ignored the man and tumbled into the backseat of the car.

"Fez, just drive me through the inner streets of the city. Try and avoid any MP checkpoints. These Military Police boys are the worst. Just drive my friend, drive. I want to see Lorr at night."

Fez, the veteran driver from Rolla Paya Luxury Rentals who had earlier driven him to the hotel from the Khan House, begged Salim for forgiveness. He claimed that he had left him at the Khan House because he was confused about whether to stay or leave since no instructions had been given to him. So, he just drove back. Expecting Salim to be furious at him, Fez bowed his head, waiting for a lashing. But instead, Salim said it was alright and shoved an entire month's salary into his palms. Then he asked that he stay with him for the duration of his trip. Shocked, staring down at his hand, Fez nodded and thanked Salim by saluting him.

"See Lorr at night? Anything for you, Saab." After adjusting the rear-view mirror, Fez slammed his foot on the accelerator, and screeched out of the driveway.

The streets of Lorr were dim at night and there were potholes that made the car's headlights bounce as objects shone in and out of vision. An occasional cyclist suddenly emerged, or a stray dog's eyes shone back in stunned stillness, but otherwise there was infinite blackness. The Canal of Fables, which used to shine with colored light bulbs at night, was invisible and curled by in a muffled whisper. There was nothingness as far as Salim could see. Until, in his bleak view, a white vehicle appeared, pulled over to the side of the road. Its doors were held ajar by two motorcycle helmets towering over a woman in a shiny outfit. Arms swung. Struggle.

Salim asked Fez to stop near the action.

"Hand me that crook-lock, Fez," he said, and made towards the helmets with the metal boomerang in his hand.

"Leave her," he roared, as the helmets turned their eyes, peering through open visors. One of them walked towards him, waving his finger like a conductor.

He removed his helmet saying, "Listen, English Saab, this is not your territory. You better get out of here before you get hurt." Looking right back at the boy, Salim tightened his grip, his white knuckles revealing his determination. The boy didn't notice the crook-lock against the black background; it reached his face rapidly and whipped his cheekbone. He collapsed on to the road. Pushing with his hands, he tried to rise but fell flat again. The other, noticing his buddy's defeat, immediately released the woman's arm, mounted his motorcycle, and bolted.

Salim walked over to the boy. A wound had opened his cheek and blood trickled down his chin.

"You'll need a couple of stitches, young man. You're not good at this stuff. I think you should choose another profession," Salim said, as the boy held his face with both hands, staring back through his fingers at his attacker. He didn't know whether to thank him or to run for his life. After a few hesitant seconds, he pulled himself up, swung his legs around his bike and disappeared into the darkness.

"Please get in your car. We will follow you to your home, Madam," said Salim, gathering the woman's belongings from the road: a bag, a couple of gold bangles, and a pack of Benson & Hedges. Fez helped the lady into her car. She looked towards Salim, like a feline confused about who her proprietor was.

"Thank you, Mister. You really are a saint. They would have taken everything had you not come. These days ... I can't tell you. It's mayhem in this city," she said, lighting her cigarette. She closed her door and rolled her window down to ask, "What's your name?" Her breath was sponsored by the brand she smoked.

"I'm Salim. You should leave. We can follow you." Through her freshly curled fringe, she eyed her savior as though she'd devour him. Then she flicked the ash of her cigarette out the window, pouted, and started the engine. Salim peddled backwards and slid into the front seat of his car. Before he knew it, she was off like a scalded squirrel. Fez tried to follow her but failed. She was too quick, even for him. After they reached a discernible army checkpoint, Fez gave up the chase. There was a look of defeat on his face, the kind one would get upon losing a sure-shot wager.

"Saab, you think it was her car or is she a good driver?"

"The hotel please, Fez Saab. She will be fine in this neighborhood. And it's her car. You're a far better driver."

Salim sank into his seat as the car weaved its way through the darkness back towards the Mall.

The hotel was prison-like at night. It wasn't the way he had remembered it. He recalled the first time he'd come to that hotel. He was with Mitti Pao. They had snuck into the nightclub in their senior year and drank martinis with socialite aunties until Mitti unfolded his dinner on the dancefloor. The guards threw Mitti out because he threatened to have them all killed. Now, in place of that old club was a sleepy coffee shop. Upstairs in his hotel room, Salim stripped off his clothes and slammed on to the bed.

The morning roared in through the slits in the curtain. With it, came a sense of urgency. Salim had two days left in the city. Meeting General Khan again was out of the question and an encounter with Laila was a long shot. All in all, he'd had a grand cluster-fuck of a time. He pictured Tamboo Charming's annoying nostrils and the way they would flare up when told about these incidents. It was something he would do when one of his many predictions became reality, as if to say, 'I told you so'. This time, Salim thought to himself, perhaps Charming and Chip were both right about returning to Pureland.

He pulled the piece of paper from his shirt pocket. The phone number had been smudged by sweat. He lunged outside to grab the morning newspaper when his eye caught hold of a headline.

Salim Agha Returns Under Fatwa

Fuck, he thought, as a visual played in his mind of his hands tied to his feet, in the back of an army truck. It was very possible. Should have been more careful, he thought. Then he recalled what Chip had said to him before he left New York.

"Be careful, Doc. I heard, in a heathen hungry country, a blasphemer is hanged to death in full view of frightened onlookers. You know, Doc, blasphemy is like poisonous gas in a windowless room!"

He lifted the rotary phone from the side table and spun the dial. After a few failed attempts, a ring tone made him sit upright.

"Hello, is this Laila Khan?"

"Who is this?"

"This is Salim," he said, fiddling with the curtains, phone receiver tucked under his chin.

"Salim? Where are you?" asked Laila. Her voice tightened his muscles. It took him a shudder to begin talking again.

"I'm here in Lorr. I want to see you."

"Salim... how did you get my number?" He told her, to which she said, "Can't talk right now. Meet me at Pasta at two this afternoon," and hung up. He listened to the dial tone for a few seconds, then jolted into action. He took a hot shower, shaved, clipped his toenails, and trimmed his nose hair. He ironed his shirt in corners he had not ironed before and laid it on the bed, then dropped down on the carpet, pumped out ten pushups and fell panting on to the floor. He rolled up into a downward dog position and managed to pump out ten more. After all that, he still had four hours to go. In a way, he felt like the boy he had once been. Weird, I know, but I guess love does that to grown men. After all, she had only given him a time and place—it wasn't like she'd asked him to run around a banyan tree in the Lawrence Gardens and make love to her on a bed of jasmines.

He called for breakfast to be delivered to his room and switched on the TV, turning the dial to the only available, nationally-run channel. In the shadowy place between waking and slumber, between day and night, which had become his habitat, he tried to watch the confusing programs; his eyes glazed with confusion.

First, there was the call to prayer, then the news delivered by an exquisite woman in a headscarf, followed by head-bobbing children reciting from religious scriptures. This carried on for three hours. As he sat on his bed, watching a TV show describing how to properly start a tractor engine, he dialed the front desk.

"Hello... yes, I would like my car please. The driver's name is Fez."

Fez had slept in the parking lot in anticipation of Salim summoning him at any moment. Fez was a simpleton who responded only to the instructions given to him; no more, no less. Salim admired this naivety of his—his unworldliness was his charm. Upon hearing a knock on his car window, Fez rubbed his eyes and wheeled the car into the hotel driveway.

"Let's see what Lorr will show us this afternoon, Fez," Salim said, as he sat down on the warm leather, rolling down the windows while Fez gave the air conditioning a kick-start. Fez's body odor had seeped into the car and, as much as Salim wanted to deny it, it made him gag. Poor boy hadn't seen a bucket of water in days. Salim held his breath until the afternoon swept some of the smell away and cool air began to blast between the front seats.

Lorr burnt under the midday sun, creating mirages that could be seen in the distance. Men on bicycles covered their faces with thin cotton scarves, breathing in their own breath. Rickshaws with roaring engines shuffled through tiny openings. Musty clouds hung loosely in the air. Traffic wardens stood sweltering at intersections, their heavy black boots baking their feet. Salim looked through the window with some sympathy for their wives who would remove those shoes that evening, breathing in that foul smell, the one worshippers swallow at mosques while touching their foreheads to the ground. It was the scent of serfdom. He had to shake his head as if to empty his mind of it.

As they drove near the gates of the Polo Ground, a stout servant-boy in the distance pulled a thoroughbred into a trot. The horse began to canter away from the boy, and Salim's mind began to wander. There was something that he could not decipher about his city—he longed for her to tear down this maddening façade and snap out of character, to return to the way she used to be. But there was something else that struck him. He thought about the time when he had first published his theorem. At night he dreamt of meeting Einstein. He remembered exactly what he had said to him about time.

"It belongs to no one," Einstein declared with an echo and clouds of vapor blooming behind his head. "Time is arbitrary. Five minutes for one is an hour for another."

Salim didn't think too much of it then. He thought it was just another random dream. But he finally understood what it all meant—it was a hint delivered from another dimension. As he looked out the window, he realized that time seemed to trudge slowly in Lorr. Rubbing the fine hair on his chin with his thumb, he whispered to himself the word for tomorrow: 'kal.' It was the same as the word for yesterday. "Kal", he said out loud, as the car came to a stop. His thumb stopped mid-stroke on his face. Lorr didn't give a fuck about time. There was no urgency. Unlike New York, in Lorr, time was not in charge—she was.

Lorr's audacity made him realize that time was able to bend as though it were on a tractable fabric. This remarkable image in his mind was pushed aside as a large billboard approached the car from above. The rodent dictator grinned down upon the people as they passed by. Like all dear leaders, this one too felt his power slipping from his hands. The ban on political parties had just been lifted. There was a rumor that the former Prime Minister, whom Zaid had brutally hanged before assuming absolute power, had a daughter who was returning to the country for elections. It made General Zaid quiver in his sleep. Salim could see it even in that phony smile of his that spread over the canal on the billboard.

This anticipation was palpable throughout Lorr. Billboards had erupted from the ground—endorsing political parties, squash shoes, and soft drinks, sometimes all three of them at once. There was a new hope struggling to break on the horizon. Revolution, on that quiet afternoon, could be heard whispering in the distance. Salim was sure of it; he knew his city and its people—chains were not their favorite jewelry.

Another billboard.

It was Salim's friend Mitti Pao this time, kissing the side of a Pepsi bottle, with his curly hair bound in a headband—sweat and condensation intertwining, dripping from his chin. Mitti Pao had come a long way. The captain of the Pureland cricket team, he was a worldly character now and his charm extended beyond the cricket pitch. Salim had witnessed it first-hand when he ran into him at a New York charity gala. There he was at Lincoln Center, draped in a tuxedo with the Duchess of York hanging from his fast bowling arms like a falcon. He ignored Salim and strolled towards the toilets. Salim followed him.

"You look familiar, champ," Mitti said at the urinals later. "Are you that Sri Lankan batsman from Kandy?"

"Yes," Salim replied. "That's me."

"See, I never forget a face. Good seeing you, champ," he said, then washed his hands and walked away.

A plump woman pulled up beside them at a traffic light. Peering into her rear-view, she adjusted her curled hair and large sunglasses that could easily encompass two sets of eyes. She was dressed like a macaw. Salim could hear her radio through the thin windows of the car. The garish clamor of pop music could've gotten her swept away into a military truck, bound for the army barracks. It was evident, though, from her swaying head and repetitive smacking of lips that she most definitely did not give a fuck.

"How far are we from this place, Fez?" Salim asked, moving his gaze from the lady who had begun to engage in an impromptu drum roll across her dashboard.

"It's near the canal. Just a few minutes more, Saab."

The signal turned green. The woman stopped air-drumming and yanked her car into gear. Salim followed her urgent movements as she rolled by.

It was known that Pasta was owned by Raja Italian—a man who requires little introduction. His name reveals his ambiguity. Rumor: he had an Italian mother who passed down secret family recipes to him in a leather-bound journal. Truth: the closest Raja ever came to Italy was the queue outside the Italian embassy, where his visa was rejected. Raja had never stepped outside Pureland. Nonetheless, in a town where deception was ushered indoors with a warm embrace while truth shivered out in the cold, Raja Italian's restaurant was where the prosperous came to dine, display fancy clothes, and show off imported cars.

Just outside the restaurant, beside a row of shiny vehicles, there he stood grinning like a village idiot—Raja Italian, chief visionary of bastardized casseroles and counterfeit lasagnas. He stood welcoming guests with his ponytail and red tie, sleeves rolled up to the elbow. Chauffeurs drove up a long ramp and deposited their patrons, parking towards the side, squatting on their haunches. Salim walked out of the car and asked Fez to order anything off the menu for himself and the other drivers. Fez responded with a confused look—one a puppy would give if asked to operate complex machinery. Salim deposited some cash into his reluctant palm and walked inside, right past the genial restaurateur.

As he entered, the restaurant's customers spun their necks towards him like ostriches, but after a few seconds of intense staring, returned to their meals. Time froze as onlookers peeled their eyelids at him, his clothing, his car, vetting his authenticity, delivering verdicts on his class. From one teenager's perspective, Salim was working-bohemian. The boy looked back at him through his floppy middle-parted hair and pursed lips—he was upper gentry like everyone else there, and quietly sipped his iced coffee with the sullen look of someone eagerly awaiting the death of aging grandparents.

Salim asked for a table for two and sat down. After a few moments, the restaurant door opened again, letting in the afternoon sun—the stares were purposely extended as an elegant silhouette stood before them. Salim was part of the welcoming committee this time. He stood while she walked in, scattering her mesmerizing scent like a crop-duster. Her hair was pulled down straight, bouncing on her shoulders. Her cheeks were delicately rouged. As always, her lips curled upwards from the corners to show the hint of a smile. It was her most astounding gift—it demanded worship. As she stepped towards Salim, Laila removed her sunglasses to reveal the eyes that had him imprisoned his entire life.

"Hello Salim," she said in a soft voice, extending her hand.

"Hello," he replied, holding her hand reluctantly as she sat down, putting her keys and sunglasses in the middle of the table. She glanced around the room with a subtle look of displeasure. She had known from the start that it was the wrong location for a meeting. But if she was to be compromised, it best be somewhere worthy of her class—a place where the Caesar salad cost more than the people serving it.

"How are you, Laila? After all these years, I wondered what I would ask you, what I would say," he said, as his breathing picked up pace. "You just left that morning without saying goodbye."

"Salim," she said, as she took in a deep breath. "I'd rather we not speak of that night. It was what it was. We talked about it. Just one night, remember? You promised we would not meet again. I'm a married woman now. I hope you understand." Her eyes met his and then looked away.

"Of course," Salim lied. "Just one night. Of course, ... I understand." He didn't. "Do you remember I gave you a bracelet?"

"Are you serious? Salim don't be a bloody child. I can't keep trinkets from you that you bought me years ago. This is not an Indian movie, you know. It's my life. I'm married and I have a son."

"You do?"

"I have a boy. His name is Sameer." A genuine smile finally arrived at her lips. As she glanced away, he grabbed her hand and pulled it close like he had done many times before on cool nights upon her balcony.

"You know, my mind tells me to speak to you about random things. About here and there, things that are of little meaning and trespass on our limited time. But there's a dishonesty to that type of talk. Laila, I want to speak earnestly. I'm still in love with you and always will be. It should come as no surprise. There's one other matter of importance to me. I want to help General Saab. It hurts me to see a man of his stature imprisoned as though he were a rabid beast. Your brother's killing him."

"How dare you?" she whispered, narrowing her eyes. "After all these years, you now care about how my father is feeling?"

"I left the Khan House with a lot of pain in my heart. At first I was very bitter. I was only a child and had a lot of anger towards everyone—you, Khan Saab ... myself. Over the years, as my life began to change, I could not hide the fact that this change was all because of him, because of what he did for me." He took a deep breath before continuing. "I always longed for this place, for Lorr. I always have. I wanted to return. Hearing about his health really shook me and made this return inevitable. In a way, I realize now that I longed for this place because of Khan Saab and, more importantly, because of you ... I've named entire libraries and scholarships after Khan Saab. Please, Laila, you out of all people ... don't fall victim to your brother's evil propaganda." He noticed her mood turning sour and tried to change the topic but had suddenly lost control of his mouth. "Laila, are you happy? You don't need to answer that. Just ask your heart. If you think even for a minute that you're not, know that I can take you with me. You and your son. To another place where you're not policed like a criminal."

"Salim," she whispered. "Have you no shame? Or have the years cooped up in a laboratory finally taken their toll on your mind? This is what you brought me here to say? I belong to someone else now. Whether Liber Ali is good to me or not is none of your concern. This is what I've chosen. Honor might be just another word for you men, but for us, it's everything. It's life itself."

A waiter interrupted them, and Laila brushed her hair aside, falling back in her chair. She lit a cigarette. They ordered. Salim even managed to force a smile. He changed the subject and asked her if she remembered the maniac who had eaten all of the Khan's pigeons and pretended to fly.

"Did you know? He asked me how he could escape his visions. I feel like flying, he said. I told him, 'Chaku, soar like the falcon you are. Go to the highest point'. Even I didn't think the bastard would climb to the terrace and jump into the garden."

Laila fought an unstoppable giggle until it came out through her nose. She covered her mouth. "I heard from Bilki many years later that he left Lorr and opened a roti stand or something." She stained the rim of her glass with a red crescent. The restaurant door opened but no one looked, it was only a waiter.

She tried terribly hard to hide it, but her eyes failed her, allowing him to see an opening to advance. Hands reached out, fingers rose from the table like spider legs engaging in an elegant dance, fingertips touched, hands jerked back again; two lovers in a Bombay Talkie—the censored version. The mood warmed. As people glanced, Salim reached over to touch her lips and she opened her legs and locked them with his.

Just when he sensed a tingling sensation, she asked him, "What are you working on these days?"

He hesitated for a moment, composed himself and spoke. "The fabric of space and time. Time is a fabric. It's bendable, malleable and, hopefully, if I'm right, it can be penetrable."

"And what does that mean?"

"We can alter destinies."

"What a load of shit," she said, as she tugged on his tie. "By the way, this isn't New York, you know. It gets hot here. Don't you feel warm in this? What did you think you were coming here for, a business meeting?" She was right. His body was put on boil by her touch. Above them, a waiter balanced a small silver tray. Salim dropped cash in it without glancing at the receipt. "And what of this fatwa nonsense. Are you even safe here?"

"Yes," he began. "I don't know... listen, when can I see you next? I can come here once a month and maybe you can come to New York. I know I'm blabbing nonsense, but I can feel your presence at every street corner, at every moment. In a way, I came here for you, to tell you that. I don't care for my safety. All I care for is you. And if I hadn't returned, I would have died not knowing. But I know now. I can see you through those eyes, through this place, these people. I know you yearn for me like I do you. What I don't know is if you would ever sacrifice it all—for a peasant."

After a short pause she said, "I'm afraid this is the last time you will ever see me, Salim." She looked down at the table and swallowed. "I agreed to meet you so you would know that I now belong to someone else. It seems that you are still as foolish as you were when we were young. It's time I say goodbye. I hope you find your destiny or time-space, whatever it is you're after." As she rose from her chair, she took a deep breath and said, "You know, you should not risk your life for this place. After all, what has it ever given you?" In that moment, as if she had a personality disorder, she had changed again. With those words, she shot him from close range in the chest, just like she had done in the past, right in his amnesiac heart.

"Wait, Laila. Please!"

Laila picked up her sunglasses and keys, and walked out of the restaurant, leaving gazing young boys smacking their lips. Salim went outside after her. As she sat in her black Mercedes, she looked back at him. The car engine roared and she floated away over the bridge towards the Cantonment.

"What has Pureland ever given me? It gave me the audacity to love you," he said aloud, standing outside as the faces in the restaurant window turned towards him.

I can only fathom the feeling that stabbed Salim like a knife at that very moment. I picture Laila's car screaming away from him and a dull pain swelling inside his chest. All the excitement that had kept him up at night, the elation of seeing her in the element of her magnificence, had been for nothing. I can also envision the helplessness which turned him to stone as he watched both, his lover and the Eden where they first met, become completely unrecognizable right before his eyes. And I can imagine he would have stood there forever if his hand wasn't tugged at by Fez and the other drivers.

The drivers sprang up from their haunches and put Salim's hand to their chests thanking him. Fez, after responding with confusion to the waiter who had earlier arrived to take his order, had pointed to the window where a child sat refusing his meal while his mother swirled her coffee chatting away with her friend. There was something appealing about the plate that sat thrust into the center of the table. Fez knew what was to become of it only moments later, as he had seen it happen many times before. It would end up in a pile of garbage. He wanted it badly. So, cheeseburgers it was for everyone, and when they arrived in cardboard boxes, the drivers picked them apart, folding the buns like rotis, swiping away at the dribbling sauces beneath. Salim met them all. He asked them their names, trying to take his mind off the pain that knocked against his ribcage. In the restaurant, the gazers muttered away as they looked at him. Ignoring the staring committee, which now included the highly confused proprietor of the fake Italian bistro, Salim asked Fez to drive him back to the hotel.

———◆———

The drowsy sun had fallen below the buildings and cozied into a red blanket for the evening. Darkness and curfew lurked around the corner, hand in hand. As she did throughout the day, Lorr changed colors. She was now red, the color of melancholy that accompanied Salim's soul as he rested his head against the window looking out at the Canal of Fables, where shirtless children did backflips from the bridge into the water. The afternoon began to replay in his mind. All the possible outcomes that could have been. What he could have said, what could have happened if he'd just kept his mouth shut. He had again managed to lose her—closing his fist too tight while she slipped out like sand.

As he looked out upon the Blisschesterson gates, a black Pajero with tinted windows blocked his vision and a hand stuck out, signaling them to stop.

"Professor Salim?" the man asked through the window.

"Yes," Salim replied. A skeletal man in a grey shalwar kameez opened his door and climbed into the back seat, while another joined Fez in the front. He pulled out a semi-automatic weapon that bulged like an erection under his clothes and rammed it into Salim's ribs.

"Everything will be fine. Just come with us. Driver, start following our car or I will shoot a bullet up your ass."

Salim cemented himself to his seat. He closed his eyes. Unlike what he had seen in the movies, his life did not flash before him. The gunman was in his twenties and built like an army truck. From his shiny golden shoes and gold Rado watch, Salim knew he was a Pashtun. The one in the front had darker skin and a face blanketed with acne scars.

"I know you might not want money. But whatever it is young man, I am not the enemy. Tell me what it is you're after?" Salim asked. When he received silence as a response he said, "At least let Fez go. He is a poor man. He has done nothing wrong."

"My Saab said that you will try and talk too much and he said to put a bullet in your knee if that happens. Please say something more so I can do that." The conversation ended.

The car screeched to a halt at a high-gated villa. Salim looked down at the car mat where a puddle had gathered around his feet—Fez had relieved himself, leaving the car smelling like ammonia.

"Get out! Get out!" yelled Golden Shoes, his gun directed at Salim's genitals. Fez buried his head in his arms and began to whisper the names of the Almighty. He tried reciting all ninety-nine of them, but only knew five. So, he repeated them over and over until he saw the two men clamp down on Salim's arms and shove him into the towering villa.

The lights were out, the room tasted like oak furniture. The kidnappers forced Salim into a chair. Droplets of a crimson sunset sliced their way through a slit in the curtains.

"Fuck me in the mouth! Where are the fucking lights in this place?" a voice bellowed, followed by squeaking footsteps.

"Sir jee, the electricity is out."

"Damn you sister-fuckers, you sons of whores! What took you so long? Were you taking a stroll in the Lawrence Gardens? Sister-fuck this place!" The voice came closer and the squeaking approached Salim. His hands had been tied behind his back with a coarse rope. It began to numb his fingers and cut into his wrists.

"Hello, Professor Agha. I hope my friends took good care in bringing you here." There was now a rough silhouette towering over him, speaking in perfect English with an accent he knew well—one shaped by marbles.

"Look, I can tell you don't need money. At least tell me my crime. If it's a blasphemer you seek, you have the wrong man."

The silhouette walked a step back. Slowly, perspiration from his captors' armpits added a subtle smokiness to the oak atmosphere.

"If I wanted to, Professor Saab, I would've had you thrown into the Canal of Fables an hour ago. Do you not recognize me, old friend?" he asked, walking towards the curtains and yanking them apart. Salim looked back emptily. The streetlight lit up a dog-like face.

"All infidels go to hell," he said, pausing after each word. Tariq had lost his hair and gained weight in places only a rich man could. He was dressed in a white shirt, blue jeans, and shiny loafers. His nose was a completely different color from the rest of his face and was surrounded by a boundary of scars. "Ah, from your look, I see you remember that phrase. It was childish of me, Salim. I should really not have written that. Really, I should've just taken a blade and slit your throat instead. Would you like some tea?" Tariq turned to his gunmen and shouted, "Why have you not served my guest tea, you sister-fucking imbeciles!"

One of them approached Salim from behind and slammed his head with the back of his semi-automatic. Salim's face hit the marble floor with a slapping sound. A wetness covered his eyes, making it hard to see. He yelled and wriggled, only to receive more blows to his abdomen.

"Stop! Stop, Tariq, please!" he screamed. Tariq raised his hand. The commotion subsided and blood could be heard dripping on the floor.

"Stop? Professor, this is just tea. Would you not like to stay for dinner? I've planned this for a long time and, when I heard you were back, I couldn't wait any longer. Take a look at what you gifted me all those years ago." He inched closer. "Sixteen. It took sixteen sister-fucking surgeries to try and reconstruct what you destroyed, you transvestite-fucker. You took everything away from me! Sorry, Professor. Stopping right now wouldn't be good hospitality."

The beating continued. Salim heard his shins cracking and his ribs bending. With each bludgeon, blood showered the marble floor. The noises came first and the pain followed. The back of his jaw broke off and fell loose in his skin. It was like lightning striking his face over and over again. His nose flattened onto his face. To breathe or to choke? It was a tough choice. The gunmen stopped as the electricity came on and the tube-lights flickered. The ceiling fan began rotating, cooling Salim's face. Tariq walked over to wipe his eyes with a towel.

"Give him some water and make sure he doesn't sister-fucking faint. I need him to stay alive for two days!" he screamed.

Through his pressed eyelids, Salim saw the moving bodies freeze as they heard a car grumble into the driveway. Tariq peeked through the window. He heard a woman's voice. Then he heard Fez, pleading. He could only make out some words through his sobs.

"What are you doing here?"

"Madam," Fez cried. "Please Madam, save my Saab." Fez's cheeks fell on to Gucci slippers. The woman took a large puff from her cigarette and flicked it into the garden as her eyes probed the villa.

"Tariq! Tariq where are you?" she yelled through a Benson & Hedges cloud, as the gunmen began to mumble amongst themselves. Tariq's eyes almost fell out of their sockets.

"Shhh—you assholes! May donkeys fuck your sisters," he whispered to his wide-eyed servants. "I thought you dropped her at the sister-fucking airport!"

Salim wanted desperately to breathe, but he could not. As he heard footsteps entering the room, and panic settling among his captors, he spat out his last breath and his body shut itself down.

———

In the hospital, Salim slipped in and out of consciousness. The state of nothingness was infused with moments of incoherent dreams. When he thought he was awake, people were there.

"I told you, son. You can become as rich as them, but never their equal," said Bally in his raspy voice, as he sat in a corner of the room smoking his hookah. Salim could smell the ash in his goblet.

"So what's this story you speak of?" chuckled Tamboo Charming, his nostrils flaring. "The pauper Raavi? He married the King's daughter, Laaj?" He laughed, slapping his knee. "Have you been taking the Floating Pir's drink again? Laaj is the curse of Raavi, you fucking idiot. He can play all the tunes he wants—she'll destroy him every time."

"I missed you, my son," said General Khan, as he peered over Salim's head and held his hand. His walrus moustache and his emeralds were looking right at him. "I could never come to terms with your leaving. I guess I wanted you to stay. You would have treated me better."

"Romeo, we never had our first wedding night," said Chaku as his sweat dripped on to Salim's neck.

Quivering, his eyes flipped open and looked around. Laila was there, asleep on a chair, wrapped in a white bedsheet. He looked down at his bandaged chest and when he looked up again, she was gone. A nurse darted towards him. Behind her was Fez the driver, whose face revealed that for days he had been a victim of short naps on concrete hospital benches.

Salim managed to utter the only two syllables he could muster, the only two that ever made sense to him, "Lai-la."

◆

Fevers weave dreams of color. Salim's breath slows down as his soul leaves his body. Up, up, up it floats into the black sky. Black is everywhere. Below his feet, the world is blue, surrounded by an endless sea of black. There lies his nation, green, among mountains, white. She is restless. His heart cries tears of red.

He glides through the black cosmos. The white stars pull him faster, faster towards them. Then it stops. His breath returns, the pain is gone and his eyes open. Now, everything is white. In the distance, mynas sing in broken verses. There are beasts huddled in the mist. Their long hair, black; their flowing capes, white. Feathers fall from their backs as they creep towards him; their eyes, white.

One extends his hand: his touch is cool.

"The journey leaves stardust in your ears, Salim Saab. Let me clean them for you." His voice is loud. The others close in, spreading murmurs into their palms, their whispers, white.

"Am I dead?" he asks.

"No, we saved you. Remember, like we did with the old witch?"

"Why did you save me?"

"So that you can save us all one day. I, Gabriel, I blew the final revelation into your nose myself," he says. His feathers are hefty, made of silver, his skin brown, his body, like a stone, presses close to him. "Something has been a bother—rattling inside your head?"

"Yes."

"Doesn't let you sleep?"

"Yes."

"And when you do sleep, it won't let you rest? Takes away your dreams?"

"Yes, but..."

"The answer, Salim Saab, is what I bring to you, like I have done many times before. I'm but a mailman, a dakia. You force two points to join through a line. Bend the page and let them touch instead." The others begin to dance, their elbows locked. Gabriel comes closer, his eyes green.

"But, what is it you want?" he asks the beast. "Surely, you have desires, too."

"Salim Saab, you are a man of great insight." Gabriel breathes, his breath is cool. "What I seek, Salim Saab, is a life of mortal immortalities, certain uncertainties, perfect imperfections. I'm a thespian, and what good is an actor without a stage?"

"So, you do have desires?"

"Yes, and one day our desires will be fulfilled and then we shall have no more desires to worry about. I yearn for that time, Salim Saab. Perhaps we will get there together, you and I." His arm stretches to pull him closer; his wings scrape the misty floor. "We have reached the cusp of this cliff, where our world meets yours. You long to be here, I long for your world. How strange these desires are that govern our hearts." Under his feet Salim sees, through the black, a room of frenzy. There's a woman of beauty; her shawl, white. There lies a still body. He takes one step forward and falls from the cliff. Down, down, down he goes, his eyes white, and the cosmos black. There below is the world, blue, and again his beloved in green. A feeling of realization flushes his cheeks red. He knows now why he was birthed upon his nation's bosom in the first place: to save her, the Eden where he first fell in love. His eyes open again—the room is white.

Recovery

On the seventh night Salim's fever broke. During these nights of agony, he could see through his cloudy vision a dark tunnel yawning in the distance, pulling him in. Like a black hole, upon whose lip time slows down to nothingness and all matter disintegrates into tiny, irreconcilable atoms, he fell deeper and deeper until he emerged out the other end, fused as one. His dreams, upon whose audacity he swam, put him back on earth. And then they went away. Reality leaked back into the blacks of his eyes. He had survived.

He began, almost immediately, to piece the series of events back together. The abduction, the gunmen with their profound smell of dried sweat and roasted almonds, the piss that pooled by his feet, the villa of darkness, the imitation nose, the beating, the woman's voice, the wife whom he had rescued the day before, his face on the floor, the floor on his face. A miracle, he thought. Has to be, right? There's no other way. He had convinced himself then, as his eyes closed, that he was gone for good.

Salim awoke to the aggravating sound of a mosquito making love to his ear. It was hot. His sheets were soaked through. The ceiling fan was inert. As the mosquito danced towards him again, he blinked hard, trying to shoo it away with his cheek, only for it to be yanked back by the wire that ran through his jaw. Letting out a yelp of agony he startled Fez the driver, a jet-lagged Chip Beetlewood, and an obese nurse, igniting a flurry of commotion beyond the half-stained glass outside.

"They're here to get your autograph," said Chip as she waltzed over to his bedside from the corner. "The lights are out in this damn place ... they're trying to get the generator working. What a place to get mended, right?"

The commotion bubbled outside as news of Salim's consciousness reached the eagerly waiting international press, who had camped outside the Ganga Ram Hospital during what was later labelled the turning point of Pureland's political revolution. Through the days of his slumber—six, to be exact—news had spread of an attempted assassination on the American scientist Salim Agha.

In Pureland, rumors held precedence over truth. One such claim made it to the top of the pile at the editors' desks. It was an account of Salim, abducted by General Zaid's men and beaten senselessly, only to be saved later by the General's wife who, it turned out, had been rescued by Salim the night before from two assailants on a motorcycle. Reliable sources supplemented the report, including:
1) A driver of a Toyota Corolla from Rolla Paya Luxury Rentals and,
2) A teenaged thief who had his face recently split open by a crook-lock.
General Zaid immediately rubbished the preposterous allegations that his wife, all 275 pounds of her, could ever be compromised by anyone, including himself. He knew this from experience, as he had tried many times, pinning her down with his arms and legs in a playful attempt to force her to conduct fellatio on him, only to have her teeth painfully snap shut around his cock.

However, this mutated rumor had escaped the tightly clenched fists of Pureland's theocracy and now the international media was swarming around the ICU doors of the hospital. As audacious as the fatwa was to the West, so too was the bravery of Dr. Salim Agha to return to face the man who had issued his death warrant. This stuff was movie-worthy. Pureland's military dictatorship was under the scanner. Diplomats from the world over demanded that Salim's attackers be tried and punished. Also, the revolution which Salim had heard whispering on the horizon the day of his capture had now turned into a bedeviling roar.

What became of his actual perpetrators? Did the world ever discover that it was, in fact, Tariq's wife who was the rescuer and not the first lady of the nation? Definitely not. Neatly rolled Pureland bank notes were tucked into the shirt pockets of local journalists, keeping the dog-faced textile scion, Tariq, and his wife out of the picture. In the coming years, the rumor became the truth, as rumors often do.

"I told you to keep out of trouble, Doc," Chip began, as Salim looked at her, puzzled, through his semi-open mouth and swollen eyes. "Usually when a dictator of a foreign country issues a bounty on your head, it's advisable not to fucking travel there!"

Salim mumbled behind his locked mouth.

"What did you say? I know, I know. I have everything worked out. The General has arranged to invite the US ambassador, dignitaries, and the press to a grand evening at the Garrison Hall. He wants to make a public statement. To set the record straight, or some shit like that." Her hand reached out to touch his. "You're a celebrity. No one can touch you now. We will be home in no time—just get some rest."

It wasn't him.

"Yes, I know it's grim. Trying to get the fucking lights on."

It wasn't him.

His mouth creaked like a rusty door hinge.

"There's one little thing, though. Small thing, no big deal," she said, pulling her hair back from her face and clearing her throat. "You need to apologize to the fucker."

Apobobize! Bor bhat!

"Easy, Doc. You want to get out of here or no? It will all be behind closed doors, don't worry. You don't have to mean it."

I bon't apobobize bor shit! And ... It wasn't him!

"I heard you, Doc. I know its grim. Gettin' the lights on, jeez, calm down."

Salim blinked, sighing.

An apology, he thought. For being excommunicated, beaten, and stripped of his identity. It was the last thing he had left to give. As he mumbled his way through an argument with Chip, the nurse entered the room and shoved a bedpan under his ass. He screamed for dear life, but she was not perturbed, and continued treating linen and patient with equal disdain.

He couldn't sleep that night as he thought of the elaborate display that was set to cap off his humiliating return to Pureland. It was Zaid's way of tightening his grip on the American handshake. He would pardon an offender of a victimless crime, show his merciful side, and continue opening blank checks in the mail for a proxy war. For him, it was win-fucking-win.

Zaid's pouch-eyed stare haunted him at night. Like a film reel, their relationship played in segments. Salim and Zaid, Zaid and Salim. First, there's the Brigadier and the boy. The cowering army man is cut down to size in front of his comrades by the young servant boy. Then there's the General, the President, the new and improved version, venomous and petty, the man who declares, through a flickering TV screen, Salim's heresy to the world. "An enemy of the republic!" he claims.

Enemy of the republic. Salim mouthed the words in his broken sleep.

There was something strange about this new dictator. General Zaid the supreme, the leader of the reformed republic, a republic safely guarded from the evils of alcohol, jazz music, and promiscuous women. What do we know about him? Zaid 2.0 was a man of God, that we can't deny. So stern was his devotion, he believed God spoke to him. Regularly. God played a huge role in the bastard's life. It all started when he was a little boy in his village of Bill-Qul. One day, perched under a mango tree, he began his first dialogue with the almighty.

"Why, o Allah, why did you besiege me with these ungainly teeth, these hollow eyes?" he cried, as tears fell from his chin. "I know there's a power you have bestowed upon me, I just know it. I feel your presence in every breath, o Lord. If you're listening, o Creator, send this mango my way. Give me a sign. Just one sign!"

Lo and behold, right at that instant a mango, ripe and succulent, dropped right on his nose. Since then, the fucker was convinced of his divine appointment. From then on, every time he needed advice, Zaid touched his forehead to the ground, closed his eyes and awaited a summoning. He believed that an invisible force had guided him throughout his life, told him what to do. It is why he joined the army, why he kept a pencil-thin mustache, and why he married a simple, heavyset woman from the village who could only converse in the Bill-Qul dialect. When he became President, his conversations with God became more frequent. The mullah, whom he had initially appointed in his cabinet to keep him abreast of all things related to the revealed text, was soon disposed of because Zaid thought he knew everything there was to know—and if he didn't, God would fill him in. It got so bad sometimes that he would leave important conferences and find an empty room to do his thing. Critical decisions were only made after divine consultation. Like the decision to ban all grape trees since grapes could rapidly become wine. Or the law that forced women to cover their heads, because we all know what happens when they don't.

This shit was funny at first, but as the years went on the other generals and brigadiers got used to it. "Where the devil has he gone now?" they'd ask when he'd abruptly leave daily briefings. "Oh, he's receiving a fax."

I believe—and this is my theory alone—that for Zaid, Salim fit perfectly into the classification of an anti-hero. There wasn't much to it really. It was clear to him: the scientist and the zealot, the yin and the yang, good and evil. That's probably how he saw it. So, it comes as no surprise that after Salim had won the Nobel and established himself as an academic giant, Zaid saw an opportunity. He could use Salim to build his nuclear arsenal, give him the biggest dick in the world so that no one would fuck with him. Nobody really told him the difference between the various branches of science for him to understand that Salim didn't know the first thing about building nuclear warheads. I don't know what he was going to do with such a bomb in the first place. He was convinced he needed one. Rumor had it that the young mullah from his cabinet advised Zaid on the matter. He said that every dictator was getting scientific toys and that he could do with one himself.

Anyway, let's move on...

The day arrived and the banquet stank of unexplainable riches. Potholes in the roads were filled with tar and streetlights were switched on. The Cantonment was dressed as though it were a bride, while reporters flashed their cameras in its face.

Meanwhile, not far from the carnival, alongside the polo ground, a manservant received a blow to the ear for eating leftover cake from the refrigerator. Behind the Garrison Hall, four children shared a piece of bread on the floor and washed it down with a glass of rusty tap water. As cars approached, a teenaged mother banged harder on their tinted windows than hunger did on her insides. A one-armed vagabond watched as a brigade of black cars trampled the sidewalk he called home, running over the pillow of concrete on which he dreamt. Children approached the flashing headlights, swarming the car windows—shirtless, their tiny crooked fingers pointing to the gaping voids in their faces.

In the luminous glow, away from where the dark-skinned people lived, generals chaperoned diplomats into the driveway, where they submitted their bodies to metal detectors. Salim's face bleeped once and his shins twice, as he was patted down.

Inside, he stared hastily at the stuffed partridges decorating every seat. A couple of lambs, roasted to medium-well and garlanded with imported vegetables, lay in the center. There were more lights in the endless hall than there were people. Fine silver cutlery lay before him— he could not eat a bite. He watched while Johnnie Walker was gulped down as if it were the last batch, and the bones of endangered birds were crushed by laughing mouths.

"Ladies and gentlemen," General Zaid began, seated at the head of a mile-long table. "It is my honor to let you know that political parties are officially allowed to contest elections in Pureland. It has been a long journey which I'm glad to have been a part of." A reluctant applause followed. "And most importantly, let's raise our glasses to our very own, Dr. Salim Agha, son of Lorr, and the pride of this great nation, who was involved in an unfortunate incident. Just a small misunderstanding. We will make sure he returns to New York safely." More applause echoed in the dense hall. From a distance, the black pouches under Zaid's eyes were so dark, it seemed like he was wearing sunglasses. But as he turned, the chandelier shone on his eyes and they ate into Salim the way they had when he was young.

The dinner concluded. Salim was pulled away in a wheelchair to a private room where Zaid stood with his back towards him. The doors shut. The General backpedaled and sat near the wheelchair, signaling for his guards to leave the room.

"Professor Saab ... I haven't seen or heard from you in years. How are you? Please let me know who did this to you. I will make sure that person is taken to court," he said, laying his hand on Salim's. Before Salim could answer, he continued, "I just wanted to say a few parting words." Salim sat up in his wheelchair. "We had this conversation after Stockholm when, let me remind you, I had called to congratulate you and you outlandishly responded with words of disdain. I admit, in the past, we might have said a few words to each other. Let bygones be bygones, is what I say. If Allah can forgive, who are we mere mortals, huh?" He paused, his left eyelid quivering. "I want you to come back to this great nation, Professor Saab. You and I, we have been on the same side of an attempt to right what was wrong. Join me again and we can make this land a better land—a more pure land."

"You ask me to return, General Saab? Return as what? A heretic? You have ex-communicated my people and hold the nation captive... Return to what?" Salim scowled, as Zaid's ardent smile pulled into a frown. His eye flickered again.

"Still as rude as you were when you were a boy. Full of words to say and no respect for whom you are saying them to."

"Buying an atomic bomb is your idea of make a better Pureland? First, I'm not a nuclear physicist. And even if I were, I would tell you to go fuck yourself."

"You should be happy you're alive. I could have chosen to have you hanged in public for the infidel that you are. I think the words you're looking for are 'thank you'."

"Thank you? For making me a supporting actor in your attempt to sell my nation?"

"Salim!" yelled Zaid. "I've shown enough patience with you!" He erupted from his chair and held up a clenched fist. "I've tried to reason with you, as Allah is my witness, but now I will see to it that you don't return to this country ever again." The room quietened as he paused and the chandelier in the distance brightened. "Even though it pains me to do this. I will release you from the fatwa. I keep my promises. You have a lot of venom still left for me, Salim. I suggest you let it go and find peace with Allah. And don't forget, it was you who instigated the first Martial Law at the command of your beloved General Khan. If it weren't for you, we wouldn't be here. You think you're better than me? No, Professor Saab. You and me are the same ... exactly the same."

"The only difference, General Saab, is that you bleed Pureland, while I bleed for her," Salim said, turning the wheels of his chair around and making for the door.

A few miles away from the Garrison, connected to a landing strip, an airplane buzzed. As he was pushed along the tarmac by a flight attendant, Salim looked back and smelled his city for the last time, knowing he wouldn't see Lorr or Laila ever again. His heart ached.

Chip held his head in her arms as he wept. Like a child torn from his mother's bosom, he watched through the window as his plane lifted off.

His soul became restless once again.

❧

When he returned to the silence of his apartment in New York, his limp body pushed through on a wheelchair by Tamboo Charming, a phone call from Deema Engine added to his pain, and he crashed to the floor in anger, his limbs trembling.

"Tell me it's a lie, Deema!" he cried. "Can he be so ruthless? That sister-fucker. Tell me it's a lie!"

"Keep a hold of yourself," said Tamboo, snatching the phone from him. "Control yourself! Your stitches haven't healed yet." Tamboo put the receiver to his ear as Deema's sobbing voice came through in broken mumbles.

"Charming ... Oh Charming! General Khan is gone. That bastard killed him!"

Tamboo Charming pulled Salim back onto his wheelchair. He held him close to his heart, while in the distance police cars wailed down Lexington Avenue.

"Khan Saab!" Salim sobbed.

That was the night General Zafar Khan left this world. It was the most difficult night of Salim's life. More painful than the day he was abducted. Not even the crushed sleeping pills, which Tamboo stirred into a glass of Johnnie Walker, could force his eyes to shut. He stared, bewildered and fatigued, out the window until the sun came up. From that day on, sleeplessness became a permanent companion.

Meanwhile, the Khan house, on the day of the funeral, the Khan house became a crowded mausoleum where everyone whose lives Zafar Khan had touched gathered to pay their respects to the great Zafar Khan. Khalil, when asked about what had transpired, immediately claimed that Salim Agha had poisoned his father. But there was no police FIR filed, no autopsy—nothing. It would have been difficult to prove such accusations, since Salim himself had been struggling for life in the Ganga Ram Hospital Intensive Care Unit. No matter how many times Khalil repeated himself no one believed him. Not even Laila. She rubbished it with her silence as she sat in the dining room with other women in dark clothing, a single black scarf covering her head, while Khan lay under a white sheet and in rose petals, his chin strapped by gauze and his nose stuffed with cotton. He had never looked as serene as he did upon his deathbed.

One by one, people kissed his cold hands and wept into their sleeves. Wannu the Weasel, Cut-Two Naii the barber, Khassi Kasai the butcher, Pappu Pipewalla, Abbas the batman, a wrinkled, timeworn Bilki—all the servants came to witness their master, enter his final resting place under the scorching Lorr sun. All but the one who mattered to him the most.

Salim knew the role he had played in Khan's death. It wasn't just isolation that had weakened him. Disappointment had crushed his spirit over the years. Salim returned to Khan his pride, that valor he had known to love as a child, and showed him that blood was a capricious adjudicator, not worthy of deciding who can and cannot be kin. As soon as he realized this, Khan was liberated, announcing to Khalil his desire to bequeath the remains of his empire to Salim's scholarship. As you can well imagine, this resulted in the most ferocious altercation a father and son could ever have. Whiskey tumblers flew where once kisses were planted. An old body fell powerlessly upon an elevated bed. A spine cracked. Shortly after, a pillow softened a breath. Any dispute about power in the Khan House, if there was one left, was settled in the same dingy room where the Evil Witch met her demise.

Furthermore, a precarious seed had been planted that day, as Laila's son Sameer watched the funeral proceedings sobbing into his uncle Khalil's white kameez.

"Just remember Sameer, no matter how much you give these servants, they'll always want more. Salim Agha's greed has no limit," Khalil whispered in his ear as the boy wept, watching his grandfather being lowered into the earth.

"This heathen Ahmadi killed my grandmother when I was young and now he's murdered your beloved Daddy-jee."

"But why, Uncle Khalil?"

"Why? Remember what Daddy-jee taught you about chess? That poem?"

"The knight may be cunning, the bishop may be sly ... but the rook? The rook..."

"Is a real prick, watching as they all die. Some people are just born to do evil in this world, Sameer. Don't forget that. These Ahmadis are called traitors for a reason."

Afterwards, Sameer returned to Khan's study, where he had painfully waited all morning for his grandfather. There, upon the mahogany desk lay an unfinished game on an old tattered chessboard. The study was locked that night, never to be opened again, and those pieces remained engaged and ready for battle. All the pieces except for one black, porcelain rook.

The Caliphate

How are we doing on time, sir? This arrangement doesn't allow me to trespass on our allotted period, so I must be careful. That's a nice watch you have there. May I take a look? Very regal, sir. Fine stuff indeed. As the hour hand on this brassy timepiece of yours reaches its highest point, I must stop.

Funny thing: time. It's an essential element in our story and only now do I realize how I've mistreated my time on this earth. I guess in these moments with you, I want to make up for it—for lost time, that is. I want to make amends. We all do, don't we? We all ponder upon alternate realities, adaptations of our past that only exist in dreams, things we want to change but can't. The best we can do is hope the future turns out better. That's why I want to tell you how I feel about this world we live in and the world that was taken away from me.

Sir, before we speak of the Scimitar, the Sword of the Caliphate, the wicked terrorist that veered you towards me in the first place, let's chat about the Caliphate itself. Let us, for a moment, assess where we are on this side of the world, where everywhere is everywhere, our tales forever intertwined. Here, in the West, we are taught to respect statehood, division of governance, judiciary, checks and balances, and what not. But that's not how it is everywhere else. Somewhere, lost in the chaotic tapestry of the East, lurks the ghost of a forgotten nation called Pureland. Over there, a new empire now blankets the land, and all that was there before is forever lost.

Alas, no one quite knows when it happened or why this havoc was wrought upon us; why our books were set ablaze, or how classrooms suddenly turned into bunkers, or where exactly our integrity was auctioned, or to whom, or when entire nations vanished into thin air, or if at all, any one of us, as it were, actually gave a shit. But indeed, a storm blew through our land, sweeping away our culture, our song and dance, ancient monuments, timeworn manuscripts, laughter.

They came at us with puzzling names—insurgents, militia, freedom vendors—spilling in from all parts into our borders. It was hard to define who they really were at first, friend or foe, missionaries or soulless tyrants. Suddenly it returned: the time of empire, the new Islamic Caliphate, stretching from the winding streets of Istanbul all the way up to the borders of India. There were no nations anymore, no countries, just one united, Caliphate cluster fuck.

We had heard of such collapses of worlds that came before us, but when it actually happened to Pureland, I felt like God was playing tricks on us. We can argue about where it all started. Many of us will blame the people of the Arabian Peninsula for exporting their nomadic Bedouin faith. But I think it has to do with more than just faith. I feel it was almost virus-like. It bore into one mind and transmitted to others exponentially. What was this virus? The promise of eternal bliss, a paradise for the zealous brethren of the Caliphate. It was a promise worth dying for and, in some cases, worth killing for.

It is impossible to know about the Caliphate without gaining knowledge of the past. So I must proceed in this way by telling you about the historical events that shaped our lives. I must tell it to you the way I saw it unfold.

A short time after Salim returned to New York in 1987, General Zaid was on his way back from his village when his helicopter exploded mid-air. As his remains rained down over the Bill Qul mango groves, the people of Pureland took to the streets in jubilation. The dictator was finally gone. But Zaid had left his footprints in our political discourse. His laws lingered longer than he did. His God, the one we spoke about earlier, remained unquestioned. Salim's fatwa had become forgotten but other prohibitions remained: alcohol, unveiled women, rock bands. Ahmadi persecution continued. It was hard for Pureland to rid itself of all this. I must confess that I blame General Zaid for a lot of things, but this whole Caliphate thing was really his idea to begin with. It occurred to him in a dream. He woke up from this vision smiling ear to ear, thinking that by uniting all Muslim countries, he would be doing the work of the Almighty. So he invited the heads of state from all Muslim nations to a conference and proposed his concept of uniting what was once known as the Caliphate. No one took him seriously at the time. The other leaders withdrew from this meeting hastily, laughing at the preposterous idea. Uniting Muslims would be like tying four cats by their tails, was their conclusion. But somehow, this whole notion of unity kept bubbling up in the distance even after Zaid's helicopter exploded.

I can pinpoint exactly when this doctrine reared its ugly head for the first time. I remember it well. Let's fast-forward a few years. It was the year *Titanic* won eleven Oscars, when Zinedine Zidane shot two headers through the formidable Brazilian defense, when Bill Clinton's infidelity became public knowledge, and when Pureland tested its first nuclear missile. The year was 1998 and love, so to say, was in the air. It was the year that I, too, fell in love.

Growing up, I had heard about those valiant warriors fighting for liberation in the country once known as Afghanistan. Armed with American weaponry and the desire for rapture, these freedom fighters defeated the Soviets and became, for many of us, revered gods in their own right. One of these heroes was a man they called the Scimitar, God's right arm. When I first heard of his heroics on the battlefield, I was mesmerized. Sitting cross legged at Friday prayers one afternoon, I became enthralled by a sermon about his valor. This fascination of mine led me to believe that I too should play a part in ridding our world of the enemies of God.

I was seventeen.

What I did then was the only act of terror I accept responsibility for. As you can tell from the way I speak, I am a product of Western education and at my high school in Lorr, there were many people from your part of the world. The Scimitar, among others, saw this as a direct threat to our society and had sounded a warning for all foreigners and infidels to leave Pureland. The Muslim brotherhood should unite once again and rule the world, he declared. I'm not sure what was going through my mind at the time, but I decided that I should play my own part in this brotherhood. Not many people took the Scimitar's threat seriously, but I echoed his warning in the form of a handwritten and illustrated, pamphlet. I made photocopies of this pamphlet and slotted them into every foreign teacher's mailbox. You can imagine what might have transpired after such a threat. It wasn't pretty. Within days, the school's foreigners were evacuated and our senior year was thrust into jeopardy.

I haven't shared this shameful story with anyone. Sorry, I'm a little apprehensive ... There's more to my cowardly act than meets the eye. When I said I'd fallen in love, it wasn't just with the Almighty. Her name was Caroline Saunders and she sat next to me in algebra. She was the most beautiful thing I'd ever seen, and every day I looked forward to that algebra class. It was the first time a girl had taken an interest in me. We would exchange notes and write long emails which ended with words like "love" and "can't wait". But after that pamphlet incident, her family, Christian missionaries from the Midwest, packed their bags and left the country for good.

I spiraled into a vortex of depression, crying for days into my pillow. I even tried contacting Caroline, but she ignored me. I could sense that she knew it was me all along that I was responsible for such a demonic deed. This only added to my woes. My parents became worried as I spent days locked up in my room. The remorse began to strangle me. Then I realized what a fool I really was. To believe a roving nomad, like the Scimitar, thinking that he held the key to my faith. I started loathing him and the people that revered him. I hated them all for misguiding me. More importantly, I hated myself for being so goddamn stupid.

Not everyone was as lucky as me. Not everyone could snap out of such blind judgment like I had. For many people my age, the idea of a unified Caliphate, heaven's utopian waiting room, became a dream worth dying for.

Things went downhill after that. Over the next few years, after the attack on the twin towers in New York, our world was turned upside down. And believers of the Caliphate, who had not officially formed yet, got exactly what they had been waiting for: a war of civilizations, one that would bring upon the end of the world. This war of theirs, needless to say, was fueled by terror. Slowly, in the early 2000s, this unification became real. And by the time I was a grown man, it had taken over the world. Yemen, Syria, Iraq, Afghanistan, Pureland ... no one utters these names anymore.

I know what you want me to say. That religion was the root of all this evil. But it's more complicated than my God versus yours, good versus evil. I am no historian, sir, but I can see how the past repeats itself. Recall the Nazi party, on whose belts were the words 'Gott min uns'—God's on our side—who stormed to power through the ballot box and then burned down the very institutions that elected them. Did they not play on the idea of purity and a promised land? Did the people of Abraham really deserve what they got? Did God really sanction the Third Reich? No. All I know is that nothing unites like hate. I think you can see how that's working out for you in this country. It's all too familiar, isn't it?

Something similar occurred in Pureland. Like all revolutions, it began at the polling stations. Before the elections of 2013 a political party, fueled by passionate young followers, emerged upon the horizon.

What did they want? Marxist reform.

When did they want it? As soon as possible.

They called their movement a 'hurricane of social reform': the Toofan-i-Tehreek Socialist Party. That's right, TITS. I couldn't make this shit up if I tried. What can I say? Politics: it's funny until it's not. But nonetheless, the supporters of this hurricane had had enough of the past. They wanted change at any cost—and their leader, a man once known for his fierce fast bowling and even fiercer good looks promised to deliver it to them. You guessed it. Mitti Pao, the former long-haired cricket captain, had become a formidable political force in the aftermath of dictatorships and military curfews.

Now everyone knew that good old Mitti was a few screws short of a hardware store, but no one could deny his charm. Every Friday leading up to the election, Mitti's followers would fill Lorr Stadium chanting slogans of reform. They were mesmerized by his powerful sermons where he used words like 'change' and 'hope'. These speeches had everything: guitar riffs, synthesizer drum rolls, and the promise of an egalitarian tomorrow. You had to hand it to him. At first, even I bought into this rock-star politics. I thought Pureland was finally headed in the right direction. We could use a bit of social equality and modernity. TITS or bust, I said to myself. How wrong I was.

Because so raised was Mitti's sail it could be ballooned by any wave of bullshit that came by. He had advisors for everything and he listened to every half-baked quack with an opinion. One doctor, his close friend, advised him to eat spinach by the kilo because of his iron deficiency. In the days following, Mitti went to town on spinach. He ate so much of it that he ended up in hospital for iron poisoning. That's the sort of stuff he would do. Spontaneity was his thing.

But one day, hesitation grabbed Mitti Pao by the neck. And this time, he didn't act on impulse. It happened a few weeks prior to the elections of 2013, when Pao's party was poised for a sweeping victory. His dearest counselor, a scumbag drug-lord turned politician, accidently walked in on Mitti while he was getting thrashed by a dominatrix. The counselor, upon seeing Mitti scream in pleasure while tied to his bedpost, let out a series of shrieks of his own. When he relayed this episode to the other party leaders, they called for an emergency meeting.

The party members warned Mitti and told him to clean up his act before he jeopardized the elections. They advised him to atone for his sins and show the public that he was on the righteous path. The best way to do that, they claimed, was to align TITS with the Islamic Caliphate which had begun to take power in cities like Kabul, Damascus and Mosul—appease the religious vote, so to speak. What's more, they promoted the idea of inducting the Scimitar, God's right arm, into the party.

Mitti, being Mitti, couldn't tell the difference between the Sword of the Caliphate and a kitchen knife, but he sure knew a thing or two about being played—shown a closed-in field and bowled a bouncer, so to say. He felt something was off. "I'll think about it," he said to his party members, and went to bed. This sent everyone into a whirling panic because they knew that thinking was not Mitti's strongest suit. The party leaders sensed that he might decline their request and cause a rift among TITS party members.

The next morning, to the horror of his supporters, Mitti Pao was found dead in his bedroom. Rumors of drug abuse and hypersexual activity were floated, but the truth was that Mitti Pao's hesitance to align himself with the Caliphate caused his demise. His party members, however, couldn't contain their excitement, knowing that mourners make the best voters.

Mitti's supporters grieved his death for days and, soon after, went to the polling booths in hordes. As expected, the TITS Party claimed a resounding victory in the elections. But as soon as they did, they announced their allegiance to the Islamic Caliphate. Just when Pureland was on the cusp of revolution, it was pulled down by the ankles. I remember watching the TV screen in shock when the leader of the Caliphate, the Khalifa of Mosul, declared that an army was on its way to plant its flag in Pureland's capital.

Pureland's own military split into two. Those who refused to join the Caliphate, formed their own militia and bloodshed became an everyday thing. The rebels put up a fight against the Caliphate army for months but eventually we, the people of Pureland, lost that war. It was January of 2014 when darkness blanketed the country.

The Caliphate's army stormed the parliament building and, as promised, raised their black flag above the pillars, announcing the end of the nation once known as Pureland. On that very day, our new leader, the Khalifa of Mosul, with his flowing black beard, issued a declaration we knew only too well. Curfew.

The Strangeness

Over the years that led to Pureland's demise, Salim's longing for a vanished homeland twisted and turned inside him like a knife. Things had not been the same since the day he left Lorr back in '87. General Khan's loss added to this pain. He had convinced himself that Khan had been liberated by death, liberated from the carcass he'd been reduced to. In his memory, however, he wanted to remember him as he once had. He thought about him a lot, to the point where he could almost sense his presence. He could see, when he closed his eyes, the stainless-steel thermos from which Abbas would pour tea into porcelain cups at the dera. Then Pappu Pipewalla would drop in no more than two sugar cubes. And while the one-eyed manager, the sly Kana Munshi, would lay out the month's sugarcane yield, he recalled how many twists Khan would give to his mustache as he plunged deep into thought. Then came the excuses.

"Wild boar?"

"Yes, Saab," Kana would say, a single astonished eye opening with each word. "First it went through the rice paddies, then it ploughed the sugarcane field, the sister-fucker. We lost it all."

"But don't worry, Saab," Billa Cycle would immediately add. "Pappu and I will catch the bastard."

"And how do you expect to catch him? On your bicycle?"

Then, laughter.

As the years went on, Pureland, along with all the people from Salim's past, started slowly disappearing. Sadly, as he watched his vanishing culture from afar, he was driven to the brink of insanity. Because the loss of a home is surely something that can make you crazy. The Khalifa of Mosul's declaration made Salim shiver. When the Caliphate hoisted its flag over Pureland, the strangeness began. He lost his ability to sleep;

weird thoughts arrived. As with the divine mystics that came before, a celestial summoning had commenced. It had been centuries since a cosmic subpoena had been delivered and, quite frankly, it was overdue. His epilepsy barked undefined voices in his head. When the summoning arrived, Salim's eyes enlarged in astonishment; his pupils expanded and the whites disappeared altogether. A look of angst permanently embalmed him. Similar to the dismayed response of Mohammed, son of Abdullah, who had looked upon the Archangel with bewilderment when asked to 'recite in the name of the Lord, thy creator'. Of course, in that instance, the illiterate prophet dashed down Mount Hira, trembling with sheer disbelief, doubting his own consciousness. In the same way, Salim felt that his mind was not his mind, his body not his body. Reality and fantasy merged. Angels and ancient jinns began whispering in his ear.

He flung chairs at walls and cursed loudly from open windows. At times he cried. He shut his ears forcibly with his palms and begged for the voices to stop. But at times he let them permeate his thoughts. Rubbing his eyes, through his feathery dreams, the only clear image that he could see was his beautiful Pureland resurrected from the dead as his heart began reciting the words over and over:

Save her, save her.

Bend time and alter history, he was told. He had to imagine it before he could make it happen. How, you might inquire, can history be altered? Ridiculous, you say. How can time be anything other than a one-way street? The answer to that question and the prophetic conclusion to this paradox is no more preposterous than the very birth of the nation Salim called home. A poet's utopia carved with a pen.

You know very well how such utopias can be vulnerable from the start. When Pureland was devoured by the Caliphate, a deranged hunger for heretics began to spread and, in the land of the pure, there was no infidel more renounced than the lover Salim Agha. The leaders of the new Caliphate sat rummaging through old file cabinets until they found the first decree, the fatwa for Salim's blood. Fairly soon, the holy order was renewed and the Khalifa of Mosul announced that justice, as delayed as it may have been, must be served. The first to submit himself to carry out this execution of the Ahmadi heretic Salim Agha was the world's most feared assassin.

You sit up abruptly, elbows on table, and your eagerness is in plain view as I hint at the Scimitar.

For a moment, sir, assume I am not who they say I am and realize that the tales you know of this assassin are not only true but are also more wicked than your imagination can muster. Because evil has never had a better representative here on earth than the Scimitar.

You flinch because even you recall that day, a few months ago, when the Scimitar arrived in New York City. There was mayhem. We all felt it. Even I knew that the Scimitar, the right arm of God himself, was no meager hit man: a mastermind of horror who had slain thousands with his bare hands; a connoisseur of deception and fear, known to make grown men piss their pants; a ghost who left no footprints, had no shadow, and no one knew what he looked like. Hence, we only know of the Scimitar through the tales of his terror. There was nothing the city of New York could do in anticipation of his possible attacks but panic.

Salim was not one of them. He was not afraid of death. Because he was bound by a promise, a divine foretelling the heavens had burned onto his brow upon his birth.

The Mirage of Promise

———•❧•———

That morning, as Salim stared out the window of his apartment, beams of sunlight played tricks through the haze. His eyes fell on the Lexington Avenue sign below and followed the mindless trek that people had embarked upon. There was no regularity, just chaos. The same pandemonium that he had learned to love in this adopted city of his, now made him weary. He had been living in the apartment building up on Lex for more than thirty years. He recalled the day he'd moved in when Brother Carl had rented a truck because Salim didn't have a driver's license, and how they had carried his belongings up six flights of stairs as there were no elevators. He'd asked Brother Carl to stay with him that night as the emptiness of the place scared him. He would look out the window and pretend that he knew everyone on the street. It made him feel like they were a part of his home. Nonetheless, there was an added urgency apparent in everyone's stride that morning, perhaps because the S&P 500 had tanked, or because Homeland Security had raised the alert to Elton John Blue, or perhaps it had to do with the series of events that led up to that day.

 A few days earlier, Murray Hill's Burnhall Building on 27th, a five-story box-like structure with barred windows, had burnt down to ashes. The first responders, brave firemen from Battalion 8, had all bizarrely disintegrated to the point where dental records were required for identification. This kind of fire, the police claimed, had never been seen before. It was as though the building sat on a geyser of gasoline. Surely, this was the work of a professional and it was, at first, considered an inside job since no one from the ground floor Kebab King store was present at nine in the morning. There was reason to believe, the Police Commissioner declared, that insurance fraud might be the motive. It was later discovered that no vendors, or eaters of kebabs for that matter, are ever awake that early in the morning. There was no insurance policy the shop owners could claim as they wept on each other's shoulders the next day with reporters flashing cameras behind them.

Then there was the other incident. The fourth floor of the Camden Building up on 45th was blown clean out of the Manhattan skyline while the rest of the building folded into itself like a wet sandcastle. The nature of the blast and the unending blaze that followed led the Police Commissioner to declare this an act of terror.

The link between the two conflagrations became immediately clear. Both the owners of Kebab King and the forty worshippers that gathered on the fourth floor of the Camden Building belonged to the Ahmadi sect, political refugees from the country once known as Pureland. This tragic affair led to the firing of multiple Homeland Security officials, security guards, NYPD officers and, of course, the Police Commissioner himself. But these events were just warning shots fired by the Scimitar. His ultimate target was and remained Dr. Salim Agha.

I can go on about those incidents and the threats the Caliphate made on the media, but I want to bring our attention back to Salim's apartment.

The weather outside had begun to turn. Almost instantaneously, a thick grey blanket began to strangle any slivers of sunlight. As Salim stared out the window, behind him, in his apartment, a tall, bald man standing aloof cleared his throat.

"Dr. Agha, we do not have much time. You should gather your belongings so we can take you to a safe house," he said, with his large hands clasping each other against his belt buckle.

"I have this event at the university, officer. I've made a promise to a friend. I have to be there," said Salim. "The mayor will be there and I highly doubt the Scimitar would attack amidst a crowd." As if he knew what the Sword of the Caliphate was and was not capable of doing.

"If you must go to this event, we will have to escort you."

"Thank you for understanding. There is no need for the safe house, officer. There's one place I know of that no one can find," he turned to look at him. "You still don't know whom you're dealing with. He will find any safe house you try to put me in. My life has been under threat before, it doesn't scare me. My lab outside the city—it's secure and no one but my assistant Felix knows where it is. I shall go there."

It was true. The laboratory was the only place where his summoning made sense. It was the only place his outlandish inklings could be uttered out in the open. He only shared the whereabouts of this location with his trusted confidant and protégé, Felix Kestenbaum. It was also where he was close to the conclusion of his prophecy—to save Pureland, to bring her back, as it were, from the forgotten corridor of history.

Save her, save her.

As he stuffed clothes into a duffel bag, he looked out from his window one last time at the teeming city. Even on a grim cloudy day, the city roared. That was New York's greatest deception. She was a mirage of promise.

As he exited his apartment, wafts of fried potatoes rushed from Mrs. Bogdonovic's apartment across the hall. He recalled when he had first met her after she moved into the building some twenty years ago. Like him, she too was from a nation long forgotten, but every time one asked, she would stretch her chest and lift her nose to say, "Yugoslavia." He admired that about her. Her husband had died early and as soon as her only son turned sixteen, he left and never returned. On occasion, Salim had spent time with her in the evenings as they watched basketball. She had taken a liking to the Los Angeles Lakers just because of Vlade Divac, the former Yugoslavian center. She would relay stories of her homeland, of Serbs, Slovenes, and Croats living in harmony, and he would in turn tell her about canals and rivers and show her photos of the Karakoram Valley, of his beautiful Pureland.

"Your country gone now? Mine just split into four," she would say, holding up four crooked fingers as though it were any better. It was a display of hope. Every now and again, he would see her standing close to the revolving door of the lobby downstairs but never stepping out, only staring through the glass. She had not left the building in fifteen years.

As Salim exited and went towards the black car that had pulled up into the driveway, he looked at the city again, at the mirage of promise that had kept Mrs. Bognodovic hopeful all these years.

Before he sat in the car, he walked over to the coffee cart on Lexington Avenue where his Bangladeshi friend Tiger put his hands to his brow in a salute and said, "Don't worry, nothing will happen to you, we will protect you." He handed him his coffee and bent low until his eyes met Salim's. "Remember that time?"

"When?"

"When I first moved to the city. When they first came after you?"

"I remember."

"What did I say to you?"

"That I was guarded."

"Guarded by angels! See this," he said, pointing to his bicep. "One hundred push-ups a day, Professor Saab. One hundred."

"Thank you, Tiger. That means a lot," said Salim, taking his coffee. He took a deep breath before entering the car. He was inhaling reassurance. He valued Tiger's concern and knew that he could barely stand upright in his old age, let alone do a single push-up, but he wanted to believe that everything would be fine, that he would be able to return unharmed, that somewhere there were angels safeguarding his life.

The car engine began to roar as he sat in the backseat.

"Sir, I wanted to remind you that we can't have you going near your residence again. The Scimitar has struck once more. A severed head was found. It's a warning."

"Yes ... yes, I know," said Salim reluctantly. "Officer, I don't want to involve you any further. After this event, I'll go to my house in the suburbs." What else was he to say to that? He could tell that the sweat emanating from under the man's collar was not because of the weather. It was fear. The severed head was the Scimitar's signature move—a maneuver to coerce the opposition to lay down their cards and surrender.

Salim stared out of the rain-stained window while he leafed through his memory, imagining the time that passed as the streets clicked by before him. New York was like that, a collection of stories at each junction reeling past you. Through Central Park, the car swerved along under tiny bridges as he thought about the first time he had fancied a jog. He had made it past the first food cart but could not escape the second.

This was the city that had welcomed him like a lover, allowing him to settle into her arms. He remembered how overwhelmed he'd felt at first and how he had to de-program himself to live in freedom, with no master, no giver of orders. He found it strange that unmarried people could copulate with such immunity. Or that television had more than one channel; he had thought how unnecessary that was. He had marveled at why chocolate had so many different kinds. Why wasn't there just chocolate? And the ice cream ... why couldn't they just have vanilla-and-chocolate-mix, like they did in Lorr? America fascinated him.

The car took a right on to Broadway at the corner where he'd met Chip for drinks many years ago.

"Doc, we got a winner here," she had said to him. "The beauty of New York City is that everyone brings their story here and makes it a New York story. And your story is definitely that." He would later find out the hard way just how good his New York story really was.

Then they drove past Lincoln Center, where there stood an edifice he remembered fairly well. It was where he was lured into casual sex by a young professor during his graduate years. Each time they slept together, he felt he had disrespected his love for Laila. But he had marveled at the young woman's blonde hair and fair skin in contrast to his brown hairy arms, and she was mesmerized by the way he spoke.

"Get laid as much as you can while you can!" was what Brother Carl would say all the time. But sex never enticed him as much as it did others. After all, he wasn't like Carl or Tamboo Charming for that matter. He couldn't understand the idea of sex without love. It was similar to the notion of eating without hunger.

When he was done clutching onto the tokens of his past, that horrid feeling crept back in. His life was not flashing but tiptoeing past him, enticing him, mocking him, insulting him. He was petrified. It was a fear he did not want to have, especially not now when he was so close, so damn close to saving his beloved Pureland. He did not want to be in a car travelling to his doom. He felt foolish. But he had made a promise to Chip.

"I need you to come to this ceremony, Doc," she had said, scrunching her Pekinese nose. "We've made a promise to each other and I need this from you. There's no way you can get whacked with so many people around."

"But, Chip," he argued. "I don't have it in me to fight any more."

Chip's eyes closed halfway. Salim knew this look. She was holding back something that could have spilled over any second had she not declined her head. She took a deep breath and said, "Remember what I had told you?"

"What?"

"When this shit happened to you back in '87. Do you remember what I'd said?"

Salim thought for a moment as he bit into his lip.

"The only way to stop terrorism is not to be terrorized," she said, as her voice became nasal. She put her hand on his and he looked up at her.

"I remember," he said. "I remember."

"Then I expect you there tonight. They couldn't get to you then, and they won't get ya now!" That was the last thing she'd said, as she put her forehead to his. Salim could feel the wetness of her eyes even though she had tried so hard to hide it, and he knew what this meant to her, to their friendship. He knew that this was not just any appearance for him and, in a way, he thought that Chip was right, that there was only one way to live.

"Not to be terrorized," Salim said to himself as the car climbed up Morningside Avenue and into West Harlem, towards the university campus where he had begun his career. It was also where the city began to change. It became noisier and the people, humbler. He felt at ease here.

The car was parked and Salim approached the Davis Auditorium where a sign read:

Celebrating our very own and Nobel laureate, Dr. Salim Agha.

As he looked around, he saw that despite the threat, people had arrived in numbers.

When the backdoor to the auditorium was opened, he saw, behind the stage, his colleagues magnetized to a small television set. It was an old TV, one with a tube, one Salim hadn't seen in years. On the screen, from a few meters away, he could see his own face and the words Caliphate and fatwa echoed off the walls. As he approached the huddle, the TV was shut off abruptly.

"Dr. Agha, I didn't see you there," claimed Felix Kestenbaum still fumbling with the remote.

"It's fine, Felix. I won't be the first man to be assassinated," he said, looking around the room of blank stares, and smiled. "So why have we turned the TV off? I want to see how it ends ... only kidding."

"Let me bring you a coffee."

As he reached out for his coffee, he spoke into Felix's ear and handed him his cell phone. "Thank you, Felix. Keep my cell phone. You will need it to get into the house. Go now. I will meet you there later."

"We're close to achieving the impossible. We can't let this stop us," said Felix with his brow arching, his pale skin stretching below his red hair. It was evident from his droopy eyes that he too was sleep deprived. Salim reached out and squeezed his arm. He needed Felix. Even though at times he felt his eagerness could compromise the experiment, he had no choice but to trust him. He was the only one who believed in his madness. The only person who truly believed that the summoning was a blessing. Felix knew, from the moment Salim's eyes had changed, that something remarkable was about to happen.

But others didn't see Salim quite so clearly as Felix. They knew that when the summoning descended, as Salim's eyes blackened, their own livelihoods were in danger of ridicule and skepticism. Like the keepers of the cube of Mecca upon hearing about a new messenger sent forth by God, they felt, to put it mildly, threatened. Because they knew that Salim had stood there once before, right on the border between sanity and lunacy, and from that border he had brought forth new claims to unseen realities, pushing the frontiers of science. Now that the summoning had begun, they saw the same fervor in his eyes, and it made them shiver. They were fucked, no matter what. Whether he would emerge with new enigmas, the secret of which he kept hidden from them, or whether he retreated permanently into madness, either way science would be held responsible and taunting fingers would point in their faces. But he was still one of them, and for him they had this special day. It was a token of appreciation for his amazing career, a recognition of support in the face of terror.

The professors put their hands one by one on Salim's shoulder, lovingly patting his blazer.

"Gentlemen, I'm not a cat," Salim roared, igniting laughter in the room.

That changed the mood. Muffled sounds from a microphone could be heard from the stage behind the velvet curtain. For a moment, it seemed all would go well. Then Salim's phone rang in Felix's pocket. He broke from the huddle.

"Yes, this is Dr. Kestenbaum. Who is this? Oh. ... oh, I see. Let me see if he's available." Felix blanketed the phone with his hand and said, "Dr. Agha, it's for you."

"Well, who is it?"

"She says her name is Laila. Do you want me to take her number down?"

"No, I'll take it." Salim's eyes peeled in excitement as he rushed towards Felix, ripping the phone from his fingers. He counted five thumping heartbeats and tried to manage his racing breath before saying, "Hello."

"Salim ... Salim, is that you?"

"Yes, it is."

"Salim, it's me, Laila. How are you? I just heard about the Scimitar. I can't believe they have gone this far."

"Laila? It's so good to hear your voice. Where are you and are you alright?"

"Salim, I've been trying to call you and get in touch with you for days."

"Laila, I cannot begin to tell you what has transpired this past week. I had asked my assistant to take all phone calls and such. Where have you been? I tried getting in touch with Gibran and you after Pureland fell. In my mind I had told myself you must all be dead by now."

"Oh Salim, I know my silence over the years has caused you great agony. Our world has become a prison. But I've been a prisoner for longer than you think and now I feel like I can take no more. Major Liber Ali has left, my son is gone, and this city suffocates me." She paused as Salim's chest began to ache.

"Salim, my son Sameer is in New York. He has been there for a few years now but has landed himself in some kind of trouble with the wrong people." Laila began to cry, choking on her words. "He needs your help. Please help my boy. He is all I have in this world."

"Laila, this may sound ridiculous, but I'm a target of a deranged hitman. Sameer would only be in more danger with me."

"Salim, call him and please find a way to protect him ... please." Laila's words struggled to escape from under her sobs.

Save her, save her.

He took a deep breath. "Somehow, even after all these years, your pain is something I cannot handle. Tell me where Sameer is. I will keep him with me and try my best to protect him."

"There's more, Salim ... I want to come to New York. To be with you. I have no one left in this world except you. Can you make that happen?" Salim closed his eyes, knowing that the cosmos had yet again found a way to pull and push at his destiny simultaneously.

"It's been so long, Laila. All this time has passed and now you call asking to be with me. What do you expect me to say? At this, the most difficult of hours, where at any moment I can disappear. I had imagined you saying these words in my dreams, knowing that hearing them would make me feel elated, but now that they've arrived ... I'm puzzled."

"I know. I am to blame for that feeling, for that anger. But there's more to it than you might assume. I left our story unfinished all those years ago, open at that chapter, that rainy night. Stockholm meant more to me than I let you believe," she breathed into the phone. "Salim ... Sameer is your son."

Evil's Most Satisfactory Treat

As you can tell by now, sir, Laila had pawned her life for her father's honor. She did it to protect the bastard, Sameer Ali, and for years she wilted under the weight of this honor with a man who could never love her, in a society that bemoaned her, with a brother who despised her, just so that shame wouldn't taint her bastard son's life. That's some sacrifice.

A brief word about Lorr and we will return to Laila Khan.

We're told that empires are not built overnight. There might be some truth to that claim. But what's also true is that empires can crumble in minutes, entire cultures can evaporate never to return again. Such was the tale of Pureland and, more importantly, the city of Lorr. We let it happen, it was our fault. We choose who we want to serve and who should serve us. Isn't that the basis of Athenian democracy? Except, the moment that faint line between the chosen state and the inherited god fades, things fall apart. When preachers become the police, anarchy begins to breathe. What more can I say? Terror and politics—it's a relationship as old as time itself.

I've mentioned this before but it needs repeating. Some towns folded way before the tanks and the black flag of the Caliphate rolled down their streets. In fact, they sent out warnings months in advance. From the pulpits of the ancient churches of Damascus and the Sufi shrines of Istanbul a warning rang out to worshippers: stay home, shop's closed. But Lorr was stubborn and, let me tell you, she didn't go down easy. Before the massacre that led to the Year of the Rolling Heads, Lorr put up a fight. The world watched the masses gather on the Mall Road in a raging protest, fists held aloft. That was when the genocide commenced. I think you can recall, too, images of the millions that were cornered, trapped, and shot like mental dogs. Blood flowed through the Canal of Fables and it hasn't stopped since—the water's turned red forever.

That, in a nutshell, was the Year of the Rolling Heads. It was said that in Lorr there wasn't a street without a severed head. The city became a cautionary example for other dominions of the Caliphate, a menacing omen, bear witness, conform or suffer. And terror made people do funny things. The people of Lorr became bloodthirsty, as if bitten by zombies; they became possessed. The Lorr Stadium, which once held the Cricket World Cup final, began hosting weekly executions for petty crimes, theft, and promiscuity, drawing larger crowds than when the Sri Lankan Lions lifted the trophy in front of adoring fans at the '96 final. For those who survived the executions and the genocide, there was the Heresy Police, the gatekeepers of victimless crimes.

Which brings us back to Laila Khan.

Laila's future in Lorr hinged on the volatile whims of her brother Khalil, who vowed to slay her if she didn't relinquish the few scraps of land she had left, leftover trinkets from their feudal past. As the country they were born in shattered, Laila saw her brother's greed overtake his soul. The fact that she had failed to see his character descend into the ditch of treachery crushed her further. Because when evil's done devouring the remains of its arid surroundings, it turns to destroy its own kin—that is its most satisfactory treat.

Over the years following General Khan's death, Khalil hawked every last morsel of the dynasty to get-rich-quick schemes and interest free Islamic Mutual Funds. The Khan House was auctioned to members of the Caliphate's regime. Where Scotch tumblers once clinked together sparking evening laughter, there now stood a solemn brick structure with the words 'Heresy Police' defining its new tenants—SWAT teams that combed the streets for conspicuously clad girls, clean-shaven boys, and radio-listeners.

Khalil had fallen victim to the Caliphate's propaganda. What's worse, he became part of the ministry that ran the Heresy Police. He was a man of unwavering honor according to the Khalifa of Mosul, a man who would stop at nothing in order to enforce the law of the Almighty, a blind follower like Abraham of Israel who, upon God's command, was willing to sacrifice his own son. He had no qualms about bringing his own family to justice. He had done so with his baby brother, Gibran, who refused to part ways with alcohol and drugs and now he was after his sister because Laila was a blemish on his upright reputation. He vowed, before a council of his peers, to bring her to justice himself.

But what was Laila's crime exactly? No one truly knows the answer to that, to what precisely infuriated the Heresy Police, and made them come after her. Perhaps it was her reluctance to cease tutoring young girls in hidden basements. Or perhaps it was because she refused to ever cover her face in public, or that she hosted too many secret disco nights. But possibly, and this could be the most accurate assumption, it was because Laila Khan didn't give a fuck—she didn't follow orders, she gave them. And her audacity only grew after her husband left. She was forced to shuffle from safe house to safe house, wherever she could seek refuge from the mullahs. When she was finally compromised, she sat to negotiate her release from her own brother in a dark and dingy basement.

"Congratulations. The Khalifa of Mosul will be proud of you once you submit your own sister to the Heresy Police. I'm ashamed of you. You're not the boy I raised," Laila said, as she sat on an obscenely colored sofa under a flickering tube-light.

Khalil shook his head in slow motion and sucked his teeth, saying, "How do you like living in squalor, dear sister? Very Anne Frank of you, no? These fine colors remind you of our grandmother? So, where is that wretched son of yours?"

"He's far away from you. I won't let you do to him what you did to Gibran," she sobbed, wiping her nose with her sleeve. Her brother watched the girl who never brushed her own hair now sniveling like a servant. "So, what now? You turn me in? Receive a bounty for a heretic? Or submit me to a mental asylum like you did our baby brother?"

"I'll make a deal with you. If you hand over the papers to the summer house, I will leave you alone, free to roam wherever you want. As for Gibran, he got what was coming to him. You inject your life with poison day after day, and Allah punishes you in his own manner. It's his will. And you ... it's no surprise Major Liber Ali left you. You're a shame to the Khan family."

Laila rose to her feet, anger brewing on her forehead, and swung her arm. Her hand met Khalil's bearded cheek causing an echo in the dusky room. A tube-light sputtered with loud clicks.

"The only shameful thing I've ever done is to raise you." Khalil was deafened by the silence that followed her words. He stared at her with the astonishment of a virgin learning she was pregnant. "One more thing you might want to hear—the last bit of my father's inheritance is for me and my son ... and his real father, whom I will be with soon. Yes, I will be with Salim, the painter's son, away from this city, and away from your so-called family shame."

"I knew it! That worthless servant, that ungrateful villager ... and you!" he howled, raising his hands in the air, questioning the ceiling. "Why, God, why did you give us such a treacherous sister?" The hairs on his arms bloomed like poppies. The color in Laila's face flushed out momentarily. Her fear of the anxious mullah who sat waiting outside to take her to the gallows was overwhelming, but to see her brother writhe in pain gave her too much pleasure.

"Yes it's true, dear brother. The son of a measly Khanpur painter, whom our father sifted out from the dirt. The same Ahmadi peasant who lived in the crumbling compartments of our servant's dens. And me, your cherished sister, the torchbearer of the family's honor, the goat you sacrificed to an impotent man ... I bore a servant's bastard child, I..."

"Stop. Stop right now! It's not true! O Allah, why? What ill deed did our father commit to get such a daughter?"

In her brother's eyes, Laila saw a torment so agonizing she could not help but feel a slender bit of sympathy. And for a moment, she forgot that he had arrived with the intent of having her arrested. In that slight second, she put her hand on his wriggling shoulder and relieved him of his torture. "You want the papers to Daddy's summer house? The Pigglesworth property?" Khalil's body froze and his eyes acquired the look one has after a successful exorcism. "I will sign the papers over to you ... but in return you will let me go to New York and get these heresy dogs off my back. Make sure I'm safe for two more days until I leave, and you can have the bloody house."

"Don't lie to me now, Laila. I have no patience for your trickery," said Khalil as he stood upright, rejuvenated.

"No trickery. I have the papers right here. First agree to what I said, and you can have them. I will leave and you will never see me again."

"Fine, we have a deal. I swear to Allah."

She knew right away that she had played a serious gamble. There were no guarantees when it came to Khalil Khan but she had no choice. While he examined the deed to the Khan Summer House upon St. Mary's Hill Station, wiping snot from his beard, she prayed in her heart. Chip had arranged a seat for her on the UN Refugee plane scheduled to leave Lorr, and all she had to do was to be there on time.

As he left the room, Khalil looked at his sister one last time and she could see it in his eyes: money had trumped all, especially honor.

"Don't forget to have a stiff drink in the evenings for Sir Pigglesworth," she said, as he was about to leave.

"Goodbye, Laila. I will pray for your soul and that you may absolve yourself of this shame one day," Khalil said, as he left the room and got into a parked car where an HP officer impatiently scratched his balls in anticipation of marking another suspect into his charge sheet.

As she sobbed in the company of her own shadow, she covered her mouth with her hands as to not let her cries escape. But her sadness could not be confined. She howled so loud the walls began to shiver. For the first time in her life, she was completely alone. There were no maids, guards, or lovers left to pick up her broken pieces. She had no one except the one who loved her with all her faults. In some way, she had known that all along. Because his love for her was untainted by shame—sinless.

But did she ever love him back or did she remember him as a mistake she had made? It's hard to tell but, in the loneliest hour of her life, surrounded by the void of her captivity, she knew she had no one else to turn to.

Before she departed Lorr, Laila revealed this secret of hers to Major Liber Ali, just one parting phone call to crush his honor so he would know that he had spent his life raising the seed of a peasant. This act of hers perplexes me to this day; for her to use that very shame she'd harbored her whole life as a tool to chastise those who imprisoned her, the spiteful brother, that callous husband. Why? If you ask me, I think this secret was all she had left in the world, her only hope, her only weapon. And by withdrawing it from its sheath and delicately spearing it into their hearts, she managed to take back something she'd lost a long time ago—her liberty.

Apostle

Sir, when you walked in here, I could tell from your face that you assumed things about me, things that are not true. Terrorist? Yes, I know. I told you, I don't like that word at all. I'd like to distinguish myself from that label. In fact, I would like you to think of Pureland differently too.

The bearded fiends who chant vehement passages of the revealed text, the ones who claim to represent us all—they want just that, that we all be treated the same. They want that we use one label for all the people governed under the black flag of the Caliphate. We can't let that happen.

So, what makes us different? Us, as in, myself, Salim, and the people of his nation. There must be something about the damn country, you ask, that drew the Caliphate in. They thought we had gone astray and needed realignment. We were, as per the words of the Khalifa of Mosul, bad Muslims. If I were to give you my honest opinion, sir, I would say it was because Pureland was a nation of Sufis, of lovers. I openly claim to be from that mystic school of thought. Yes, there is no doubting the fact that I am a man of faith, and this faith has guided me throughout my life. We Sufis are vehicles of love, travelling through this wilderness of malice, swaying our heads to the hypnotizing beat of the dhol, whispering the name of our beloved. That is devotion. We worship through art, not through bowed heads. In our world, God can only be found through love, for a companion, a paramour and, most importantly, a mentor. For in our world, it is the mentor who guides us to nirvana. We don't worship mentors, no sir, of course not. That would defeat the purpose. Allow me to give you an example.

The poet Rumi once said of Abu Bakr, Prophet Mohammed's most trusted friend and his premiere convert, that he was essentially the original Sufi mystic who relinquished his worldly belongings on the path of devotion, on the path of his sage, his *aaka*. It can be safe to assume that Abu Bakr's resilient support for Mohammed, son of Abdullah, helped the Prophet deliver his message. This mystic relationship is important to understand as I begin to tell you about the final days of Salim Agha's life.

I will talk about Salim's achievements a bit before I return to the matter of mysticism. We know that our modernity rests on the foundations of some rare achievements in the realm of science. Our understanding of the world today has been shaped by such discoveries. Surely, you can't launch a rocket if you don't know the renowned edicts of Sir Isaac Newton. Nor can you contemplate relativity without Einstein. Salim Agha's elegant formula of universal energy, the one that creates harmony between our known world and the cosmos, is one of those fundamental contributions I speak of, and practitioners of science would agree that Salim's impact on the advancement of our species is undeniable.

In the early years after Salim had won the Nobel, the university found it difficult to hold his lectures. The halls were too small. So many students would fill the auditoriums, they became potential fire hazards. And when the fatwa added to his stardom, Salim found it almost impossible to walk the campus without students asking him to scribble on their book covers. But when the summoning began in 2014, all this changed.

It happened almost suddenly. The lecture halls began emptying out. Peculiar notions began creeping into Salim's lectures, concepts which were far removed from the syllabus. Actually, far removed from reality itself. His abnormal beliefs in time travel had started rumors amongst the other professors. They believed, as any skeptic would, that he had lost his mind. Like Stanley Weinberg, he began to develop a reputation. At times even Salim thought he had gone completely bonkers, but at other times his thoughts were too persuasive. He just didn't know how to prove them; they seemed too bizarre. He knew no one would regard the dream sequences that had begun to occupy his mind. So, he became, as he had once before, a recluse. He trusted no one, not Brother Carl, nor Chip Beetlewood—no one but the long-nosed freak, Felix Kestenbaum.

There was something odd about Felix so a word or two here suffices. At first sight, he looked like someone had put a garden hose in his mouth and let the water run. His peculiar body sat on two twig-like legs and his hair was like thousands of fiery red corkscrews escaping his scalp. Most peculiar of all, however, was his skin, scattered with red spots, galaxies of celestial freckles lathered over a pale white universe. Oh, and the nose, what a nose it was! A spiraling roller-coaster which had the most disgusting of moles nestled under its shadow. Yes, one could imagine how challenging it was for Salim, or anyone else for that matter, to have faith in Felix Harman Kestenbaum.

While other students pointed fingers at Salim during lectures as he droned on in absurd soliloquies, Felix's eyes widened with eager appreciation. He would be the only one in class to raise his hand as high as possible and bark responses to Salim's inquiries:

"Say we were to combine the two points of time on a linear field by folding the paper," Salim would say to a soundless lecture hall. "What would we need?"

And even before Salim could finish, Felix would answer with an exigent liveliness, "You need energy. Enough energy to pierce through the fabric of time-space!"

To which Salim responded with an enthusiastic smile as some confidence trickled back into his depleted heart. After the lectures, Felix would continue to engage him in these uncanny dialogues, urging him on the notion of ultimately piercing the space-time fabric.

Thus, when the summoning began and the strangeness engulfed Salim, Felix's voice was the only reassurance he had. He was his only apostle, his *mureed*. Similar to the encouragements Abu Bakr had given Mohammed, son of Abdullah, of his sanity and steadfast character, suggesting to him that he, in fact, might be the courier of a celestial message, Felix impelled Salim to dive forth into the realm of uncertainty, to pull off the unimaginable, to conquer time itself.

"If you don't try, Dr. Agha, how will you know? Isn't experimentation the basis of our discipline?" he asked one day.

"Why can't we..." Salim had responded in a trance.

In that moment, clarity had shocked Salim like a bolt of lightning. He retracted immediately to his suburban home, to his secret laboratory, and didn't return for days. Leafing through old papers in his basement, ones that he had deemed too laughable to share, yet too unique to throw away, he stared into space, with pieces of his past pulling together immaculately, revealing to him his predestined fate. Images of a boy pointing to the stars, the archangel Gabriel whispering in his ear, the city that owned time itself, and a promise he had made to his beloved of conquering the unconquerable.

I can't imagine what would have happened to Salim had he not met Felix, but I do know that the two of them set forth on an unthinkable journey. But why did Felix choose Salim as his mentor? Your question is legitimate, because I, too, asked myself the same thing. Well, because there was more to Felix Harman Kestenbaum than met the eye.

He was born to first generation Polish-Jewish immigrants in Brooklyn's Borough Park. His father was a timid and dull individual who drove his wife into another man's arms. Adina was a real attraction, a woman of high cheekbones and sunset skin, a glaring opposite of her grotesque son, Felix. She was classy and instilled in Felix the meaning of status. She threw fancy cocktail parties and decorated the house with expensive flowers. Felix would examine the looks on people's faces when he would emerge from behind her long dress to present himself. The guests would often jump backwards in shock, as though Adina had sprung a snake on them. Yet she took nothing but pride in her son. Especially when she heard the callous limerick that followed him at school:

Felix the Feeler Kestenbaum sucked every dick in town,
When all the dicks dried away Felix the Feeler ran away.

"Don't you pay attention to those nasty children, Felix," she would say. "Your mind is far greater and more beautiful than anything this world has seen. You can conquer everything."

She knew that nothing attacked dignity like a child's cruelty. And her son's dignity was stomped on every day.

But one day, when Felix received a phone call from the police summoning him to the Pennsylvania Hotel, his life changed forever.

He arrived at the scene of the crime to a body bag peeled opened to reveal the angelic face he had loved his whole life, with its celestial hair and teasing grin. His mother had made a death pact with her lover, leaving him with haunting questions that were never answered. On silent nights, Felix would lay blinking at the ominous red flashes on his window from the street below. He felt his mother disappearing from his memory. He feared that one day he would awake and not remember that Adina smelled like oatmeal in the mornings, or how warm her palms felt on his face. He felt like he would forget the only person that had ever loved him, and to bring back his mother was a promise he made to himself each night before falling asleep. He shared with his mentor the same resilient dream—to take from time what it had stolen from him.

When the summoning began, Salim and Felix constructed a secret lair in Salim's basement and began to conduct experiments that bordered on insanity. Thousands of attempts to penetrate time failed. Small mass objects—tennis balls, pencils, paperclips—were shot through with volts of energy. With Deema Engine's help, they manufactured an apparatus so ridiculous, it should have, under normal circumstances, initiated phone calls to mental institutes asking for vacancies.

After each unsuccessful attempt it was Felix who was the optimist. "More energy, that's the answer. We will try again!" he exclaimed.

The evening they learned of the Scimitar, Salim and Felix sat in the bowels of the laboratory. A heated exchange had unsettled them. The freckles had darkened on Felix's face. It was what happened when he was angry, or if he had eaten a habanero pepper.

"I'm telling you Dr. Agha, there's no other alternative. We've been through this thing several times and..."

"Oh stop it now, Felix! I heard what you have to say and we cannot increase the damn energy. This is bloody preposterous. We will be singed!" he yelled, pacing up and down the control room like an expecting father in a delivery room. "Just do as I say and run the damn thing at eight like we did before."

Felix gave him a look of disgust and waited until he turned his back.

"Logging mission. Energy levels are at eight of ten. The destination date is set." With the image of his mother returning to him through a misty haze, his hands swiftly moved to the lever, pulling them to towards the number ten.

"Activating levers now..." said Felix as he heard Salim drop his mug of coffee and pummel his way towards him, leaping into the air like a puma.

"You bastard! You will kill us both! Are you insane?"

Crimson locks fluttered in the air as they both crashed on the ground below, rattling a nearby shelf. Felix held Salim's hand and twisted it towards his own back. Salim turned around and thrust his elbow in Felix's face, causing his glasses to leap off his hooked nose. Meanwhile, in the reactor a beam of light shot through, zapping an old tennis ball with the word 'Adina' written in black marker.

The ball disappeared.

When I initially heard of this occurrence firsthand, it bombarded my mind with puzzling questions. I believe you feel the same way right now. I can't tell you for sure whether all this was true, whether that bizarre experiment succeeded or not, but I can imagine the feeling that enveloped both Salim and Felix. They knew then that whatever it was that they had to conquer was so close they could touch it. I can imagine tears rolling down their faces as they both looked at the vacant space where Adina had left a cloud of smoke. I can imagine that, for Salim, the smell of his village after the rains, blew through the room and in the background, he could hear the sounds of the euphoric dhol of Lorr's marble shrines. I can imagine both the *aaka* and the *mureed*, the mentor and his disciple, wrapped in the ecstasy of their triumph. I can also imagine Salim's eyes. The pupils shrinking back to normal as the summoning finally concluded.

The Bastard

———• ⚜ •———

Sir, I've chosen this moment to introduce you to the bastard. I see you have been eagerly waiting for him. So here goes...

The bastard Sameer Ali was conceived on that rainy night in Stockholm in 1979. 'Just one night'. The only night Salim could recall with meticulous clarity: the rain drumming lightly on his hotel room window, a Nobel medal on the bedside table, a princess asleep in his arms; two prizes on one miraculous evening. He had made love to Laila slowly, preciously, as if not to break her, and when he climaxed, she giggled underneath him.

She left early the next morning though, before he awoke—away to Lorr to engage in the courtship her father had chosen for her: a lifelong bondage with General Ali's son, Major Liber Ali. For General Khan, it was a proud moment as she was gifted to Major Ali in a ceremony lasting five long days, a grand gala, one that Lorr had never witnessed before.

When she discovered she was pregnant, wiping her morning sickness from her chin, staring at her reflection in the mirror, she feared the worst. Because she knew that Liber Ali was many things, but a penetrator he was not. It was too late, because at the first hint of this familiar nausea, the families began to celebrate the possibility of an all Pashtun prince, heir to a double dynasty, a future army man.

But it was not to be. Sameer Ali's birth widened eyes and made brows quiver with astonishment. And mouths, well, they started whispering—Major Liber Ali's bride had brought with her an unwanted dowry. The baby didn't look anything like the Major. It was a peculiar rumor which was dangerous to repeat, an awkward torment that kept burning in Liber Ali's gut. He also doubted whether his wife had been a virgin when she'd arrived in his home. Even though she had done such a convincing job on their wedding night, cunningly squeezing sheep's blood from an eyedropper on to the sheets and squirming as though she was being had for the first time. But he never spoke of any of his concerns to her because he thought saying something would make his worst fears come true.

Of course, Laila had many lovers before him. Some random ones too, at extravagant parties in dark corners of inner-city havelis where she had lost her virginity to a textile scion in the bathroom, pushed against the wall as onlookers peeked in, tiptoeing from the window, hands over mouths. She remembered how she'd felt afterwards—guilty, dirty. She loved it. This was followed by her hypersexual years when, allegedly, she had the entire city of Lorr in the palm of her hands and could turn the manliest of men into vulnerable puddles. Suitors, from feudal princes to businessmen, lined up outside the Khan House pleading for her hand in marriage. She used them all. Every single one of them was on the hook for something or another, competing for her love through gifts and generous parties; parties where she was the central figure. That went on for a while until Khan decided that it was best if she was married off. So, her marriage put an end to all sexual enterprises, as marriages often do. She was handed a prescription for a new life: to uphold the honor of Major Liber Ali. She took on this mission from the very morning she left Salim's hotel room, quietly packing her clothes like a zombie, half asleep, stepping from the wet streets of Stockholm straight on to a Lorr-bound airplane.

Laila tried hard to be the wife the world wanted her to be, she truly did. She even tried to exercise her illicit passions with her husband in bed. But he was as absent under the covers as he was in life. Thus, she went about her days devoting herself to her son Sameer and would only relive her past in short bursts at the occasional party when Liber Ali was not around, in bright living rooms where Scotch-and-soda laughter was a contagious thing. She would sit eyeing young polo players in their tight jeans and husky voices, rub up against dim middle-class male models on the dance floor, and even give the odd hand-job to former lovers behind the bushes. That was the extent of it though. She never slept with anyone, lest her honor be compromised.

As the years progressed, Sameer became a souvenir of the mistake she had once made and for Major Liber Ali, he became a stain on his lineage, a disgrace to his pedigree. He never questioned Sameer's legitimacy but never denied it to himself either. With his painful silence, he did to Sameer what no father should ever do to a child.

"Why are you always putting Sam down? He yearns for your love," Laila would ask.

To which Liber Ali's response would be, "When he becomes captain of the cricket team, then we will see." Or, at times he would say, "When he becomes number one in his class, then we will embrace him." And his worst response: "When he becomes the youngest major in the army, then he will make us proud."

Liber Ali never used the word 'I' to describe himself. By 'we' he meant his tribe, his race, his feudal lands and everyone who had the audacity to live on them. He spoke for all of them. He never kissed his son, never hugged him, nor did he ever speak to him for longer than a minute. Had he been Liber Ali's own seed, it's quite possible Sameer would have endured similar treatment, because Liber Ali was that kind of man—love confused him.

As a child, Sam would walk up to his father in the evenings when he'd have friends over, when Liber Ali would be at his most vulnerable and say, "See, Abba, my report card. Teachers say I'm the best artist in all of Blisschesterson. They say I can paint anything I want."

Whereupon, his father would look from under his brow, jaw jutting out and say, "Sam, you should be the best in *proper* classes, not just bloody drawing and painting," and return to his conversation with his guests. That was the extent of the father-son relationship.

Sameer hungered for approval and for love, which he ultimately found in eyes like ocean-deep emeralds, a place where once another child's heart had sought refuge. It was General Khan who knew early on in the boy's life that there was a void which only he could fill. His fondness for his grandson was something greater than he had ever bestowed upon his own sons, and Sam too loved him to the point of madness.

The reality that Sam was unlike his father didn't matter to Khan. In fact, he thanked the Lord for it. The one thing he was sure of though, was that the boy's mind was sharper than the Major's. Khan didn't care that his skin was brown or that his hair curled into rebellious spirals. He tried to spend every moment possible with his grandson. On their trips to the village on Sundays, he would take the boy's hand and point it beyond the sugarcane fields, far into the distance where the canal dipped into the horizon.

"This is all yours, my son."

"Are you sure, Daddy? All of it?"

"Of course, my boy. Everything."

The General couldn't help but see that the boy's eyes did not lie. Somewhere deep in their alluring glimmer, tucked far away, there was Salim smiling back at him. He had to shake his head each time he had this vision. Laila, too, saw this every day. And no one could ignore the boy's ability to construct the most accurate depictions with a paintbrush. His hands were made to create, and with the most intricate of pin-prick touches, he could produce astonishing and intricate paintings. In the silence of Khanpur's Ahmadi cemetery, deep beyond the kino trees, Jaaji's chest expanded with pride each time this took place.

Of course, Liber Ali never expressed such delight. He was an emotionless man—an impassive cyborg wandering the arid wasteland of a dreary underworld. He barely spoke to Laila, barely touched her. In fact, after their wedding night, the Major developed an unexpected case of impotence. What's worse, he blamed her for it. She, too, felt disposed like her son, lonesome, abandoned, reduced to afternoons of melancholic gin-and-tonics, playing solitaire in the veranda, wrapped in the rueful guilt of thinking it was her fault that her husband couldn't get it up, that she was not as beautiful as people had been telling her all her life.

Sameer Ali had a childhood seeped in anguish. He didn't have many friends at school, and bullies constantly had their way with him. His nanny, Bilki, who had arrived at Liber Ali's home as a part of the dowry, was the only person he admired as much as General Khan himself. Hers was the first face he'd laid eyes on at birth, and when Laila, panting from labor pains, handed him to her, Bilki immediately understood the job at hand. She'd done it many times before. From his very first night, and for the nights that followed, Sameer slept tucked against her bosom. She was, in every way imaginable, his mother and best friend. She taught him everything: how to make a slingshot from banyan branches, knot a double-breasted kite and, his favorite, burp the entire alphabet in one go. And whenever the boy fell sick, she would hold his hand at night and tell him a story. By the time morning came, his illness would vanish. Magic story, they called it. It worked every time. The old hag loved the bastard to death. She had raised Laila and her brothers and cared for them deeply, but there was something special about Sameer. The minute he came into the world and wrapped his tiny fingers around hers, she had fallen in love.

One day, when Sameer was seven, he returned home from school with a purple eye. Bilki was so enraged she didn't sleep all night. The next day, she marched right into his classroom, grabbed the bucktoothed bully by the collar, and pointed at his crotch saying, "See this little thing? If you touch my boy again, I will cut it into little ribbons and feed it to you! Understand?" Nodding as he gulped, the shivering little shit got the hint and, from that day on, left Sameer well alone.

However, time began to catch up with Bilkis Kaur, and with time came remorse. Around the spring of '89, a couple of years after General Khan's death, Bilki began losing her marbles. A recollection from her youth, of the brutal Partition and Khanpur's riots of 1947 began to make her tremble in her sleep. The same nightmare, every time:

A furious mob approaches with swords held aloft. They've come for honor, and the teenage Sikh boys, with their elbows locked, are there to guard it. "God is great!" the mob chants, as turbans fall to the ground. Then there's her father, the kino farmer, pushing his kirpal dagger into his own throat. Her sisters are there too, queuing up behind the well, jumping into it one by one before the horde gets to them. But Bilkis

Kaur, the shameful, the coward, sits veiled behind a tree. She makes a dash towards the fields. Now she sits crouched between sticks of sugarcane, biting her fist, silently listening to the mob do what they'd come to do. Fast-forward to the next morning: the coward emerges, tiptoeing towards the aftermath, stepping through a mist of flies over motionless corpses.

This vulgar dream stirred in her mind until she could smell her family's blood and feel their blank, vacant eyes stab her heart. She became a mute, her mind serving a life sentence in a prison of nightmares, and a constant tremor began running through her arms. The doctors declared that she was suffering from trauma; what kind exactly, they were unsure. She'll be fine in the morning, they concluded, and sent her on her way.

"Don't you worry, Bilki Ma. You'll be alright," Sameer said to her that night, caressing her forehead. "Nothing will happen to you. You sleep right here with me until you get better. Remember the magic story of Laaj, the princess of Shalm? I'll tell it to you, and tomorrow you'll be as good as new. You sleep now, Bilki Ma. You sleep." While he lay there next to her, holding her shaking hand, Sameer recited the magic story until he dozed off.

The next morning, when he awoke, with Bilki's fingers still in his hand, he jumped up in excitement.

"Bilki Ma! See, I told you. Your hand's not shaking anymore. Mummy! Come see ... Bilki Ma is fixed. I fixed her!"

Bilki's hand had indeed stopped moving but Sameer still didn't let go of it, rubbing it with his thumb as he repeated the magic story over and over again until Pappu Pipewalla and Billa Cycle arrived from Khanpur, snuck up behind him and placed a single white sheet over her face. That's when the boy began to scream.

"Take that off her, you bastards! She'll suffocate. Are you crazy?"

Laila yanked him away, wrapping him in her arms until he stopped wailing. When Billa carried the lifeless Bilki on his shoulder out into the garden, Sameer walked to his room, locked the door and went to sleep. From that day on, he never talked about her again, nor did he ever visit her grave. Khan's death was hard enough on the boy, the idea of his alleged murder weighed down on him unforgivingly but after Bilki left his world, his heart turned to stone.

Years later, as the city around him began to crumble, he locked himself in his room and drowned himself in art. He spent hours in isolation, dripping oil paint onto canvases, and every once in a while, he would display his work at exhibitions. Other than that, he remained indoors, smoking cigarettes, drinking, and making art. Laila let him. It was the only thing he loved that hadn't been taken from him yet. That was until the Caliphate arrived.

"Sam, if the Heresy Police discovers your paintings they will have you taken away," she said to him.

"Fuck the Heresy Police."

"Sam, you are all I have left in this world."

"Fuck your world."

It took some convincing, but finally Laila put Sameer on a New York bound plane. She had no choice. But she also knew that over the years, he had taken from Liber Ali the worst of his character. He had absorbed his arrogance and carried it with him to New York. Petty remains of his mother's inheritance saw him through for a few years, but soon enough, his funds evaporated, and when his paintings were repeatedly ignored at art exhibitions, he turned to alcohol and cocaine.

He refused to find a job and continued to bleed his mother for money. As Laila had feared, Sam fell deep into debt with the type of people that extracted fingers as recovery payments. That's when she sought Salim's help and, a few days later, that was when Sameer arrived at Salim's doorstep.

"Salim Saab!" Sameer cried with outstretched arms as the door opened. "Finally I meet the great Salim Agha. I've heard so much about you all these years. Quite frankly, sir, I am an admirer of yours."

Stunned, Salim stared into his son's eyes for the first time. There, all his previous doubts, if he had any, of Sameer's authenticity, were put to rest. Because there was no question that he was his blood, and that Jaaji peered at him through the brown of his eyes. And similar to the painter's, Sameer hands were angular, with square fingertips.

"Salim Saab, are you alright? You look like you've stopped breathing."

He lunged at him and held his son without courtesy, pulling him close to his chest. The same way Jaaji had done with him the day he'd left the village.

"Okay, okay, sir. Take it easy. I'm not going anywhere." Salim found it hard to pull away from him.

"Please, come in. I've set everything up for you. You can stay in the guest room." He started walking with urgent steps. His hands began a nervous fidget.

Felix's jaw dropped to his chin as he stood behind Sam in the doorway. Here he was, in the lab of secrecy, with a stranger clinging to Salim's shoulders. This was his lab! Humiliation painted his face pink.

"I've arranged for your mother to be here soon. My friend Chip is very resourceful, you see." He went to the kitchen and pulled out a dish of macaroni from the fridge, as Sam sat on a bar stool slapping his hand on the granite counter.

"That's all fine. Just tell me, Salim Saab—may I call you Salim Saab? Would it be alright if I smoked in here?"

"No!" cried Felix.

"Well ... yes, I think it will be fine. I will just open the window." He didn't know how to respond to this inquiry. What was he to do? Say no to his only son? His only trophy of a love lost in a timeless memory? "Here, I can turn on the exhaust on the stove."

So, this is how it went.

Felix's annoyance grew over the days before Salim's murder. He would mutter to himself and roll his eyes at the new guest. Sameer, on the other hand, lazed about the house like he owned the damn place. Salim constantly picked up after him and made sure he had all the comfort he could provide. He took care of all that needed to be taken care of. He watched him closely as he ate, with his left hand of course, noticing how his mouth had the curve of Laila's lips, and how uncanny it was that he spoke with the painter's raspy voice. Just as Salim was eyeing him, matching his attributes to himself and the people he loved, Sam did the same. Like sleuths, they examined each other. But while

Salim would turn away smiling, Sam would pout, raising his brow. No one noticed this strange expression except Felix.

"A bloody drink would be good right now, no Salim Saab?" he said one evening.

"I don't think we should be…"

"Oh ho, Salim Saab. This is America. Please, I'm a grown man. What say you, Red? We could all use one."

"I don't want a drink."

"See, you got Red all upset for no reason. All day you two spend downstairs. All this anxiety of the Scimitar and all. Bullshit, I say. You need to let loose, Salim Saab, and Red, my boy, I think you could do with a whiskey as well. My mother said I shouldn't leave your presence until she arrives … but I'm so bored, Salim Saab."

Salim thought to himself for a moment. Stepping out of the house was something he didn't want; it was too dangerous. He couldn't afford jeopardizing everything. All for what? Why was he even thinking about it? But he had this desire to give into anything the boy asked for. Felix had noticed this change in him from the moment Sam first walked through the door. His mentor had become a servant again from a time long ago. Orders were made and he could do nothing but obey them. But Salim felt enough was enough. He wouldn't just roll over to any demand. Son or no son.

"What would you like to drink?" was all he was able to say.

"Johnnie Walker, Black … breakfast of champions!" Sam smiled back at him and turned towards the TV in the lounge. Salim sprang to his feet and began looking for his keys. Felix came up behind him.

"Have you lost your mind?"

"Excuse me?"

"Where are you going? Your'e going to get killed, old man. We're so close. So damn close! And you will sacrifice it all for what? A stupid kid?"

"What do you know, Felix? What do you know about anything? About me, about who I am? About all the sacrifices I've made to get here?"

"I am the *only* one who knows about those sacrifices!" The silence became heavy. Their breathing quickened. "I don't know who you are any more," he said as he made for the door. "I think I'll just leave."

"Wait, Felix, wait." Salim held on to his arm. "They are after me, whoever they are. But they don't know Sam. Why don't you take him to the city? Go for a night. I think we're all tired of being in this place. Just lay low and be back tomorrow morning. You asked me when we're doing this? Tomorrow is the day."

The creases in Felix's brow flattened immediately. "You're not just yanking my chain, are you?"

"All these years ... have I ever lied? Tomorrow it happens."

"Fine." He looked over at the living room where a leg swung back and forth on the sofa. "I'll take the brat out. But tomorrow, we are fucking doing it."

———◆———

It was not a situation he would have liked to be in. However, Felix Kestenbaum sat quietly, scarlet curls forced into a wave along the top of his head—ponytail blooming from behind. His gut, girded by a colorful belt, spilled over his khakis as he slouched in the booth. They were in a dingy room that smelled of leftover beer.

The bastard Sameer grinned and grabbed Felix by the arm saying, "Great place, huh?"

"You're joking, right? What the fuck are we doing here? Is this the best place you could find? I said we have to lay low, not be trapped in a dungeon."

"Look, Red," Sam began, running his tongue over his teeth. "Aren't you happy I convinced the professor to let us out of that house?"

"I convinced..."

"Whoever. We've been locked up for days. I needed a drink, and ... let's face it. It's his life in danger, not ours. The Scimitar wants him, not us."

"You know," Felix said pausing. "I thought to myself, who is this proud fuck, coming into our lives, invading our privacy. Maybe he has something to contribute. Or maybe he will help us catch the fucking Scimitar. Dr. Agha just let you in the front door as if he were waiting for you his whole life. One phone call and here you are. I thought you would be someone of value but you're not. You needed his money to bail you out. And you don't care for him. This is all a joke to you."

"Fine, fine," said Sam. "Yes, I did need the professor's money to sort out a couple of loose ends and what not. But I'll have you know, it was my grandfather who made him the man he is today. In a way, the professor is paying back an old debt." He let out a sinister giggle. "You won't get it. It's how it worked in the old world. But forget that. I see you're getting irritated. Look, Red. You've been wary of me since we met. You watch my every move. You have your head so far up my ass I can taste your yarmulke."

"I don't wear a..."

"That's not the point. Give me a chance ... you might like what I have to say." He extracted a Zippo lighter and a pack of Marlboro Lights from his sweatshirt, lit a cigarette and said, "As to your earlier inquiry, my boy, this is why I come to this fine establishment. They let you smoke. It's the only place left in the city." He let out a puff towards the ceiling. "So, this contraption that you have built, what does it do precisely?"

"Well, let me see... It does none of your fucking business is what it does. I'm not Dr. Agha. I don't have to put up with your nonsense," said Felix, pushing down on the table with his palms, raising his large frame up from the booth.

"Come now," Sam said holding on to Felix's freckled arm, pulling him back down. "I can see you're getting redder by the second. I have a proposition for you." He looked around, blinking ever so slowly and said, "There's something disturbing you, Red. I don't know what it is, but I see it every time you two emerge from the lab. Like you're being forced against your will. It works, whatever the hell it is, and you want to get in there on your own. Am I right?"

Felix let out a deep sigh. The kind that escapes your lips when you lose energy, too tired for anger. "I want to. Yes." Felix peeled the label off his beer and twirled a lock of hair behind his ear.

"You need to get in there and do your own thing. You can't afford to waste the one chance you have on what Dr. Agha wants, do you? He runs an airtight ship. We both know that. No one gets inside without him punching codes and fingerprints and what not. Also ... if he senses the slightest bit of trouble, he'll make the whole thing implode," he said, making a rising mushroom cloud with his hands. "But he envies you, Red. I can see it in his eyes. Why?"

"Because he is an old fool who doesn't..."

"Doesn't trust you? I know, it can be an infuriating feeling. Believe me, I know. He doesn't trust anyone. But he trusts me. Like I said, in a way he owes me," he said, putting up two fingers at a waitress holding a vacant plastic tray. "What if I had a solution to that? Let's get one more drink, shall we? It's been a rough few days. No one knows where we are. My apartment is safe. I'm a nobody. The least we can do is have a good night, go to my apartment, rest, and head back with a clear head in the morning. And of course, with a solid plan to let you in that lab—alone."

The Dreamer, the Thespian

———•⚹•———

Since the summoning began, right after his nation vanished, Salim's prophecy became clear to him. His adversary was the very monument he longed to summit: time. He had to conquer it before it was too late. That's how he saw it anyway.

I'll try and be impartial here. But to truly understand what Salim was going through, we must assume what he assumed, try and see with his eyes. Only then can we truly draw a conclusion on this prophecy. During those days, on the cusp of summer, after that incident of the vanishing ball, where he believed he had finally achieved the impossible, he lay pondering the solitude, the sacrifices that made it all possible.

It was a loneliness so intense that even his shadow begged to part ways—a laborious time with nothing but him and his thoughts. This was the prison he had endured for so long. As he lay in bed, he heard crickets in the garden singing into the night. After all those failed experiments, he felt at ease. All the time he had spent doubting his sanity had finally yielded something. His time in confinement was about to end. But even he had to ask the one question that had been troubling everyone since the summoning began. Was he insane? Was this all part of a never-ending daydream? I can't reveal the answer to that. I can only tell you that, in an attempt to save his nation, he was, in a way, trying to save himself.

There were many things that had perturbed him during the years I speak of, the years of isolation. He thought of his epileptic seizures that, at times, left him in utter pain, bleeding from his ears, and how they made for remarkable visions. Visions which, as absurd as they were, inspired him. He never repudiated these miracles, but almost reasoned them out of existence. He convinced himself that his hallucinations did not hold weight in the real world, his world of evidences. He was a man of proofs and experiments. He didn't care for the tyranny of the revealed text that plagued the world. When he was awake, he rejected all dogmatic mystery but, in the stillness of sleep, he longed to seek patterns, give in to superstitious transcendence.

When the strangeness began and the summoning commenced, his rendezvous with the archangel Gabriel became quite regular. He learned to be a good listener and a friend to Gabriel. The angel spoke to him of rebellion in the heavens and said, "Believe you me, Salim Saab, here is a world where humans struggle to be angels and the divine long to be human." Bizarrely, the archangel himself had the most aching desire to live on earth. Salim thought this to be an absurd aspiration for God's most beloved angel, who lived in paradise without pain or suffering.

But Gabriel argued once, sitting cross-legged, hand under chin. "When the role of archangel was up for grabs, Salim Saab, believe you me, I was the first in line, application under my arm, only to realize I was the *only* one standing when God raised the question with us winged councilmen. The others closed their eyes, lifting their noses snobbishly. They despised the idea of speaking to men in coveted sonnets, in dark caves and lecherous deserts. They thought it beneath them to be called upon during inane dream sequences as counsel: how to wage war, conquer tribeswomen, how to make love, in what position, how to wipe bums. But, it was exactly what I wanted. A stage where I could express my talents."

Gabriel spoke of ancient epochs, of prophets, of evil spirits, concubines and wives, wars and crusades and, most of all, love. He believed in love.

"With love," he would say, "Salim Saab, mankind will realize that their desire for one another is all that matters. And the humility of their beginnings as risen apes will put them in harmony with other living things. They will forget that once upon a time they thought of themselves as fallen angels and learn to care for their world. Only with love, Salim Saab. Only with love."

He was surely a dreamer.

Salim sighed, turning on to his side, staring at his bedside clock as it flashed bright red numbers. In his suburban house he felt safer than he did in the city. He could not help but worry for Sameer and Felix, though. He felt guilty for allowing them to go to the city unchaperoned.

"Salim Saab," Sam had said. "No terrorist can possibly know about my apartment. Sometimes even I can barely remember where I live. Haha!" He slapped his thigh and then Felix's back, his laugh coming through his nose. "Red over here knows how to get back to the city. He's done it a million times. We will be fine and, before you know it, we'll be back."

How could he suppress the desire to give in to his son's request? And tomorrow, his beloved Laila would arrive and they would be together as a family. But deep down, he had brutal visions of the Scimitar's sword slicing through his son's neck.

Having his life under threat from an assassin had become something of a banality. In a way, he felt he had to live until he died. The minutes could not go by any faster though. He pondered upon the joy Laila's presence would bring to him, and of what she would say when he revealed to her the means by which they would change the world. To take her to the nation they once knew, to save Pureland from the brutes that had swallowed her whole. He would bring back the Lorr as he remembered it to be and live a life of harmony with his family. These enchanting visions tickled his mind as his eyelids closed for the night.

Verily, the dreams that are the most vivid are the ones when you feel pain, happiness and sorrow. Then there are those dreams that give you the impression that you've been abruptly awakened by a loud pounding noise on the front door. The alarms do not ring and you have the precipitous feeling that your life has finally been sabotaged. This was not a dream he wanted to be in anymore. The knocks grew louder as he rushed towards the door with the hair rising on his arms, his eyes blinking through the misty hue. Looking at his phone he tried to decipher the identity of his intruder; the surveillance camera images were blurry. He couldn't recognize the naked figure with flowing long hair, shivering, covered in mud. He switched on the light, counting ten pounding heartbeats, and opened the door. The man tumbled into the house like a draft of wind and began breathing in short bursts, feeling cool to touch, smelling of corn chips.

Salim tried to open his eyes wide, a measure he employed when trying to escape his dreams. His brow pushed hard against his scalp and, in some way, he could still feel his pillow under his face. But he also heard quivering cries from below.

"Oh, Salim Saab! I haven't felt these shivers before, what should I do?" Gabriel sat on his haunches, hugging his knees, trembling on the floor.

"Gabriel, what are you doing here? What has happened to you?" said Salim, rushing to his closet to retrieve an overcoat. The doorway was muddied, as was the main entrance towards the kitchen. There was something different about Gabriel. He no longer had cape-like wings and his chiseled body had acquired a rather large organ between his legs.

"I've been telling you, Salim Saab. God of Abraham has finally allowed me to have my dream—to be here on earth. Please, I'm feeling cold. How do I get this stuff off of me?"

Salim's heartbeat had now raced to proportions that were not conducive for sleep, and at any moment now, he thought, he would be relieved to find himself on his bed. So, he tried once more, opening his eyes wider, but nothing changed. He led Gabriel to the bathroom and let the water run in the tub. Gabriel's eyes were grey and his skin was almond colored, darker than Salim had remembered from his dreams. He sat in the tub reluctantly at first, but later splish-splashed away, giggling like an infant as he played with the bubbles.

"This stuff is fantastic! Believe you me, I love it!" he yelled, as Salim tiptoed backwards out of the bathroom. "Oh when the saints, oh when the saints!" As he closed the bathroom door, Salim dug his nails into his forearm until he winced with pain. Looking down, he saw a crescent of blood. This could not be, he thought.

He ran to the pantry near the kitchen and shuffled violently through old newspapers and behold, what did he find: a bottle of Johnnie Walker, breakfast of champions. He swigged five gulps down before coughing.

The whiskey rolled out from his eyes. In the backdrop, he could hear the archangel gurgling, "Oh when the saints go marching in!"

His heart now was about to burst through his ribs. There lay an opened box of sleeping pills. He popped two out of their pods and tossed them into his mouth followed by another gulp of whiskey. Then he heard a loud splash that made him rush back to the bathroom.

"Salim Saab, this stuff is remarkable! Now I know why you guys can't live without it!"

Salim, with his body relaxing before him, asked, "Why have you come to me? Is it my time? Am I going to die?"

"No, no Salim Saab. Like I told you before, I've made a deal. It was God's parting gift to me, a golden handshake, believe you me. I've always told you I wanted to be an actor. Here I am!"

"Why?"

"Why not, Salim Saab? Being an actor is all I know. I'm going to Hollywood—to be a movie star. I have everything I need. I wanted to meet with you before I left, because you helped me through this whole thing like my own personal life coach, believe you me." He cleared his throat and squinted, speaking with a heavy voice. "How do you like my new actor voice? It comes with an American accent."

Salim pulled Gabriel out of the water and handed him a large towel. He saw the archangel tumbling on the ground like a child as he became accustomed to a wingless body. He also handed him a pair of fresh pants and an old shirt. "Gabriel, you need to leave soon. Felix will be here any minute," he pleaded.

"Don't worry, my car will be here. I just came to meet you and to thank you for being such a good friend. And I wanted to tell you..."

"What? What is it?"

"Oh ... I keep forgetting ... damn it!" Gabriel said clicking his fingers. "I will let you know once it comes to me. I had it a second ago."

A car honked outside as Gabriel leapt up. "I should be off, Salim Saab. I will send you a postcard." He reached out to embrace him in his long arms. He was in a state of unreserved urgency, the kind one would be in if they were strapped to dynamite and the fuse had been lit. Another honk, and he was out the door.

Salim breathed in short bursts. This was the most bizarre experience he'd ever had. He felt his eyes closing. The second hand on his kitchen clock slowed down. He felt his face on his pillow again. And the warmth that whiskey brings to the blood and the heaviness that comes with it, where your body feels like it belongs to someone else. He had not remembered being so deep in sleep before. It had been too long, but his body thanked him for it as he lay on the living room couch, his cheek stuck to the leather.

Then another dream arrived. Or so he thought.

Shameless

The one thing I can't figure out is was why Salim chose that particular day to conduct his experiment. I thought about it a lot, sir, I really did. I can't seem to understand. I don't know how all this works, to be honest. How he was going to pierce the time-space fabric and what not. Or whether he even could. I didn't know whether Felix would be able to do it either. But he was adamant about having it all to himself, have the whole thing go his way. Two pasts needed altering, I guess, and something tells me they only had one shot at it. What I do know is that in the days that led up to his death, just prior to Laila's arrival, Salim was a different man. He whistled to himself, sang songs, that sort of stuff.

Laila had finally boarded the plane and was on her way to him. Salim had been counting the days. The hours stretched further than either of them wanted them to. As you and I both know, sir, one cannot simply arrive in New York anymore. She had been delayed by interrogations. In Europe, she bought a brand-new cell phone. She hadn't seen one in a while but Salim explained that a video call was necessary and that he longed to see her face. They'd set a date to see each other before she was to arrive in the US.

Salim, on this date, bathed and shaved against the grain in anticipation. The screen came on, there was a time lag. Laila was in a hotel room, where the morning had begun to breathe a yellow hue into the room. She looked around and back at the screen, her feet swaying in excitement. After all, the last time she was in this city, she had left without a farewell. Stockholm.

He could see a shadowy silhouette in the sunlight. Her hair was burgundy like wine and had the texture of a thousand red serpents that locked neatly about her neck. Even the sun of thirty summers had failed to ravage her face. Her eyes seared his soul like they always had. After all these years, Salim's heart still changed its rhythm, and like a snake swaying in front of its charmer, he was stunned. He'd spent his life rehearsing the words he would say to her, the clothes he would wear when and if this moment were to arrive. He knew his obligation was to mend her and to love her like his heart had told him to do many years ago, from the moment they had first met.

The first thing she said to him was, "Your friend was very helpful in getting me out. But what kind of name is Chip for a woman anyway?"

Salim snickered. He saw her lips burn through the screen of his phone. "When she was young," he said. "A couple of boys made fun of her for the way she walked and how she loved to play sports. Called her a butch bitch. She took a baseball bat to their mouths, chipping their front teeth. Since then people started calling her Chip. Weird story, no?" He tilted back onto his pillow. "Brother Carl moved away from New York, some years ago. She's the only friend I have left. She and Deema Engine of course."

"What strange names your friends have. Speaking of which, where is Mr. Charming?"

"He's here—lives upstate. In a town called Woodstock. Sells love potions and conducts sex seminars. He's done quite well for himself."

Laila smirked, shaking her head. "Tamboo Charming ... what a man. Do you know, years after you left, he had an affair with one of the Christian maids? I forget which one. I think even Bilki was hot on him—never understood why. Anyway, do you think Sameer will be safe in the city?" Through the open window of her hotel room, Salim saw the curtains sway as the cool air pasted goosebumps across her arm. In the old days, at the first sight of this, Bilki would have rushed to the trunk to bring out the shahtush shawl, while Abbas would line up the fireplace with newspaper and burning coals. But this time, she just rubbed her hands over her arms.

"Yes, yes, of course he will be safe, my darling. Felix is a responsible boy and I just thought they both needed some time away from here. And don't worry, this place is well protected. No one knows where it is."

"Is Sam still in trouble?"

"No. He is fine. I helped him settle his debts. In fact, I gave him more money than needed just to make sure. Can never be too careful with these drug dealers."

"My poor boy," she whispered, closing her eyes. "He's inherited his uncle Gibran's love for intoxication."

"And my father's," Salim was quick to add. "The painter was seldom sober."

"We have to help him, Salim. He's all we have left."

"Don't worry, my love. You're both safe now," he sat up and fixed his robe. He loved what she had just said. It made him feel a part of something. "How is Stockholm? Do you remember anything from the last time we were there?"

"Of course. Everything," she whispered. It was a lie. That night was nothing but a hazy dream, a last hurrah before a life of imprisonment and quite possibly an act of impromptu rebellion. But it had been so long since someone had looked at her so lovingly, she wanted it to continue.

"Laila, if I was not the son of a Khanpur peasant and just like the other boys in Blisschesterson, would you have fallen in love with me ... married me when we were younger?"

She thought for a moment, because it required some thinking. "It depends. If you were General Ali's son, remote, aloof, dim as a dying lantern, then no. But if you looked at me the way you do now, with no shame, nothing but unconditional love, and would go to the ends of the earth for me, then yes, of course I would have married you."

"May I ask you a question," he said, clearing his throat. "How many lovers have you been with?"

"Why do you ask such a stupid thing?" she shot back, pushing her phone away and tucking her feet underneath her as she sat up.

"Oh no, never mind. Just a silly question." His heart began to thump.

"You know, sometimes all you men have the same feudal mentality. Really want to know? Only two," she whispered loudly. "You and Liber Ali. Happy?" She looked away towards the window, as silence settled upon them from thousands of miles away. She counted two long breaths.

"Although that prick could never make love to me, so that doesn't even count."

She didn't know what, in that impulsive moment, inspired her to lie, but deep down she did not want to show him that side of her—her powerful side—her ability to control any man's heartbeat. She had kept it from the Major, and she wasn't about to let it all out in front of Salim.

"Let it be now, it was a silly thing," he said. "I always wanted to ask you. When I came back to see you, the time I was hurt, did you visit me in the hospital?"

"What do you think?"

"I couldn't tell. I thought I saw you sleeping on the chair when I woke up once."

"I guess you will never know now, will you?" she said. "How's your epilepsy?"

"Hard to say. Sometimes I feel as if I'm losing my damn mind. That's why, when your face showed up on my phone, I pinched my arm. At times the line between reality and fantasy is blurred. Especially when it comes to things as beautiful as you."

"Oh stop it, so *filmi* you are."

"I have a surprise for you and Sam. When you arrive tonight, I'll show you then ... I'm so happy today. I can't wait. All my life, I've yearned for a family and today all my wishes have come true."

"What surprise?"

"Lorr," he answered. "Lorr like you remember it. Our city, our people, the way it used to be."

"Oh spare me please, Salim. I just escaped that hellhole and you want to send me back?" she asserted, sitting up abruptly. She reached over to the nightstand and flicked open a pack of cigarettes in anger, lighting one up, blowing smoke away from her phone as Salim shook his head. "What? I'm going to quit you know. But I never quite understood something." She paused. "After all you've achieved in the world, Pureland remained silent about you, issued a death warrant for your blood, never named a single street after you. Kids no longer read about you in school, no one knows you exist. Yet, you have this passionate, almost pathetic, desire for that shithole. Even now, when it is no more."

She blew away his proposition like the smoke from her lips. It was outlandish to promise a city from the past. But surely she, like everyone else, must have had at least one desire that time had stolen. He wanted to bring that back for her, whatever it may be. This perfect day could not become any better, he thought, knowing that with the twist of a dial he could change everything.

"I think I hear the doorbell. It must be Sameer."

The Sword of the Caliphate

A few miles outside of Manhattan, in the borough of Queens, there is a neighborhood no queen would dare visit. Music blared from its streets one morning as teenage boys loitered around corner shops, their feet against the walls, baseball caps swiveled at an angle. Nearby, subway station crowds with oversized coats and large boots sieved through like grains in an hourglass, while in the distance, railway tracks zigzagged into each other. Here, the houses were sewn together in rows, as if by an invisible rope. On the third-floor bedroom of one of these houses, shriveled buttocks wobbled on what used to be muscular legs. Once upon a time, they could squat a military truck multiple times, but now they quivered into a pair of pants.

His skin had become pale over the last few weeks; the poison that flowed through his blood made it pasty white. He felt weaker than he had when they'd first discovered the tumor in his lungs. His hair had long escaped the torture of the chemotherapy, leaving a dotted scalp in its wake. He wondered what kind of treatment this was, one that left you worse than you were before. He tried to concentrate, this being his first attempt at wearing pants. It wasn't easy. Grey tumbleweeds that had decorated his face for forty years, now lay on the wooden floor, cut clean away from his cheek with a straight razor. He fell to the ground with a loud thud, both feet finding each other in the same leg. He stared up at the ceiling, cursing loudly.

"Everything fine, Lala?" a voice bellowed from the stairs below.

"Yes, yes. Everything is fine. Just get someone to clean up this mess. I will be down in a minute." The Scimitar let out a deafening sneeze. "Aaaachoooo!" He waited a few seconds, then said, "Thank the Almighty," as one often does after a sneeze, because you never know when it could be your last.

He jostled with a leather belt as though it were a snake and buckled its pin over the loops of his pants. He let out another sneeze and then another, splattering mucus on the floor.

Thank you, Lord.
Allah the merciful.
Praise be to God.

The spring breeze, seeping through a cracked window, scraped the back of his throat. Breathing wasn't easy. It was mating season, according to the weather report: maple, grass, and oak. Love was in the air. The struggle with this alien outfit and his inflamed sinuses added to his anger. After all, he'd only worn one kind of shalwar kameez his entire life—the Pathan suit—this new guise confused him. As he saw his clean-shaven self in the mirror, he made a menacing grimace. His new look was too innocent for him. He didn't like that, especially before a big kill. But his sketch had been floating around in news reports. He needed to change things up.

He wondered whether the two incidents, the explosion at the Ahmadi congregation, and the burning of the kebab shop, gave him the practice he required. And that warning sign, that severed head he elegantly placed on a spike outside the 17th Precinct—was it enough? Was he ready? He was a perfectionist, you see, who conducted scrimmages before the actual match.

Slowly, he took on a frozen expression as he readied himself for another sneeze, gushing green on to the mirror. He analyzed it with a look one might have when, during a sky jump, the parachute malfunctions. It was unlike phlegm from a cough or cold, which he had seen before. After all, he had survived for many years huddled in the foothills of the Hindu Kush. His body was immune to petty viruses. But this was different. His mind began to wander into the mist of superstition. Surely, someone had to have been thinking of him. Such vicious sneezes cannot just arrive without someone's longing for his company. In his mind, far away planets were tugging at the strings of his destiny. It excited him.

As he finally made his way downstairs to the breakfast table, an inauspicious laughter welcomed him. The team of four pointed at him, amusement choking their words.

"Haha! Lala you look like a peeled potato."

"So innocent you look. Are you going for a *rishta*? Too old to get married, no?"

"By God, if any of you laugh, I will cut your throat and bury you with the professor." Silence swiftly swept up any lingering chuckles. One of them rose from the table to help him. He shoved him away and sat down to a plate of toasted Eggo waffles. Breakfast was an important meal for him, especially when he had a long day's work ahead.

It was well known that senior members of the Caliphate respected him to the point of believing he was divine. Someone with this many kills in God's name was surely a giant among mortals. Many claimed that he held sway in matters dealing with access to heaven. After all, he was the head of Law Enforcement. He made sure celestial laws were obeyed. The Khalifa of Mosul put him at the helm of this group himself. This was the most important division of the Caliphate according to him. They were warriors blessed by the Almighty. The Khalifa even designed their uniforms himself. Uniforms make a proper army, he claimed. But outfits were never important to the Scimitar. He didn't see himself any different; he'd been a soldier from the start—God's soldier. Taliban, Freedom Fighter, Law Enforcement—these were just empty words to him. He was the best in the business. But, according to the doctors, he had a year left before the cancer had its way with him. He wanted that year to count.

"No sugar for me," the Scimitar said, as tea was poured into his cup.

He recalled the time when he'd first joined a group known as the Freedom Fighters in 1980 as a meandering, homeless drug-addict. The Central Jail was where word of such an organization began to spread, where skilled inmates were selected to fight a holy war against the Soviets. Of course, he was there, first in line to offer his talents. He believed he had found his life's calling, a guaranteed path to paradise. He developed an enormous reputation. Many years later, after Mitti

Pao's sudden death, he was inducted into the TITS as a senior advisor on religious affairs. Back then, when they aligned with the Caliphate, the TITS became an attraction for idle young hands. One could say that young boys couldn't wait to get in TITS. The Scimitar knew this and built his division with young new recruits who were willing to die for any cause the Khalifa of Mosul declared.

Over the years, as the Caliphate grew, varying offshoots and spin-off coalitions had come and gone, but slowly, organizational structure was needed, departments were created. A screening process determined which department to place applicants in. But the Scimitar remained in the branch he knew best. Because one cannot simply make a career switch from assassinating heretics to marketing or human resources.

Not to say that the human resource department of such an establishment was an easy place to work in. In fact, it was quite demanding to deploy talented assets for terror plots; employee turnover was very high. So you could well imagine their surprise when the Scimitar called up the Khalifa of Mosul and volunteered himself as the sole executioner of the Salim Agha fatwa.

Professor Salim Agha had become something of a prized scalp in the Caliphate. Over the years, the propaganda against him had grown to new heights. At every sermon, the infidel Agha was described as the devil himself. Of course, the Scimitar knew that this assassination would top off a remarkable career. The Khalifa of Mosul jumped from his chair when he heard that his highest-ranking assassin had taken it upon himself to carry out these operations and that, too, in the United States. The planned attack on the Ahmadi refugees and the assassination of Salim Agha were the first strikes the Caliphate would be conducting in the US. And there is nothing that brings people together more than the death of the most loathed heretics and their unsaid leader. The Scimitar's plan was impeccable. The HR department arranged for his travel to the US as a cancer patient—seeking treatment for a real disease under a fake name. No one would recognize him, they thought, and his old age would allow for a hassle-free entry at customs. In order to make his job simpler, they sought the help of their American cell, the local recruits, to make sure he received all the assistance he required.

A word about these dimwits. For the recruits, who were lured in through social media campaigns, terrorism was not a strong suit. Let's just say they were fan-boys who shot paintball guns at strip clubs, hustled young kids at Friday prayers, sat huddled in a basement while getting aroused by assassination videos. None of them ever killed as much as a slug. Their only failed attempt at making a dirty bomb had left them staring at each other eyebrowless. Frustrated, armed with a grenade he'd bought from an online auction, one even decided to blow up the Home Depot from where they had bought thirteen bottles of bleach for the failed bomb. After shouting the Almighty's name, when the grenade ceased to ignite, he quietly walked back out amid chuckles and pointing fingers. That was the extent of their experience, sadly. Bombings and assassinations were something like folklore to them, and to be in the presence of the greatest ever, to be taught by a true pioneer of brutality, was incentive enough to assist in this glorious crusade.

The Scimitar finished his tea, wiped his beardless face and said, "The kebab shop was a success, thanks to Allah. And that heathen prayer hall too. Everyone is proud of us for that. Now one last thing left. Let's go over the plan, brothers." A young Bangladeshi boy in his early twenties, with a pencil thin beard, brought out a marked map of Nassau County from under his sweatshirt.

"Where did you find his location? And how sure are you of the house?" he asked as he popped a piece of buttered waffle into his mouth.

"Lala, the professor been buyin' coffee from my Uncle Tiger every mornin' for thirty years. Uncle Tiger is the only one he trusts. I followed my uncle one day and I saw the professor," he said, raising his eyebrows. "You have to be careful though. I heard him say he got all sensors and alarms and shit. If you trip 'em you ain't gonna get to him."

"Just tell me where I have to go, son, and I will do the rest. And no one follows me. I do this alone," said the Scimitar, who in his youth would have included the young recruit in his body count for the day. But his old age and frailty had brought a sense of calm. The others jumped in and wrestled to identify the exact location of the house. By the end of a long tussle, they collectively narrowed it down to two houses.

"You mean to say you idiots haven't even figured out which house he lives in? I thought your uncle told you the address?" asked the Scimitar. "Wait till I tell human resources. Or better yet, the Khalifa himself. He will cut your fees to half!"

"No Lala," they all barked in unison.

"Lala, the security over here has increased after you blew up the kebab shop. We couldn't follow him for long. We came to this street, sometimes as pizza delivery guys, sometimes as gardeners. Shit, it's really impossible to know where he is exactly. But the young one here saw the target. He be hangin' with two other boys. One of them looks full Jewish, Lala, with red hair and all. By God, take him out and we're all in heaven."

"Yeah, that Jew is the assistant. Take him out, Lala!"

"Take out the fuckin' Jew," they all chimed in.

"Alright then. Drop me off two hundred yards from both houses and meet me at our starting point exactly thirty minutes after ... Now, more importantly, did you get the weapon?"

"Just like you asked, Lala," said the young recruit, pulling out a duffel bag stuffed with newspapers and a black handgun. He pulled out a cylindrical tube and displayed both items on the table, like offerings to a god. The Scimitar admired the weapon as it shone in the morning light. Some butter from his finger slipped onto the nozzle. He cleaned it with his shirt and put it back on the table. He respected the tools of his trade.

"What's this? Is it not assembled?" he asked, picking up the cylinder.

"I'll just fasten it for you," said the boy, as he twisted the tube on to the nozzle.

"Is it in working order? It's not too loud, is it?"

"Lala ... when you shoot, you won't hear the gun. Only the one you shoot, hahaha," he said, causing unanimous laughter around the kitchen table as the Scimitar peered through the silencer into the soul of the gun.

"Good, then. God willing, I will succeed. I want to do this alone. I want you all to be far away, you hear me? I don't want any lookouts. I can't share this with anyone. Allah requested me to carry this out alo ... alone ... Achoooo!"

Wiping his nose with his sleeve, the Scimitar walked to the window facing the street below. His eyes began to water and his nose felt as if a large rock were attached to it. His lungs ached. Despite the fact that his veins throbbed with poison that had been pumped into him earlier in the day, he felt rejuvenated. Neither a runny nose nor a failing lung was going to get in the way of his final mission. The assassination of the infidel Agha would be a monumental achievement for the Caliphate. It would re-galvanize the public's sentiment; send a passionate throb through their hearts. To claim responsibility for bringing to justice an absconder, an enemy of the Prophet, was something he'd dreamt of his whole life.

He looked out the window. His eyes flew up from the street, over the sliver of water towards the small island which had once been bought for a few clams. A soulless land only a few hundred years old. Pathetic, he thought.

"These infidels have no sense of direction," he began as the others looked on wide-eyed towards the window. "Unlike theirs, ours is a culture of undeterred legacy, of an imperishable people. And I'm convinced that the Caliphate will reclaim what we have lost. An empire that had once laid the foundations of a truer reality; a complete submission to the Almighty. Brothers, pray with me."

He turned and raised his hands to his face, as the others followed. "Oh Allah, in my final undertaking, make our success possible and anoint us with eternal transcendence unto rapture."

Ameen.

The Final Sneeze

———— ❦ ————

I remember that day. How could I not? If I close my eyes, I'm there again.

The sky is bluer than blue. The sun stretches its arms, declaring morning's end. And, there he is, the Scimitar, God's hitman, making his way uphill, carelessly limping along the sidewalk of a winding cul-de-sac. There's silence in this neighborhood and the air is brittle. He's heading towards the corner houses, sneezing his way past the trees.

"Oh Allah, be kind," he says to himself, squinting through a haze of tears. "Which asshole is remembering me so much today?"

The doorbell rings.

"It must be Sameer," Salim whispers.

"I'm going to the airport now," Laila responds. "I'll see you tonight."

Salim hangs up. With tepid excitement, he makes for the door. His guard has fallen. Without hesitation, he opens it.

A bald, clean-shaven old face with brutal eyes stares back at him. It carries the menace of a thousand famished savages. A gun is extracted from a pair of loosely held pants. Salim's blood thickens as he raises both hands. Determination has made a single solid crease on the Scimitar's forehead. He walks in and closes the door behind him.

Salim knows immediately who he is. It's not the gun that gives him away, but his eyes. He has seen this look before. The resolve on his face can only be brought about by hatred alone. So close to achieving what he wants and here he is, staring down the barrel of a pistol.

"I thought you'd be younger," Salim says to him, pedaling backwards.

"I was once. But don't underestimate what I'm capable of."

"Never said I did. What makes you hesitate?"

"Nothing," he says, walking closer. "I wanted to see the fear in your eyes before I killed you. But you are, like they say, shameless."

"Just this day. Let me live for just this day and I'll be at your mercy tomorrow."

"I've waited too long, Saab. I can't spare you for even a minute, let alone a day."

The Scimitar's gun now reaches the softness of Salim's cheek. Slowly, his raised arms begin to fall. He takes another baby-step back and says, "I've always wanted to know. What makes you people hate so much? What did those poor people, whom you blew out of the sky, ever do to you? What have I ever done to you?"

"Wah, Salim Saab, wah. You commit the biggest sin of all and ask why we hate you? All this knowledge you claim to have and yet you're completely illiterate. The Scimitar hesitates for a moment as he puts his sleeve to his nose. Then the gun is lowered before his nasal words return. "Look at how you're looking at me, like you think I'm beneath you ... how you're talking to me. You think because I didn't read the books you read that I'm somehow an animal, a beast, but I follow the one book that matters. You're the ignorant one, Professor Saab, not me."

"And you believe that your book tells you to kill people like me? What's my sin? I want to know?"

"Your people are shameless blasphemers who defy the finality of our God's prophet. I've spent an entire lifetime bringing justice to infidels, but there's no kaffir in my eyes bigger than you. Do I need to tell you how you shamed our Pureland, our ... Why are you laughing?"

"Because you claim to be a lover of our nation, just like me, and here we are, trying to prove to each other whose love is greater."

The Scimitar walks close, puts his gun to Salim's temple and says, "In the name of Allah, the merciful..."

Then the door opens. The gun goes off. A piece of the ceiling falls to the floor. The Scimitar is down. His gun slips from his hand.

"What's going on here?" Sameer says, extracting a pistol from his bag.

"Dr. Agha, are you alright? Who is this?" asks Felix.

The Scimitar reaches for his gun and takes aim again. Four people and two guns greet each other at Salim's entrance, with the door still wide open. The spring air waltzes into the house. Sam, with his Walter .44 Magnum, an agitated Felix Kestenbaum, the Scimitar, and Salim echo loud threats: a mistimed orchestra deprived of a conductor.

Aaaaachoooo!

The Scimitar cannot seem to concentrate. He should have been out the door by now, leaving three dead bodies in his wake. He cannot see anything. His eyes are watering.

Sameer's gun changes its direction.

"Sam, why do you have a gun pointed at me?" screams Salim, "Felix where are you going?"

"I ... I'm sorry Dr. Agha." Felix snatches Salim's phone from him and unlocks the basement door.

A small irritation has begun to crawl down the Scimitar's nostrils. Down, down, down it goes. His nose itches and he blinks but can't prevent the dribble sliding down to his lips. He is losing focus now, he tilts his head back. His gun spins in all directions. He opens his mouth wide and gives birth to an intractable expulsion. The Sword of the Caliphate, God's right arm, pulls on the trigger with a blink as he prepares to carry out the work of the Almighty.

God is great.
Aaaachooo!

Epilogue

When the chambers emptied and my eyes opened, it was all over. They were all gone. In that moment of undue frenzy, my breath raced faster than I could control. I looked down at the pistol burning in my fist, and in my other hand, pressed tightly between my knuckles was a solitary, black ceramic chess piece—a rook from an abandoned game.

I claimed Salim Agha's murder immediately. I don't know to this day whether it was my gun that ended his life, but as soon as I pulled that trigger I was swathed in guilt. I did it, I said, and my hands went up when the uniforms arrived. They pulled me up from my elbows and carried me away. Since then, these wrists have been wrapped in jewelry.

I didn't say a word to anyone when we reached the station, quietly nodding as accusations were flung towards me. Agonizing words like 'the Scimitar', 'terrorist', 'assassin' rained upon me and fingers were thrust into my chest with immense force, bruising me instantly. But I didn't move. I was planted in a field of nothingness, barely breathing, silent. It was only later that evening when I put a telephone receiver to my ear that a woman's voice on the other end jolted me into existence. My mother, Laila Khan, didn't enquire about the catastrophe that took place but instead she sobbed, uttering unbroken apologies over and over again, "I'm sorry, Sameer. I'm so sorry. I should have told you years ago. I'm sorry."

It was then that my legs found new-born vigor and thrashed against my captors, claiming my true identity. Only then did I realize the nature of the crimes I'd been accused of. But it was too late. Boots pinned me to the floor and a vaccine of electricity made me quiver until I was motionless.

That night, in the soundless hush of my chamber, in the misery of my confinement, I began to dream. Dreams of color. Angels, with eyes as white as clouds, whispered in my ear the tale of my deceased father. The walls suddenly vanished and I appeared in earlier epochs in a land long forgotten. I began to unfold my father's legacy and follow him through his remarkable journey. I cried into my palms the next morning, knowing that I'd murdered a man whose only crime was trying to save the woman he loved and the nation he had once belonged to.

So, here we are, sir, I've told you everything. Many might think that this story's nothing but make-believe and these dreams of mine, well, they don't exactly go down well in court either. But justice, for my father, is all I seek. And you're the only jury that matters to me now. Like I told you when you first walked in, I'm not the monster people think I am. I'm no terrorist. Just a confused man whose entire life has been a lie. Vile words were whispered into my ear by my uncle Khalil while I was growing up; words that made my fists tighten with anger. And those years of systematic hatred that we, the children of Pureland, had breathed; hatred for a people we believed were so evil they destroyed everything in their wake. Yes, the Ahmadi was an enemy we could only envision in dreams. I believed that to be true. And this treacherous Ahmadi, the one my grandfather raised, the one who ended up strangling him, the traitor Salim Agha, who was now after my beloved mother? I just couldn't help it, sir. That spring morning, as all this tumbled in my mind, that trigger pressed itself. I guess I was on my own prophesied path, and like I mentioned before, my victim and I had our destinies folded together from the very start.

Your face has hardened from when you first walked in here, sir. You have questions, many of them, about what really transpired, whether I am a liar, or just plain mad. Please, sir, explain to me, what became of Felix Kestenbaum? No sign of where he went. Did he just vanish into thin air? You want to argue that he never existed in the first place, that he was a figment of an imagination powered by the supernatural. But it's true. I saw it with my own eyes. That magical apparatus of time, which has kept you on the edge of that unnerving chair, sucked him away.

I know what you're thinking. That I, too, like my father, have lost my goddamn marbles. You regurgitate the facts of the case before me and the most unequivocal element of them all: Salim's house never had a basement to begin with. You can further state the testimonies of the university faculty members about the curious state of Salim's mental health. You might argue, like them, that, a few years ago, when the summoning commenced, he had begun speaking to himself in empty corridors, laughing at his own echo, banging his head against the walls. You would be right to assume all those things. Yet, your coffee remains untouched and you listen to my implausible confession with unmoving interest, knowing that there is an element of truth to this story.

Sir, this is why I chose to invite you here. We're both artists, you and I. I know you very well, the world knows you. The masses that have gathered outside these walls in anticipation of this testimony, most definitely know you. I've followed you throughout your career and I know that no one else would believe me but you.

What happened to Salim Agha? Despite all warnings, Tamboo Charming and Deema Engine flew his body to Khanpur and buried him next to Jaaji, the Painter. The people of Salim's nation have desecrated his gravestone since then, chiseled his name right off. The word "infidel" now specifies who lies below, and feces and trash are flung onto it in a piling heap.

Sir, a black fire consumes the world I come from and, here, in this, the so-called realm of liberty, a similar reckoning has begun to peek out over the horizon. The people here, too, have begun to accentuate the elements that make us different from one another. There's a destructive branding underway. The world has got itself wrapped in distasteful animosity. And I fear that it will burn through my father's legacy. Please, don't let that happen.

You ask whether I think Salim ever got to fulfill his prophecy. What do you think? You really want to know the truth? The answer is that it's up to you what happens to that foretelling. Soon, I will be gone, put to sleep like a mad dog. Please, present this story to the world. Relieve me of this burden.

I trust that you will find a way and, in doing so, finally set me free.